VALLEY 10/27/2006
50690010558200
Read, C
A field

W9-BVW-419

A FIELD OF DARKNESS

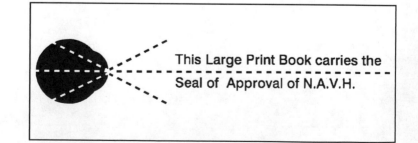

This Large Print Book carries the
Seal of Approval of N.A.V.H.

A FIELD OF DARKNESS

CORNELIA READ

THORNDIKE PRESS

An imprint of Thomson Gale, a part of The Thomson Corporation

THOMSON

GALE

Detroit • New York • San Francisco • New Haven, Conn. • Waterville, Maine • London

Valley Community Library

739 River Street

Peckville, PA 18452-2313

THOMSON

GALE ™

Copyright © 2006 by Cornelia Read.

Quotes on page 8 and page 518 are from Old Money, by Nelson W. Aldrich, Jr. © 1996, 1988 by Nelson W. Aldrich, Jr. Published by Allworth Press. Used by permission.

Thomson Gale is part of The Thomson Corporation.

Thomson and Star Logo and Thorndike are trademarks and Gale is a registered trademark used herein under license.

ALL RIGHTS RESERVED

This book is a work of fiction. Names, characters, places, and incidents are the product of the author's imagination or are used fictitiously. Any resemblance to actual events, locales, or persons, living or dead, is coincidental.

Thorndike Press® Large Print Reviewers' Choice.

The text of this Large Print edition is unabridged.

Other aspects of the book may vary from the original edition.

Set in 16 pt. Plantin.

LIBRARY OF CONGRESS CATALOGING-IN-PUBLICATION DATA

Read, Cornelia.
    A field of darkness / by Cornelia Read.
      p. cm. — (Thorndike Press large print reviewer's choice)
    ISBN 0-7862-9017-X (alk. paper)
    1. Upper class — Fiction. 2. Cold cases (Criminal investigation) — Fiction.
3. Syracuse (N.Y.) — Fiction. 4. Large type books. I. Title.
    PS3618.E22F54 2006b
    813'.6—dc22   2006021194

ISBN 13: 978-0-7862-9017-8

Published in 2006 in arrangement with Warner Books, Inc.

Printed in the United States of America on permanent paper
10 9 8 7 6 5 4 3 2 1

For Grace and Lila, who are both
sweetness and light.

PART I
SYRACUSE, 1988

■ ■ ■ ■

The Old Rich may all too easily describe a trajectory through life that, graceful and composed though it may be, is not in touch with the common ground of reality. Their bodies lack traction, their spirits lack consequence. Nothing they do makes any difference. Their noblest gestures, most beautiful arrangements of self and setting, greatest accomplishments, are all quite reasonably attributed to their unearned money. Deprived of the pain and pleasures of risk, they lose a large part of experience itself.

— Nelson Aldrich, *Old Money*

CHAPTER 1

There are people who can be happy anywhere. I am not one of them.

When the house on the next street went
up in flames for the second night in a row, I
wondered again what the hell I was doing
in Syracuse.

Let me say right up front that those fires
had nothing to do with the murdered sisters.
They'd been dead nineteen years by then,
their throats cut one state-fair night back in
1969 when I was three thousand miles away,
about to start grade school in California.

Still, if I think of those girls, of everything
that happened once I knew, it's the image
of that twice-burnt house I flash on first.
Like maybe it was one long sly Dada-
surrealist wink from the universe, a warning
I should have been hip enough to catch.

The first night was already hot, so still the
whine of a neighbor's dog carried right

through our bedroom window. I heard a screen door yaw wide to let him out, the tired spring slapping it closed behind, the click of canine toenails on sidewalk. I kept turning my pillow over and over, trying to find one cool spot on which to rest my cheek, but by the time that dog scratched to be let back in, I'd given up on sleep and rolled my grumpy ass right out of bed.

Wandering through our apartment, I wished for a breath of air from the second-story porch, just a shred of stray breeze meandering this far inland. No such luck. I ducked my head under the kitchen faucet and stretched out along the seven-foot leg-less purple Naugahyde sofa my husband Dean dragged home from a train car he'd rehabbed.

I hated this object, if only because the thing made my frail Waspy castoffs look even more ridiculous. The pair of Hepple-white demi-lune tables. The painted Bavarian linen press. The stately between-wars globe amidst whose black oceans you could still find Ceylon and Formosa and the Polish Corridor.

I was twenty-five that summer, and every-thing I owned was scratched and warped, ring-marked by generations of abandoned cocktails. It was pure jetsam, the crap that gets thrown overboard on purpose. My money is so old there's none left.

In that sense, Syracuse and I deserved each other. The place used to churn out everything from rifles to soda ash, helicopters to typewriters, but by the time I showed up they'd paved over the Erie Canal and gutted the great mills.

There were still traces of those glory days if you knew where to look, things like our radiator covers, made of the steel sheets from which Remington and Smith-Corona letter-key stems had been punched, leaving behind a delicate herringbone tracery. The ghosts of history are in the details, in the negative space.

I scrunched my pillow against the sofa arm and started reading a garage-sale paperback of *In Cold Blood.* Four pages on, I heard this long, dull *fwhooomp* from outside — noise so deep it echoed in my ribs.

There was a pillar of smoke framed all majestic in the porch doorway. It twisted black against the city-pink night sky, billows delineated by hundreds of thousands of red-gold sparks, pinpoint gems helixing up to join the stars. Exactly three a.m., if you believed the clock in the stove.

Soon there were fire trucks in the distance,

their Doppler-effect wails punctuated with staccato chatter-and-yelp as they barreled through each intersection. When the engines rolled into the next street, they cut the sirens but kept all the lights going.

I stood up, dazzled by flashbulb pops of color from between the tight-packed old triple-deckers — strobing to pick out every dent in the alleyway garbage cans. I chucked the book and snaked on my flip-flops.

Outside, an ancient Oldsmobile muttered up the hill. It crossed the bright alley's mouth, caught in momentary silhouette: exhaust blue with oil, wheel wells rusted to filigree. The fire sucked moisture from the air, tightening the skin along my cheeks.

I cut across the tar-soft street and between the woodframe hulks facing ours. For just a second, coming out the other side, it was like stepping into one of that guy Weegee's photos from a forties copy of *Life:* black-and-white, some police-scanner tragedy back when everyone wore hats and cars were bulbous as the *Hindenburg.*

I blinked and it was just my neighbors milling slack-jawed, tank tops and stretch shorts bursting with that translucent flesh I always attribute to Kool smoke and government cheese. I stepped in among them and chastised myself: *no worse snob than a poor relation.*

Helmeted firemen, sweat-slicked in rubber coats, rushed to yank down equipment. They raised a ladder and we sighed, our eyes fixed on the rooftop flames, the heavy hose-arcs of water. We stood mesmerized until the trucks left, then stumbled home with that aftermath smell of bucket-doused campfire caught in our teeth. Insult to injury.

How absurd that it should all happen again the next night, the absentee owner maybe wanting to squeeze just that little bit more from his insurance. Three in the morning and there I was back out on the sofa, reading Capote and looking up in response to the onslaught of crackling noise.

For a minute I thought I should peel myself off the Naugahyde and shake Dean awake, but it was only an hour before his alarm would go off, even on a Sunday. For him that summer was all dawn-to-dusk welding and invention, at his family's farm or with a railgrinder crew in Canada.

I should have gone to bed myself, but waited until after they'd put out the second fire. In the quiet that followed, there was the thump of a great storm sweeping in from the west. I knew the air would chill and sweeten in its wake.

A crack of street light spilled inward when I opened our bedroom door. Dean's long legs were tangled in the top sheet, his summer-gilt hair bright against the pillow. I sat on the edge of the mattress and he stirred half-awake, pulling me in close when I stretched out beside him.

I'll say again that the fires had nothing to do with the dead girls, but still those two nights are what kicked it all off for me. They were the last time I found sleep without first having to acknowledge, in the hollow dark, at least partial guilt for someone else's murders.

CHAPTER 2

By the time I really woke up the next morning, Dean was long gone. I'd surfaced briefly as he kissed me goodbye, then listened for him to kick-start his Harley — its *potato-potato* idle all basso profundo in the predawn quiet.

Around eleven I shuffled into the kitchen. I'm an ideal candidate for a caffeine I.V., a liter bag of the stuff set to a fast drip and hung off a wheeled chrome dolly so I could drag it around. I settled for a pint glass of blistering-strong French Market coffee, cut by half with milk and finished with a fistful of sugar. Light sweet crude.

I sucked it back fast, already late for lunch at my in-laws'. Dean was home maybe a week, this time. I'd hammered him into promising he'd take the afternoon off.

His Canada gigs were brutal. Couple days' notice from this local outfit Speer-O-Matic and he'd be off to moose country for weeks, the lone scab shoehorned into an otherwise-union crew car. No phones. Nothing but endless, blue-treed vastness and the mind-fracturing screech of grit tearing into steel.

If you've ever laid a penny on a track, you know how trains punish metal. They leave a shiny, paper-thin oval of copper, Lincoln's face smeared clean out of existence.

Same thing with steel: trains mash microns of rail forward, like taffy in front of a rolling pin, leaving a series of regular waves behind. Each passing boxcar, hopper, and passenger coach exaggerates that pattern, until finally the track's "corrugation" gets so pronounced that momentum along its distorted surface starts to batter equipment and burn extra fuel. At that point, you can either replace it or tackle the distorted bits. The second option is, not surprisingly, cheaper.

Enter the railgrinder, basically a locomotive fitted with twin rows of spinning, abrasive discs. Because track isn't flat on top, the grinding crew had to angle these discs by hand, positioning each to shear a discrete ribbon of corrupted metal from the railhead's convex surface. Even so, existing grinders couldn't quite mimic the original half-teardrop profile.

Dean's work meant we could never plan stuff. Not just because there was no telling how long he'd be home, but because he crammed pent-up months of invention into the downtime. On the road, he kept the old grinder up and running. At home, he was hell-bent on designing ways to automate it.

He'd programmed a computer to adjust each grinding head from inside the cab. Speer-O-Matic was ready to buy, but Dean thought a different linkage might replicate the railhead's arc. If that worked, they'd get years' more use from the same track, but the computer alone meant two guys, not twenty, could run any grinder in the world.

He could sell it to Speer-O-Matic, the Southern Pacific, anyone . . .

The union, of course, pretty much wanted him dead.

Dean didn't care. He was too excited about how this was the "ideal opportunity to provide structural integrity for our future."

I called it "a ticket out of this shithole."

Spot the English major.

I looked at the stove clock again and hustled toward the bathroom sink, where I slammed a brush through my hair and some paste on my teeth.

If you want a visual for me, Madeline Dare, I'm five-five but lie and add an inch on my driver's license. When I was fourteen, old guys in bars started telling me I look like Ingrid Bergman. In daylight among the sober, I'd pass for her hockey-playing cousin, the one who's just a touch too fond of the creamed herring but still has the cheekbones and the narrow hips.

I confided this once to Dean. We were standing against each other, and since he's exactly a foot taller than I am, the top of my head fits perfectly beneath his chin.

"Fuck Ingrid," he said, insinuating an arm around my waist and peeking down the front of my sweater. "I vastly prefer a more buxom woman." In that regard, he will never find this marriage a disappointment.

I grabbed the tabouleh I'd made the night before out of the icebox. Well, okay, "fridge" or whatever. I come from that tribe of verbal conservatives who still say "Victrola" and "toe-*mah*-toe" — Old High Long Island, my first language.

From the broom closet, I took my grandmother's shotgun for a little after-lunch shooting. This was a beautiful object, a side-by-side 20-bore Holland & Holland Royal Brevis from the thirties, sent by my father two weeks after my twelfth birthday. It had been his mother's, one of a pair, the barrels so true a fingernail flick still made them ping like crystal.

It was worth a great deal of money, and I should have sold it. Dean had accrued a tidy savings account from years of family agricultural labor, but other than the gun and my crappy furniture, I didn't show up here with much in the way of dowry.

Dad had probably sent the gun less out of generosity than as one more way to expunge traces of our robber-baron ancestry. He meant well, but I think passing as a regular guy among the trailer-dwelling potheads of Malibu counted more with him than his daughters' birthdays, most years. Still, I couldn't bear to sell it.

I had long cherished the hope that if I gathered up and held on to all the stuff he'd abandoned — maybe while scrunching up my eyes and thinking only good thoughts — I could conjure him home. We'd get a do-over, him and me. Just keep hitting the rewind button until we landed back at the part where he walked out when I was four, then erase all the broken crap that happened after.

Not bloody likely.

Real life was him unfolding a director's chair in the dirt outside his rusty VW camper every morning, ready to throw the I Ching with a fine Pacific view once he'd smoked his Wake-and-Bake joint.

Real life was me in Syracuse, broke and walking down to my rusty VW Rabbit with an appallingly expensive shotgun and a bowl of tabouleh, amazed again that I had come to rest here between Oyster Bay and California, the former poles of my existence.

Before I was fixed up with Dean by my friend Sophia, during a party at her parents' place on Central Park West, I'd never set foot in this town. It is a testament to how much I adored my husband, despite what he called my "debutante sensibilities," that I had stayed.

I cranked up NPR and leadfooted it out along 690 and 481, passing a dozen cars with 1988's stupid suction-cup–pawed Garfield stuck to their rear windows. People were not yet so sick of them they'd begun slamming the heads in the trunk, letting the fuzzy cartoon corpses flop around in the slipstream.

It had been that kind of year — mostly froth. Sure, you had Benazir Bhutto and Solidarity. Summer Olympics in Seoul. Iran-Contra. But pretty much if you were American all you'd remember is shoulder pads and a lot of hair gel, a blur of photomontage color.

Dukakis was still kind of in the running. I kept telling Dean that Ollie North was a flaming asshole, and he'd say the guy was just following orders. I'd retort that those had included upholding the Constitution, whether Reagan liked it or not, and that once Just Following Orders was considered a valid excuse for perfidy, it was all too easy to end up needing a rerun of the Nuremberg trials.

NPR agreed with me, which is what made Dean call it "The Voice of Managua." Some commentator was still jawing on about Admiral Poindexter when I downshifted into the decreasing-radius turn at my in-laws' exit.

I soon pulled into their driveway, coasting past the cow-shaped "The Bauers" sign and up through the gravel until I was almost under the eaves of their wide blue house.

Dean was in the cool garage, rubbing crud

off his hands with a scoopful of Gojo, the tin standing lidless beside his neatly folded coveralls. In green work pants and white undershirt, he could have been the central figure of some Soviet mural. All he needed was a wrench to brandish as he strode into the sunrise, red hightops glowing with promise.

"Hey there, sweaty young bronzed god," I said, cocking a hip under the tabouleh.

"Bunny, my dear." He smiled, wiping his hands on a shop rag, and leaned down to kiss me.

There was a constellation of tiny burns along his biceps, points at which welding sparks had singed through the coveralls.

We raced up the wooden steps to the kitchen, jostling each other through the door.

Dean called a breathless "Hey, pal" to his mother, Dot, throwing an arm across her shoulders.

"Oh, now, Deaner . . ." she protested, beaming.

She reached around him to pat my hand and give me a peck on the cheek. I asked if I could help with lunch and she took the tabouleh, saying "Now aren't you sweet," and "Doesn't *this* look nice," and assuring me that everything was taken care of. She shooed us both on inside so she could finish taping a four-color Sunday-paper portrait of Billy Graham to a cupboard door.

Dot was always so calm, so chatty with a little edge of laughter to every story, and yet got more work done in a day than any other ten people I know.

With me there's always crap all over the place and it takes half an hour to find car keys or socks. Here everything was orderly, sparkling, and covered with cow pictures.

My mother-in-law has a serious weakness for Holsteins. From the "Happy Moo Year" kitchen calendar to the ironing board cover to the holder for spare rolls of toilet paper, everywhere you looked, there were pink-nosed, piebald, cud-happy faces. I don't think she'd ever forgiven her husband Cal for switching from heifers to cash crops.

Cal and firstborn son Scott were sprawled out across the tweedy mustard plaids of the living room, watching a promotional video for a John Deere baler that would, the announcer promised, "virtually eliminate plunger-head slap."

I always experienced a little vertigo on the threshold of this room. It was the epicenter of the heartland, that terra incognita whose existence I'd intuited as a child only when I wondered if there were people who actually watched *The Lawrence Welk Show* on purpose.

I envied them. Denied irony, I would have lasted about five minutes. And as an older Bavarian friend had long ago confided, "One was impressed if the men in my family knew how to shave themselves."

This was bedrock, all concrete utility and economy of perspective. But it was in these rooms Dean had discovered William Blake and the Velvet Underground, from here that he set off for junior year in Kathmandu.

Dot called us to the table. She'd laid out a bounty of sliced turkey and ham and roast beef and Swiss, Jell-O salad, soft kaiser rolls, Miracle Whip, French's mustard, homemade sweet pickles, and bowls of chips. My tabouleh looked kind of obscene.

Cal helped himself to a courteously big serving, but he scrutinized the first forkful, halfway to his mouth, pronouncing, "When I was a kid, we called this 'silage.'"

I smiled weakly at him, never having had my cooking compared to grain fermented for the winter sustenance of cattle. In defense of my culinary talent, he also described all Chinese food as "dog in crankcase oil," and Syracuse is annually among the nation's top four cities for per capita consumption of Cool Whip.

Cal's mostly salt of the earth, but he's got moments when he harshes out on whoever's available, and to be honest he enjoys the hell out of them. Probably the closest thing he had to a hobby, an indulgence: tossing out spiky little grenades he could back away from, all innocent, if anybody yelped.

He kept it right on that sneaky edge where it was kind of funny if it was happening to anybody else, especially if they got huffy. Then it was your turn to remember his knack for arming a joke with that rock-in-the-snowball touch of hurt.

Firstborn Scott sat across from me, dark and pinched as a young Nixon. He was still wearing his meshback DeKalb cap and waiting, pissed off, for someone to notice his empty glass, to walk the four feet from his chair to the kitchen and rectify the oversight.

He was older by five years, but had beaten the crap out of Dean daily until the afternoon he got his ass handed to him in the hay barn. Cal walked in to find Scott blubbering on the floor, twelve-year-old Dean all smiles and holding a pitchfork to his neck. My husband has called his big brother Wimpy ever since.

"I was down to that car lot this morning for a new truck," Wimpy said. "Got-damn

Cuomo wants to jack up the taxes again, and then that Goldstein at the dealership wants to hose you on everything from power steering to tires."

Dot leapt up. "Iced tea or cranberry, Scottie?"

He leaned his chair back and crossed his arms. "What can you expect from a Hebe?"

Such an asshole. "Exactly what I'd expect from anyone else in the world," I said.

He turned to Dean. "Real sorry. Keep forgetting your wife's one o' them Jew-lovers."

Dean ignored him and found my foot with his beneath the table, tracing the very tip of his shoe slowly up the inside of my ankle. Wimpy got the farm, Dean got the balls.

Wimpy exhaled and turned back toward his mother. "Might as well give me that cranberry, if we don't have anything better."

I would have decked him and told him to take his damn hat off. She smiled and bustled to comply, pouring a winking, back-lit stream of ruby liquid from the cow-covered pitcher into his cow-covered glass.

Dot placed a second hand on the larger vessel, raised it without spilling a drop. Her neat, brisk steps toward the kitchen were first muffled by carpet, then sharp against vinyl floor. She returned to perch on the leading edge of her chair, poised for the next request.

We all chewed, accompanied by the occasional clink of fork against plate.

I fanned out my pitiful canasta hand of inoffensive topics: zucchini glut, humidity, recent Amtrak debacles.

My relatives consider lack of small talk the most profound moral failure of which a woman is capable, but the Bauers didn't mind lapses in conversation. Long silences were the norm here, punctuated with sudden and rather alarming gouts of speech, like eruptions of long-range artillery on a slow day in 1916.

Cal put down his fork and looked us all over.

Dean winked at me, mouthed "Incoming . . ."

The patriarch cleared his throat. "So I hear they're selling everything off up to Johnston's Tuesday," he said.

Dot sucked in her breath, no longer smiling.

I tried to catch her eye but she had become entirely focused on a fold crease in the tablecloth. She frowned at it. Tried to iron it flat with her palms.

This was a woman, her younger daughter once remarked, who took Tilex and an old toothbrush with her for her daily bath, scrubbing and whitening the grout instead of relaxing into the water and steam. I wished her drive would rub off on me, that I could have absorbed it by osmosis, proximity — a little Calvinism to buttress my over-bred moral laxity.

With dogs the hips go first. With people it's the backbone.

"Johnston's gettin' on," said Cal, reaching across to spear some turkey slices. "Funny he should sell right around the fair. We've been leasing most of the place since he had that stroke."

"I still wish you wouldn't ever've set foot on it," said Dot. She twisted in her seat but wouldn't look up, had to make that table-cloth behave.

A wicked grin started at one corner of Cal's mouth. "Decent price. Good land for corn. Don't see why you'd complain."

"Izzy running the auction?" asked Dean.

Cal nodded.

Dean laughed. "Size, shtyle, condition, und *breed*-ing."

"I beg your pardon?" I said.

"There's this great old auctioneer," Dean explained. "Izzy Fleischmann. Used to push heifers on us when I was a kid. He'd slap one on the back and say, 'This one, she's the one for you . . . size, shtyle, condition, und *breed*-ing.' Kind of like you, Bunny."

"I'm *so* flattered."

He smiled at me. "Izzy used to butter up Uncle Weasel something fierce. Knew exactly how to work him. 'I vant you to know you're a schmaht man, Vendell,' he'd say."

"Only time anybody ever said it," Dot murmured, good humor creeping back.

Dean had a feel for diplomacy. No topic could bond the people around this table more profoundly than Why Weasel Is Such a Jerk. All you had to do was speculate on the number of socket wrenches gone missing after he walked through the farm shop and heads would bob in happy unison.

Dean leaned back. "Guy could sell Weasel anything. He'd have a truckload of these cows all humped up and shivering, snot dripping out their noses, three tits and skinny and everything. Weasel'd buy 'em all."

I took a bite of tabouleh, which was magnificent, I'll have you know: lemony with a lot of cracked black pepper and minced flatleaf parsley.

"Izzy knows his business," Dean said. "He'll make sure Johnston sees some solid cash out of the deal."

Dot started sweeping up crumbs with the

edge of her hand. She made little square piles of them. "I just don't like to think about that place."

I wanted to ask her why but Cal turned to me and said, "So, you work for that paper — maybe you'd be interested in something I found up to Johnston's a couple years back. . . ."

Next to Dean, the best thing about living here was my job: staff writer downtown at *The Syracuse Weekly.*

Dot looked up. "Now, Cal —"

He waved a hand to cut her off. "Back in 1969 there were two girls got their throats cut. Last seen alive with a pair of soldiers at the state fair. Johnston found the bodies."

Dot shoved away from the table and stood up.

Cal took a long sip of iced tea and smiled at me. As she marched for the kitchen, he swiveled to follow her progress, draping an arm across the back of his chair.

"I remember seeing him later that week," he said. "I'm driving the tractor back down the road and there he was, sitting on a stump, piss still knocked out of him."

Dot cranked the kitchen sink taps open. Cal raised his voice to compensate. "He was trying to finish up in that field and couldn't do it. Just stopped in the middle of a row."

He paused while Dot snapped on rubber gloves, so she wouldn't have to miss a word. "Told me those cuts were so deep you could see bone at the back of their necks. Couldn't stop picturing it every time he shut his eyes. Got sick as a dog right there in front of me."

Dot looked back toward the table and I could tell she wanted to clear but Wimpy was still eating, so instead she walked to the stove, knelt, yanked the broiler door open, and pulled out the drip pan.

She walked the thing back to the sink, shoving it under sudsy water so hot it turned her forearms pink despite the gloves.

"So of course now Johnston's gettin' on," drawled Cal, "and we started leasing from him, couple-three years ago. I was fittin' ground that first spring, and when I knocked off for lunch I noticed something shiny caught in the spring-tooth of the drag. Turned out it was a set of dog tags. Same field where I'd seen him that time, right along where he'd found the bodies."

Dot pulled out a box of Brillo, grim, but Cal was undeterred.

He turned to zero in on me. "Still got those tags down-cellar. You're a writer. Might be some use to you."

I almost said no, thanks. Not just because I didn't want to further rile my mother-in-law, but because I really wasn't the investigative type. I did the puff-piece stuff: book reviews, food columns, articles on city lore, events calendar "picks." You'd never have found me with a press card in my fedora, jostling to the front of the pack. I wasn't built with that kind of hustle.

So I was about to tell him not to bother, but he was already heading for the garage, clapping Dot on the shoulder as he passed. The cellar steps were out there, railing partitioned neatly off with plywood, shelf across the top stacked with cases of Mason jars. Cal's descending footfalls echoed back, lug-soled boots on the riserless plank of each tread.

Wimpy shoved his chair away from the table, off to commandeer the bathroom.

I looked at Dot. "Cal never gave those tags to the police?"

She pressed her lips tighter and started clearing.

I stood to help her, walked from chair to chair, stacking plates.

Reaching for Dean's, I leaned down close and said, "Why the hell didn't he?"

"Busy guy," he said, enclosing the phrase that followed in air quotes: " 'Hay to get in and we're burnin' daylight.' "

Dot returned for the condiments, the platter of luncheon meat. I became fiercely concerned with the harvest of those remaining plates and forks.

When she was back in the kitchen, unfurling Saran Wrap with the water running again, I squatted down by Dean for another second. "Something like this, I'd picture him getting on the horn lickety-split."

"Fast Cal?" He laughed, shaking his head. "Thinks cops're about as useful as tits on a bull. Government boys."

I mulled that over as I went to scrape the plates and load the dishwasher.

When she thought I wasn't looking, Dot grabbed all the silverware back out of the Maytag's little cutlery basket and put it in the sink to hand wash. Didn't want to hurt my feelings.

An intricate dance, this in-law thing.

The dishwasher's industrious hum masked Cal's return. I flinched when I looked up and saw him across the table, a strand of cobweb in his hair.

He stretched his arm across to me. I held up my hand and he let the chained bits of metal slither and clink into my palm.

I looked down. The name "Lapthorne Townsend" glinted up in stamped relief.

All the blood dropped out of my head and coursed, rank and sour, into my gut. The little letters got blurry and I blinked a couple of times, hard.

Lapthorne Townsend. My second cousin. My favorite.

Must have read it wrong.

But when I looked down again, there was only that exact name, a serial number, and the words "B Neg," and "Episcopalian."

Dean stepped up behind me, trying to get a look. I snapped my fist shut.

Think fast. Of course we were all Episcopalians in my family, it went with the rest of the *Mayflower* bullshit. But weren't a lot of people? Maybe Lapthorne wasn't that weird of a name?

I wanted to wish it all away, but Rh-negative type B blood is the second rarest in the world. I have it too.

I turned back to my father-in-law, trying to sound casual. "So you never showed these to anyone?"

Cal shrugged.

I stepped into the kitchen and grabbed the notepad and pencil kept next to the phone. Turning away from everyone, I did a rubbing of both tags, then shoved the slip of paper into my pocket.

When I felt a little steadier, I looked around with what I hoped was a grateful smile on my face. Normal. Relaxed.

"I don't know if I can do anything with these," I said to Cal, "but I appreciate your thinking of me."

I gave them back, looking straight in his eye with all the sincerity I could muster.

He shrugged again.

Dean and I walked silent along Collamer Road, uphill toward the farmyard in its moat of jadeite corn. Cars shot by close and fast, buffeting us with air so muggy it felt like getting towel-snapped with a hot wet sheepskin.

All I could think was *Lapthorne . . . no way.*

I was jittery, suddenly longing for the ocean. Everything smelled of melting tar, aromatic as summer dock-piling creosote but without the soothing counterpoint of brine.

Two lead-heavy boxes of shells pulled at my left hand. I'd checked to make sure my shotgun wasn't loaded, but still cradled it "broken" over my right arm — veed open at the hinge for safety.

I walked faster.

The farm outbuildings betrayed no quaint Vermont-calendar or Shaker-coffee-table-book conceit. These were barracks for hay and tractors, old cars and older tools. They got swabbed down twice a decade with a soup of household paint-job tailings. Different batch of colors every time, but it always came out Cream of Ugly — baby shit or mustard or day-old guacamole.

I reached the shop's cinder-block wall and leaned back against it, closing my eyes in the thin stripe of blessed shade.

"I remember Cal talking about how he'd found those tags," Dean said from beside me, "but today's the first he ever dragged them out to show."

A single drop of sweat rolled down the inside of my left forearm, quick and twitchy as a ball of mercury.

Dean nudged against me, making my shirt stick to my skin.

"You've got a Cousin Lapthorne," he said, no lilt of question in his voice.

He'd seen the name. I was totally screwed.

CHAPTER 3

Dean laid a hand on my shoulder. His voice was gentle. "You want to tell anyone? The cops?"

Still leaning back against the shop, I didn't open my eyes. A breeze came up, rushing through the corn. It sounded like water and I wanted to savor the illusion.

"Bunny?"

I blinked and looked up at him. "The cops? Okay, this is going to sound so . . . Jesus . . ."

He eyed me, patient.

"It's just that . . ." I said. "He's a really good guy, Lapthorne."

"Good meaning like, what, in this instance?" he asked.

"Good meaning . . ."

I could see Lapthorne's face, another grownup leaning down to shake my hand when I got sent east for custody visits as a little kid, but he'd actually *looked* at me after asking how I was. We'd probably spent a total of seven hours together in our whole lives: one game of chess around when I was eight, then — maybe the following summer — an afternoon fishing for trout in an Adirondack guide boat.

Last time I'd seen him was for half of some other cousin's bridal dinner, right before I started senior year of boarding school.

Dean was still waiting for me to finish.

"I can't give you a concrete reason," I said, "except, if it were anyone else, the rest of the clan? You could pretty much take your pick and I would've called the cops from your parents' kitchen. Just not Lapthorne."

Dean looked out toward the horizon, considering. "This guy come to our wedding?"

"His mother did. Binty."

"Blonde strip of beef jerky, plays too much tennis?"

I had to smile at that. "Exactly."

He shivered, shaking out his arms. "Bitch needs a cheeseburger."

I pressed a toe against his shin. "*Please* don't make me laugh, it's too damn hot."

"Swear to God, your family —"

"Oh, right, and Jesus wants *Wimpy* for a sunbeam."

He shrugged in concession and cracked a grin at me.

I looked up into his eyes, wide set, the clear caramel of strong tea. He leaned down to nuzzle into my neck.

"You're crazy," I said.

He pulled back a couple of inches. "Why exactly?"

"Kissing a sweaty chick with a gun, exactly."

"A sweaty chick with a gun who's avoiding the issue of whether or not her favorite cousin got away with murder." He nipped my earlobe with his eyeteeth.

I straightened up, moved away from him. "Oh, so suddenly this is *my* responsibility?"

"What, suddenly?"

"Well, I mean, how many years has Cal had those dog tags? Doesn't seem like any of you were in a great hurry. Now it's this huge looming issue because my cousin's name comes up?"

"Who said huge and looming? I'm just broaching the idea of the cops."

I looked away from him, out across the inland sea of corn, toward the scrim of dark woods. The piles of cargo inside my head shifted, just the tiniest bit.

Because, hey, if I was absolutely convinced of my cousin's innocence, why wouldn't I call the cops, just march inside the farm shop and pick up that old black Bakelite receiver and dial away? Indeed, if he were innocent, what would it matter if I called them or not?

And Lapthorne was a great guy. I meant every word I'd just said to Dean. It was just, you know, *history.* I couldn't suppress that little flicker, that little tickling edge of doubt. Two girls dead. One of my relatives in the vicinity.

I imagine most people would deny the possibility of a killer in the family. With us, start counting at Plymouth Rock and you'll run out of fingers before Paul Revere. Take Captain John Underhill, who directed the massacre of Connecticut's Pequot Indians. Before dawn on May 26, 1637, his troops set fire to the tribe's wigwams and wooden palisades. He reported, "Many were burnt in the fort, both men, women, children. Others forced out, and came in troops . . . twenty and thirty at a time, which our soldiers received and entertained with the point of the sword."

Governor William Bradford later wrote, "It was a fearful sight to see them thus frying in the fyer, and the streams of blood quenching the same, and horrible was the stincke and sente there of."

They killed between four hundred and seven hundred people in under an hour. Underhill boasted that the young soldiers with him were sickened by "so many souls gasping on the ground, so thick, in some places, that you could hardly pass along."

When asked why they had not spared the women and children, he said only, "We had sufficient light from the word of God for our proceedings."

He was paid a bonus by the crown, used it to buy a chunk of Long Island, an estate he named Killingworth.

The only known depiction of Underhill isn't from life, it's a bronze plaque at the foot of a memorial obelisk erected in 1901 by a society of his descendants. He's shown seated on a throne, reading from a great book to the Indians crouched adoring at his feet. You can just make out the text beneath which his finger trails: *Love One Another.*

You might argue that he's just one guy, that lighting all those little kids and their families on fire took place four hundred years ago, that perhaps I should consider moving on.

My answer is that he's a random pick, the slip of paper pulled first from a tragically full hat . . . nothing up my sleeve.

Not like we don't have harmless people, too. Needlepointers. Bow-tied collectors of scrimshaw. In Mom's branch we've pretty much universally devolved into a slough of ineffectual bohemianism. We say it's the "circus blood," her mother having been adopted.

But still there's this disturbing frequency of bad guys. I could give you the whole timeline rundown, from "Blankets, Smallpox" through "Napalm, Profits to Dow Shareholders From," but it doesn't matter where you start or where you finish, what volume you pull off the shelf or which page it falls open to. One minute somebody's signing a check to help knock off Allende or whoever and the next you've got some dowager confiding over her pre-luncheon bourbon that "Hitler had the right idea," right before she tosses the Pekinese an ice cube to chase around the library rug.

After a while it's all a blur. Everything starts to crowd in on everything else, like those tigers running around the tree faster and faster until there's nothing left but a pool of butter.

I wanted to believe Lapthorne was different, but I wasn't going to say shit to anybody until I knew for sure. Not the cops, not my paper.

Dean nudged me again, said softly, "Bunny, what — you're into this guy?"

"Let's start shooting," I said. "I need to think."

CHAPTER 4

The first artificial trap-shooting targets were blown-glass balls thrown up by hand. Sometimes these were filled with feathers, and I always thought it would be spectacularly satisfying to nail one, making it explode in a shower of down and glittering shards.

We had cases of clay pigeons, stout little Frisbees made of pitch and chalk. I handed the gun to Dean, stock first. While I loaded the trap, he thumbed a shell into each barrel and snapped the breech shut. We had earplugs in, pretty much precluding conversation, which was fine with me.

Dean yelled, "Pull!" and I sent the first disc winging across the corn. He hit it dead on. One second you could see it and the next there was nothing but smoke — just a mist of black powder against the sky.

I knew he would have preferred shooting woodchucks and rats, to placate his Swiss-Scots compulsion for industry, but my interest in guns has never extended to taking out anything with a heartbeat.

When it was my turn I tried to stand loose, a little bend to my knees.

You don't have the gun at your shoulder when the clay's released. You have to "mount" it from a resting position, remembering to bring the stock to your cheek, not vice versa.

Sight down the barrels and imagine the clay's leaving a trail of smoke, like a dogfight biplane. Draw a bead on that ribbon of hypothetical vapor and swing up it, pulling the appropriate barrel's trigger just as you pass your target.

You want all of this to be one smooth arc, but if you think about it too much it breaks into all these separate pieces. I read once that King George V kept a shotgun in his bedroom so he could practice this lift-and-swing over and over, whenever he couldn't sleep. No mention of whether or not he kept it loaded.

I called, "Pull!"

Gun to cheek, swing, pull the first trigger, follow through . . .

You can't stop moving when you fire, since everything takes a few fractions of a second — the finger's response to the brain's command, the flight of the shot down the barrel and through the sky. You've got to shoot ahead of the clay, at the spot your little pigeon *will* be flying through by the time your reflex's shit is packed.

I missed it. *Concentrate. Visualize the sequence again, see yourself hit it. Start over. Deep breath . . .*

"Pull!" I followed up, up . . . pulled the second trigger and smoked the thing, making Dean whistle through his teeth.

I broke the gun and the empty shells clicked out an inch. I hooked a thumbnail under the rims and tossed them into the little pile Dean had started.

I was all jumpy, ended up taking the rest of my shots totally spaced out.

Of all my cousins, why Lapthorne? Why not porcine Ogden with that horrible laugh? Sulky

Jake of the short, damp fingers? Binty, even . . .

Dean's turn. He was shooting way better than I was. Even with earplugs I flinched at every crack of the gun.

We kept going until the sun was halfway down the sky, the day cooling but still muggy.

Dean stood up and stretched. I went to gulp warm water from the spigot.

He followed, touched my shoulder. "The dog tag thing. You want to just let it go?"

I shook my head, wiping the back of my hand against my mouth.

"Those girls who died," I said. "It would drive me crazy. I have to know."

"Let the police handle it, then."

"What if it's just some really weird coincidence?"

"What if it's not?"

I dropped my head and sighed, scuffing my shoe across the clods of dirt. "If it's not, if he did it . . . I mean, come *on*. Of course I'd go to the cops. But I want to check it out first."

He looked away.

I started pacing. "Maybe he was in Paris in '69 dropping acid, or doing some investment-banker training program, or whatever."

He cocked an eyebrow. "And?"

"And I don't *know,*" I said, taking his hand. "I need to see how much I can find out on my own. Honest to God — like just whether Lapthorne was even here in the right year, okay?"

I tried my most winning smile and Dean was completely unmoved.

He handed me the gun. "If you find anything, you have to tell the cops."

"Scout's honor," I said, holding up two fingers in the Brownie benediction.

"Jesus. You chicks from downstate." He shook his head, kneeling down by the trap.

We plugged our ears again and started up.

I hit the first two.

On the strength of that I figured I'd practice the only trick thing I knew, but had never mastered. I wished Dad had kept it together long enough to teach me how to shoot from the hip, something he'd learned from the guy who was Sean Connery's *Thunderball* gun coach.

Instead I'd heard the story from my mother, whenever it was James Bond Week on the Million-Dollar Movie.

I tried it for all the shots on my last two turns, and missed every goddamn one.

We got takeout from Sal's Birdland, "Home

of the Sassy Sauce," and ate cross-legged on our Naugahyde, dunking the greasy wings in sweet yellow syrup and scarfing down potato wedges in batter savory with black pepper and sage.

"I think I need to talk to Kenny," I said, when we lay groaning amidst wadded paper towels and Styrofoam clamshells piled with glistening bones.

Kenny was an old friend of Dean's, an ex-cop who tended our favorite skanky dive bar downtown.

"Probably Kenny and Mom," I said.

"There's a terrifying combo." Dean put his head in my lap and dangled his feet off the far end of the purple sofa.

I ran a fingertip along his jaw. "I need to know more about those girls, and more about Lappy."

"Lappy?" He emitted a snort of derision.

"So I don't call my relatives Wimpy and Weasel. You want to give me a hard time, go after Winthrop and Roderick."

He closed his eyes and smiled. "You married beneath you."

"All women do," I said, leaning down to kiss him, but he was already fast asleep.

I edged out from under him and tucked a pillow beneath his head. Married, the two of us. How weird was that? I mean, when I was a kid and someone asked what kind of husband I wished for, I always answered, "The kind that pays child support."

Not cynicism, exactly, just resignation. An honest appraisal. Dads who stayed on the team for their kids once things went to shit were a rare species in my childhood landscape.

Grownups didn't seem to pick spouses very well. No one had immunity. No one ever saw it coming. They had weddings and kids and houses and obviously thought it would turn out okay. I figured I could get away with minding my own business for a few years, building forts and what have you, but at a certain point you got overcome by these powerful and irrational forces that made you fall in love with someone who could turn out to be ridiculous to spend a life with, even if you were both otherwise perfectly decent people.

My parents hit the fan in 1967. He stayed on Long Island and she lit out for Honolulu, me and my sister in tow. California was the geographic compromise Mom struck with Michael, the second husband she'd acquired on Oahu.

Mom and Michael had my little brother before they broke up in '72, around the time Dad decided he didn't want to be a stockbroker anymore. By '76 he was in California, too, working at the Chevron in Malibu and living in his camper. He built a big bed in the back and kept all his stuff underneath it. That's when he started giving me castoffs, things from his past life that didn't fit anymore.

He needed room for the alfalfa sprouts he'd learned to grow in Hellmann's mayonnaise jars with Handi Wipes rubber-banded across their tops. He stopped paying child support. He discovered pita bread, made sprout-and-tuna sandwiches when my sister and I came to visit on school vacations. She was short enough to sleep in the hammock that hooked into brackets on either side of the windshield and I got the fold-out cot under the pop-top. We went to Disneyland a lot, which must have been hard for him to swing.

These days, Dad was still out in California, but Mom had moved home to Centre Island, the spit of land hooking into Oyster Bay on the north shore of Long Island. Her family had been there since 1698, but she lived with this guy Bonwit. Had they gotten married, he would have been stepfather umpteen. Not the nastiest of the bunch, to date, but he was close.

A car rattled up Green Street and Dean

stirred in his sleep on the sofa beside me.

"I got lucky," I said, quietly so he wouldn't wake up all the way. "I fell in love with you. It might turn out okay forever, but even if it doesn't I'm lucky right now."

He straightened out one leg, and I stroked his hair until he settled down again.

I stood up, thought about calling Mom to find out more about Lapthorne, but I had an article to crank out: "Hot Drinks for Winter" — not a topic I really wanted to tackle on another machete-humid evening, but it was due first thing and my boss was, to be kind, a loathsome and unforgiving prick.

I cued up the Allman Brothers instead, speakers pointed away from Dean. While the computer booted, I made myself a tall iced coffee and broke out my handy-dandy International Bartender's Guide to find some cocktails fellow Syracusans might want to drink après-ski, après-skate, or après-shovel-off-le-driveway.

I was flipping pages: gin, rum, cider, bup-kes. . . . Not a peep from the journo-muse until this punch called "Flames over New Jersey" snapped the bitch awake like a pistol start. I hit the keyboard at a dead sprint straight off the chocks, caffeine and "Whipping Post" blasting me through the finish tape hours later.

I stood up, all jangly, printed the file and cracked my neck and looked at the clock. Just shy of midnight, way past any hope of calling Mom. The street was quiet, Dean was still conked on the sofa, and I didn't want to think about dead girls.

Fresh pages in hand, I stepped onto our rickety porch to proofread. Once tipped back in a wicker chair, I just stared up at the mackerel sky instead: all those fat little clouds, bright and regular as abacus beads.

The moon glowed from a pocket of nacre, mother-of-pearl pinks and blues and silvers. Seven years since I'd last seen Lapthorne, the night before Cousin Ogden IV's wedding.

I propped my feet on the railing and let my fistful of paper sift to the paint-thick floor.

It had been a Labor Day weekend Friday. I flew into LaGuardia from California, seventeen years old and about to start my last scholarship year at boarding school — never suspecting Mom would ditch Carmel for Oyster Bay by graduation, that we'd all be sucked back into the ancestral maw.

The rehearsal dinner was black tie, held in the gardens behind the great stone house

Ogden the First had erected in Locust Valley, acres and acres of them, stretching down to the Sound.

It must have looked like a circus from the water: thousands of fairy lights twining through boxwood hedges, strings of paper lanterns arcing between stands of maple and copper beech, brick paths shimmering from folly to terrace to allée.

The seating diagram had me at a Table 16, off to the side of the first tent and behind a pole. I hadn't recognized the other names, so when I saw Lapthorne lounging in one of the little gold chairs, I figured I must've gotten the number wrong.

He saw me and stood up, crooking a finger to draw me over. Same easy slouch, even in a tuxedo. He sported a black raw-silk eyepatch, to match the cummerbund, and his dark hair curled at the edge of his collar.

I looked at his hooked blade of nose, the face just barely shy of too long, too narrow — thought of a Byron couplet: *One shade the more, one ray the less / Could half impair that nameless grace.*

The table was empty but for him, our fellow guests preferring the bar. Unoccupied chairs faced expectantly inward toward low, candle-spiked arrangements of ivy and white lilies.

51

"Chère cousine," he said, "over here, right next to me."

I must have looked a little confused, because he added, "Don't tell me you've forgotten poor old Lapthorne. . . ."

Impossible idea. From, like, the moment I turned eleven, I'd dreamed of winching every possible limb around the guy so as to spend at least a week licking his neck.

Judging from the little half-smile now playing across my cousin's mouth, this wish had not exactly been a secret.

"Couldn't forget the man who so kindly baited my first trout's hook," I said, cool as I could manage. "I just didn't see your name down for this table."

"I switched the place cards," he confided.

"Wicked thing," I said. "Hope the lady's worth it."

"She is indeed," he answered.

Then he leaned down to kiss my cheek, pausing long enough to say, directly against my ear, "Christ, Madeline, you turned out stunning."

I blushed in my sham finery — cast-off tux pumps with grosgrain bows, thrift-store black cotton caftan slit up the sides and decked with gold braid at the neck and wrists. Around my waist was the burgundy satin sash off an old brocade dressing gown, and my string of fake pearls fell to my knees. It had all seemed kind of sardonic Moroccan when I put it together, but I now felt full-on Sgt. Pepper doorman.

Lapthorne straightened up and pulled out my chair. The moment we were seated, staff in drip-dry livery arrived to grace us with salads.

I watched my cousin open his napkin with an impeccable flick beneath the table, then select the correct fork without so much as a glance at his choices. When we'd finished, he and I would each leave, alongside the identically angled cutlery on our plates, exactly one piece of lettuce as a testament to the salad's quality.

I'd described this custom to Dean in a restaurant once. After he finally stopped laughing, my husband assured me that the busboy would be deeply impressed.

When our salad plates were whisked away, Lester Lanin cued up the band in the next tent, starting off with "Night and Day" as he always did.

"Promise me a spot on your dance card?" asked Lapthorne.

Oh shit. No no no no no.

"Never went to, ah, dancing school," I said. "California and everything . . ."

"Dancing school's a load of crap," he

drawled. "Spent years myself under the stern eye of Mrs. De Rham. Only useful thing I learned was that one can flush lit cherry bombs down the toilets at Piping Rock."

"Still, I can't . . . I mean, even the *box-step* . . ."

"Don't be nervous," he said. "You *know* better. Have since you were five years old, Madeline."

He glanced around the room. "This is all just . . . perfume," he said, dismissing the Merchant-Ivory splendor with a casual wave of his hand. "Nothing to be afraid of, unless you confuse it with sustenance."

"You don't . . ."

He turned to look at me.

"It's different for you," I said.

"No."

"It is. Fundamentally. You're in it. You could walk away and this would all still be waiting, any time you wanted. . . ."

He shifted in his chair. "So can you, any time —"

"No," I said. "*Really.* I mean, no matter what, your place is assured."

"No more than yours," he said. "You have my guarantee."

And I didn't have to answer that, because they started sliding a new course in front of us, the dinner's acme: chilled lobster salad spooned back into the shell.

Lapthorne leaned in over his gilt-edged plate and picked the creature up with both hands, standing it on its tail so that clumps of pink meat plopped onto the porcelain below.

"I give you Julio Crustacean," he said, waving its claws around as though they wore little castanets, "Flamenco Dancer of the Sea . . ."

"How absolutely *cunning*," I said, in my very best lockjaw.

"Ostentatious," he sniffed, slipping into bitch-perfect clubwoman falsetto. "Ogden was *always* vulgar."

I shrugged, stuck a fork into my plate's mound of creamy shreds. "Beats hell out of airplane food."

"Honestly," he continued, voice still fluting as he batted his eyelashes at me, "you'd think his mother was a *hat-check* girl."

"A little gainful employment might have improved her sorry ass," I said. "Yours too."

Lapthorne laughed so hard he dropped the lobster.

"Don't be a snot," I said, pointing my fork at him, "or I won't give you a place to hide, come the revolution."

He bowed from the waist. "Consider me

chastened."

I nodded, then polished off my excellent supper, savoring the last bite's aftertaste just as Lester and the boys segued into "Cheek to Cheek."

"Playing our song," said Lapthorne.

He stood up and held out his hand to me, drawing me smoothly up the moment I took it.

He turned a little toward the bandstand, so our hands were behind his back, and then he did this subtle shift of the wrist, rolling his thumb slowly into the hollow of my palm, pressing it there for a long moment before he started toward the music.

This early the dance floor was populated entirely by the ancient — female dreadnoughts cruising in the arms of their silver-haired escorts.

When we'd reached the exact center of the parquet, Lapthorne turned toward me and transferred my right hand to his left, raising it to the height of his shoulder. I tried to dredge up some clue about how to comport myself, no matter how trivial. The only thing I could remember was hearing Mom once remark that she always turned that hand palm-out, at the nape of her partner's neck.

"Gives your fingers a nice loose drape,"

she'd said. "Far more elegant than clutching their shoulders."

So that's what I did when he pressed the small of my back and drew me in.

"Never done this," I said. "You've been warned."

He smiled down at me. "Nothing to it."

Close up, Lapthorne smelled of limes and woodsmoke. He kept his right hand low, applying serious pressure just above my tailbone. Guy knew what he was doing. It was like that spot unlocked the secret, shot some rays through my teenage-white-girl hip-socket chakra.

I stopped thinking and my legs disappeared. Nothing but glide.

Pretty soon he made us spin so the hem of my dress flew out.

"See?" he said. "You're a natural. Must get it from your mother."

"Always thought I'd take after Dad. He used to go up to girls at deb parties and say, 'Excuse me, would you like to sit this one out?' "

Lapthorne laughed and the band continued with "This Could Be the Start of Something Big." More people came out on the floor and Lester started tossing out those trademark little party-favor beanie hats, his name painted on each in script.

They spun out over the crowd, pink and red and powder blue and pale yellow. Hands reached to snatch them out of the air.

"That's my cue to exit," said Lapthorne. "He makes me nervous with those damn things. Only have one eye left, after all. Wanna go smoke a joint?"

I was just relieved to get the hell off the floor without having crippled him. We walked away from the heat and the light and the low hum of the crowd, Lester's mellow horn section made bouncy with a little piano and electric guitar — soulless music, reverberating through the trees.

We made our way down a gentle hill toward the water, following a stone path into a long rose-draped pergola that curved around a fountain.

Lapthorne took an old monogrammed cigarette case out of his pocket and lit a little hand-rolled number, taking a hit and passing it to me. I took a couple of really small tokes and turned it down the third time he offered.

Weed can make me hideously self-conscious. One hit's kind of okay, unless you're talking some sticky monster African bud, vat-grown in Maui with red hairs all over it and so resiny it smells like a parking lot full of Christmas trees. That stuff kills me if I so much as walk by a house where someone's doing a bong hit.

I'm such a lightweight that I stick to a single hit of even the lamest pot. Seriously — it could be dried-out Mexican crap stolen from somebody's mother's Woodstock-era stash and half cut with oregano. Two hits and my knees get creaky, then I start obsessing over the stupidity of every word that leaves my mouth.

I could say something innocuous as "That looks yellow" and hear it echo around my skull for half an hour in different intonations.

The only thing that gets me over this THC angst is eating an entire bag of Doritos and going immediately to bed for about fourteen hours. I would have made a really lousy hippie.

Lapthorne's stash seemed like typical East Coast junior-varsity shake. A decent buzz, nothing freaky. I reached up and picked one of the roses — deep pink and thornless.

I pressed my nose into it, caught the heady perfume of the antique Bourbons, the note of raspberry . . .

"Zephirine Drouhin, you think?" I said.

The petals started falling out, drifting to the ground.

"I think it's a good color for you." He

raised his hand and plucked another, tucking it behind my ear. "Belle of the ball."

I thanked him, half expected him to lean down and kiss me. Didn't know whether I wanted him to or not. *Liar liar pants on fire.*

He crossed his arms. "How old are you?"

"Eighteen," I said. "In March."

"Too young to be unchaperoned, I'm afraid. Especially with an ancient bachelor of thirty-two."

"Old enough to smoke your dope, though."

"Point taken," he conceded, but still he tucked my hand through the crook of his arm and started leading me back up the hill to the dancing tent.

If it had all happened a year or two after, I would have just laced my fingers into his lapels and planted one on him.

Soon as we stepped into the light, Lapthorne's mother and father came scything toward us. From a distance they looked so perfect, elegant as something only Avedon could have captured on film.

Binty's dress was more architecture than couture — strapless shantung the exact shade of her dark sapphires. Her white-gold chignon, cranked tight at the nape of her neck, set off skin tanned as a catcher's mitt.

She stopped within two feet of me. That

60

close, the woman was so goddamn thin she looked like a stocking full of hangers.

I gazed at her face: loooong upper lip and tiny eyes . . . Really. Black. Eyebrows.

Cat in the Hat.

Oh, man . . . I was so stoned it was just ugly.

"Couldn't you at least have gotten a haircut for this, Lappy?" Binty cut off her son's hello, narrow hand gripping a tall pale glass.

She didn't acknowledge me, just turned to present a shoulder blade slopped with freckles. I shifted my eyes to her husband.

Didn't take much to figure out which parent had the dough. Kit's contribution was entirely decorative.

He was the source of Lapthorne's looks, sporting the same finely hewn features, the dark hair that might have betrayed some curl of its own if he hadn't always kept it so very short.

He wasn't looking at any of us. Just stood there, smiling — the perfect arm-job, striking but so bland his wife never had to get rattled over it. Nothing of his son's spark, of the sly hips or hint of slouch.

"Mummie," said Lapthorne, giving Binty's cheek an obedient near-kiss, "you remember Cousin Madeline?"

I held out my hand to shake hers, but she was focused on her son.

"The Trotters have been here for *hours*," she said. "Daddy wanted you to *meet* them."

My knees started to feel weird. I kept shifting my weight and I could practically hear the cartilage grind.

Binty got more Dr. Seuss by the second. Goddamn *sleeper* dope, the kind that just kept getting worse no matter how "too high" you felt already.

I bit the inside of my cheek. My hand was still sitting in midair, ready to shake.

Finally, Binty deigned to acknowledge me. "*Lovely* to see you, dear. How *is* your mother?"

"Fine, thank you, Cousin Binty. She asked me to send you both her regards."

Like hell.

I looked from her to Kit and back, tried to peel my lips off my cotton-mouth teeth for a smile. When would I learn that the marijuana gods were *not* my friends?

"Are you having a nice evening?" she continued, frowning a little as those tiny eyes raked me up and down.

I flexed each knee in turn.

She gave me demerits for the flower behind my ear, then X-rayed through to the tiny gold pair of safety pins that were knitting up my raveled sleeve with care.

"I'm a little nervous —" I began, about to compliment her son's dancing.

Binty shifted her glass so she could pat my still-just-idiotically-sitting-there hand with drink-chilled fingers.

"Don't worry," she said, in a smoker's whisper all could hear, "I was fat when I was your age, too."

She spun on her heel. "Kit . . . the *Trotters* . . ."

Lapthorne watched her go, face tight.

"My apologies, Madeline," he said. "There goes proof one can be both too rich *and* too thin."

I dropped my head and started blinking really fast, so he wouldn't see me cry.

"None of that, now," said Lapthorne. "After all, she's . . . well, I take it you're familiar with her nickname?"

I shook my still-hung head.

"Ice Cunt," he said, and I couldn't help it, the image was so perfect it just yanked these hard little pieces of laughter out of me, like I was barking.

"Your Uncle Hunt's invention," he explained. "Says it's because the ambient temperature drops five degrees whenever Mummie enters a room."

I peeked up at him and he was grinning, all conspiratorial.

"Plus," he said, "I would imagine she's consumed with envy when she sees someone who looks like you. Dad makes her wear heavy veils at home, and it's widely known that he prefers the embraces of the pool boy."

"Kit?"

"May I get you a cocktail?"

I nodded, still stunned.

Lapthorne tilted his head back and smiled, tracing a slow finger along my collarbone before he drifted off in his parents' wake.

How could anyone fail to defend a man like that?

Okay, so from my Syracuse porch it seemed like a thousand years ago, but then anything to do with those people always feels like some Edith Wharton time warp.

It takes effort, afterwards, to shake the money out of my head so I can resume my actual life.

I went back in to the sofa, nudged Dean awake, and propelled him gently to bed.

In the dark I kept thinking about Cal's description of the murdered girls, kept seeing Lapthorne's face when he welcomed me to the table.

I wanted the night to be over. I wanted to get cracking.

CHAPTER 5

I was late for work, stuck again at the five-way Erie Boulevard light. Most mornings I'd drum my fingers on the wheel and wonder why the hell they'd filled in the canal, still down there under the Boulevard's wide stretch of asphalt. I'd inspect the once-proud buildings, spiky with imperial turrets and crenellations, and imagine how much better they'd have looked from the water, from a barge deck's slow glide behind a mule.

Now I just thought about the dead girls. Necks cut to the bone. The sight enough to make an old man vomit even days after he found them.

I couldn't stop the video loop, kept groping for a distraction. I scrunched my eyes shut and tried to picture my favorite photograph of Syracuse. It was taken not far from the intersection at which I was stopped, a grainy old shot of ice-skaters on the frozen canal. There were young boys in knickers and knit hats with pom-poms, arms swinging as they raced through the crowd. A dancing woman in a picture hat. Spectators looking on from the streets above.

The figures cast long northeasterly shadows across the ice, so it must have been taken toward the end of that afternoon. It would have been cold, no doubt with the slicing wind I knew from having lived through two raw winters here, but still there's a sense of possibility, of wonder.

You look at that crowd and you know they were aware of being *spectacular* — worth looking at, deserving of record.

With the canal gone, the city's best-known body of water is the one east of town: Oncas Lake, the most polluted in the United States.

One hundred years ago, its shores were dotted with hotels and pavilions. A four-hundred-foot steel pier beckoned to ferries and pleasure boats, and "Oncas" salmon and whitefish were prized by chefs across the state.

A confession: my great-grandmother Dodie came from the family that killed this lake. Her father discovered a miraculous chemical manipulation, the "Lapthorne Process."

I read once that a single thermometer-full of mercury is enough to make 10,000 one-pound bass unfit to eat. His factory pumped

165,000 pounds of it into the lake.

By the onset of World War II, Oncas was dead — literally suffocated. Anaerobic reactions in the muddy bottom produced carpets of fizzy, sulphurous bubbles so powerful they could break off acre-wide rafts of sludge and buoy them up to the surface. When the wind was right, the stench of brimstone made people gag all the way "down-city."

By that point, of course, Dodie's family had sold the company, embarking downstate on what I'd once heard referred to as "the Schlep of Tears." I suppose for my relatives you'd have to rename it "the Long Dark Cocktail Party of the Soul," or talk about fleeing the Trust Bowl.

When I hated living in Syracuse the most, I told myself I'd returned to perform ancestral penance, long overdue. Lapthorne's parents, meanwhile, had named him to honor that branch of the family.

I'd sooner christen a child Thalidomide, or Triangle Shirtwaist Fire.

The Erie Boulevard light went green again, and at long last I was first in line.

When I climbed out of my car, it was so muggy the sky looked like a slab of gray-veined marble. I ran up the stairs to the third-floor offices of the *Weekly,* collapsing in ecstasy at my desk since the air conditioner was working again.

Editorial was empty, but there was a note on my keyboard: "See me immediately. Ted."

That would be my skinny red-haired boss, the loathsome and unforgiving prick. Dean called him "the Angst Lizard."

I booted up my computer and thrust the floppy from home into the A drive. If I had to tangle with Ted first thing, I wanted to do it with work in hand.

I sent the hot drinks article to the printer, two desks over, then took an infusion of painfully bad coffee while my pages wheezed out of our dot-matrix behemoth.

Looking at Ted's door, I was pissed all over again that my buddy Karen, the old department head, had lit out for Boston.

She would have liked "après-shovel-off-le-driveway." She would have kept Ted off my back about whatever the hell it was this time.

Ted was usually stoned, spending a lot of time in the parking lot with Wilt, the senior writer. Syracuse University had a fine journalism program, the Newhouse School, and Ted and Wilt had met there in the sixties. The *Weekly* was a free paper, but a good one — packed with a lot more New-house grads in every department.

The printer finally finished spitting out my article, a task that could have been done faster by medieval illuminators. I grabbed my coffee and walked over to Ted's door, opened just a crack.

He barked "Get in here!" before I could knock.

"Chief," I said, noting the six-pack of Visine, the red hair skinned back into a ponytail.

He had his back to me. Just as well. Even from behind, Ted was all pointy angles, like something with an exoskeleton, or Ichabod Crane.

He scratched the side of his head frantically. Every jag of his fingernails snapping a few hairs from the gray rubber band. I watched them spring into coils.

He spun around. "Those goddamn pictures of you didn't come out."

Simon the photographer and I had spent the previous Friday afternoon in the parking lot below, with me wrapped up in all the winter clothes we could find in the office lost-and-found. I'd had to smile over an earth-toned mug of boiling water in the midday heat while passersby made pro-foundly unwitty comments. I'd posed since we had zero budget for models and everyone else on staff had appeared in the paper too often.

"Simon says steam doesn't photograph," he continued, "so he's looked up some other way to make it look like you're holding a hot mug of delicious whatever."

I wanted to say, "And this is my fault by what stretch of your pitiful imagination?" but mumbled instead, "Um, how?"

Ted glared at me, a stoned praying mantis steepling its fingers.

"Cigarette smoke," he said. "We'll have Wilt kneel down next to you and blow it through a tube. You can probably hold it under your thumb, once you've got those mittens back on." He grinned like that was the most entertaining image he'd ever considered, and the only thing better would be if I bitched so he could have the satisfaction of ordering me to suck it up.

"Can't wait," I said.

Ted was right to get the shot now. We'd be freezing our asses off soon enough, and any lead time was a good thing. Still, he didn't have to be so damn happy about it.

I couldn't figure out why he hated me. The guy either wanted to jump my bones or was utterly repulsed. I couldn't tell. Not really something you could discuss without sounding like a complete idiot, so I just let it all fester.

Half an hour later I stood sweltering in the parking lot, in a fur-lined Mad Pilot cap, a wool muffler, and Ted's brown tweed overcoat. Tall, rangy Wilt was down on one knee next to me, just out of the shot. He had a British Invasion mop of hair and a Fu Manchu mustache. George Harrison on stilts.

"Wilton, man, you're killing me," I said as he blew another lungful of smoke through the tubing I held to the edge of my mug.

"America's favorite health kick," quipped Simon, snapping away.

The fingernails on our photographer's chubby left hand were blackened by near-constant immersion in the developer Amidol. One of my more odious stepfathers had been a photographer. Same creepy manicure.

In all other respects, Simon reminded me of a Hummel figurine: big head and belly, dimpled pink cheeks and rosebud mouth, eyelashes longer than my arm. He was almost totally bald, but the dark strip of hair left to him was all fluffy, glistening curls, like the tonsure of a Disney monk.

Even his personality was pure kitsch — shy, cherubic, unfailingly helpful.

He spent most of his time in the *Weekly's* basement, where the back-issue "morgue" and his darkroom were. He maintained an extensive photo archive down there, could turn his hand to virtually anything needed upstairs, from an eight-by-ten of the Miss Syracuse Diner under construction in 1932 to one of Mick Jagger backstage at the Carrier Dome.

His own photographs were the *Weekly's* strongest feature. Never a grainy shot, never anything done in less than perfect focus and contrast. His blacks were dark inky voids, the mark of a true pro.

The only trouble was that he made everybody look psychotic, even the little kids in the back-to-school issue. And here I was all sweaty, squinting in Wilt's fumes. There was no way around it, appearing in forty-two thousand free newspapers was going to hugely suck.

"You guys take a break," said Simon. "I need a reflector."

Wilt rocked back on his heels and then sat, stretching his legs out along the asphalt.

I put down the wretched cup and took off my hat and scarf, gulping down fresh hot air.

"Goddamn mittens," I said. "Today I'll really earn that $23.70 after taxes."

"Today you should ask for a raise."

"No way."

Wilt tilted his head from side to side, cracking his neck. "Ted's a pussycat."

"You get high with him all day."

"He likes you," said Wilt. "Likes you fine."

I rolled my eyes. "How's Lee doing?"

Wilt was covering the mayoral race, had picked another doomed liberal favorite.

"Tanking," he said.

"They do another poll?"

He shook his head. "That buffet yesterday," he said. "No shrimp. Hotel Syracuse brings out the baked ziti, might as well go home."

"No shit."

"Such a drag, man. I've had my eye on Lee like forever. Good guy. But what can you expect from a place that reelected a mayor under indictment, twice?"

He shook out another Pall Mall. Lit it.

I sat on the ground next to him, Indian style. Might as well just jump in and ask him. "Hey, you were here in '69, right?"

Wilt nodded.

"So, uh, you remember that double murder? Two chicks at the fair?"

"My first cover story." He blinked and looked down at the cigarette, stoner-pinched between thumbnail and index finger. "The

Rose Girls. Horrible."

"What?"

"Comes from how they were found. They had, like, wreaths or whatever around their heads . . . blossoms all twined together. Garlands." Wilt took a drag and held it for a second, leaned back to blow a ribbon of smoke straight up. It hung there, curling slowly outward in the thick air.

"Hell," he said finally, "Simon can show you. He's still got all the pictures."

He looked back at me, then dropped his eyes just a notch.

I was covering my throat with both hands.

CHAPTER 6

Roses and Lapthorne. It wasn't just the blossom he'd tucked behind my ear at that wedding — the connection went deeper.

Our great-grandmother Dodie had had several hundred rosebushes planted in the family cemetery after her husband Jake burned to death at sea — the victim of a purser's arson on one of his passenger liners, the *Glamis Castle*.

The ship's hulk ran aground at Atlantic City, floating up in the surf along with a couple of hundred charred and bloated bodies. They never identified his.

There was no other memorial for him, just that garden Dodie'd woven in amongst the crooked aisles of headstones.

When I was sent east in the summers, I spent hours there. It was a cool, fragrant haven overlooking Oyster Bay, and I'd memorized flower names from the little bronze plaques next to each bed.

Tipsy Imperial Concubine's pink cabbage-head blooms hung drowsy on stems too weak to hold them upright. Paul's Himalayan sprawled along the surrounding brick wall, a single plant encircling the whole acre. Ferdinand Pichard was a clear white, striped with crimson and purple, and bloomed all summer — a rarity in this collection of old garden roses, most of which had a big "flush" of flowers in the spring and a second smaller one in early fall.

When the blossoms were less profuse, well through July, the cemetery smelled of cool green boxwood. I could lie on the grass there just staring out across the bay, watching the tiny Junior Club catboats crossing back and forth as the young sailors rounded their marks in an afternoon race.

I had to see the flowers from which the dead girls' garlands were made. If they had the slender pointed buds of hybrid teas, those scentless blooms you find in Miss America's arms and FTD bouquets, I could breathe easier.

Darkroom chemicals gave the morgue a doctor's-office reek. Wilt had told Simon what I wanted to know, so after lunch he was ready with a fat manila folder and an old *Weekly* laid out on his worktable.

He motioned me to take a seat next to him, then nudged the yellowed paper toward me with his black-nailed left hand.

It looked totally sixties, down to the journal's name rendered in a font so Art Nouveau it might have been lifted off a pack of rolling papers.

I examined the cover photo. "This one of yours?"

Simon nodded. It had been shot indoors: rose petals scattered around a photo-booth picture strip, all on a background of seamless paper. Half the petals were glowing white, half must have been a true red, which photographs as black.

Two young women — one fair, one dark — appeared together in each little frame of the strip. In the first, they were as stiff and serious as that *American Gothic* farm couple. In the second, they had dissolved into a fit of giggles, the blonde making bunny ears with her fingers behind the brunette's head. Frame three showed them vamping it up, one pursing her lips in a Marilyn Monroe shut-eyed smooch, while the other swooned, hand against her forehead, glamorous as a young Gish sister. In the last shot the pair just grinned — young, relaxed, and vibrantly enjoying themselves on a long-lost late summer night. Behind their heads was a cheesy banner reading "1969 New York State Fair" in bowling-alley-snackbar script. There wasn't a rose in sight.

I'd been expecting bouffant *That Girl* flips, but these were slick-looking hippie chicks — long straight hair and middle parts. Syracuse had never been a fashion haven. Photos from here tended to look about five years behind those from downstate. The girls weren't local.

The brunette was in a beautifully embroidered peasant blouse with big hoop earrings and a wide jet-beaded choker, while the blonde wore a French sailor shirt and what looked like an ebony figa, a tiny carved fist, hanging from a short necklace of rawhide thong. In 1969, that's the kind of stuff only rich city kids were wearing. Here in the outback, high school girls were still indistinguishable from Tricia Nixon.

Sure, they might have been downstate

chicks who'd gone to SU, but then someone would have identified them in a heartbeat.

The headline read "Who Are These Lost Girls?" Who indeed?

"Where'd you get this?" I asked, pointing at the images of the pair.

"They gave out copies to everybody, all the papers. TV. Trying to identify the bodies."

He leaned across me and carefully opened the pages to a section he'd marked with a strip of white paper.

"These are mine," he said, tapping in succession shots of the cornfield, the farmer, the grove of trees encircled with crime scene tape, all laid out alongside Wilt's text. He'd only touch the edge of each, as though the inked halftone renditions were still real prints that could be marred by the oil from his fingertips.

Not a one showed the bodies, the garlands. By the time he'd been given access, the coroner's van was long gone.

As though he'd heard me thinking, Simon said, "Of course, these were shot after they'd, ah, finished processing the scene."

So there was no way I'd be able to check out the roses.

"I guess you'll want to read Wilt's stuff," said Simon, with a shy smile. He left the table, and I could hear him puttering behind me.

I started in on the text:

The Rose Girls
by Wilton Shakely

When Harvey Johnston set out to harvest his corn that morning, he wasn't expecting anything other than a long day's work, but as he came up an outside row, perched high atop the seat of his corn-picker at roughly 10 a.m., he saw something no one should have to.

Two girls lay side by side in a tiny grove along the western edge of Johnston's acreage. They were on their backs, about a foot apart, and holding hands. Each girl wore a crowning garland of roses.

"At first I thought they were asleep," he said. "They looked so pretty. It didn't strike me for the longest time that their throats was cut. I guess I must have seen it, but just didn't want to know."

Johnston ran to call the police. Investigators were on the scene by eleven o'clock.

Officer Jack Schneider reports that the girls had been dead less than 24 hours when his crew arrived, and credits Mr.

Johnston with having found them so quickly.

I glanced at a photo of Schneider in the margin. Brush cut and a grim face — his mouth drawn crooked, with no lips to soften the edges. Something wrong with the eyes, maybe too much ink?

"If he'd been finished harvesting," said Schneider, "we might not have found them 'til spring. That patch of trees is hidden from the road."

The girls have not been identified. Photos found in their possession place them at the New York State Fair the previous evening. Carnival workers saw the pair walking in the company of two Camp Drum soldiers.

Mrs. Ruby Finegarb, who operates the Whack-A-Mole game, said that the soldiers tried to win stuffed pandas for the girls by playing several rounds, but had not succeeded. "They was all laughing and giggling," she said, "but they run out of dimes before they won a dang candy dish, and I couldn't break a fifty. Them soldiers must have just got paid."

Another man claiming to have seen the foursome is Archie Sembles, a silhouette artist working some hundred feet beyond Mrs. Finegarb's booth. Sembles remembers cutting portraits of all four young people near the close of the fair that night. "I had one of the girls put her hair up with a Spanish comb, as I thought it would add to the elegance of the depiction. The other girl had lovely thick dark hair, and I asked her to braid it quickly and to pull the braid over the top of her head, imitating another old-fashioned style. They were all quite pleased with the results." The silhouettes have not been found.

On the next page, bland police sketches accompanied the text — two guys in uniform. They seemed so generic that either could have been Lapthorne, really, or anyone.

. . . Police sketches of the two soldiers have been circulated but have not, thus far, led to any positive identification.

An enlargement of the last image from the girls' photo strip was centered amidst the columns of print. Another image appeared below, one more shot of where the bodies had been found, a close-up.

You could see the police tape, some tree trunks, a few small rocks in the dirt — but not a single flower.

I closed the paper. Simon was behind me, rolling heavy file drawers open and shut.

"Hey, Simon, can I ask you something?" I looked again at the petals on the front page. "How did you choose these roses for the cover? Did you make them red and white just for the visual, or did the cops say what color the garlands were? Wilt doesn't specify in the article."

Simon walked to the table. In the fluorescent light, he looked like library paste. Dude needed to get out more.

"I thought Wilt explained in the parking lot," Simon said. "I have *all* the photos."

He sat next to me again, reaching for the manila folder that rested on the table's far edge. He dragged it over but didn't open it.

"What do you mean, 'all,' Simon?"

He looked down and away, a little more color coming to his cheeks. "I knew some guys. Cops. Buddy over there slipped me a set of his prints, for the archives."

The real roses had to be in there, but Simon wasn't letting go of the file. He started stroking it, running his fat hand across the cardstock. He sighed.

I crossed my arms, squeezing my hands against my ribs so I didn't just rip the thing from him. His little paw went pat, pat, pat.

"Simon?"

He sighed again. "Sure you want to see these? They're, ah . . . detailed."

I nodded.

He lifted the cover to reveal a pile of eight-by-ten glossies.

The first had been taken from the corn-field, facing the grove. It was black-and-white, shot from the same perspective as one of Simon's, only in this the girls were still there. While it was in sharp focus and well lit, it was done from such a distance that you couldn't tell much about the bodies, other than that they were barefoot, and holding hands.

The second shot was from just to the right of their feet, giving a three-quarter view of them. The girls' hair fanned out prettily along a bed of moss, as though carefully arranged. You could see the dark gashes in their throats, but the garlands were camouflaged — white against blonde, near-black against brunette.

There was something odd about the darker roses, an uncanny reflection, maybe moisture catching the light. Not enough detail to tell.

Next was an extreme close-up, in color, showing only glossy mahogany hair set off by cupped blooms in a deep red.

It hadn't been the lighting. Each petal was limned with that narrow band of white known as a "picotée edge." Unmistakable: Baron Girod de l'Ain, a French hybrid perpetual introduced in 1894.

Simon lifted the glossy carefully away. Beneath was a shot of blonde locks, tiny clusters of snowy rosettes. Félicité-Perpétue? Didn't matter. I was hip-deep in shit.

CHAPTER 7

I pushed my chair back from Simon's worktable, sickened. Unless I could come up with compelling evidence to the contrary, I had to work from the premise that my cousin was a murderer.

I pictured myself going to the cops, pounding my fist on some bureaucratic Formica until they reopened the case because of my gardening know-how.

Cha. And then they'd crown me Homecoming Queen and drive me around in a convertible. Even when you threw in the dog tags and the blood-type stuff, it sounded crazy.

Simon was obviously expecting me to say something, but I just couldn't. I mean, first because I was terrified that if I opened my mouth I'd puke, but mostly because I really couldn't tell what it would all sound like, bunched together.

Was I just being paranoid? Would anyone else see meaning in this weird little fistful of data? I was so shaky, I couldn't tell.

It was another genealogical trip on my part, to be honest. I mean, in addition to the Indian killers and the nuke-the-commies-back-to-the-Stone-Age types, we were prone to delusion. Dad's whole elaborate deal with the KGB agents sneaking around his camper, that Winthrop guy his wife had to keep in a cage, my paternal grandmother's predictions of snowballing disaster, always taglined, "and then you'll get to the hospital and the anesthesia won't work."

With genes like that, you want to keep a damn close eye on the things that make your guy-wires twang. Seek outside verification. Get a professional opinion.

Nip things in the bud.

Oh crap.

I really, really, really wanted to throw up.

"You okay?" Simon laid his black-nailed hand across mine and I flinched, yanked down from high orbit.

I swallowed bile, then took a deep breath. "It's just horrible. Those girls."

I could tell he expected more, but even though I was desperate to ask him what else he knew, I couldn't trust my ability to sound detached. I needed to think this through, get some distance.

"Listen," I said, standing up. "I'm, uh, really grateful you took the time to show me this stuff, but it's kind of . . . I mean, I think I need some air."

I was all wobbly and he smiled at me, suddenly beatific, his tiny white teeth wreathed in that fat pink blossom of a mouth.

He moved both hands to his lap, beneath the table, and for a second I had this flash of conviction that he wasn't trying to be reassuring or sympathetic, that he was instead kind of *into* how freaked out I was — feeding off it.

And then I thought, *Jesus, Madeline, will you just fucking get over yourself already*, and started for the door.

I didn't actually throw up, but it required force of will and several minutes barricaded in a bathroom stall, cross-legged atop the toilet with a wet paper towel over my eyes, trying to remember breathing stuff from high school gym class yoga.

Desperate measures.

Back at my desk, I wanted to take some

86

action. Use up the nervous energy.

I dialed Mom in Long Island. Just for groundwork, I told myself. Nothing direct until I saw her in person.

She picked up, effervescent as always.

"Hey, it's me," I said.

"Well, what's *happening* in fashionable Syracuse?"

"I think they've finished the butter sculpture for the fair," I said, and she laughed. "How's it down in the actual world?"

"Eight women for lunch, so I made my *new* gazpacho. So easy, holy crow: just a can of V8 and last night's salad in the blender. A little shake of parsley . . ."

Usually she ate all that slimy black lettuce for breakfast. I pictured it whirling in a glass carafe and had to lean away from the receiver for a second, lips shucked back and tongue sticking out in a Trader Vic's— fiberglass-vengeful-tiki-gargoyle grimace.

I tuned out until the gazpacho all-clear had sounded, waving the phone back and forth past my ear, making her voice fizzle and surge like the BBC on a short-wave.

". . . done in *petit* point, of all things," she was saying, "and only a couple of burns in one toe. But of course Bonwit's still in Newport with Rafe — finishing touches on that little steam launch and home Saturday."

Mom lived with Bonwit. He hadn't divorced his second wife, merely invited her to move out. Number two groused until he tossed in a bunch of consolation houses and a freaking ginormous allowance.

Mom didn't care about his money, she was in love with him, had been since practically forever. He was twenty-five years her senior, but she had a thing for older married guys. You could trace it back to when she was in ninth grade at Greenvale, the moment she first necked with a friend of her parents named Dealie Van Couvering.

I met him once. Major asshole, same as Bonwit.

Mom is just wired that way.

"They've torn down the Gubelprechts'," she burbled, "great big Dumpster out back, so I have the most mag-*nif*-icent curtains for you. Peach moiré. Thought I'd drive them up Friday."

"Can't wait," I said. "What time?"

The reply was a dial tone. Typical.

Mom's like double-dating with Zelda Fitzgerald.

I wedged a shoulder against the receiver, dialing for Dean. We agreed to meet at the Crown Hotel so I could talk to Kenny, but only after Dean had finished up with his welding.

"Seven o'clock," he said. "Very earliest."

I'd have time to run home first, after work. Kick back and think.

I stared at my computer screen, thought about the rest of the shit I should be doing, such as actual work.

Couldn't stop running through Simon's collection of images. Something about them bugged me. Not the violence they recorded — awful as all of it was. This was different. A peripheral itch, a detail that wasn't quite right. A subtle wrongness, but one that mattered all the same.

It cranked up what Judith Goldiner had peevishly called my "photogenic memory" one afternoon in tenth-grade Chemistry. This was part talent, part affliction: I retained gobs of information so well I never took notes in school — maybe because I never remembered to bring a pencil. Poor Judith was thoroughly sick of lending me hers.

I closed my eyes, ran a slide show of the images in Simon's folder. Close-ups: each girl's hair, each girl's garland.

There. Click. Recognition . . . the ill-paired colors: blonde with white, dark with red. An off-kilter choice. One you wouldn't make without a reason.

And I knew what it was.

CHAPTER 8

"Shirley Temple?" asked Kenny, from behind the bar.

The man was thick as a Minotaur through the neck and shoulders, with a profile straight off some Byzantine coin.

I shook my head. "Someday I'm going to say yes to that, and then what the hell're you gonna do?"

He rolled his eyes and nipped the cap off an Old Vienna for me.

I gave Dean a peck on the cheek and climbed onto a tall stool, after checking the seat's duct-taped vinyl for anything untoward.

The Crown was a B-movie dump. Kenny tried, but he couldn't root out the intrinsic bouquet of emphysema, stale cabbage, and vomit. The walls were just varnished too deep with misery, and every dip in the floor brimmed with cigarette bouillon.

A tacked-up sheet of paper read "Hamburg . . . $1, Cheesburg . . . $1.25."

I figured it was just for show, like the pickled eggs and pig knuckles suspended in their respective gallons of cloudy brine.

This was no place to eat. Most people came to the Crown because a disability check covered the monthly cost of brown liquor down here and a thin mattress upstairs.

Dean had used it as a litmus test for chicks, in his bachelor days. He'd brought me on our second date.

I'd asked for a boilermaker, lit a Camel straight, and stepped up to the jukebox.

Kenny had set our glasses down as the needle dropped on my first-pick 45. Don Helms twanged into "Hey, Good Lookin' " with his Gibson Console Grande, and poor Dean was hooked before Hank Williams sang a word.

Debutante sensibilities my ass.

Later that night, I'd asked Kenny where he'd gone to college.

His answer won my heart: "Vietnam. It was pass-fail."

The man radiated such heavyweight calm that there were never brawls at the Crown, and yet if he didn't know you, he'd drop the final *s* from his last name, to make it sound Italian.

"Lot of people around here," he confided, "they think the Greeks aren't actually white."

Posers acting all buddy-buddy called him Ducatelli. True friends never let on it was really Doukatelis.

I respected his desire for camouflage. He let me get away with mine.

Dean put a hand on my shoulder and brought me back to the present. "So what's the word on Cousin Lapdog?"

"Saw the crime scene photos and wanted to puke," I said. "You told Kenny?"

They nodded, and I took a long and welcome sip of my beer before telling them about the colors.

"The blonde girl had white flowers," I said, "and the dark-haired one had red. It was backwards, aesthetically."

I expected Kenny to smirk at that, but there wasn't an iota of humor in his face.

"I figured out why that bugged me, why it felt so familiar," I continued. "It's a fairy tale . . . 'Snow White and Rose Red,' sisters named after the roses growing around their cottage door, white for blonde and red for brunette. I looked it up at home. It's one of the Grimm stories, and a lot of the details fit. . . ."

I pulled a piece of paper from my pocket and read aloud, " 'No evil ever befell them; if they tarried late in the wood and night overtook them, they lay down together on the moss and slept till morning,' and 'The two children loved each other so dearly that they always walked about hand in hand whenever they went out together.' It's almost like whoever killed them was setting up a *tableau vivant*."

Dean said, "Which is?" but Kenny got it.

"Kind of elaborate charades they used to do," he explained. "People dressed up and posed together, some famous scene — classical, something from the Bible. No one moved, no dialogue. Just the image —'live tableau.' The audience had to guess what they were supposed to be."

"Those photographs," I said. "It all looked like that. Like somebody arranged it for an audience. Kenny, does that make any sense?"

"Officially? Different jurisdiction, and I wasn't homicide. I don't know anything you could use for the paper."

"Dude, come on. If this was about work, I'd be asking you for a souvlaki recipe."

He glared at me.

I lowered my voice. "Lasagna . . . whatever. I'm sorry. You know what I mean. I don't write hard news. This is just . . . it's *family.*"

His face relaxed and I realized that by floundering accident I'd hit on the magic word.

A guy down the bar called for a couple more beers, but when Kenny came back he leaned in close between the two of us.

"We all talked about it. It was a big deal, that case. Strange. This isn't the South Bronx, but we're not fresh off the turnip truck, right? You get your bodies up here. Your nasty shit."

I waited, didn't touch my beer.

"Okay, I'm trusting you, Maddie. That fairy story? Maybe it fits. Something was up with this guy. Usually, your killer wants to get away from the scene. I mean, sure, very rarely, you get your necrophiliac for whom the main event is postmortem. This guy, though, he took his time prettying things up. He washed them. He put their clothes back on . . . no blood spatter on the fabric."

"All that in the dark?" asked Dean.

Kenny shrugged. "Maybe a flashlight. Maybe he waited for the sun to come up."

Somebody yelled for bourbon, and he poured out shots, still talking. "This gets into what you call 'staging.' Parents do it when they've killed a child, a lot of times . . . cover the body with a blanket, put a favorite stuffed animal in their arms. An apology, trying to comfort them after the fact. But this guy . . . something else there. More to it."

"Guilt, or showing off?" asked Dean.

"We had all kinds of theories," said Kenny. "I thought he was cocky, that it gave him a thrill. This was not a rookie. You can be the sickest bastard in the world, but the first time you kill somebody, it's sloppy. This guy knew what he was doing. It had the feel of a pattern to it."

"Ever see anything else like that around here?" I asked.

"Never once," he said. "Nothing before, nothing after. A lot of people were on the lookout . . . still are. They'd know this guy."

I thought about that. "Weren't there two soldiers? How could one guy kill two women?"

"I'm not saying there wasn't a partner, but a couple things pointed to a single killer. First off, the wounds were nearly identical. Made by somebody left-handed, from behind."

I shivered. The intimacy of that, the embrace.

"Knife was thrust in from the side and pulled forward," he said. "Takes a lot of strength, but the vic can't scream. It's the kind of thing a pro knows: Special Forces shit . . . wet work. A couple of us were back from 'Nam already. We'd seen that."

Dean whistled, said, "Must have been some nasty-ass blade."

"Combat knife. There's all kinds of specialty stuff, custom. Guys who did that kind of crap, they didn't depend on military issue, your Kabars . . ."

Kenny paused to chuck me under the chin. "You okay? Looking a little pale."

"Just those pictures . . ."

He cocked his head, considering me. "Look, all of this? Not an area I ever wanted to study deeply. Anybody talks about killing as something glamorous, gets off on the details, I'm gonna move right on down the bar. Might just be why I'm not a cop anymore."

I looked at him. "You know I'm not digging into this for the thrill, right?"

He nodded.

I took a deep breath. "Then I'd like to ask you one more question."

"All righty," he said.

"You said there were a *couple* of things pointing to a single killer. The knife, the cut — they're still pretty much one detail. What else?"

He tilted his head back, looked up. "Main thing was the uniforms. . . . From the witness descriptions, you could tell pretty clear those boys at the fair were cherry, never been 'in-country.' Army doesn't teach all that *Soldier of Fortune* hooey in basic. . . . Some eighteen-, nineteen-year-old draftee? Lethal as a Cub Scout, if he's still stateside."

Lapthorne would have been that young. And they weren't doing any hand-to-hand combat training at Junior Club, between regattas. Sharing somebody's mother's Virginia Slims in the bushes, maybe, or running a weenie kid up the flagpole by his boxers, along with the burgee . . . *Please God let this all be the fault of some other guy, some mystery SEAL badass with a chip on his shoulder.*

"Maddie," said Kenny, "all I can tell you is shop talk, rumor. Guy who'd know the whole picture is Jack Schneider. Lives down near the Rez now. Retired, but he was the lead on the case."

"Schneider? There's a prick," said Dean. "Shows up when the Kingsnakes do a show anywhere and gets drunk off his ass. Always looking for a fight."

Last thing I'd done at work was proof band listings for the events calendar. "Kingsnakes're playing down in Jamesville a week from Saturday," I said. "Blues night at STD's."

Dean shook his head. "I'll be in Canada."

"Still?" I asked, counting off days in my head. "If you're going Wednesday, isn't that —"

"Wednesday to Sunday this week," he said. "Then a couple days home. Back up there Tuesday, I think. That'll be for a good stretch. Two, maybe three weeks. They're not sure."

"I hate this," I said.

"Work is work. Long as it lasts . . ."

"It's *great*," I said. "*You're* great for doing it. Just, you know, life sucks when you're away."

He shrugged and then a white-haired little guy who'd been sitting quietly down the bar from us started screaming and waving his canes around.

"Fred!" boomed Kenny, banging a fist on the bar. "Knock it the hell off. How many times I gotta tell ya this ain't goddamn Inchon."

Fred gulped air and ducked his head in apology, then limped up the back stairs to his room. It was so hushed you could hear the canes' rubber tips squeak against the linoleum.

"Goddamn guy thinks it's Korea in here every goddamn *night*," confided Kenny. "I look like a gook to you?"

Back home, we finished off the leftover tabouleh and Dean fell asleep with the fork still in his hand. I propelled him to bed and returned to the porch, sat in a wicker chair and leaned the thing back until it shuddered and creaked.

The neighborhood dogs were doing bad canine barbershop harmonies.

I thought back over what Kenny had said, tried to glean out stray grains of hope. Like maybe Lapthorne's dog tags were his only link to the dead girls — maybe he pissed someone off at Camp Drum. Had he even been there? They called it Fort Drum now, anyway . . . underscoring how much time had passed, as if I needed any further reminder.

I shut my eyes and tried to picture him again as I'd last seen him that night in Locust Valley — the near-effeminacy of his manners, his evening clothes. You could see how somebody like that might rile a drill sergeant or returning vet — but enough to get him framed for murder?

I mean, to paraphrase the old Fitzgerald saw, the rich are different from you and me. They're just so damn clueless when you get them out in public. Like Grandaddy Dare having his chauffeur carry a hundred-dollar bill during the Depression, because none of the toll booths could make change so they'd get to drive through for free.

Lapthorne and I differed mainly in that he came from a side of the family that had managed to hang on to money the old-fashioned way, by marrying it. My view of Green Street was more than enough to remind me that my own branch had wedded for love.

Hard-core family wealth almost universally starts with one man. A guy who's solitary, poor, nasty, brutish, and short. You don't usually, after all, invent the safety pin or apply rocket science to the bond market if you're busy dating and having friends.

This guy, Ancestor X, makes his pile, whereupon he lands a very attractive and outgoing woman who's most often quite stupid. With a small American fortune, three generations gets you biggish blond people who have to strain for the gentleman's C, but are as calm as a herd of flatulent old Labradors.

Really big money nets you marriage with at least one rarefied European, and by generation four you get Dobermans with the Hapsburg lip, which is why I've never liked Southampton.

In my case, Ancestor X was my great-grandfather Jacob Townsend. He started out by hating farming, the genesis of more than one American fortune. At seventeen he went to "town" for a clerking job with a liner company. They were into freight and passenger ships, and Jake rocketed up through the ranks, becoming powerful enough to acquire sway with the government. I'd heard it mumbled that it was he who made sure the *Lusitania* blew up, because he thought World War I was a good idea.

At thirty-two he met my great-grandmother, Dodie Lapthorne. She was nineteen and a hot number, liked swimming across the family lake in the Adirondacks each summer and riding fast horses for the rest of the year.

Dodie first saw Jake Townsend across the captain's table on board his liner *Agassiz,* traveling with her family to Cuba.

Not much for romance, Jake hollowed out a peach in the *Agassiz* galley their last night aboard, popped in the hefty engagement ring he'd picked up in Havana, and wrapped the whole thing in a twist of newspaper. At the captain's table that night, he tossed it into her lap, saying, "Here, a peach for a peach."

I could never reconcile the great-grandmother I'd known with the woman whose tall portrait hung above the sideboard in her dining room.

This painted Dodie looked back over a perfect white shoulder, as though she'd been turning to walk out of the frame but thought of something amusing to tell the artist at the last possible second, before she'd altogether lifted her hand from the crude stone pillar he'd posed her beside.

She wore a velvet flapper dress, deeply green and backless. An emerald-and-diamond bar pin flashed from the hip still tipped toward the painter, the audience.

Some weekend guest had christened this work "Nice to See Your Back Again." I always thought there should have been a small brass plaque on the frame, engraved with the word "Before."

"After" was a silent, gray, and forbidding woman who always confused me with my cousin Skippy.

It wasn't just that she was so much older by the time I knew her. When she was two weeks pregnant with her last child, Dodie saw Jake blown up on the bridge of Townsend's newest liner, the *Glamis Castle.* The next explosion threw her clear.

A fire at sea is a terrible thing, because fuel will continue to burn as it spreads out over the surface of the water. Dodie was hospitalized for over a month. I remember overhearing, as a child, that it was there she'd become an addict, that Jimmy the chauffeur had then kept her in drugs for decades.

I always imagined a large box of Blue Tip

needles and vials of morphine in her dressing room closet, alongside her bazillion pairs of Belgian shoes.

It was late, and I tried willing myself to feel tired. Over dinner, I'd begged Dean to take me to the Johnston-farm auction, so I wouldn't have to go alone the next morning with his Uncle Weasel.

"Only if we get up at three," he'd said. "Otherwise you're on your own."

CHAPTER 9

"Of all the goddamned pissant jerry-rigged piece-of-shit ways to run a place," Dean fumed, throwing up the hood of a third tractor.

It was just before Tuesday's dawn on Collamer Road. Dean and his Uncle Weasel were trying to figure out which vehicle contained the farm's only working truck battery.

I was trying to stay out of their way.

"Wasn't me took it out the truck in the first place," complained Weasel. He ran a hand over his white crewcut, sucking his lower lip high as a bulldog's.

"You might still for once get your thumb out of your ass and help me," said Dean.

"Ain't seen *you* out balin' much hay this summer," said Weasel.

"Didn't see any of *you* pay me for last year."

Weasel strained for a comeback, whining, "Well . . . month ago when *I* used that battery, *I* left it right in that truck."

"Last time you did a lick of work, you still had your own goddamn teeth," muttered Dean.

He slammed the tractor hood back in place and moved on to the safety-yellow bulk of a prewar Hyster forklift.

Weasel put a cigarette in his mouth and shuffled outside, then scraped a kitchen match along the doorframe.

The air was still, but he cupped a hand around the flame, making his face shine copper in the dim blue.

"Bunny," said Dean, "you okay? Eyes look like two holes burned in a blanket."

"Last time I was up this early I was still at the party," I said. "Want some coffee?"

"Nope."

"Could we use the battery from my car?"

"Nope."

"Want me to drive to Sears and buy you one?"

"Oooh," he said, smiling and aping that drawn-out upstate pronunciation, brimming

104

with secret umlauts and flattened midwestern vowels, "now you wouldn't want to go'n do *that*. Might get a perfectly good battery from Weasel's wife's second cousin, the one with the broken dryer, if you could find her husband half a fan belt for his brother's lawnmower."

"So his brother would fix the dryer?"

"After he got around to, y'know, that *snow*-m'bile on the front lawn," he said, giving up on the forklift.

"Wouldn't want to rush him."

"Oh, gaaad no. Them snow-m'biles're no Swiss picnic."

"Yut," I agreed, taking a gulp of my coffee.

He moved on to a small red Case. "Not in this one it must be out in the damn pole barn."

"Tractor drove into a bar," I said. "Pulled up a stool. Leaned on its front wheels, *weeping*. Bartender said, 'Jesus, you look *terrible*. What happened?' "

Dean nodded and folded up the dented hood.

"Tractor looked up," I continued, "said, 'I got a John Deere letter.' "

"Bingo," crowed Dean.

He smiled and flipped the leads off with

his thumbs, lifting the battery up like a grail.

We drove slowly, rattling down godforsaken roads as the sun came up. I was in the middle, and every time Dean had to shift, the gear knob mashed his hand into my knee.

Weasel popped a square of nicotine gum in his mouth and lit a Marlboro chaser. There was no radio, and I knew the two of them could have ridden in silence for days. I wanted to go back to sleep, but every time we took a curve I was afraid I'd end up in Weasel's lap.

"So how old is Johnston?" I asked Dean.

"Must be in his eighties," he said. "His daughter's mom's age, I think. I played football with a couple of his grandsons. Big fuckers. Nice enough. One of 'em told me in 4-H that if you picked up your calf every day, you'd be able to lift it when it was a cow."

"That work?"

"Never really found out. Something always makes you miss a day. Next thing you know, it's too big."

I laughed. I could just see him tottering around the barn, thin as a length of bamboo, short hair bristling blond, arms full of baby cow, wanting to get tough enough so his big brother couldn't kick his ass anymore.

Primogeniture rankled him still, but if the farm had been earmarked for Dean instead of his brother, it would have created terminal drag on our escape velocity.

He denied wanting to go. Told me Syracuse was Real Life, and that I should get used to it, that I'd been raised in the airless Potemkin villages of the rich where there would never be true sustenance — arguments always tinged with his Sparta, my Athens.

But Dean was still that kid who garnered a broken arm flying his bike off the barn roof. The desire to get the hell out had been there long before I showed up, he just needed a little help staying airborne.

I wove my fingers through his and let my head rest on his shoulder. He rubbed the back of my hand with the edge of his thumb. It would happen.

"Johnston wasn't ever right after he found them girls," said Weasel, suddenly.

I looked over at him, surprised as hell.

He didn't turn his head.

Started futzing around with the latch on the wind-wing. His thumbnail, a bloom of red-black, had recently stopped a hammer.

"Kinda let the place run down," he said. "His daughter's husband run it, mostly, till he got his hand caught in that old baler. And Johnston had some stroke. Not any of 'em much good after that. Them boys're down-city, workin' for wages."

Workin' for wages: the yeoman-farmer's vilest epithet, one Dean's father applied to us often.

"You ever talk to him about finding the girls?" I asked.

Weasel swung his head slowly left and just looked at me, chewing away.

"Why'd you wanna do that?" he said, finally.

I could see Dean biting his lip to keep from laughing and had to look at the truck's ceiling myself or we would have both lost it.

I pressed my thigh against his as hard as I could, and he pushed back.

"John Deere letter," he said, grinning and sputtering. "Not bad."

"Little slow on the uptake," I answered, and he gave my hand a squeeze.

"You're a schmaht man, Vendell, I vant you should know," said the fabled Fleischmann, eyes twinkling as he hooked a hand around Weasel's elbow.

We were standing on shit-spattered concrete, the edge of a cattle pen alongside one of Johnston's barns. Pickups wheezed into the dirt yard behind us, disgorging passengers in bib overalls or shiny high-waisted jeans. They were quiet — no shouted greetings, no Kiwanis-meeting jollity — just grim knots of men pushing back feed-caps, scratching their heads and commiserating about wheat and soybeans and mud. The price of Atrazine. The goddamn government.

"So, Vendell, you ready for getting back in the dairy business?" crooned the auctioneer. He was a little hunchbacked, with a nimbus of white hair.

Weasel shrugged. Chewed his gum.

"Got for you some real beauties, here . . . size, shtyle —"

"Condition and breeding," I mumbled, smiling.

Fleischmann grinned at that, made me a conspirator with one broad wink over the turtle-shell curve of his shoulder.

He wore a lime windbreaker zipped to the chin. Long sleeves, despite the heat.

"And you are the new Mrs. Bauer?" he asked, releasing Weasel and taking my hand in both of his. "Izzy Fleischmann."

"Madeline Dare," I said. "A pleasure to meet you, Mr. Fleischmann. Dean's told me you're the best in the business."

"Please, call me Izzy. We dispense with

formality in such a setting, yes?"

He looked me up and down, eyes pausing on my chest for a second. "A nice *gezinta* girl." Izzy pointed his chin at Dean, not letting go of my hand. "So, *nu,* how you do so good, young Dean, in the marriage department?"

"I showed her the real America — red necks, white bread, blue eyeshadow," said Dean, putting one strong arm around my shoulders and sweeping the other through the air to present the cow pen's expanse for my delectation. "Whole new world."

"*Quelle* epiphany," I said, rolling my eyes.

"Won her heart," continued my intrepid spouse. "Danced her into the ranks of white trash."

"I prefer *garbage blanc.*"

"French," said Dean. "Candyass language."

"Please excuse my husband," I sweetly countered. "He studied German in school. After years of work and dedication, he can open his mouth and make rocks fall out."

Izzy pinched my cheek. "You," he said, "I like."

Weasel, too long ignored, spat his gum onto the ground. "She wants to talk to Johnston 'bout them two girls was killed on his place. Works for that newspaper." He kicked up a little pile of dirt and mashed it over the wrinkled wad of Nicorette, then walked away down the long railing.

"Oh, for chrissake," said Dean, setting off behind him.

Izzy watched them go, then turned to me. "The newspaper?" he asked.

I shivered, a little "goose walked over my grave" tremor.

"It's not for the paper," I said.

He crossed his arms. "For what, then?"

I looked away. "I'm just, uh, curious."

"So, Mrs. Curious," said Izzy.

He waited until I was uncomfortable enough to glance back, to find him squinting in appraisal of me.

"He's in the barn over there, Farmer Johnston," he said. "In a wheelchair. My opinion, I don't think he can tell you much, anymore. I don't think he knows what day this is. Today, his own what-they-call-it, *heartbreak* auction."

"Oh, you know . . . that's okay," I said.

"So, then, you don't care about knowing, why come here?" he said, cocking an eyebrow. "Is a little fishiness. A puzzle."

"Indeed," I said.

"No, really," he said. "Now you make *me* curious. Now I am actually fascinated."

I smiled at him.

He ducked his head a little, sideways. "You don't want to answer me? So, don't answer."

I didn't. We both stood there until the silence started making me jumpy. He was good at this.

I couldn't stand it, blurted, "So, Izzy . . . That's short for Isaac?"

He nodded. Maybe warmed a little.

"I had a great-great-grandfather Isaac," I rattled on. "Always liked the name. Makes me think of whaling captains . . . all those Yankee guys."

"Me it reminds of little old men in Brooklyn, or maybe Vilnius," he said, smiling so his crows'-feet got all crinkly. "Always having an argument . . . still with herring in their beards, shaking a finger in the other one's face."

He raised both hands, right index fingers bent.

The gesture made his sleeves pull back, revealing the start of a bluish scrawl down his left forearm.

1436 . . .

I flinched.

"The four," I said.

I lifted my hand, resting a fingertip on his arm, just beneath the spot at which that second numeral's crossbar terminated.

The tattooist had taken the time to ink a neat little perpendicular stroke there. A flourish. "How could anyone —"

Fleischmann cleared his throat. "Long time ago," he said.

My hand fell away, and he tugged the elasticized cuff back over his wrist.

"I beg your pardon," I said. "That was thoughtless of me."

"No," he said. "Not thoughtless. I don't believe you could manage that, to stop thinking. Such a state, such a condition . . . I don't believe you are quite *capable* of it."

Fleischmann passed his hand slowly across my line of sight.

"Watch," he said. "Follow . . ."

He worked his fingers through an odd pose, a stage gesture, drawing my gaze with the motion until he'd brought that same bent index finger to the corner of his own eye.

"Look here . . ." he said, smiling again. "You like, I tell your fortune."

"Right now?"

"You don't believe? Oh, but I am very good. With this I made my living, first year in America. Just like the lady who taught me promised. She said, 'If you can tell people *part* of the truth about themselves, you never again go hungry.' "

"But if you tell them more than part?"

"Ah," he said, "I asked her the same question. She said, 'Most cases they kill you. My advice, you want to hold something back.' "

"Very wise," I said.

"Of course wise, because she was old like you can't believe," he said. "So old she was growing backwards. Everything shrinking, even her head. Her nose touched her chin, almost. The Rom, sometimes you can't tell what age, but this lady —"

"Rom?"

"A Gypsy," he explained.

"Thought they hated outsiders . . ."

"Me and this lady," he said, "in the war it happened that we got jammed together on a train. A journey of several days, during which we faced some uncertainty . . ."

I swallowed.

"She was with her youngest son — youngest but older than me, back then, maybe even old as I am now."

A small gaggle of farmers walked by. Fleischmann's eyes flicked over them, and he kept silent until they were well past us.

"Very ill, this man," he continued, "and I was able to do him a small kindness before he died. His mother was grateful. She wanted to give me something in return. We had nothing, you understand? We had been left nothing, for this journey.

" 'Another time,' she said, 'I would have given you a horse or a fine coat. But I do not have even bread, and so I will give a secret. I will teach you to know the future.' "

"With cards?" I asked.

"We had no cards," he said. "I told you, we had nothing."

I waited, didn't want to interrupt.

He was quiet for another moment, glancing away before he spoke again. "She taught me how to study faces. 'It's not difficult,' she said, 'but you have to look and look, until the secrets come out. They cannot stay hidden, if you are quiet for long enough, because the secrets are foolish, and they have no patience.' "

He stopped, looking at me. "She told me to practice on her," he said, finally. "I complained that it was too dark to see her face. 'For this you need no light,' she said, 'just to look. Just to wait.' "

He sighed.

"What did you see?"

"Everything," he said. "I saw everything."

"And did you hold something back?" I asked.

"I told her nothing," he said.

"Why not?"

"Because she died, while I was watching.

The real secret. Her gift to me, even. She took with her my fear."

I believed him.

"As for you, Mrs. Curious," he said, "you got a good face. More than pretty . . ."

I could feel my cheeks flush, and I looked down at my shoes.

"So, you don't believe it?" He tilted my chin back up with the tip of his finger. "Just look," he said. "Don't blink. Try for me, long as you can. Hold your head still."

I couldn't relax, having someone peer at me so intently. The only way I could stand it was just to let my eyes go unfocused.

He laughed. "Of course you don't believe it," he said. "Or maybe you think you don't deserve it, but people always gonna look at you when you walk in a room. Men. Not a common face. Too sad, though, too serious, and maybe a little scared now, like you taking on something big, something you're not sure about . . ."

He looked thoughtful and leaned toward me, raising my head another half inch. "You think you got no protection. But I see strength here, determination."

He tapped twice on the center of my chin and then took his finger away.

"What the hell you doing in this place is another question," he continued. "Not your people here. You think I'm kidding when I say I know condition und breeding . . ."

That made me look him in the eye.

"There it is," he said, "you come here because you got no place else . . . not yet. Maybe you gonna find . . ."

Fleischmann stopped and shifted his eyes away, looking past my shoulder.

"Wait," I protested, "when you say I might find . . ."

"*Not* everything," he said. "Already I told you —"

"Just *that*. Not everything. Just if 'not yet' means 'someday.' "

Fleischmann looked at me, hard. "Truth?"

I swallowed again. Nodded.

He put a hand around my wrist, gripping it tight from beneath. The gravity of the gesture made the back of my neck buzz.

"You want to find a destination, you gotta take a road," he said, "gotta start walking."

He kept talking, faster now. "Some people, they pick the soft one. The easy one. *You* gonna take the hardest road. Only thing you can do."

I closed my eyes, and this time he didn't tell me not to blink.

"But when you start," he said, "could be you don't come back."

"Come back here?" I asked, hopeful.

Fleischmann shook his head, dropped his voice to a confidential hiss. *"Zei gesund,"* he said. *Go in health. Survive.*

He made it a blessing.

"Thank you," I said.

"And here is coming your husband," he said, voice louder, slipping back into professional bonhomie.

He laid a hand along my shoulder and turned me to face the approach of Dean and Weasel.

"Now to business, to selling heifers," he said in my ear. "Not much of a living from telling the future, anymore. Not here."

"So don't let Weasel get away," I whispered back, "your perfect customer."

"Oh, sure, and *this* is news," he said, laughing. "You can write for me the headline."

Dean reached us first.

"Listen, Izzy," he confided, "you want to pawn off a cow on Weasel, it's okay by me. Just don't let him trade it for any of those magic beans."

Izzy, again the perfect audience, threw back his head and cackled magnificently.

"So you have an admirer," said Dean as we walked away and left Weasel to his fate. "I've never seen Izzy talk to anyone that long without some sorry-ass livestock changing hands."

The rising heat gave the cowshit's ammonia a stinging intensity. The ground seemed to shimmer, and I could hear cicadas starting up in the distance.

"He wasn't trying to sell me anything. He was . . . I dunno. I think I give off some kind of orphan vibe. Older guys get all worried about me the moment they're introduced. At least the nice ones."

He leaned close and put his mouth to my ear. "I think it's because you make them all flustered," he whispered.

His breath tickled, and I laughed. "He told my fortune."

"And how'd you do?"

"Um, actually? I have no clue," I said. "Let's go find Johnston."

"You even know what you want to ask him?"

"Not the least glimmer of an idea," I said. I didn't expect anything more than what I'd already read in the paper, and given the man's health, maybe not even that much.

We walked through a giant doorway and into the cool darkness of the barn.

My eyes started to water. "Couldn't there be at least a couple of horses?" I asked. "Their shit smells better."

"Better than this?" He sucked in a great lungful of air through his nose, threw his arms wide. "This is perfect. And horses are so goddamn stupid."

"Sure, like cows are prize-winning Dante scholars. *Darling I love you but give me Park Avenue.*"

"Uppity," he said, grinning and flicking a finger against the side of my neck.

"Uppity your damn self," I said, batting his hand away.

We came out from the low passageway between cow pens, into a high-ceilinged room where the pre-auction scrutiny was under way. People were milling around, and in a far corner I could see the glint of a wheelchair, a wiry old man hunched down in it.

His knees were drawn up, the stiff cuffs of his new overalls folded back, glossy and high-laced workboots beneath resting on the steel paddles of the chair's footrests. I always worried about the feet of people in wheelchairs, afraid they might fall off those little ledges and drag without anyone noticing. I felt a sudden bolt of shame for being young, for being able to walk.

Beside him stood a broad woman with hair in tight, short, blue-white curls. She wore glasses, a flowered smock, and dark stretch pants, and had one hand firmly on a chair-grip beside his tilted head. She looked determined.

"There's your man," said Dean. "Go easy."

CHAPTER 10

Dean didn't have to warn me to go easy. It was all I could do to take another step into the barn. No need to worry that I'd storm over and rudely buttonhole a crippled old man about a decades-old double murder hc'd been unfortunate enough to stumble upon — right on the very morning he was going to have to watch his life's work broken up and carted off by shamefaced neighbors.

"It's sad," I said.

"I bet the boys are just as happy to see it go," answered Dean. "Make a nice clean escape to a house on a cul-de-sac, shiny Buick LeSabre out front. No cows to milk at four a.m. and a desk job where you don't have to wash off the stink at the end of the day."

"That what you want?" I asked.

"I can just see trying to talk my fancy wife into a Buick."

I smiled. "I don't think she'd go for that,"

I said. "But isn't it kind of hard on the grandfather, giving up the place?"

"Old Johnston?" Dean turned to look me full in the face. He knew me too well. "What's up — you want to blow this off?"

"It just seems like a harsh time to be going after information."

"Look, you want to drop the whole thing, I won't begrudge you dragging me out here. But if you're going to pursue it, do you think you'll ever have a better excuse to get a word with the guy?"

Of course not. The question was whether I had the guts to do it at all and the brains to finish it right if I started.

But then I pictured the Rose Girls themselves. How vibrant they'd looked in the last pictures taken of them alive. How they'd looked dead.

You gonna take the hardest road. Only thing you can do.

"No, you're right," I said. "I can't drop it."

"Well then, you're burnin' daylight." He took my hand and led me into the room.

My stomach shrank to an acid fist. "Tell me about the rabbits, George."

That made him laugh. "You *are* the rabbit, Bunny."

As we drew closer to Johnston and daughter, I saw a clear, thin oxygen line snaking across his face, with little side-segments of plastic spurting enriched air up each nostril. I could hear the rattle and whistle of his ruined lungs. He didn't look at Dean, just stared at me.

Dean introduced the daughter, Mrs. Ulene, and they started to chat. She didn't bother including her father.

Johnston was still staring at me. I stared back. He looked mean as a cornered ferret.

"What you want?" he finally wheezed at me.

"I wanted to ask you about the Rose Girls," I said.

"Can't hear you," he said, then coughed for a minute. "Get down." He pointed to the ground next to his left foot with a shaky hand. I squatted, rocked back on my heels.

"I wasn't sure you could still talk," I said.

"Dying," he said. "Not stupid."

"The Rose Girls," I said. "That's who I want to ask you about."

"Outside."

"You found them outside . . ." I coaxed.

He squinted his eyes shut, impatient, then

flapped his hand toward the doors of the barn. "Take me."

His eyes opened again. He reached a claw toward his daughter's hand, pointing at me when she turned to look. "Outside," he said.

"Now isn't that nice," said Mrs. Ulene. "Dad doesn't like just *anybody.* Why sure, honey, you can take him outside for a while."

She fitted a too-large hat on his head, a stiff-brimmed Agway gimme cap.

I got behind his chair and grasped the warm black rubber handgrips. It rolled along pretty well, but then Johnston couldn't have weighed more than about ninety pounds. It was impossible to reconcile him with the bulk of his daughter.

The minute we cleared the barn doors and got around the side of the building, he scraped my hand with his yellow nails. I put the brake on the chair and hunkered down next to him.

"Smoke," he said.

"Excuse me?"

"Get me one."

"A cigarette?"

He nodded, looking fierce.

"You'll blow up," I said. "The oxygen."

"Haven't yet," he said, and smiled, revealing too-perfect false teeth.

Where the hell would I find a cigarette? I looked around the yard. Weasel.

"Get a light," Johnston said. "Don't forget."

I found Weasel on the other side of the barn, and he looked at me funny, but finally parted with a Marlboro and a match. I trotted back around to Johnston, put the butt in his mouth, and dragged the match along the barn's cement foundation. He had barely enough breath to suck the thing to life as I held the flame to its tip, but his eyes narrowed with bliss as he gummed it and puffed down a drag.

"Better," he said.

I was certain a spark was going to rush up his tubes and into the little tank of pure oxygen. Serve me right.

"What you want to know?" he asked. The nicotine seemed to ease him a little. He could say more words at once.

"You found them," I said, and he nodded. "What do you remember about it? Maybe, you know, something you didn't think to tell the police right off?"

"You family?" he asked.

"No," I said, *at least not the girls'.*

"So, what then, Lois Lane?"

"Sure," I said. "Lois Lane. What the hell."

He coughed up a little laugh, took another

drag. I waited.

"Haven't seen too good for a long time," he said. "Can't tell you if I saw something right, even back then."

"You seem pretty sharp to me. I mean, especially for a guy who's had a stroke."

"Didn't have no stroke."

"And here you've got everyone convinced you don't know what day it is. Even Fleischmann."

"That Jew?" he said. "Why's it matter?"

"Seems like it matters to you."

"How's that?" he said.

"Why else you talking to me?" I said.

"Wanted a smoke."

"Why else you hinting you know something?" I asked.

"Want another after this one."

"Might have to tell me something to get it, then."

"Figured as much," he said, and hacked-laughed again. "Saw a man."

"That morning?"

"Nope. Near dark that same day. I come back up there by foot with a jar . . ." The old man paled, breath whistling. He closed his mouth and his eyes and sucked the straight oxygen into his nose until a little color came back into his cheeks.

"A jar?" I asked, when it looked like he might live.

"Holy water," he wheezed, "from that Catholic church up West Yates. Never . . . been in one before. Methodist."

This made perfect sense to me. How could he not have wanted to purify the ground from which his family's sustenance came? Grape juice in little paper cups might be fine for his spare, demystified Wesleyan communion of a Sunday. Removing the taint of that much blood and malice called for deeper, older measures.

"And you're, what — coming through the woods?" I asked.

He nodded, settling his head back. Didn't embellish.

"So," I went on, "you see some guy —"

Another nod.

"Recognize him?"

Nothing.

Johnston closed his eyes.

"Maybe a cop, following up?"

I didn't want to say "soldier," not unless he brought it up first. "Like if he was in some kind of uniform —"

His eyelids moved, just a bit of twitch.

"Dressed regular," he said, a little spacey, like he was actually picturing it.

Not a rookie cop, then. Not a soldier,

either — or at least not one who could risk anybody knowing it.

"What's he look like?" I asked.

"Dark hair. Brush cut," said Johnston, wheezing a little.

"Big guy?"

The cigarette was burning down between his fingers, ash an inch long. "Can't see him any too clear. Gettin' on towards night."

"What's he doing?" I asked.

"Looking for something."

"Where?"

"In the woods, behind where them girls was, then out front in the furrows. Cursing a blue streak."

He snorted more oxygen.

"What was he looking for?" I asked.

He opened his eyes, smirking up at me.

The cigarette's spent length of ash quivered and fell across his fingers, revealing a fresh hot point of orange. Johnston raised the receiving end to his mouth and sucked hard, then tossed it at my feet.

He'd smoked down far enough to singe the filter's dappled golden-brown paper.

"Step on that."

I mashed it under the ball of my foot, grinding back and forth until there was nothing left but a mat of shreds.

"Now pick your mess up," he said.

I didn't.

"Scared it's gonna bite? G'wan . . ."

I raised my eyes to his. "Deal's a deal. You got your smokes, now answer the question."

He smirked. Made like he was locking his mouth with some invisible key, which he then pretended to flick at me.

"Mr. Johnston? You sure you want to be pissing me off, here?"

Old man hadn't expected that. Liked it even less.

I crossed my arms. Waited.

He started wheezing a little harder.

I looked around. Took my time inspecting the whole yard, inch by inch, like we had all day.

"People're starting to head for the barn," I said. "Bet it'll get kind of loud, once things are under way. Hard to get someone's attention, from out here."

Johnston closed his mouth, lifted a hand to push the tube tighter against his nose.

"You're not sounding any too good, there, sir. Probably shouldn't smoke, you don't mind my saying. . . ."

He stared at me. Didn't want to blink.

"Anything I can do?" I asked, voice sweet with concern.

He shook his head.

I eyed the fat black knob on his oxygen

tank. "Wouldn't be any trouble, and your daughter must have her hands full."

"No need," he said. Kind of a whisper.

"Okay, then. . . . You need help, though, just say the word."

Johnston was inhaling with vigor, now: quick hard draws off his plastic lifeline.

He watched me, I watched people amble inside.

Nobody was in a rush, yet. Just ones and twos, looking for shade, maybe, as the sun picked up steam.

After a while, I glanced back at him. "Your color's a little better," I said.

He nodded, wary.

I looked at the barn. "Want me to run inside, see if they're starting? Happy to, unless you'd rather just chat. . . ."

"Chatting suits me fine."

"Well then." I smiled at him. "Guess when we left off, I was asking whether you knew what that guy was looking for."

Johnston let go of the tube and lowered that hand to his lap, considering. "Might've been after them dog tags."

I flinched, and he shot me this mean-edged flicker of smile.

"What," he said, "you think your father-in-law didn't trot over and squawk, soon as he churned 'em up? Bent my ear about *you*, too, minute you come upstate."

So the guy'd strung me along like a champ this whole time, and made me cadge butts for the honor.

From *Weasel,* goddamnit.

"Called you a 'buxom heifer,' Cal did," he went on, squinting to make a closer inspection. "Guess that's true enough."

Had there been a cliff handy, I would've whistled "Farmer in the Dell" and shoved him over, chair and all.

"Now run-go-fetch-me another cigarette," he said.

He flapped a claw to shoo me along.

I stomped off, muttering "prick" under my breath until I nearly plowed into Fleischmann.

"No," he said, looking past me to Johnston, "I'd call him a *mensch.*"

The way he leaned on the word made it no compliment.

"More like *mamzer,*" I said.

"So, the *gezinta shiksa* knows the Yiddish for 'bastard.' "

"The *gezinta shiksa* is ticked."

He grinned. "Go on inside, then. Cool off a little."

"Think Johnston's daughter'd notice that I came back alone?"

"Let me bring him," he said. "You go find your nice husband."

"A generous offer, Mr. Fleischmann."

"It would be my pleasure, Mrs. Bauer," he said.

"You're very kind to say so."

"Not at all," he said. "In fact I am being quite sincere. Would you like to know why?"

"Yes indeed."

He leaned closer, dropping his voice. "Because in about ten minutes, Johnston will lose everything. And for that he should have a front-row seat, the old shit."

I wondered aloud over dinner who'd been wandering around Johnston's field that long-ago night.

Dean just patted me on the head and said he was sure I'd figure it out. He had a dreamy look, and when I asked him what was on his mind he said he thought he might have worked out the enduring conundrum of how to construct his railgrinder linkage at long last.

"Trapezoids," he said, and I knew I was on my own for the rest of the night.

I cleared the table, and he went to work at our big desk in the front room, X-Acto—blading up more minuscule pieces of balsa wood with Teutonic precision and gluing them to odd shapes of cardboard. If I'd tried anything like that, I would have ended up wearing it all in my hair for the next week, but I knew he'd happily putter with it for hours, and that he should be allowed to try out his theory in peace, his last night before he was back in the crew car.

Later I lay awake in the dark, worried that I'd revealed too much without knowing enough, that I'd talked to too many people. Izzy, Johnston, Kenny . . . even Weasel, for God's sake.

I hadn't made measurable progress, out at Johnston's, but something in the pit of my belly told me I'd caused a tiny shift, had dislodged the first grain of sand in some Rube Goldberg universe.

Dean, dead asleep, muttered and turned toward me, his well-muscled arm wearing bracelets of light from the street window.

Already, it felt like I'd put something precious at risk.

CHAPTER 11

Dean was gone the next morning and the rest of the week dragged ass. I knocked around the apartment at night, talking to myself, staying up way too late reading and then slamming into work all cranky and fogged in.

Mom sailed in Saturday morning, having left Centre Island before dawn.

She was now standing on top of our kitchen-stool–stepladder thing with a half-dozen nails in the corner of her mouth, arranging folds of faded peach silk moiré around the living room's biggest window. In profile, Mom looks exactly like Queen Elizabeth on the Canadian penny, but head-on she's way more of a babe.

"That the middle?" she asked. She pinched up a swag edge, hammer poised.

"Two inches to the right . . ."

Mom elbowed the piece in place and basted it to the wall with three quick taps.

She nipped down from the ladder. "That works, don't you think?" she asked, hands on her hips.

"Perfect." I was cross-legged on the floor, cradling a glass of coffee in my lap.

Mom was shortly back up on the top step with a pair of pleated jabots. "Hand me that one on the table," she said, her back to me.

I looked around the room. There were four tables heaped with undulating yardage. My sister would know exactly which "that one" she wanted, but I've never been as fluent in Constance-speak. She was never

"Connie," except to overfamiliar salesmen.

"The *staple* gun, Madeline."

"A staple gun is a 'that *thing,*' Mom."

She extended her hand back toward me without looking down from the window frame, one neatly shod toe tapping on the stool's red seat. I found the gun buried under an excrescence of silk and handed it to her.

"This will work here, don't you think?" She tacked up a jabot to cover a seam. "Oh yes . . . your mother is a wizard."

"A goddamn genius."

I headed through the archway to the kitchen and grabbed celery and bell peppers out of the icebox, thinking it was a good day for gazpacho. I've always said I learned to cook in self-defense.

"So tell me about Lapthorne," I said. I'd told her about the dog tags, sworn her to secrecy. I grabbed a good knife and the chopping block to set up on the tall island table, so I could keep talking to her.

"Lappy was an okay kid. It's not like he wandered around pulling the wings off flies or anything. Just quiet. You'd have to be with a father like Kit. Kit was always looking for order after growing up with Uncle June. June turned everything into chaos, and he was such a nitpicky bastard. . . . You never knew when he was drunk, except that he really always was."

She started experimenting with ways to drape the curtains along the sides, trying the tiebacks at different levels.

"Lawrenceville was a godsend for Kit, because it got him away. Then he met Binty. One of those Westbury girls. Always in organdy, at dancing school, all floaty and perfect. We just had boring velvet. . . . A *lot* of dough, Binty — right up Kit's alley."

"What'd they have, three kids?"

"Lappy's the youngest. Always running to keep up, never quite marching in step well enough. Kit likes everything precise. We used to call him 'Hospital Corners.' "

She came into the kitchen for a glass of iced tea.

"I made Kit nervous," she said, smiling. "I don't think he really *likes* women. Always dated girls with figures like ironing boards. Clotheshorses. Well, I mean, look who he married — Binty, never a hair out of place and she doesn't eat in public. 'The really chic women *smoke* for lunch,' she told me once.

"I remember coming east for Aldrich's wedding," Mom continued, "and afterwards some of us went to Rothman's for dinner. We took a bunch of cars to East Norwich"

— she pronounced this *Nahr*-edge — "and I ended up at Kit and Binty's table . . . with his partners from the firm and their wives. I was down at the end near Lappy and one partner's boy, who were about seventeen. I guess it was right after I married Michael, '67? '68? They were talking about taking a semester off to work for Eugene McCarthy —"

" 'Go Clean for Gene'?" I said, dicing three nice beefsteak tomatoes from a plate on the counter.

"Exactly, which I thought was a lot more interesting than the discussion at the martini end of the table, so I was asking them about it when the partner stood up and pointed at me, livid, and said, 'Lay off my son, you *pinko!* "

"Perfect moment," I said. "How did Binty take it?"

I dumped my tomatoes into the bowl and juiced a couple of lemons. I always like my gazpacho with some of the zest, too — cilantro if I can get it fresh, but that never happens upstate.

"Oh, you know Binty — she'd already read me off in the receiving line because my skirt was too short."

"The good old days," I said.

"I'm hip," answered Mom.

I started broiling slices of French bread to go with the soup, in an attempt to develop a reasonable facsimile of crust on the flaccid local baguette.

"With all Binty's dough," said Mom, "you'd think she might . . ."

"What?"

"I don't know . . . be happy? Stop picking on everyone? Kit, her sons . . ."

"Us?"

She laughed.

I checked the toasting progress. "Have you ever seen anyone happy, because of money?"

"Not once. People with big dough, anyway — with our background. Maybe if you'd made it yourself? Maybe the new people are happy? If it were still all shiny and fresh, instead of something to live up to, something to lose . . . All the WASP shit, the Puritan ethic . . ."

Everything she'd tried to escape by going west. Everything she'd come back to.

"Mom, I just . . . I mean, we're *all* fucked. We're all crazy. But can you see Lapthorne doing this? Even with Binty as a mother. It's not like she was sticking him with forks all the time. . . ."

"Of course not. She hired a nurse for that. Awful little woman."

"Gerdie? I remember she gave me a cookie

once. Like when I was four. Watched me eat the thing and then told me she'd poisoned it, after I swallowed the last bite."

"Horrible," said Mom.

I put the finished toast in a basket. "But even so —"

"Even so," she said, gathering bowls and plates and napkins and spoons, "I can't picture Lapthorne polishing his own *shoes,* for God's sake. Much less knifing anybody."

"I know. And I *like* the guy."

I started taking stuff to the porch.

"Well," she said, following me out, "we'll just have to throw a cocktail party."

Her answer for everything. I ladled soup into the bowls.

"It all comes around on the guitar," she said, perkily misquoting Arlo Guthrie for the thousandth time.

Chapter 12

It was Monday, opening night of the New York State Fair. Dean was home for a too-small window of time and Ted wanted a midway-food "Eats" piece by morning. He'd begrudged me two comps for Jerry Lee Lewis at the Budweiser Pavilion.

I'd been psyched, but the playlist was all

flabby B-side ballads, each tinkling plink so low-rent Liberace I was ready to throw a candelabra at Lewis's head. There was none of the flash, none of the raw swagger. His trademark forelock barely moved.

It was pissing me off and I was dying to hear "Breathless," but God knows I can't imagine having to play something I'd written thirty years ago over and over again for yokels reliving their DA'd and Brylcreemed youth. Closest I'd ever get to being a musician was dubbing the occasional mix tape and knowing that you never want that last seat on the hastily chartered small plane, even if Plan B is a crowded station wagon through midnight Arkansas.

The show seemed over, until Lewis leapt back onto the stage, catapulted into an encore by our tepid applause. He launched into a searing, lock-up-your-daughters rendition of "Great Balls of Fire." He hammered the intro chords, growling, "You shook my nerves and you rattled my brain . . ." The piano shuddered, ready to levitate.

Before he could inhale, every last person in the bleachers was standing up, screaming like the Beatles had just taxied up in a DC-3.

Lewis's long curls broke loose and danced across his face. He slammed the keys with his feet, his fists . . . he jumped around and played with his ass for a beat or two, then twisted back and hunched over the keyboard, elbows jumping as he threw off a flashy progression.

We were all hoarse by the time he banged to a close, and he just stood up and looked out at us all with a smirk, like "Yeah, got your damn seven dollars' worth," before stalking off the plywood stage.

Five minutes before, I'd been ready for a nap, but now my blood felt carbonated. "He's still got it," I said to Dean, "but what a strange way to show it, huh?"

"Oh, I dunno, I always liked 'Middle Age Crazy.' "

"Gross."

"Just because you grew up listening to that Joni Mitchell–Baez estrogen crap. If you'd spent your summers with a crewcut riding around in the back of a pickup, you'd have a little more appreciation," said Dean.

"Oh, right . . . and then I could delight in hearing Wimpy go, 'Your wife one o' them girl-fags, like Kristy McNichol?' "

He laughed. "Want a Pizza Frite?"

I groaned. We'd had spiedies, the Binghamton specialty sandwich of blandly marinated sliced meat. We'd had bites of souvlaki, lobster egg rolls, and sausage, onion, and pepper sandwiches. By the time we got to Ye Olde Ox Roast, we could do no more than take one half-mouthful each of a tepid "Ox Burger" before balancing the plate atop an overflowing garbage can and slinking away.

Waddling like a pair of *Charlotte's Web* rat Templetons, we'd dragged ourselves past the hawkers of cotton candy, Karmelkorn, Hawaiian Sno-Kones, and Sugar Waffles, but had given in to temptation at the NAACP Chuckhouse, sampling sublime greens, sultry ribs, and a thin wedge of platonic-ideal sweet potato pie. Two hours of Jerry Lee and flat beer, however, hadn't rekindled my appetite.

"How about a ride instead? The Cortina Bob, or the Ferris wheel?" I asked, steering him toward the sawdust and flashing lights. "Maybe if we jiggle everything around a little we'll have room for a quick funnel cake."

Dean nodded and we walked toward the rides, but I was arrested by the sight of one of those games where you swing a sledge-hammer and try to ring the bell at the top of a pole.

"I can't believe they have one of these," I said. "It's like straight out of *Popeye*."

We watched the line of local swains smashing the hammer down, trying to win their sweethearts a stuffed animal, but none were successful. The guy in charge of the game climbed off his stool every five customers or so, hitting the thing one-handed and dinging the bell without a change in his flat expression. Dean watched until he figured the angle needed to make the clanger jump to the top.

He stepped up to the plate and won me a small cobalt-blue teddy bear, but when he gave it to me I shivered, having a sudden flash of the Rose Girls and their soldiers standing right in this spot, before this same tattooed carnie in his greasy undershirt.

The Cortina Bob whipped around its canted oval track, Led Zeppelin's "Whole Lotta Love" cranking, and I felt like if I just squinted hard enough, all that frosted and overpermed mall hair would become Aqua Net–lacquered beehives, and it would be 1969.

I turned around slowly, saw a small trailer wedged in between the Ferris wheel and the Tilt-a-Whirl. The thing had been mocked up to look like a Gypsy wagon, with red-spoked wheels and a peaked roof shingled in cedar. A sign over the doorway read "Classic Silhouettes by Professor Archibald Sembles."

There were little lightbulbs screwed into this legend's frame, all the way around, like some old backstage makeup mirror. The clear globes winked on and off in sequence, except for three burned out at one corner.

"Bunny, you okay?" asked Dean. "You're white as hell. Pillar of salt."

"That's the guy," I said.

"What guy?"

"Archie Sembles. He did their portraits the night of the murders — Rose Girls and the soldiers. It was in Wilt's article."

"Wanna talk to him?"

"I should," I said.

"So get him to do one of you."

"Dude," I said. "Way too creepy."

He shrugged. "Okay," he said, "so *don't.*"

"But I should."

"So go ahead."

"Really?" I asked.

He shook his head, then grabbed my hand and towed me over to the trailer.

I looked down, the steps' turquoise paint all chipped craquelure at my feet. I couldn't move.

Dean gave me a nudge, and I put a foot on the first tread. He gave me another nudge.

"Lay off," I whispered, raising my eyes to the threshold, the white-and-gold sheet vinyl floor buckling where the door had leaked.

"Look, you don't want to go in," said Dean, "let's leave."

"Fine," I said, still whispering. "Be impatient, Mr. 'I'll be in goddamn Canada' —"

"Your choice," he said, not taking that bait. "Go in, or just go."

So I climbed the stairs, then looked back at him. "Aren't you coming?"

He shook his head. "You don't need me for this."

"Of course I need you. . . ."

"No," he said. "This is your deal."

"Dean . . . what the hell?"

"Look, I don't agree with this, but I'll respect whatever you decide to do, here. Just don't ask me to coax you into it." He wasn't acting snarky, just annoyingly calm and reasonable.

"But I'm *not* asking you to —"

"Bunny, if you *really* want to talk to this guy, then you don't need me as a cheerleader. I'm gonna go buy a soda. The rest of it's your call. I'll be back in a minute, but I'm staying outside."

I watched him go, the shithead. He disappeared into the crowd.

I took a deep breath, then slipped my face and one toe past the doorframe.

Archie Sembles dozed in a wing chair. Light from a standing lamp reflected off the worn-shiny patch of brocade around his head, off the greasy white hair raked across his scalp in Zen-garden-gravel stripes.

The tabletop next to him held an ashtray, ripped sugar packets, and shreds of foil and brown paper — Hershey Bar remains.

I caught a whiff of something sweetish in the heat, familiar. Saw a thread of perfumed smoke rising from one of those chalky green spirals you light against mosquitoes in the tropics.

Sembles hadn't moved. But for the spots on his hands, he was opaque as tallow, like some figure at Madame Tussaud's they hadn't yet painted to resemble flesh.

I cleared my throat.

Guy didn't even twitch. Maybe he was dead and I wouldn't have to talk to him.

"Sir?" I asked, voice all quavery.

Sembles blinked — eyes chicory blue, pupils small as fine-print punctuation. He raised his head and turned it slowly toward me.

"Step into my parlor," he said, in a measured contralto.

Then he smiled, teeth black as a Japanese courtier's.

CHAPTER 13

"Seven dollars, dearie," said Sembles. "Or ten for the special, which includes a mat and frame."

He gestured toward the wall behind me, closely packed with examples of his work. There were silhouettes of children, couples, men in glasses, women in hats — black on white.

I counted out the last of my crumpled bills. "I have eight," I said. "Not enough for the frame."

"It's been slow tonight," said Sembles. "I'll give you the special for eight."

He had me sit on a tasseled piano stool, then jacked me up three lurches with a foot pedal. I thought of Bugs Bunny in that barber chair.

Sembles spun me a quarter-turn on the stool, centering my head against a piece of black felt tacked to a row of cabinets.

He switched on an old gooseneck lamp, then angled its head so I was caught in the glare.

"I thought you'd use backlight to throw my shadow on a screen," I said. "Doesn't 'silhouette' mean shadow?"

"Shadow cutting is strictly for amateurs,

my dear. . . ." he said. "Housewives . . . the untrained."

I snuck a look at him. He squinted, moving half a step backwards.

"The word 'silhouette,' " he added, "has nothing to do with shadows."

Satisfied with the position of my head, he resumed his seat in the greasy wing chair.

"Well, what *does* it mean, then?" I asked.

He blinked at me, twice. "What?"

"Silhouette," I said. "What does the word 'silhouette' mean?"

"Silhouette," he sniffed, "is the surname of the man who first practiced paper-cutting as portraiture . . . Étienne de Silhouette, French Minister of Finance."

"Fascinating," I said, trying to sound like I meant it.

He sniffed again, offering no further comment.

"And may I ask," I said, "by whom you were trained?"

"I learned from my grandmother, who was instructed at the knee of the master: Augustin Amant Constant Fidele Edouart. He revived the art, perfected it."

"Where did they meet?"

"He was often at Saratoga, when my grandmother was a girl," he said. "Edouart traveled to all the top resorts, in season."

He yawned. It made his eyes water.

"And she was from Saratoga, your grandmother?"

"Ballston Spa," he said.

Sembles peered at me, then adjusted the lamp again.

"Better," he said. "Now we begin."

He reached into some lower shelf of his little table, producing a piece of matte black paper and folding it exactly in half, so that only its white backing showed.

He looked up and caught me watching him.

"You must hold *still*," he said, leaning across to reposition my chin with a bony finger.

"Why do you fold the paper?" I asked, trying to watch him without moving my head.

He took up his scissors. "One achieves better detail cutting against white than black."

"Remarkable," I said.

"Every profile is captured in fifteen cuts," he continued. "A true likeness requires precision, nuance. I rely on German scissors and doubled paper — both of which are nearly impossible to get in these sorry times."

"A lost art."

"I rather prefer to think otherwise."

"My most profound apologies," I said, looking at the profiles arrayed in front of me. "You are quite gifted. Does your work require a great deal of travel?"

"No," replied Sembles. "I'm a local boy, as they say. I used to do corporate events and private parties, but now I'm semiretired. I still like to work the fair, however. Such a lovely variety of faces."

He began looking from me to the paper, alert now and making deft snips with the tiny blades. He worked the scissors with his thumb and middle finger.

I was trying to think of a good way to introduce the topic of the murders, but Dean's absence made me even more self-conscious.

"Are these portraits on the wall of people you know?" I asked. "Family?"

"Merely likenesses with which I was particularly pleased."

"Of customers?"

"Certainly."

"But didn't they want to keep them? I mean, your work is so lovely," I said, gesturing toward the wall. "It must have been difficult, convincing people to part with these."

"Doubles," he said. "Another benefit of folded paper: one completes two likenesses at a go."

I tensed up, feeling my pulse in my throat. "What do you do with the spares?" Please, let him say he'd saved them all . . . that he still had likenesses of the Rose Girls, of the soldiers. . . . "Are these the only ones you've kept?"

He laughed, affording me another glimpse of those black teeth. "I have every one. Even my first sorry attempts preserved, Grandmother saw to that."

Just ask him. . . .

Maybe Dean was back by now. Maybe he'd change his mind and come in, which would be great because if *he* asked Sembles about the Rose Girls, it would come out sounding all casual and charming, like he didn't really care but it was just kind of interesting . . . because he *didn't* really care, and because he was very talented at coaxing.

I wasn't. I sucked at it, especially when it mattered.

I tried to make my voice sound relaxed, offhand. "So, all those doubles . . . do you keep them here?"

"In those cabinets behind you. Album after album, sorted by year. I hope to equal Edouart's record — thirty-eight hundred cuts, though he lost nearly all of them at sea. So far I've amassed some twenty-seven hundred."

I wanted to rip the felt backdrop down and throw all the doors open, start pawing through those albums until I found the right year. Instead I tucked my hands under my thighs, squashed them against the piano stool.

Sembles had finished cutting. I watched him reach for a piece of cardstock. He fixed one slip of black to it, after laying the other on the arm of his chair.

"Mr. Sembles . . ." I was all croaky. Nerves putting asphalt in my throat. I tried to cough before continuing. "If you could spare the time . . . I'd love to see more of your work."

He looked up, pleased. "Only if it wouldn't bore you."

"I'd be honored . . . and if I . . . I mean, may I ask you . . ."

"Fire away."

"You said you have every portrait. . . . Did you keep your doubles of the Rose Girls?"

Sembles's hand jerked, and the second cut fluttered from his chair to the floor.

He tried to smile, but it wasn't a tremendously convincing effort. "Who, dear?"

"The Rose Girls?"

He looked at the doorway, like he was

checking to see if anyone could hear us.

"In my line of work, dear . . ." he said, eyes dropping to the card with my profile on it. "Really, to recall any specific person . . . one meets so many. . . ."

Oh great. I was totally blowing this. . . . Maybe act decisive?

"You cut silhouettes of them in 1969," I said, trying for a little sternness, "and of the two soldiers they were with."

He glanced around the room, focus lighting on everything but me. "I'm not familiar . . ."

"Mr. Sembles?" I said. "You were quoted in the papers about it. In fact, you gave a detailed description of each person and each of those silhouettes."

Sembles brought his hands into his lap. He looked down at them, then made fists with his thumbs tucked inside.

"I've told you. Over twenty-seven hundred people," he said. "A great *many* people . . ."

"How many were murdered the same night you completed their portraits?"

He didn't answer. And then I just felt mean. What a horrible thing to say . . .

"I'm sorry, sir," I said, leaning toward him. "I just can't believe that would slip your mind. Even if you didn't live here . . . even if you traveled to different fairs all summer and this was just a stop on your circuit, I don't believe that. . . . And you're local. Anyone who lived here then, anyone old enough — they all remember what happened to those girls."

He opened his mouth, then closed it.

"Sir, it wasn't just what you said to reporters. The police had to've questioned you, probably more than once. . . ."

His legs started trembling, right when I'd said "police."

"Please," I said. "If you still have those doubles . . . if you can tell me anything . . ."

Sembles shook his head. He opened his fists and pressed both palms against his quivering knees, trying to steady them. It didn't work, just made the palsy spread to the rest of his fragile body.

Great. I had successfully terrorized an old junkie. Totally ham-fisted, stupid, lame-ass thing to do. And now I had no idea what the hell else to say.

"Mr. Sembles . . . I am so sorry," I said. "I've obviously upset you, and that's not at all what I wanted to do."

He checked the door again.

I couldn't get him to look at me. "It must have been tremendously disturbing, and I feel awful, asking you to revisit something that's obviously still very painful. . . ."

I tried to make my voice softer. "It's just that you're the only person I can ask about this. You must have been one of the last people to see them alive, and I don't understand why you're so . . ."

He turned back toward me, legs going double-time.

"I don't mean any offense, sir," I said, "but somehow I've frightened you, bringing this up, and I don't know why that is."

He started to sweat. Upper lip, then forehead. His hands slipped on his jiggling legs, revealing wet palm-prints beneath.

"Because," I continued, "you weren't worried about talking to reporters, after it happened. I've read the articles. . . . You even explained how you asked the victims to style their hair before cutting their silhouettes. You gave one a mantilla and a comb to wear. . . ."

I climbed off the piano stool and stepped toward him, very slowly.

"Mr. Sembles?" I leaned over to touch his hand, wanting to reassure him, but he yanked it away so my fingertips only brushed his thumb.

At that contact, he swiveled sideways, like he was going to bolt from the trailer.

He closed his fists over his thumbs again.

"I'm sorry," I said. "I didn't mean to

155

startle you."

Silence. Sembles wincing like he was trying not to cry.

"You know something," I said. "Please . . ."

I crouched down by the arm of his chair. "You should tell me," I said.

I wanted to reassure him . . . tried reaching toward his nearest hand again. He crossed his arms, shoved those fists under his armpits.

"Don't you touch me," he said, voice low.

"Mr. Sembles —"

He turned his head away.

"Why won't you talk about it?" I asked. "You weren't worried about it back then. You weren't afraid to tell people. What changed? What happened, afterwards?"

"Nothing happened."

"Something did. Some*one.*"

"I don't remember. I'm an old man. You have no right to threaten me. . . ."

"I'm not threatening you," I said, then felt like a jerk because I'd obviously made him *think* I was, which was what mattered.

"I'm sorry. I don't want you to . . . I'm just asking for your help. I mean, you make your living studying people's faces, committing their likenesses to paper. You're a sensitive man, a keen observer —"

He closed his eyes. I was just making it worse.

My legs were cramping up from squatting. I lowered myself to the floor, gingerly.

"But what you said . . . it's part of the public record. Has been for decades. Plus it didn't lead to any arrests, any solution. So all those details, the things you were quoted saying . . . they turned out harmless. They didn't change anything, didn't have any effect. They had no power."

"Then there is no point in bringing those details up," he said. "Whether I recall them or not."

Okay, so I was a total loser, and he was staring at the doorway again — craning forward to get a better view, like he thought someone was going to jump through it.

"Please," I said, "I'm not a threat. If you have those doubles . . . if there's anything you can tell me . . ."

Sembles turned back to me. "I want you to leave."

We stared at each other, and finally I just said, "Why?"

He shook his head.

I'd blown it. Didn't matter what else I said, and I was so pissed at myself my next words came out all testy.

"See, we're up against the central question," I said, "that 'why?' That whatever-it-is, making you want me gone."

Sembles sat up straighter.

"In that assumption, you are mistaken," he said. "The central question is not why I yearn for your departure. The central question is why you came."

"I came because of those girls."

"And what else?"

"Nothing else."

"I don't believe you."

"It's the truth."

"They've been dead for twenty years," he said. "You couldn't have known them. You're too young. So who told you? Who sent you here?"

"No one sent me here. I swear . . . if I knew any way to convince you of that . . ."

We stared at each other again. I struggled for something else to say, some hook to win him over, some way not to come off like an idiot for once. . . . Then I realized he hadn't seen Dean.

"I'm alone. You keep checking the door. No one's there. No one's listening. No one even *knows* I'm here," I said. "And no one will. It's just me."

"Then leave it alone," he said.

"Mr. Sembles, please believe me . . . I wish I could leave it alone. I wish I'd never heard about you or those girls or any of this."

"It doesn't matter what I tell you. Nothing will change."

"It does still matter . . . what you know is still important. To me."

"Those girls . . . It's finished. You won't bring them back."

"Please, just show me the doubles. That's all you have to do. It will never be traced to you."

Sembles shook his head. "I can't," he said.

"Why not?"

He dropped his eyes, started scratching at the back of his spotty hand, kept sneaking looks at the table next to him.

His nails were ragged. He knocked a little scab off his hand, then moved the scratching away from it, started attacking another patch of skin. Blood welled up in the tiny crater.

"Why the hell *not?*" I said. "You can sit there and let the whole damn thing fester, let whoever was responsible get away with killing two women? Those girls don't even have *names* anymore. What about their families? What about the people they never went home to? How dare you tell me you won't show me their portraits?"

"I didn't say *won't*. I said *can't*. It isn't possible."

He sighed, still scratching, gaze flicking over to me, to the doorway, back to the table. "They no longer exist. I had to burn them. A long, long time ago."

"You burned them. You just . . ."

"The slips, the backing. Everything. I had no choice," he said. "That was made quite, quite clear."

His nails wandered back to the center of his hand, to where the scab had been. He pulled the dome of blood out into a thread — back and forth, back and forth — each pass smearing the red streak wider.

"You're bleeding," I said.

He stopped scratching, but he didn't look at his hands, or at me. "And so there's nothing left for you to see, nothing left to learn," he said. "Nothing to delay your departure."

"Why didn't you have a choice?" I said. "Tell me that, and I'll go."

He leaned forward and started examining the floor. When he located the little card with my silhouette on it, he kicked it at me.

It skidded, spinning, coming to rest beside my knee.

I didn't pick it up. "Who made it clear? Tell me. Answer that one question, and you get your wish."

"Struwwelpeter."

"Who?" I asked. "Mr. Sembles? Who is

Struwwelpeter . . . one of the cops? One of the soldiers?"

"Your one question has been answered."

"Please . . . I just . . ."

Sembles pulled open a drawer in his little table.

"Get out," he said. "Now."

"Please."

"I am an old man, but I am capable of forcing you to leave."

I stood up.

Inside the drawer, I could see the spoon. The stub of candle. The tip of a syringe.

"All right," I said, moving toward the doorway. "I'm sorry."

I backed down the stairs, right into Dean.

CHAPTER 14

The trailer door banged shut, and we could hear the click of the latch. The winking lights around Sembles's sign went dark.

"So he's done for the night?" asked Dean.

I just stood there.

Dean gave my shoulder a squeeze. "You okay?"

"Kind of," I said.

"Kind of?"

"Kind of not."

"Want some soda?"

"No," I said. "Just let's go."

"Find something out?"

"Kind of," I said.

"Like?"

"I don't even know."

"Tell me," he said.

"Let's go. Come *on*." I started walking.

The wind picked up, heavy with sugar and grease. Smoke. Rancid beer.

"Bunny?"

I whipped my head back toward him. He hadn't moved.

He started toward me. Long strides. "What the hell happened?"

I turned full forward again, kept going with my back to him.

They had the Cortina Bob loaded full, some bored guy walking along the snake of sleighs, clanking down lap-bars one by one. Then he threw a big switch and it all started up, the riders in a whirl faster and faster, with "Freebird" blistering from the speakers.

Dean caught up, falling into step.

I went faster. Couldn't shake him.

We finally reached my Rabbit in the parking lot. I went for the driver's door, Dean for the passenger's. I dug in my pocket for the keys, still wondering who the hell Struwwelpeter was.

"Bunny, you're shaking."

Taking a deep breath, I turned toward Dean, locked eyes with him across the car's orange roof.

He looked worried. "What did he say? Did he tell you it was Lapthorne? What happened?"

What happened was I proved to myself that I was just as scared and sorry and stupid and useless as I suspected.

What happened was I had no fucking idea what I was doing, which was exactly why I'd wanted Dean to go in there with me, only the whole thing was so pointless he'd been right to make me do it alone.

I opened my mouth to tell him that. Everything.

But what came out instead was, "You are such an asshole for ditching me. You really are."

"Bunny, look . . . it's time to get someone official involved."

We were sitting in the car, still parked.

I'd told him what happened with Sembles. Bad idea.

"You want me to call the *cops?*"

He didn't say anything.

I could see the top of the Ferris wheel. It

was stopped. The seats were rocking.

"That's so stupid," I said.

He crossed his arms.

"No, really," I said. "I tell you this name that might *be* a cop for all we know, and your response is I should talk to the police?"

"This is bullshit," said my husband.

"This is *not* bullshit."

"Don't get all pissy with *me*," he said. "I didn't goddamn kill anybody."

"*You're* the one getting pissy," I said. "I'm totally fine."

So then we had to sit there, glaring at separate points on the windshield to prove how not-pissy we were.

Which, sadly, just allowed me to reflect on how totally psycho I was being. I have a weakness for snark but I normally really pride myself on not acting like a bitch, even under duress. I felt guilty, lashing out at Dean.

Plus, the cranky thing wasn't doing crap to buttress my argument.

"Look," I said, "I'm sorry. I mean, if it's . . ." And then I just stopped. Had no idea what to say.

I shoved my fingers into my hair and then made fists, strands sticking out everywhere from between my knuckles. I could see my reflection in the windshield: Portrait of the Artist Totally Losing Her Shit.

I growled.

"What?" asked Dean.

"I don't know," I said. "I. Have. No. Clue. There's just a big swirling nest of crap in my head. . . ."

I put my hands in my lap. Tried to look vaguely sane.

"Like," I said, "um . . . what if this means that Lapthorne's —"

"You don't know what *any* of it means. You *can't* know. That's the whole point. That's the only thing that matters."

"So you're telling me to just give up, just hand over the dog tags?"

"You said you would. You said the *first* thing you found out . . ."

"But this *isn't* finding anything out," I said. *"Nothing's* more definitive. *Nothing's* clearer. This is just *more."*

"You want to start qualifying a bargain . . ." he said, letting the thought trail off in a particularly annoying way, all fakey-fake lighthearted and reasonable.

I resisted the urge to bash my forehead against the steering wheel. "What if it *was* someone else? Maybe it's the Struwel guy, but maybe it still leads back to Lapthorne.

You're telling me you'd call the cops on one of your cousins if you weren't totally sure?"

"My cousins are busy wrenching on their cars or making Jell-O salads or crocheting incredibly ugly afghans. You know, *normal*."

He was so tall, even sitting, that the ceiling's proximity made his hair all staticky, standing up so it stuck to the headliner.

I put a hand on his elbow. "What if it was Rotten Charlie?"

"R.C.?"

Dean's right-up-the-road first cousin, so named to distinguish him from his father, Just Plain Charlie.

"If it was R.C. . . ." he said, reluctant. "Okay. I'd probably wait until I *knew*."

"Of course you would," I said. "You guys'd be doing bong hits in his parents' shed and practicing New York Dolls riffs and figuring out how to sneak him into Mexico. . . ."

Dean closed his eyes and started rubbing his temples.

"And I, as your loyal wife," I continued, sensing weakness, "I would *totally* respect that. I'd make goddamn sandwiches for the trip. Iced tea. I'd probably end up *driving*."

"You probably would."

He tried to stop himself from smiling at that image. Couldn't do it.

"So you just need to lay *off* me for a minute," I said, "while I figure this out."

Dean glanced up at the ceiling for a second, resigned, then turned his head away from me and nodded, giving in.

It took a second before I realized that I hadn't wanted him to, after all.

My stomach felt like one of those fruit-punch dispensers they used to have on Woolworth lunch counters — a flared aquarium down whose walls you could watch the bright icy liquid cascade endlessly, in sheets.

CHAPTER 15

I was cranking out the food piece for Ted the next morning — "Eating Your Way through the New York State Fair: A Grease-hound's Guide to the Midway."

My writing was shit. I was too rattled about Sembles. Wondering who the hell Struwwelpeter was.

The name tugged at me. I'd heard it before. It gave off this little nagging blip of familiarity, but every time I tried to zero in on a context, the teasing spark of recognition darted to the periphery and winked out.

I kept typing.

You're probably under the illusion that you go to the State Fair to win a Kewpie doll, dunk that stupid clown who makes fun of your shorts, scream your lungs out on the Cortina Bob, or eyeball Li'l Muffin, World's Smallest Horse. But let's face it: When you come home at the end of a long day on the midway, what you spent most of your shekels on was food — and lots of it.

Dreck. I needed more coffee. I stood up, about to grab my mug for a refill, but then just stood there with my hand on the back of my chair.

Struwwelpeter. The answer was so damn close, right on the tip of my brain. Somebody Kenny'd mentioned? But if I'd heard about the guy at the Crown, if he was a local, wouldn't Dean have remembered, too?

I looked at the phone. He was working at the farm today. I could call, could run it by him again.

Just thinking of Dean's voice made me realize how quickly he'd be gone — so soon I felt lonely already, and here I was stuck at work. Not like he had time to just kick back, but I wanted to be hanging out with him, even if all I got to do was sit there watching him weld trapezoids to each other.

Maybe I could run out there during lunch,

bring him a sandwich. Ask him about the stupid name.

Who the hell *was* it? I shut my eyes, trying to think back over how things had unfolded with Sembles. There was no logic to it, the way he'd reacted. So much easier to admit he remembered the girls, and leave it at that.

If he'd done that, I would have figured he was a dead end, a source already milked of insight and possibility. Instead he thought I was checking up on him for someone else, making sure he still abided by whatever promises he'd been threatened into keeping. I wanted to believe that identifying Struwwelpeter, the source of that threat, would put Lapthorne in the clear. I wanted to believe I had the name of the killer.

I could ask Kenny or anyone at the paper if that name rang a bell. But what if Struwwelpeter wasn't the killer? Sembles got freaked out when I mentioned the police. What if it was a cop trying to cover things up? What if Struwwelpeter was the other soldier? What if asking about it led to finding out that Lapthorne was involved after all? That he'd been right at the heart of everything . . .

Well, fuck it. Then he'd deserve no protection. He'd deserve whatever happened, the very worst outcome, and I'd help make sure he got nailed, with all the trimmings.

But what if he *wasn't* involved?

Until I figured out who this Struwwelpeter was, figured out one way or the other whether that knowledge could drag the still-entirely-possibly-*innocent* Lapthorne into this mess for no reason, it didn't change shit for me.

I could ask Dean. I could run the name by Kenny. I could try looking the guy up in the phone book. I didn't want to ask Wilt, or anyone else here in the office. Not straight out. Not yet.

I shuffled over to the coffeemaker.

Wilt was watching brown elixir drip into a glass Bunn pot. He was wearing a tie three feet wide, peace signs all over it.

"Reaganomics trickles down with greater speed," he said, by way of good morning. "How was the fair? You get to see Jerry Lee?"

"The fair was the fair. Jerry Lee was hugely lame up until the last possible moment, then he was great."

Wilt nodded, eyes still locked on the carafe.

I hesitated, suddenly wanting to reveal my little nugget of dirt, to find out whether he'd ever heard the guy's name.

Same stupid rock. Same stupid hard place.

But if I kept it looser? Didn't mention Struwwelpeter specifically?

I twisted the mug in my hands. Cleared my throat.

Wilt looked up at me.

"So, um . . ." I said, tilting the mug so I could stare into its depths. "I did see this . . . you know . . . *guy.*"

I lifted my eyes.

He smiled, waiting for me to continue.

No sound but the drizzle of coffee.

I checked the bottom of my empty mug again, hoping to find some dregs of reassurance. "Someone you quoted in your Rose Girls article."

"Yeah?"

"You remember that guy Archie Sembles, who does the silhouettes?"

"Sure," said Wilt. "See him at parties every couple of years — gala-event-type deals. New Years. Always brings this, like, booth. Sets up in a corner. Freaky little dude."

"Yeah," I said. "Kind of nervous."

Wilt nodded. "So, d'you talk to him?"

"While he was doing my silhouette. A little."

"Ask him about the Rose Girls?"

"I did. Yeah."

"Story's got you going, huh?"

171

I shrugged. "My father-in-law was talking about it a while ago. It just got stuck in my head, you know? Morbid curiosity."

"That's the kind that haunts you. Keeps working you over."

"Exactly," I said.

"You should write about it. A follow-up piece — nineteen years and still no answers . . ."

"Wilt, I write about, like, collecting old hubcaps . . . 1,001 ways with chicken wings . . . hot drinks for winter . . ."

Wilt patted my head. "Don't sell yourself short."

"I just . . . I don't really like interviewing *people.* Phone calls, beating the bushes . . . all that hard-nosed investigative stuff you're good at. I get serious agita when I have to order a pizza. . . ."

"You'd pick it up, though, Maddie. A little practice, you'd be fine. You'd start to dig it."

"That's, like, ulcer material. Just talking about it with you. Remember when Ted made me write that piece on couples who'd met through the personals ads? It was supposed to be a nice sweet little fluffy thing for Valentine's Day?"

He nodded.

"And then I kept getting phone calls from

172

wackos for months afterwards — that guy who became a transvestite in prison and wanted me to write his life story, how he wore pink satin hot pants and toenail polish and curled his hair? I mean, he wanted me to call him Betty Lou over the phone and he started breathing all heavy. . . ."

The coffee was done. Wilt filled his cup. "You get used to it. Couple of times more, nothing would faze you."

"Wilt, all those manila envelopes I got in the mail, filled with clippings from the *National Enquirer* and toilet paper coupons, for God's sake? With little notes on scrap paper wondering did I ever notice that after playing tennis for an hour a woman's breast on the racquet side gets bigger. . . ."

"This is different," he said, pouring coffee into my mug.

I shook my head. Not different at all. My sorry-ass performance with Sembles last night proved it.

He laughed, put the carafe back on its warming plate and then tapped one long finger against his temple. "Trust an old hippie."

"I'm way way way too wussy."

"This whole thing's got its teeth sunk in you good and deep, Madeline. I recognize the signs."

"It's not like that." I gripped the mug tighter, so he wouldn't see my hands shaking.

"It *is* like that. This kind of shit's a virus, not a choice. The Rose Girls, they've got you all infected with their story. . . . They're going to keep pushing at you until you go after it, egging you on, poking their heads into your thoughts whenever your guard is down. Only gets worse. Why else would you be questioning this fair guy, for chrissake?"

"Questioning who?" asked a small voice behind me. I jumped, squeaking.

I turned around. "*Jesus,* Simon. You almost gave me a heart attack."

"You're ready for this, Maddie," said Wilt, "and I'm telling Ted to give you the assignment."

"Really, Wilt," I pleaded, "don't."

"What assignment?" asked Simon.

"The Rose Girls," answered Wilt. "Redux."

"Oh, I think that's excellent," said Simon, with a shy smile of encouragement. "It's always good to push yourself, Madeline."

Easy for him to say, I thought, he gets to hide behind a camera.

By the time I was finished with the fair piece, Wilt had run his inspiration by Ted, who gave me a great lizardy leer and told me he thought it was a great idea. *Yeah, goddamn brilliant.* I wanted to get home early, since Dean was leaving the next morning, but Ted called me into his office to hammer out the details.

"You've got a lot on your plate . . . those book reviews and the apple festival and your thing on the Adirondacks . . . so I'll give you until Novemberish for this. I would have run it as an anniversary piece, but it'll be good around Thanksgiving. People always want a little morbid pull on the heartstrings while they're suffering through their own family gettogethers. Couple of dead chicks . . . just the ticket."

Asshole.

"Wouldn't you rather just have a nice piece on stuffing recipes?" I said, grasping. "A history of green bean casseroles with mushroom soup and canned fried onions on top? Nice tongue-in-cheek illustrated evolutionary sidebar . . . I mean, Ted, this is just not my line of country, you know?"

"Of *course* I know," he said, rocking back in his chair and folding his arms behind his head, practically flicking his tongue in reptilian glee, "but what have you done for me lately?"

I went back to my desk. Could have puked

all over it, frankly.

Why the hell had I mentioned Sembles to Wilt in the first place? Idiocy.

I dialed the number for the workshop out at the farm. There was still time to get out there with a sandwich for Dean, even if I couldn't imagine eating anything myself.

The phone rang and rang and rang.

As I cradled the receiver in defeat, I started obsessing again about Struwwelpeter.

Inspiration. Eureka. Yee-ha.

I pulled open the bottom drawer of my desk and took out the phone book.

For all I knew he'd be listed, and I could just call up and say "Listen, you annoying nemesis bastard, I want to know what the hell you did to freak out the silhouette guy and then I want you to tell me my cousin had nothing to do with the dead girls."

And of course then he would and my conscience would be clear and I could just write about potholders instead of murders, because that's exactly how perfect my life always turns out, since I am the silver-lining poster girl champion. Not.

I flopped the directory open and snapped through pages . . . Sargent, Siemanski, Smith, Smith, Smith . . . but on the Stokely-to-Suma page I found exactly nothing. Not a single murderer-to-solve-all-my-problems between between Strunk, Larry D., and Stryker, Patrick, DDS.

And it was only then that I realized how crazy it was that I knew how to spell "Struwwelpeter" in the goddamn first place.

That's why its initial consonant's mushy Teutonic sibilance didn't prompt me to look first under S-H, why I knew perfectly well there were two *w*'s, and that there was no point in backtracking to "Streww . . ." or any other variation.

Because I'd seen it, not heard it. Only I couldn't remember where.

Photogenic voodoo, biting me in the ass.

Dean was exhausted that night. I wanted to tell him about the Rose Girl assignment, but over dinner he started describing how he'd done some work down at the Speer-O-Matic shop and the union guys tried to light him on fire.

He'd been lying underneath a tank car, welding, and someone poured gasoline into one of the steel tracks crisscrossing the concrete floor, so that it flowed across the room and down near his head. A spark from the welder ignited the stuff, but he rolled away fast and grabbed a fire extinguisher.

My hands started shaking. "Did you see anyone?"

"I think I heard a truck pulling out of the lot, but after I put the fire out there was no one there . . . just wind blowing through the yard. Scary as shit."

"Is it worth it? I mean, last time you were there they'd spray-painted 'scab' all over everything, and now they're starting in with the flammable liquids. Are you sure you want to do this?"

"It's an open shop, says so right there in the contract. This isn't work they can do, and they're trying to screw me out of a living. The union can suck my dick."

I wanted to weigh in with Cesar Chavez, the Haymarket riots, to point out that unions benefited us all, raised the bar for everyone. But I knew part of my vehemence was family guilt for screwing over "the working man" in the abstract, while here was an actual and specific working man who had an opinion of his own, thank you very much.

Plus, we'd had the same argument like twenty times already over the years, starting with a heated dinner conversation on our third date.

So I just carried the dishes to the sink, not even turning on the kitchen light. And then I started to cry because what the hell was I pissed at him for, when he could have been hurt or even died — the stupid heartrendingly dear scab fascist shithead.

The worst possible thing. Even the idea he was in danger, at risk of any kind of harm . . . and I wondered if that same feeling was making him stonewall me, talk me out of pursuing this whole deal with Lapthorne. So I started crying harder, feeling guilty but maybe also deeply cherished, getting my face all snotty and everything.

Dean came into the kitchen and stood behind me, in the dark. Wrapped his arms around my shoulders and pressed his chin down on the top of my head.

"If anything ever happened to you," I said, my voice all weird and gummy, "anything made you get hurt . . . I would just roll up and die."

"Anything? Like a hangnail anything?"

"If it was a hangnail anything, I'd punch you really, really hard first. Before the whole rolling-up-and-dying part."

"You could just punch me, skip the rest of it. I'd be cool with that."

"Yeah?"

I thought he'd keep going, say something nice back, but instead he went, "Ewwww . . ."

" 'Ewww'? You're kind of sucking the romance out of the moment, here."

"Well, you're kind of dripping snot on my arm."

"Oh," I said. "Sorry."

"It's okay. Probably some kind of Eskimo foreplay, if you think about it."

"Only among extremely depressed Eskimos."

"Best kind," he said.

"Sure," I said. "Famous for having constant rad sex."

"Exactly."

"So, look, Dean — promise you won't die, okay? Don't let anyone light you on fire. Stuff like that."

"You promise first."

"Okay," I said.

"Okay," he said, digging his chin a little harder into the top of my head. "Then there's something I should tell you. I wasn't sure, but since you've promised not to die it's probably safe."

"Is this about Eskimos?"

"No."

"About what, then?"

"Struwwelpeter."

"You found out who it is?"

"I knew."

"Last night?"

"Pretty much."

"You suck," I said.

"I was worried. I *am* worried. This whole deal . . . I don't want anything to happen to you."

"Okay, I'm sorry. You suck slightly less."

"Thank you."

"But you still have to tell me who it is."

He sighed. "It's not exactly a person."

"Shit," I said. "Shit shit shit shit."

"It's a book."

A book someone had given us in a box of discards when I was a kid.

"That creepy German thing with all the poems about what happens to children who misbehave," I said.

"Yes."

"I am so fucking stupid. The thumbs . . ."

Dean pressed his chin down again. Tightened his arms around me.

"In one of the poems," I said, "this kid's mother tells him not to suck his thumbs. He starts up as soon as she leaves, so a crazy tailor with giant scissors runs in and cuts them both off."

"*Die Daumenlutscher,*" said Dean. "I think it's 'Little Suck-a-Thumb' in English, but I don't get the connection."

"Sembles makes his living with scissors. He kept hiding his thumbs every time he

181

got nervous — wrapping them up in his fists, shoving them under his arms. That story's the perfect threat to keep him quiet. I should have put it together. It's just I wanted it to be some bad guy's name. A substitute for Lapthorne."

"It's time to tell the cops."

"No."

"Bunny, there isn't any question. This has to be your cousin. The rose thing is German, too. Brothers Grimm."

"I think it *was* the cop. Not Lapthorne."

"You just don't want to see it."

"If you'd been there, with Sembles . . . he was totally fine until I mentioned the cops. That's what freaked him out. Before that, he was just calmly denying he remembered anything. The minute I said 'police,' he lost his shit."

"And some upstate cornhead cop is so fixated on German literature he runs around killing people to enact children's stories?"

"Some upstate cornhead cop with a name like Schneider? Why the hell not?"

Dean flinched.

"What?" I snapped.

"Schneider."

"What *about* Schneider?"

"It's the German word for 'tailor.' "

"Ha!"

"Bunny . . ."

"So there," I said. "Neener neener neener."

He dropped his arms. Stepped away from me. "Bunny, Jesus Christ . . ."

"I was right. You're just pissed because I was *right*."

He turned on the lights. " 'Right' doesn't come into it."

I put my hand up to shield my eyes. "But don't you see how this —"

"You have to tell the police," he said. "Tomorrow. I'll come with you. We'll go down and give them the goddamn dog tags."

"Are you *crazy?*"

"This is too goddamn dangerous. I don't care who did it. I don't care what happens to your cousin. This is way over your head. It's time to tell the cops."

"*Schneider's* a cop."

"Not anymore."

"Like that would make a difference . . ."

"Let it go. Let them sort it out."

That would be when I told him to rot in hell.

He went to bed.

I didn't.

CHAPTER 16

I was still pissed the next day, not to mention cranky and self-indulgent and freaked and brooding. Too little sleep. Too much coffee. The whole subjective-depressive Tar Baby.

Plus I had that live-action Howard Cosell interior voice-over going, in stereo, telling me what a jerk I was for feeling like such a jerk. Couldn't snap out of it, even when Mom called me at work to announce that her invitations had gone out, that Lapthorne had already RSVP'd a firm acceptance, and that she'd decided at the last *minute,* holy crow, to make the thing a costume party.

But it was my last afternoon with Dean, probably for weeks. I was so utterly devastated by the prospect of my beloved's impending absence that I left work a little early. I got all choked up and teary on the drive home, swearing up and down that I'd send him off with a kind supportive word and a smile on my face, even if it freaking killed me.

I found him just finishing off his packing, and invited him to come with me to shop for the makings of a little home-cooked meal before it was time to hit the airport.

We'd be cutting it tight, so I decided to drive up to this place on Butternut — a market I'd dubbed The Outpatient Grocery Store. It was always like shopping in a methadone clinic, but it was the closest.

The owners knew most people in the neighborhood couldn't afford a car to get to the nicer, cheaper stores out in the burbs: the solidly clean P&Cs and Big Ms, the Wegmans in DeWitt with the big "international" cheese section. So, just because they could, these guys stocked The Outpatient with nothing but nasty old crap at lunar-colony trade-embargo prices.

I muscled past Dean and yanked a rattle-wheeled cart from the front-door pileup. The handle was greasy and the kiddy-seat basket thing was rusted shut, but it made a great battering ram. I smashed it through the busted "Automatic CAUTION Door," into the fuck-you-you're-on-food-stamps reek of Pine-Sol and cheap fish, badly refrigerated.

Pretty much every supermarket in America is designed to make you go right when you come in the front door. My cart pulled to the left, balking when I tried to maneuver it over the pitted, sticky brown flooring.

I fought that cross-eyed axle with all my

weight, hell-bent on the produce aisle.

Dean walked ahead, hands in his pockets. When he had about ten feet on me, he turned around to wait, resting a hip against the cantaloupe bin.

It was at this point that my husband casually mentioned how he wouldn't be back from Canada in time for Mom's party, which was fine with him because it was a really stupid idea.

I just said, "Oh?" and smiled at him, while body-slamming my cart toward the lettuce.

"Yeah," he said. "Bernie from Speer-O-Matic told me yesterday. I forgot to mention it."

I was determined not to let my pus-filled mood infect our last few hours of blissful togetherness.

"Hmmm," I said. Calmly, honest to God, with absolutely no inflection that could be construed as negative in any way.

I gave up on the cart and just walked the rest of the way to the lettuce.

"Of *course* they have nothing but iceberg," I said, slapping one of the sad little brown-tinged balls. "Like nobody's ever heard of romaine, let alone endive."

"*On*-deev," echoed Dean. "Who died and made you Marie Antoinette?"

"Heh heh," I gamely chuckled, "like *you'd*

condescend to eat this shit even with a gun to your head."

I waved my hand over the aisle's gallery of deflated oranges, wizened turnips, and beets that had seen better days.

"This could make you give airplane food five stars," I said, still the very model of lighthearted spousal repartee. "Chef-Boy-goddamn-Ardee wouldn't shop here. My *mother* wouldn't shop here."

"Of course not," he said. "There's no dented stuff on sale."

I whipped a head of iceberg at his chest as hard as I could.

He caught it one-handed.

"I am just so sick of this town," I said. "It's like some mental dust bowl filled with people who didn't have the gumption to get in the goddamn truck with Granny and the chicken coop strapped up top so they could drive the hell away. What are we doing here? What will we ever be able to do here?"

"This is real life. You just don't recognize it because you got brought up in pretty little Disneylands. You wouldn't know real life if it fell out of the sky and knocked you flat on your ass."

"You are just so —"

"Look," he said, calmly, "I don't want to fight with you. You're just spinning your wheels with this whole murder thing."

He was right. But I felt so defeated and horrible I couldn't admit it. Couldn't let it go. I looked at him and snapped, "What the hell is *that* supposed to mean?"

"Your cousin, this party at your mother's . . . I won't even get into how goddamn stupid it is, how goddamn dangerous."

"Good. So don't."

"The rest of it . . . above and beyond . . . You've been completely unbalanced since the whole deal with the dog tags came up. The house is a sty, you're not concentrating on your work — everything is falling apart and I don't even know what's in it for you if you figure out who killed those chicks."

Nothing was in it for me, because there wasn't a chance in hell I *could* figure it out. I was a big fat loser, and all I could do was make us both miserable until I caved in and said so out loud. Except of course I was too miserable to do it.

"Maybe it'll be my ticket out of here," I said.

"Bunny, don't *cry*. . . ."

"Maybe if I'm writing about something that matters, I could get a job someplace other than bumfuck upstate."

Okay, so I *was* crying . . . right in the

middle of the stupid grocery store.

"I used to be good," I said, wiping a sleeve across my nose. "In high school, in college. I was generally recognized as having wit and talent. Now I'm an unemployable piece of garbage in the middle of nowhere, and the only thing that matters to you is that I'm not wearing a starched apron while mopping the goddamn floors all day." Which was patently unfair of me to say, as he always did the mopping, stripping off his shirt while blasting "Ride of the Valkyries."

"That's not what I said."

"It's what you *meant*," I said. "I am *not happy* here. I've been telling you that for two years and you think I'm an idiot because of it. I'm *not* an idiot and this place *does* suck. Admit it, because you know it's true."

"The trouble with you is you think if your existence isn't being documented in *Town & Country* it doesn't count, and now you're spinning out this Lapthorne thing so you'll have something to talk about at cocktail parties."

"In Syracuse? Vienna sausages out of the can and warm Labatt's do not a cocktail party make, no matter whose garage you're in."

I was disgusted with myself even as the

words left my mouth. What the hell was I doing?

"I just think," he said, thankfully ignoring that cheap shot, "that you're messing around on the edges of this thing because you want some thrill to lively up your existence. This isn't it. This is just ugly and dangerous."

"Are you listening at all? I meant it when I said I wanted to find out just enough to know whether I should give the dog tags to the police. Let's just go to the stupid party at Mom's and see if Lapthorne means anything . . . that's all I'm asking. That's not dangerous —"

"I can't take off for some party," he said.

"But you can go to freaking *Canada?*"

"That's work."

"Yeah, yeah, 'you're burnin' daylight.' "

"And you want to move someplace else because you think you'll like yourself there," he said. "Doesn't matter where you live. It'll still be you."

"That's just great. That's just goddamn beautiful." And absolutely true.

A vested biker with two kids in his cart took one look at us and opted for another aisle, horrified.

"If you're so set on pursuing this bogus crap, why haven't you told them at the paper?" he retorted.

"I did," I said. "I have an assignment, as of yesterday."

"So why didn't you tell *me?*"

"Because you didn't goddamn ask me. Because nothing *I* do matters."

"Everything you do matters to me, Bunny," he said. "That's why I can't understand this. I just want you to be happy. We have a good life. This project is going to make it better. . . ."

"Please stay," I said. "Just a few days. We could go out to STD's on the weekend and talk to Schneider . . . the Kingsnakes are playing."

"I can't. You know I'm right."

I did indeed. And I also knew that I was married, that I had made my bed, that every moment for the rest of my life would be spent beating my fists against a reality I would have enjoyed if I'd been a better, deeper person.

I didn't want to be my parents, to throw it all to the winds if it ceased to entertain, to go for the highs of newness over and over again. But Syracuse forever?

Standing there, staring at that stupid pile of lettuce, I thought about how there was only an hour left until I had to drive him to the airport.

So I apologized. I meant it absolutely sincerely, and despised him for it anyway.

By the weekend I wasn't pissed anymore, just numb and tired and lonely. Dean hadn't called from the road.

Of course not. I was such an asshole, I wouldn't have called me either, not for a million dollars.

There I was on the sofa, Saturday night, reading *The Big Sleep* and eating a WASP-soul-food dinner of Ruffles out of the bag with sour-cream-and-onion-soup-mix dip in a cracked bowl.

My latest mix tape was cranked way the hell up: Puccini interspersed with the English Beat, the Kingston Trio, and Jello Biafra's "Viva Las Vegas" cover. Lou Reed was singing "Wild Side" but would get interrupted halfway through with the price of gold at the London fixing because I'd forgotten I was making a tape and switched the stereo over to NPR for a second.

This was all designed to keep me from putting Joni Mitchell on, because I was depressed enough as it was. My worn cassette of *Blue* kept winking up at me from the picnic basket of tapes near the stereo, saying "You know you want me," and I was weakening even though the opening bars of her lament for distant California would put me over the edge.

I mean, look out any window in Syracuse and see if you can keep from losing it while somebody starts singing "Sitting in a bar in Paris, France." You'll go through an awful lot of Pernod just thinking about it.

I never listened to Joni when Dean was home, because he said he could feel his chest hair falling out. It was sort of a pact between us — her and Judy Collins on my side and Captain Beefheart and the Stooges on his, to be played only in each other's absence.

Maybe I deserved a good tear-filled folkie wallow, though, since I was stranded on my plastic Green Street sofa, missing out on the chance to question Schneider.

Or just missing out on the chance to screw up questioning Schneider.

If I were a better person, I thought, I'd either have gotten to know a bigger gang of local people upon whom I could call in such emergencies or have developed the social courage to head out to a bar by myself.

And right then there was all this pounding on my front door. "Madwoman! Open up!"

"Ellis?" I said, getting up off the sofa.

No one but Ellis ever calls me Madwoman.

CHAPTER 17

Ellis breezed into the room, a dark-haired green-eyed gamine, coltish in the summer rich-girl uniform of the eighties: white linen shorts, white T-shirt, black lamb's-wool Eurotrash sweater vest, black loafers.

She was a Cheever girl, a Salinger girl. She should have been stepping off a fall-game-weekend New Haven train in a long squirrel coat, or contemplating a young-married affair on some moonlit club terrace.

"So," I asked, "what brings you to fashionable Syracuse?"

"I was in Utica, breaking up with Alec at his dad's. I mean, what's another hour on the thruway once you're in this godforsaken neck of the woods. Got anything to drink? My teeth are wearing sweaters."

Alec, the coke-dealing stonemason. Into Eckankar. I grabbed two beers out of the icebox while she plucked the bottle opener from a long-familiar drawer near the sink.

"This place really is the asshole of nowhere," she said. "I mean, what are you, like three hours from Williamstown and six from the city?"

"Alec is really history?" I said.

They'd been living together for over a year, had broken up four times already but she always gravitated back to him out of inertia or loneliness or the need for bill consolidation. It was like watching a small and very beautiful bird fly over and over again into a plate glass window.

In between times she'd show up here with interchangeable slicky-boy tennis players. Dean and I categorized them by their training programs — Goldman Sachs, First Boston. None of them keepers, but the world was short of Cheever and Salinger boys.

She looked at the ceiling. " 'History' is such a big word for such an infinitesimal man. Let's just say he's over."

"Alec was over before *either* of us slept with him."

"Well," she said, "at least you had the perspicacity to do it first, and only once."

"Perspicacity would have involved keeping my clothes on."

"You were young and drunk," she said.

"I ran out of quarters for pinball. What's your excuse?"

"I liked him, and he gave me a place to live."

And her father had just died when they moved in together. I handed her the beers.

Ellis opened them, gave me one, and jumped up onto the counter. She crossed her tan, pretty legs and swung a loafered foot.

We have the same tattoo on our right ankles, a cent sign. I got mine first, after my sister got a dollar sign.

Ellis's was backwards, as she didn't trust the tattoo chick to draw it "the right way" and made her redo the trial sketch before it was inked. She came up with the best reason for them, though, saying we stood "for change."

"Hey," I said, "he's okay. It could have worked."

"Oh please." She looked at me, generous mouth turned up at one corner. "Saying Alec was a shitty boyfriend is like saying 'this toothpick made a lousy sword.'"

"Here's to *good* boyfriends," I said, raising my bottle.

She clinked it. "Here's to swords."

We had no hometowns, no permanent allies — nothing but the involuntary vagabond's glib knack for establishing beachheads at each pause in our parents' orbits.

They'd deployed us cash-free into top-notch trust-fund schools, short of socks and warm-enough winter coats. We drank too much and never just-said-no to anything, a pair of pretty, fatherless girls who most often saw a hard-on as an applause meter.

Then I met Dean: right guy, wrong town. Now the world pulled at me, and the promise of a real haven beckoned to Ellis. We wished each other across that divide.

The phone rang. I balanced the handset under my chin. "Hello?"

"Hey, Bunny," said Dean through a load of static. "Wanted you to know I got up here okay."

"Hey, Ellis just walked in." I twirled the phone cord on my index finger. Neither of us would mention the fight, we always just picked up a different conversation.

"Oh great. . . . You *know* when you guys get together it's like a couple of frat boys with tits."

"I'd like to think slightly smaller and funnier."

Dean was silent.

"Is he calling us frat boys with tits again?" said Ellis, taking the beer from my hand. "Hi, Dean!"

I could tell he'd heard that but was ignoring it. "Listen, I don't want you guys going to STD's."

"Yes, dear." And I would have meant it, except Ellis made it all seem a lot better. Possible.

"Bunny —"

"Well, now that she's here, it would be kind of nice to check out the Kingsnakes."

"You *hate* the Kingsnakes."

"I *adore* the Kingsnakes. I am a dedicated and lifelong blues fan."

"You called them 'pompous derivative white boys' at Tom and Maripat's wedding."

"Only because they wouldn't turn down the speakers and they were scaring your grandmother. I mean, they were playing at eleven — that's one more than ten. And I did ask them once, politely."

He sighed.

"I should go," I said.

"Just be safe, all right? Don't do anything stupid."

"I love you."

"Yeah," he said, and hung up.

"I take it we have plans?" asked Ellis.

"Cornering a corrupt ex-cop at a seedy roadhouse in order to solve a decades-old double murder that may have been committed by my second cousin."

"Perfect," she said. "What are we wearing?"

CHAPTER 18

Ellis damn near fractured an axle on a bad chunk of parking lot. My teeth snapped into a corner of tongue — ice-cold pain flashing white down a thousand alleys of nerve and synapse.

I shouldn't have let her drive, especially since she'd shown up in a borrowed Toyota pickup.

Ellis yanked the wheel hard left, skittering to a halt between an Econoline and a rusty Pinto.

"You," I said, tasting blood, "are a menace."

She shrugged. I leaned across and grabbed the keys from the ignition.

The Kingsnakes were pounding away on a little John Lee Hooker from inside STD's. *Boom boom boom boom.*

Ellis waved a hand toward the sign glowing from the only visible window: "Budweiser" centered in an electric shamrock.

"Why, look," she said, "it's the international symbol for cheap beer and shitty food."

"There *is* a God." I arched my back, slid the keys in my pocket.

"Sure," she said, swinging her long legs out of the truck, "he's malicious."

Outside, a barn lamp hung off a pole near the street. Gnats swam lazy in its cone of light, rising toward the galvanized-coolie-hat shade. Hot as hell but they wanted more.

I raised an arm, swiped my forehead across a patch of T-shirt sleeve. Here I was with my trusty sidekick and suddenly the whole idea seemed beyond ridiculous.

Ellis leaned against the back of the truck, draping her arms along the tailgate. "Okay," she said, "tell me again what the hell we're doing."

I'd filled her in on most of what I knew during the ride over: dead girls, dog tags, Lapthorne, roses . . . the full catastrophe.

"Kenny told me the local cops figured the killer had to be experienced," I said, "somebody who'd seen combat. That could exonerate Lapthorne, if he actually *was* one of the soldiers at the fair. Those guys were really young, supposedly — hadn't shipped out yet."

"How old was he in '69?" asked Ellis.

"Nineteen."

She nodded.

I looked toward the flat-topped building across the lot, scrubby woods grown hard against three sides. "This guy Schneider was lead cop on the murders. Kenny told me to talk to him, said he'd know the most about it."

Three big-haired girls spilled outside and the music went all crisply dimensional — drums and guitar dialed in with the bass for as long as the door was open. I watched the trio clatter across the lot, all done up in acid-washed stretch denim.

"That band's local," I continued. "The Kingsnakes. Schneider's way into them. Dean said he never misses a show."

I didn't say anything for a minute.

"Okay, so . . ." prompted Ellis.

"Okay, so . . ." I said. "Okay, so . . . the thing is that Kenny . . . um . . . doesn't know what I found out from the silhouette guy."

"About the thumbs?"

"Right."

"Which is a problem because . . ."

"Because now that I know Schneider's involved somehow . . ."

"So you're pretty damn sure," said Ellis, "that Kenny'd retract the suggestion, considering."

I nodded.

She waited for me to say more, but that

201

was pretty much it.

"Um . . . so Maddie," she said, "do you have, like, a *concept* here?"

"I guess just to chat him up. Kind of . . . generally. Or whatever."

She smiled. "And you're opening with?"

I looked away. "No clue."

"Something will turn up," she said.

"I'm such an idiot."

"Hey, if you knew what you wanted to find out, there'd be no point having the conversation."

"So you vote we go ahead?" I asked.

She looked at me. "Last time I said no, I didn't hear the question."

"My mother always says that."

"I know."

"You scare me," I said.

"I know."

"Maybe I'll get lucky," I said, "and he won't show up."

She punched my shoulder. "Chickenshit."

I punched her back.

"You know what this guy looks like?" she asked.

"Just seen a couple pictures. Old ones, but he has a look."

She raised a speculative eyebrow.

I shook my head. "Not, like, a *good* look."

"You're buying, then."

"I've got six bucks. After that, we'll need to make friends."

Ellis stood up, spanking grit off the back of her shorts.

"Yeah," she said, "like the two of us've ever had trouble with *that* in a bar."

Inside it was all knotty-pine walls and cheesy Styrofoam dropped ceiling. We bashed through the crowd and climbed a pinball machine to get up into the neon-shamrock window, having ordered two Rolling Rocks each.

The Kingsnakes were slamming out a loud but mournful little number. I checked the shoving bodies below for Schneider's hard face and crewcut, relieved not to see him.

The bouncer looked over, ready to order us down from our perch.

Ellis blew him a kiss and he winked instead.

"Oh *please*," I said.

"He'd be doable if he had a neck."

"Would not."

She swung her foot against mine. "Seen you go home with worse."

"And better."

"Sure," she drawled, "*lots* of times . . ."

The band was cranking up to a flashy crescendo right then, so I just grinned, leaning to chuck my first empty under the pinball machine.

The Kingsnakes thrashed out a final chord, brimming with upstate-Caucasian angst.

I looked up and saw Schneider.

He'd been there all along. I'd missed him because his hair was longer, Brylcreemed high with a greasy hank dangling front and center. Plus he'd grown a beard to soften that slash of mouth.

Now, though, I could see his eyes. I should have remembered how literal Simon's images always were, known that Schneider's newsprint gaze — flat as a shark's — wasn't any trick of ink or light.

The guy kept both elbows cocked, vain about those biceps. Tight T-shirt, stiff jeans with cuffs rolled doo-wop-wide. He'd asked the dice for Brando but thrown a Jack La-Lanne.

"That's him," I said, "with the redhead chick at the bar."

The girl was a touch taller than he was, not pretty but younger.

I watched him survey the crowd — eyes fathomless black, clicking from point to point slow as a schoolroom-clock second hand.

Ellis lifted her chin. "Ozark Fonzie," she

pronounced. "Guy should lay off the Grecian Formula. Mongolians don't have hair that black."

When the Kingsnake fans surged forward, I could see Schneider cup the redhead's ass and squeeze. She fussed at that, waving a sloppy finger in his face.

He did it again and she tried to shove him away, knocking only herself off balance. She clutched his arm and fought gravity, ankles bowing out over white spike heels, legs sheathed in "suntan" pantyhose. Her skin was otherwise so pale it had the blue tinge of skim milk.

The band was blasting again, so Ellis put a hand on my shoulder and yelled into my ear. "Think they know each other?"

He slid his hand from ass up to waist and the girl pressed into him, crotch first. She dropped her head and looked into his eyes, whispered something pouty.

"Signs point to yes," I said.

Schneider shoved a hand deep in his jeans pocket, retrieving something small which he then tucked down the front of her shirt.

She touched his cheek, mashed her mouth against his jaw for a second, and turned toward us.

The ladies' was just the other side of the pinball machine. Schneider's date brought tremendous concentration to the effort of reaching it. Every bobble on those heels making this Moby Dick of a purse thump against her hip.

Slow as her progress was, she nearly made the door before she puked.

Ellis tapped my beer discreetly with hers. "Madeline, the gods have smiled."

The girl shuddered and spewed another bright plume.

Schneider sipped his drink, watching.

"Poor Vomit Girl," said Ellis. "Not a friend in the world."

We jumped down, buoyed her up by the elbows, and whisked her right the hell on into that bathroom.

"M'okay," she said more than once, but we kept her moving toward the handicapped stall.

We had the choreography down: Ellis hooked the stall door wide with a quick toe so I could angle in. I kicked up the seat and we muscled Vomit Girl into range.

It was tough keeping her vertical, especially one-handed. The actual bouts weren't so bad — her body arced with the effort, and we just had to keep her balanced.

Slack, however, the bitch was a moose.

Soon as things slowed down, we let her sink to her knees. Vomit Girl hugged the rim, head flopping onto a shoulder.

I tucked a last strand of hair behind her ear and rubbed her back. She kept her eyes shut, breathing in short Lamaze-y puffs.

"You ladies're wicked awesome," she said finally, voice echoing out of the bowl.

Ellis looked at me. "Boston?"

"Hyannis," croaked VG.

She raised her head and opened her eyes, dragged her hand across shiny lips.

I got my first good look at her face: pug nose and a vixen chin, lashes gummed with too-black mascara. She was tired and no-where near sober, but you could tell she was finished.

"Man," she said, "that was *some* fucked up."

She drew her knees to her chest, reached a milk-glass arm past orange legs to grab her purse, pulling out — what else — Virginia Slims.

Vomit Girl got one in her mouth and thumbed a metal lighter going. Her hand shook and she had to shut one eye before aligning flame and tip, but she managed a French-inhale by drag three.

She dropped the lighter to the floor and squinted at her nails. "Busted off a damn tip."

"How you holding up otherwise?" asked Ellis.

Our charge smiled at us, head lolling back against the wall. "Have to say I'm feeling just ducky."

Her unbuttoned shirt revealed blue veins tracing the swell of each breast. Older than us, I thought, but then I wasn't sure. She looked sixteen and fifty, all at once.

Vomit Girl took one more drag and pitched her cigarette into the toilet, only a third smoked down. It hissed and went instantly dark to the filter.

I watched her weasel a Jack Horner thumb into her bra, then extract a brown glass vial with a black plastic top.

"So," she said, "you ladies up for doin' a little coke, or what?"

CHAPTER 19

There'd been so goddamn much blow in the Berkshires, I always pictured the Mass Pike choked with round-the-clock dump-truck convoys. The only plus for me and Ellis was we'd never paid for it, if you don't count that whole year we squandered.

In retrospect it was always February, five a.m. in some ugly condo with everybody blurting "Okay, okay, but wait — this one time *I* . . ." while a razorblade tick-ticked against a mirror and those android chicks with patent-leather hair pranced around Robert Palmer on MTV.

Not exactly a high-water mark for Western civilization.

I looked down at Vomit Girl, half repulsed by the vial. Then thought how awfully nice that aspirin-flavored drip down the back of my throat would feel if, you know, we all just did a quick line.

"Love to," said Ellis, right before I went, "Should we tell that guy you're okay?"

"Schneider?" snorted Vomit Girl. "If he didn't already ditch me, the prick."

"I'll find out," I said.

I drained my beer and shoved it into the Kotex bin.

Ellis took out a credit card.

Vomit Girl gave her the vial.

I flipped the stall-door latch.

"Hey," Vomit Girl called after me, "could you give him this?"

Her nails clicked against the floor and I looked back. When she reached to hand me the lighter, an old Zippo, the motion made her shirt slither down her right biceps.

She yanked it up, but not before I caught the fist-print, black and green, tucked beneath the nexus of collarbone and shoulder. Schneider must have been wearing some big-ass ring to leave a cut like that.

"Thanks a bunch, hon," she said. "He'd kill me, that got lost . . . had the damn thing forever." Fuh-*ev*ah.

Ellis raised her AmEx, a mound of white balanced on one corner.

"You wanna chop that up on something?" asked Vomit Girl, hand quick to purse.

Ellis shook her head. "Open your mouth," she said.

The redhead obeyed like a baby bird and was rewarded with a sharp gust of powder — straight to the back of her throat.

A little trick Ellis had learned from me, not so very long ago. I won't bore you with a description of the unpretty circumstances in which I'd picked it up myself.

I flipped the Zippo into the air and caught it.

"See you guys," I said.

They didn't look up, nor had I expected them to.

"Not like it's the first time," Schneider confided at the bar. "Trouble is, we came down on my bike. She's this drunk, I sure as hell don't want to ride her home."

Ice was melting in his drink, brown liquor

gone paler than tea. He raised the glass and swirled it. The ring *was* big. Ugly, too. One of those free-form nugget things, with random diamond chips.

"Shit," he chuckled, "I'm about ready to put 'If you can read this, the bitch fell off' 'cross the back of my jacket. Know what I mean?"

I attempted a smile, took a pull off my fresh beer. "Bet she's fine by now," I said.

The whole point of being here was to buddy up and coax him into talking, but I couldn't get past the image of his fist slamming into Vomit Girl.

The band wrapped it up, and everybody started crowding against us at the bar.

Someone shoved into me, pushing me closer to Schneider.

He smiled.

Then he tipped his glass, straining bourbon dregs through his teeth. Opened wider, tossed in the shards of ice. Chewed with his mouth open.

Through the slush: "You and your friend got a car?"

I waited for him to swallow. "Truck," I said.

He laid a finger alongside his nose, then tapped a nostril. "Bring her home, I'll be sure to make it worth your while."

He looked into his glass, then at me. "Get you another?"

"I'm good, thanks."

"G'wan . . . little something for a chaser?" He snapped twice and the bartender stepped up. Big guy with a mullet.

"Another Jack rocks," Schneider told him, "and a bit of the same, neat, for the lady."

He turned his head half back at me and winked.

"Appreciate it, but I gotta drive," I said.

"Don't you worry," he countered. "I know where all the cops are hiding. Used to be one."

Two glasses appeared and he dropped a twenty on the bar, then reached for the smokes rolled in his T-shirt's right sleeve.

Schneider smacked the pack against his fist, a pair of Camels popping up like bamboo fortune sticks. He nipped one out with his teeth before tilting the other toward me. Shrugged and rolled them back up in his sleeve when I declined.

When he started slapping his pockets, I produced his lighter.

"This what you need?" I asked.

The Zippo was centered in my palm, engraving made plain by a stray shaft of light. "HUE," it said, right above the words "DOUBLE VET."

Hue, imperial city on the Perfume River: Vietnam's answer to Dresden. I remembered reading about all those lace-fragile wooden palaces, burning to nothing after they got bombed to shit in the Tet Offensive.

"What's Double Vet?" I asked.

Schneider smiled but didn't answer. He brought a finger to bear on one edge of the Zippo, flipping the thing onto its back.

The B-side read "GET MORE IN '64" with a naked chick splayed out beneath. I might have called it a beaver shot had the engraver's talent allowed him to render female genitalia bearing any less resemblance to the muskrat family.

And then there were those five cuts in the lighter's bottom edge.

I looked up, caught him savoring my disgust.

"Notches . . ." I said. "Those're for what, villages? I remember watching you guys on the news at night, when I was a kid. Lighting huts on fire, big-ass grins for the folks back home . . ."

Schneider's fingertips slid down around the edges of the Zippo. He pulled it away, dragging a slow knuckle along my hand — a sensation so exquisitely repulsive I wanted to penknife a pair of X's into my flesh and suck out the venom.

He lifted the lighter so I could watch him run his thumb fondly down between the cartoon legs.

"Miss those little bitches," he said, unlit cigarette still in his teeth. "Go all night, fit like a goddamn glove."

The Zippo's flame was blue and the fluid smelled sharp.

Once Schneider had a good lungful of smoke, he expelled it against my shoulder.

"Work 'em right," he confided, "you'd always leave a little blood on the sheets. . . . Souvenir."

I watched him put the lighter back in his pocket. Left-handed.

He smiled, raw mouth peeling wide as the skin around his eyes crinkled up.

"Nice tits," he said. "Bet I could make you beg for it."

I smiled back. "Why don't I just go see how those two're getting on."

Schneider drew his heels tight. His dismissal was silent, just both hands arcing through a matador's veronica pass.

I shoved into the crowd. Didn't start to shake until I got halfway across the sticky floor, praying for a window in that damn bathroom.

Behind me he just laughed and laughed.

CHAPTER 20

There was a window, but there was also an audience: a woman rehabbing her spiral-permed coxcomb with moist fingertips.

I stepped up to the vacant basin. The handicapped stall was latched and I didn't want to draw attention to any group activity therein. I considered sliding under from next door, but it, too, was *ocupado*.

Scoping out the window by mirror, I plotted defenestration technique. If you stood on the back of the nearest wall-mount toilet, you could maybe hoist up onto the partition and rotate on your belly to get both feet out. The opening was so chintzy-ass small a five-year-old couldn't have turned around in the thing, and headfirst was a nasty proposition, that high up.

It could work, if we had the bathroom to ourselves for five minutes. If we tied Vomit Girl to a toilet and taped her mouth shut.

"Jeezum Crow, Arlene," Perm Doctor called out, "what're you, makin' *sculpture* in there?"

"Them damn tacos," Arlene lamented.

"Should've had the wings," clucked Perm, touching up the trompe-l'oeil slash of brown beneath each cheek.

Arlene flushed and slammed out of her stall, horning in on the mirror.

"You just better hope Mike and Courtney're still asleep, out in that car," said Perm.

"Told you," Arlene shot back as they bustled out, "once they're in jammies, you won't hear a peep till morning."

The door swung closed behind them.

"Nice loafers," said Ellis, from inside the stall.

"How's our friend?" I asked.

"Napping."

"Good. We need to get out this window."

"Your little chat was productive, then?"

"Schneider thinks we're carpooling. I'd . . . ah . . . prefer not. You guys finish that vial?"

"Oh please. I am so sick of cocaine," said Ellis, opening the stall door. "Damn 'War on Drugs' made it so cheap it's tacky. . . ."

"We gotta *go.*"

She eyed the aperture. "Cool," she said, walking into the stall beneath.

Ellis hopped onto the back of the toilet. She launched herself up so she could swing a leg over the partition, and shoved at the window.

"Thing's painted shut," she said. "Any chance you're holding a Swiss Army knife?"

"Top of my bureau."

"So look in her purse."

I lifted Vomit Girl's head with a safecracker's delicacy, then unzipped her bag.

She didn't travel light: Certs, Suave mousse, toothpicks in cellophane . . . cardboard nail file, rat-tail comb, tube of Clearasil . . . My arm started to cramp. Woman's head weighed more than a bowling ball.

"Christ," I said, "she could, like, launch an assault on Everest."

. . . Little redhead girl's school picture in a clear plastic sleeve, bottle of white shoe polish with a nurse on the label . . .

"Anything?" asked Ellis.

"Crochet hook," I said, "roach clip with feathers, Secret roll-on . . ."

Someone pushed the bathroom door in a few inches, then thought better of it.

"Oh my *God*," said Ellis. "Find me something or I'm going to kick out this damn glass."

I smiled. "Bingo."

"What?"

"Razorblade." I held it in my teeth and shoved the rest of the crap back in the purse.

I lowered Vomit Girl's head by the smoothest increments I could manage, wrist sparkling as blood shot back into my hand. She brought a fist up to her mouth, but didn't open her eyes.

I stood up and walked the blade to Ellis.

She snicked it along the foot of the window frame, sliced down the left-hand edge, then the right. "Latex. We lucked out."

Ellis punched at the base with both hands. The window popped out and up, awning style. *"Et voilà,"* she said.

She scooted back, then swung her legs up, toes pointed, to scissor neatly onto her belly.

"Slick," I said.

"Bet your sweet ass."

Ellis pushed out fast, hand over hand. She paused, elbows on the sill.

"Hey, know what?" she whispered, grinning down like the Cheshire Cat.

"What?"

"You're prettier," she said, "but I'm thinner."

Then she dropped like a stone down a well.

I had one foot up on the toilet when hands latched onto my earthbound ankle.

"Hell you think you're going?" croaked Vomit Girl.

"Home," I said. "I'm tired."

She pulled herself under the partition, using me for leverage. "Better not be a damn thing missing from my pocketbook."

"Your razorblade. Stuck right up here in

the window frame."

She dug her nails into my flesh. The busted one hurt like a bitch. "What's with you sneakin' out, then?"

I shrugged. "Your boyfriend's creepy."

She slitted her eyes, working that ragged nail sideways and deeper. "Yeah?"

"No offense."

"Tell him go get fucked," she said. "S'what *I'd* do."

I thought about kicking loose, yelling for Ellis to get the truck while I hauled myself out the window.

Then I realized the keys were in my pocket, which meant she couldn't get any kind of head start unless I tossed them out into the dark scrub behind the bar.

Then I realized the keys meant we hadn't needed the razorblade at all.

Then I had an attack of conscience.

I looked down at Vomit Girl. "You live with that guy?"

She stiffened. "None of your business."

"It's just . . ." I faltered, groping for something that would sink in.

"Spit it out," she said.

"That picture in your purse? Pretty little girl, all those gorgeous red curls?"

"Tiffy," she nodded, face going soft.

Her daughter, then, but not Schneider's.

Tiffy's dad was black.

"What he said to me tonight?" I said. "He reminded me of this one stepfather. . . ."

Vomit Girl's eyes clicked back to mine.

Maybe, I thought, you'll do for your kid what you won't for yourself.

"Listen . . ." I said, "promise me something?"

She swallowed hard. Didn't blink.

"I want to know you won't leave Tiffy alone with him," I said.

Her throat turned pink, then her face.

I kept staring at her, hard.

"Ever," I said, aching right then to take her with us, to go get her kid so they'd both be safe.

Vomit Girl shook her head. "He loves her like his own," she said. "Buys her stuff. Clothes. All these books from when he was a kid. Reads her stories every night. Brushes her hair. Treats us like gold —"

Books. Stories.

"And does he make sure she's asleep," I asked, "before he starts slamming you around?"

She took one hand off my leg and touched her shoulder, covering the spot right where I'd seen that bruise.

"You don't know shit," she said.

"Oh, sweetie," I said. "Shit's what I know

220

best. What I know by goddamn heart."

"Just pissed 'cause he wouldn't look at you twice."

Someone banged on the door, then I heard Schneider boom, "Hell's taking so damn long?"

I kicked free and launched myself out that window, headfirst.

Ellis, bless her unsuspecting soul, broke my fall.

"Chrissake," she said as we ran for the truck. "Just 'cause I said I was thinner didn't mean you had to go prove it."

The truck's back end broke wide, coming out of STD's, but I punched it and we straightened out.

How long would it take Vomit Girl to go narc? I'd been stupid to piss her off.

I looked in the rearview mirror. Narrow lanes behind, everything black beyond the taillights' reach.

I wanted to get the hell away from STD's, onto something more anonymous than the skinny old turnpike. We had a good few miles through the woods yet, no side roads to duck down.

I checked again. Saw a flicker of light way back just as we dropped into a hollow.

Up the next rise and there it was. Closer.

But the mirror was vibrating. I couldn't tell what I wanted most to know.

"Look out the back," I said.

"What?"

"Is that one light or two?"

"Don't tell me," said Ellis, "Schneider's a biker."

"How many?"

"Can't see it now," she said.

We were coming up on a curve. I tapped the brakes going in and then gunned it.

"If you thought he was gonna come after us," she said, "why the hell'd you talk to Vomit Girl so long?"

"She's got a daughter," I said. "They live with him."

"And?"

"And I think he killed those girls himself," I said.

Ellis was silent.

"I mean," I went on, "the idea of a little kid . . ."

"Yeah," she said. "Okay."

She was still looking out the back. I told myself it would be good luck if I didn't check the mirror. I held my breath down the straightaway, counting silent thousands like I was waiting for thunder.

"There it is," she said.

"It?"

"It," she said. "One light."

CHAPTER 21

Ellis kept checking the cab's rear window.

"Not gaining," she said, "but keeping up."

I just looked ahead, willing us forward. I could see lights. Civilization, so to speak.

"Oh my God!" said Ellis.

"What?"

"It's a van," she said, bouncing on her end of the seat. "With a headlight out."

She turned around and laughed and collapsed against the door.

We didn't speak, not until we were rocketing north on the raised stretch of 81, past SU's shoulder of hill.

It was overcast, sky aglow from the city beneath us. I slotted into a tight pack of cars with Ontario plates — you want to go fast, tailgate a homebound Canadian.

"Hey," I said.

"Hey."

"Sorry for landing on you."

"Sorry for saying you were less than svelte. Which is not true in any meaningful sense," she said.

"It's okay. You pretty much only *implied.*"

"Yeah, well. What are friends for?"

"Breaking one's fall."

"Exactly."

I checked the mirror.

"See him?" Ellis looked out the back.

I shook my head. We were both twitchy with adrenaline.

She crossed her legs, started jiggling a foot. "So, you really figure he did it?"

"Not like he *definitely* did it, just more like *could* have."

"Which you weren't thinking earlier. Going in."

"Would've told you."

"So now he might have *because?*"

Eye-flick to the mirror. "I'm not sure anybody would seriously buy it."

"I would."

"Okay," I said. "He's left-handed. He was in Vietnam really early — 1964."

"He told you that?"

"It was on the lighter Vomit Girl made me take out. One side had a city name on it, 'Hue,' with 'Double Vet' under it. The other said 'Get more in '64' with this picture —"

"And it would be *good* if he did it, right? I mean, we're hoping for that. As an outcome."

"I'd be pretty psyched, sure . . ."

She nodded.

"Okay, so Hue, that early?" I continued.

"I think you're talking *up* there — Ultima fucking Thule. Like you'd have to be all Martin Sheen, persona-wise. Jungle patrol. Face paint. Throw a rat on the barbie . . ."

We were coming up on the MONY Towers. They had masts up top with colored lights on them, supposedly coded to the weather. Orange now, whatever *that* meant. There was some rhyme about it, but nobody could tell me how it went.

Taillights flashed ahead and I braked. "So maybe Schneider knew the kind of techniques Kenny said the killer used — how the girls' throats were cut, stuff like that."

"Which is good because you *like* this cousin."

"*Like* like?" I looked straight ahead. My cheeks had to be flaming.

She shook her head, tsk-tsking. "Christ. You are completely *transparent.*"

"He was just always really kind to me. . . . As a kid."

"Give it up," she said. *"Seriously."*

"You're doing that thing with your hair."

I immediately put both hands on the wheel. "Nuh-uh."

"That *thing,*" she said. "That little annoying flippy *thing.*"

"I told you about the fairy tale, and the thing with the silhouette guy, right?" I asked. "The old German poem with the thumbs?"

"*Struwwelpeter,*" she said. "Yes, you did."

"Okay, so Vomit Girl said Schneider buys all these books for her daughter, things he liked as a kid, and that he reads to her every night. . . ."

"He must be a total babe, your cousin."

"Ellis . . ."

"No, really," she said. " You are *so* not over this guy."

"Dude, shut *up.*"

She turned toward me, grin predatory in the dashboard glow.

"I'm driving," I said. "I'm not going to look at you. I can see you out of the corner of my eye, and you're being an asshole."

She crossed her arms.

Kept jiggling that foot.

I sighed.

"He has an eyepatch," I said. "Tall with dark hair, kind of curly. Taught me to dance."

"You must have totally wanted to jump him."

I ignored her, me and my Canadian posse flying past an entirely too sedate Crown Vic. Methodist Blue, Dean would call it.

"What were you," she said, "like twelve?"

"You do it too," I said. "That flippy thing."

"It's universal. See a guy you'd drop trou for, play with your hair. Some hardwired ovary deal. Even thinking about it."

I gripped the wheel.

"Nice try, fighting the impulse," she said. "Your knuckles went all white."

First sign for Adams and Harrison. I flipped the turn signal.

Ellis sighed. "Just wanted to point out that you may be lacking a certain amount of objectivity."

"Duh."

"And that you should probably bring me along if you're going to talk to him."

"Party at Bonwit's," I said. "Next weekend. Lapthorne's already RSVP'd."

"Perfect," she said. "What are we wearing?"

"Costumes."

I shot down the ramp, toward that circular Holiday Inn. Nipped through an intersection just as the light went yellow.

"You sure you want to keep going?" I said. "After tonight?"

"He straight?"

I stopped for a red light and looked her full in the face. Lifted an eyebrow, Belushi-perfect.

She stared up toward the headliner. "Oh sure, just because *you're* married."

"You would hit on my most tragically un-consummated huge childhood crush?"

Ellis cleared her throat, arms still crossed. She started drumming her fingers in rapid sequence along her upper arm.

Didn't look at me. Didn't have to.

"Oh," I said. "Right."

Tit for tat. There was that guy Pete Schiller, first of all. Not that *I'd* hit on *him* . . . And Gary . . . um . . . Gary *whatever*. In Vermont. Alec didn't count.

"Only thing —" I started.

She looked at me, mouth tight.

"Those were still his dog tags," I said, "where they found the girls."

She tried to keep a straight face but sputtered once and then lost it, cracking up so bad she couldn't breathe.

"Dude," I said, *"harsh."*

"Totally had you going, though, didn't I?"

The light turned green.

"Okay," I said, slamming the stick into first, "yeah. You totally did."

I hit the gas, went under 690. By the time we passed the Kleen-Food at the foot of Green Street, we were weeping with laughter, practically blind.

■ ■ ■ ■

"Hey," she said, hours later, cozy in the bed I'd made up on the sofa.

"Need another pillow?" I walked from lamp to lamp, groping under shades for the little pull-chains, each equipped with ancestral tassel.

Ellis yawned, shaking her head. "What'd 'Double Vet' mean, on the lighter?"

"I asked him that. He never told me."

"So you should find out."

"Yeah. Could be something."

"Could be," she said, closing her eyes.

"Ice water? Anything?"

"Go to bed."

I extinguished the last bulb. "Sweet dreams."

"Yeah," she said. "Sure."

By morning, she was gone — an eventuality I'd expected, long used to her habit of arriving without announcement and leaving without a goodbye. Ellis just got too fidgety to be bothered, and I'd never seen her sleep more than five hours, which had made us crappy roommates in the Berkshires.

The purple sofa was empty. She'd folded up all the bedding and put it back in the linen closet. The only sign she'd been in town was half a paper towel, duct-taped to the coffee machine:

4:30 . . .

Couldn't sleep so thought I'd drive home. Call re party. Must get you out of this fucking town ASAP. It does not deserve you.

Love, EBC

p.s. Do the dishes. You're turning into my mother.

She still had my earrings, and the rest of the weekend sucked.

CHAPTER 22

By Monday night I was wallowing in the mood pool's deep end.

I stood useless on the sidewalk outside work — still daylight, even though I'd been the last one out of editorial. The prospect of another Dean-free evening at home was too onerous to bear. Ellis blowing through had only made it worse.

All weekend, I tried to get up the nerve to

drive downtown, ask Kenny's opinion about the Schneider stuff. Didn't happen. I was just glued to the damn sofa.

I'd checked my old paperbacks from A.P. U.S. history with Mrs. Laupheimer at Dobbs. Hue was indeed pretty high on the map.

In 1964, Americans were still supposedly there in a strictly "military advisor" capacity, going out on patrols with the South Vietnamese Army. LBJ was quoted as saying, "We are not about to send American boys nine or ten thousand miles away from home to do what Asian boys ought to be doing for themselves." And then the USS *Maddox* was fired upon in the Gulf of Tonkin, or so we're expected to believe.

I had to stop reading. Not just because it got me worked up about Schneider, but because I was still pissed off about the whole war. So goddamn depressing. So useless. I sat on that sofa, staring into the abyss, wanting to bitch-slap Kissinger and all the grownups who'd abandoned righteous anger for consciousness raising and chardonnay.

Never made it to the laundromat, a block and a half downhill. I kept thinking Dean might call, every time I considered the door.

And here it was Monday.

I told myself to go home. . . . My car was one of three in the lot. I stared at it, then started walking up toward the Crown.

Kenny got ticked before I'd even told him anything serious. Just "Schneider's creepy and we climbed out the window," and he went all old-country on me.

"Time you left this alone, Madeline," he said, begrudging me a draft. "You sneaking out the back? All that? Dean not in town, I feel responsible."

"Schneider doesn't know my name. Even if he'd seen us leave, we were in a borrowed truck with Mass plates."

He filled a pitcher for two guys down the bar. "That Ellis is trouble. Said so the first time you brought her in."

" 'That Ellis' is my friend, so lay off."

"Friends like that . . ." He shrugged and walked the pitcher down, returning with a ten.

"You're being a dick."

He turned his back and punched some register keys. "Kiss your mother with that mouth?"

"Annually."

Kenny shoved a thick finger into one last key and the cash drawer popped. He licked his thumb to make change, then took a fistful of singles down to the pitcher guys and chatted a good five minutes.

He came back and dropped an elbow for anchor right in front of me, leaning onto a leg-of-lamb forearm and staring over the top of my head. He even tried to whistle a little something.

"You're the one who told me I should talk to him," I said.

The whistling trailed off. "I tell you to go alone?"

"I wasn't alone."

"All practical purposes."

We glared at each other.

"Two girls going in a bar. How that looks," he said, raising a finger, "your husband out of town."

"You're fucking kidding."

He dropped his hand and looked away, bull-exhaled through his nose.

"Kenny," I said, "there were two hundred people. There was a band. It's not like we were cruising South Salina in hot pants, leaning in car windows going 'You boys dating tonight?' "

He made this minute gesture with his head. Just a sly inch of motion, richly endowed with inference. Byzantine.

I nudged a fist against his hand. "Anybody even noticed me and Ellis walking in, they probably thought we were a couple."

No response.

"Or, I dunno, *Canadian*."

Okay, so he smiled a little, around the edges.

I tried to move into his line of sight. "I mean, I'm *here* alone, right?"

"I look happy about that?"

It hadn't occurred to me, but indeed this was my first time solo at the Crown.

"This place, you're chaperoned," Kenny said. "Some guy comes within ten feet . . ."

I looked to my left: eight empty stools between me and the regulars. I felt bad, all of them squished down at the end like that.

"Aside from issues of propriety," he continued, "Dean would have my ass, he knew I agreed to you chasing around on this. It'd be goddamn dangerous even if you actually had some idea what you were doing."

I pressed both palms against the sides of my glass, rolling it slowly between them. . . . Clockwise . . . Counterclockwise. "You gonna tell him?"

The motion of my hands was so slow the beer barely climbed the sides of the vessel. Slender ribbons of bubbles continued to rise, undisturbed.

"I mean," I said, keeping my eyes on the golden liquid, "it's not like you can just pick up a phone. He's in a crew car, halfway to White Horse or Yellow Knife. Saskatoon."

Spin . . . spin . . . "Last time he called, they'd driven seventy-five miles for a cup of coffee. Some breakdown, dead moose or whatever, so there was time to kill. Took the truck out with a couple of guys. Nothing but trees for an hour each way."

I looked up. "That was Friday. I told him Ellis was here, that we were going out to see the Kingsnakes. Dean's the one who said Schneider was into them, right?"

"He know the rest?"

"Would if he'd called since." I stared down into the glass, shrugged. "Guess he wasn't too worried."

I raised the beer and drained it.

He didn't offer a refill.

"Please, sir," I said, ducking my head in supplication, "may I have another?"

"Damn it to hell," said Kenny.

He put my glass in the sink, reached for a fresh one.

I took that as a good sign. "So can I talk to you about what actually happened?"

Kenny couldn't resist pausing mid-step to patronize me. "What, you called everybody into the library and someone confessed, like those pinkos on PBS?"

He had the nerve to chuck me under the chin.

I considered biting him. "I'm serious."

He grinned, hands and my as-yet-unfilled beer glass raised in mock surrender. "No need to get testy."

He pulled the tap, glass tilted to keep the head slight.

"Oh, g'ahead," he said, all bogus expansive, "ask me anything."

"Fine," I said. "What's a double vet?"

He swung his head toward me, beer still running. Liquid bulged above the rim of the glass, then broke and washed down over his knuckles.

Kenny shoved the tap shut, slopping more foam to the floor. He ignored it — stepped right back in front of me and leaned close, free hand gripping the bar.

"Where'd you hear that?" he said, very quiet.

"I read it," I answered, voice pitched just as low. "Why?"

"*Where'd* you read it?"

"Off Schneider's lighter."

Kenny's skin went from gold to gray-green.

"You okay?" I touched his hand.

"What you said, it's apocryphal. God-damn Jane Fonda horseshit that never happened — hippies made it up to smear us."

"If it never happened, how come Schneider had it engraved on his Zippo?"

Kenny looked at the glass in his hand. He set it down with exaggerated care.

"According to the lighter, he was in Hue," I said. "In 1964. Same year as that crap in the Gulf of Tonkin. Back when it was all still 'advising' the ARVN. . . ."

Kenny wouldn't look me in the eye.

"So he was a Green Beret or some shit, right?" I said. "Just like you told me all you cops figured it was, when those girls got killed."

I waited for him to answer. He didn't even exhale.

"Chrissake," I said, "be straight with me. What the hell's it mean?"

He raised his eyes. "Double vet?"

I nodded.

"You want to believe the long-hair propaganda, it means he killed a woman in 'Nam," Kenny said, "right when he'd finished balling her. That straight enough?"

The guys down the bar kept chatting. The compressor on one of the coolers clicked alive. I could feel it shudder before it settled into a steady hum.

"That lighter had five notches on it," I said. "Schneider's left-handed, and he buys all these children's books. . . ."

I waited for him to comment, the silence stretching out.

"I know it isn't any kind of proof," I said, "but it's something, right?"

He turned his back on me. Picked up a towel. Ran it around the fat neck of the pickled-egg jar.

I could see his face in the mirror. "Kenny?"

Soon as he noticed I was watching, his gaze flicked away.

"Turns out it was a local guy," he said, "you can ignore it, right?"

"Ignore it, *hell*," I said. "I came to you. Just like I did about the dog tags."

Kenny turned around. "This cousin, he's loaded?"

I hunched my shoulders, wrapped both arms tight across my belly.

He leaned in, hand in my face, pad of his thumb running back and forth across fingertips. "Isn't he?"

I tilted my head away. My throat hurt.

"Fancy schools," he said. "Some hoity-toity accent. Just like you."

Snick. That familiar sound. Cut from the herd.

"So if it looks like Schneider killed those girls," he went on, "your boy's off the hook."

"That's not —"

Kenny held up a hand, shaking his head. "You found your scapegoat," he said. "Word to the wise, though, Madeline? Watch out you don't let anything about this town actually *touch* you."

I stood up.

"You really believe that's what matters to me?" I asked, my voice so quiet even I could barely hear it.

"Only thing matters to you is finding some reason to get the hell out of Syracuse," he said. "Doesn't make a difference what it is, who it hurts — long as you end up back with your kind."

"I had hoped 'my kind' was you, Kenny."

I pressed some bills on the counter and turned to go, but he wasn't finished.

"Be sure you tell 'em, back home," he said, "that I think your finishing school was worth every last penny."

"Back *home?*" I swung around, stared him full in the eye. "Where the hell's that? Think I'd be here at the Crown, I had *anywhere* else to go?"

He lost the smile. The certainty.

"Look at this place . . ." I said, "have to be goddamn desperate . . ."

"Aw jeez," he said. "Aw jeez . . . don't *cry.*"

Kenny reached a hand toward my shoulder, but I twisted out of comfort's way. After shoving my crumpled singles toward his side of the bar, I put my glass on top, like they might otherwise blow away.

■ ■ ■ ■

PART II
CENTRE ISLAND

■ ■ ■ ■

Ralph sometimes called his mother and grandfather the Aborigines, and likened them to those vanishing denizens of the American continent doomed to rapid extinction with the advance of the invading race. He was fond of describing Washington Square as the "Reservation," and of prophesying that before long its inhabitants would be exhibited at ethnological shows, pathetically engaged in the exercise of their primitive industries.

— Edith Wharton,
The Custom of the Country

CHAPTER 23

Friday I threw my backpack in the Rabbit so early it was still dark — stars overhead shivering bright in the dew-point chill. By Ithaca it was pouring.

I called in sick from a piss-rank Catskills phone booth, so the guys at the *Weekly* wouldn't try me at home and hear how I'd left Bonwit's number on our machine, just in case Dean called.

Just in case he didn't remember the number, or where Bonwit lived, or how to call Information, or was lying alone and sick by the railroad tracks somewhere in the Yukon, or had actually really *wanted* to call his wife all along, but was the captive of Maoist polar bears.

Wilt picked up in editorial, and he was totally onto me. "Nothing undercuts a good flu story, Maddie," he said, "like the sound of eighteen-wheelers downshifting in the rain."

"Don't tell Ted, okay?" I said. "Be a pal?"

He promised to swear I was home in bed, suffering. I dropped the phone in its greasy cradle and shoved out for air.

Back on the road, the wipers left a widow's peak on my windshield, rain coming down like hammers until just before the Tappan Zee Bridge. Suddenly it was clear, both Hudson and sky saturated with that poignant cusp-of-fall blue, perfect gateway for descent into lush Westchester. I accelerated for the Throgs Neck and the Long Island Expressway — five hours down, one to go.

You smell Oyster Bay before you see it — air growing rich with salt tang on the curve before Mill Hill Road, then everything on your right drops away but the old seawall's metal railing, the beach grass below, West Harbor and Centre Island beyond.

This island used to be the family farm. I was the tenth generation, matrilineal. Its main charm now was how well it concealed the "embarrassment of riches" from prying eyes. Only a handful of houses can be seen from the tree-canopied road.

Bonwit's gravel driveway was good for a couple tenth-of-a-mile odometer ticks, downhill toward the water. The house was old-school Abercrombie and Fitch, back when they outfitted Roosevelts for safari rather than rent boys for Fire Island. It was all creamy stucco and white shutters, under a blue slate roof.

No cars out front. No one home.

I walked into the green-walled mudroom, past piles of rubber boots and field hockey sticks and tweed caps and bicycle-polo mallets and an umbrella stand filled with rain-bent tennis rackets.

Above the inner door was a warthog-head trophy, sporting a gold hoop in one ear. I gave it a salute and cut through the "bier-stube," a small dining room of such Bavarian flavor that you half-expected to catch the St. Pauli Girl filing her nails at the head of the table. I lugged my pack up to the third floor. Bonwit had welcomed us kids to live in the northern part of the servants' quarters. Actual servants rated rooms in the half of the house he'd pay to heat, come winter.

I washed my hair, then made my way back to the kitchen for iced coffee and the *Times* crossword.

I was stuck on 13 across when Egon the Nazi gardener came in. He was white-haired, buff, and close to seventy-five. Bonwit found him working in a German boat-yard after the war. Brought him over and set him loose in the camellias.

"Morning, Egon," I said. "Any ideas for a Latin American capital, seven letters?"

His blue eyes narrowed. "Trouble with Latin America is the Jewish bankers."

"I like Jews, Egon. They're nice to me. Plus they don't put Spam on a Triscuit and call it dinner, which is more than I can say for some people."

"*Ja,* okay," he said, rocking back onto his heels. "When I work bartending around here, is always the Jews who are generous, you know? One time I have a guy, tells me, 'Egon, you give only one ice cube in a cocktail, or it's your ass.' You never have a Jew tell you some crap like that."

Egon was a shithead. For instance, he delighted Mom's boyfriend Bonwit by calling me and my siblings *die lumpen* — "the most degraded stratum of the proletariat."

But the guy loved to gossip. If Lapthorne had secrets, Egon'd spill them faster than he could throw up a *Sieg Heil* arm.

"You must see an awful lot, working around here," I said.

"Oh, *ja,* plenty," he said, nostrils flaring with satisfaction.

"Stuff people wouldn't want known," I said.

He grinned. "*Ugly* things."

"People can be pigs, can't they?" I said.

"All the time messes," he agreed. "Sometimes they want me to clean it up."

I nodded.

"*Ja,* so," he said, eyes shifting around to check the room for a broader audience.

I nodded again, and he sidled up to the table.

"It's the money," he confided. "You or me, we do wrong, there's no protection. For them the story gets all smooth, after. If it's suicide, maybe the police just say 'accident.' If the police say suicide, then probably two people involved, you know? How many suicides you know some guy shoot himself and falls *forward?* I seen people shot in the war. Only time you go face-first, the gun is behind you, understand? You tell me, how a man shoot himself in the back?"

I shook my head. Then nodded and shrugged at the same time . . . shocked at these revelations. *Shocked.*

Egon, visibly touched by this show of awed disbelief, continued.

"Is because they don't love their children," he said. "Big house, too many servants. The mothers . . . *useless.*"

"That's like my cousins, Lapthorne and those guys. They always got left with this woman Gerdie."

Egon's face pinched up in distaste. "That one, she give the Nazis a bad name —"

Bonwit walked in, dressed in a herringbone railroad cap, his typical threadbare wide-wale corduroys, and the seersucker busboy jacket he'd "liberated" from a 1930s-Havana-restaurant garbage can. The latter now sported buttons embossed with the Hohenzollern crest. Twenty-four karat. It was the sort of sartorial nose-thumbing that once landed him on Cholly Knickerbocker's "worst-dressed" list, sandwiched between Gandhi and Howard Hughes.

Bonwit inspected my wet hair. "Have you been *bathing* again? Don't suppose you have *any* idea how expensive hot water is. . . ."

I looked across the broad expanse of lawn, toward the private dock to which his latest boat was moored, then handed him a quarter.

"Here you go, Uncle Bonny," I said. "Don't spend it all in one place."

CHAPTER 24

Mom bustled past us with a load of groceries, giving me a peck on the cheek.

"Thought we'd have lunch on the terrace," she said. "The cook's at a wedding, so I'm making pork and beans with Mummie's coleslaw from Thursday before last. You can take some plates out, Madeline."

Pork and beans with week-old coleslaw needed a little window dressing. I opened the pantry cabinets that held luncheon plates — considered an Imari knockoff in vivid rusts and deep blues, the chunky majolica cabbage leaves, the cartoony spouting whales from "that little woman on the Cape" . . . fifteen patterns.

I chose the Luneville because it was Mom's, because I missed eating in our kitchen in California. I loved the familiar bright nosegay centered on its white ground, the thin raspberry stripe piped along each plate's scalloped edge.

Bonwit came out while I was setting the terrace table. He dropped his railroad cap beside his plate and pulled up a chair. Mom followed with the wheeled cart, Van de Camp's lukewarm in a big Lowestoft tureen up top.

"Lapthorne called," she said as she took her seat. "Wanted to let us know he'd be coming by water, around eight-thirty. . . . Maybe you should meet him on the dock?"

Coins of light spangled through the fine old trees. Mom served Bonwit first.

He poked around with his spoon and pursed his lips.

"Pork and beans, pork and beans, I'm Captain Jinks of the Horse Marines," he said. "Seem to have been eating an *awful* lot of this lately."

"They had a whole *case* at Foodtown, dented," chirped Mom.

"*Well* then," he said, breaking into a smile, "let's have some for this party. Might make *quite* a nice little pâté."

I passed my plate to Mom, not wanting to get involved. Mealtime conversation here was like watching Fellini and Wodehouse drop acid.

"So, Madeline," said Bonwit, "your sister tells me that poor people eat rats —"

"Not *again,* Bonwit," said Mom, handing my plate back. "For chrissake, *how* many times have you dragged this up —"

"I wondered," he continued, "whether they take the *fur* off beforehand, or leave it on and eat that *too?*"

"Fur on," I said. "For the roughage."

Egon started up a chain saw. Thank God. Ellis arrived right then.

"Awfully good to see *you,* dear," Bonwit said, over the racket.

He reached across the table to give her

hand a welcoming squeeze. It always seemed like he went out of his way to show how much he preferred her to me. But I knew how painful it had been for her to lose her dad, so I didn't begrudge the attention, most of the time.

It made me ache to see her face light up at the merest approval, to see how quickly she could draw sustenance from even Bonwit's barren landscape of affection.

The chain saw motor cut out.

"Can I interest you in a plate of these delicious pork and beans, dear?" Bonwit asked Ellis.

"Ah, can you smell?" called Egon, from across the lawn. "The linden tree is in flower again. . . . In the Hitler Youth, we make tea from the blossoms."

I helped Egon carry a couple of folding tables up from the cellar, then he put me to work slicing lemons and limes.

"I was thinking about what you told me earlier," I said. "That woman, Gerdie —"

"Not one to be with children." He snapped out a white tablecloth so it hovered in the air for a second, perfectly horizontal, before fluttering down.

"Why, you think?"

Egon shrugged. "The war."

"She was Swedish?"

"Danish. From the Jutland."

"Was it bad there, in the war?"

Another shrug. "Took it early, *Fall Weserübung.* Not real fighting . . . two hours, they give up. Then we just move through quick for Norway."

"So if it wasn't so bad there . . . I mean, it's still a war and everything — hard times. But *you* came out of it a solid guy, straightforward . . . real sense of honor . . . kind. . . ."

Fond of torchlight rallies, known to whistle "The Horst Wessel Song" while lopping blooms off the hydrangea bushes . . .

"For her, different. In the war she got . . ." He stopped himself, filled the pause by hoisting a case of tonic water onto the table. Then he started totting up cartons of liquor.

"She got . . . ?" I coaxed.

Poor Egon, so conflicted. Lips pressed tight to keep back the rest of the story, eyes already guilty with the pleasure of knowing he'd tell. It had to be something particularly nasty. Private.

He tapped the top box on a teetering stack. "Gonna need more gin."

"Let me get it, after these limes," I said, pretending absolute dedication to the precision of my slice cutting.

252

He sighed and shifted around — couldn't stand holding this morsel back.

"She got . . ." He drummed his fingers, looking sideways. "She got . . . passed around, you know?"

He pitched his voice just a notch above a whisper. "Walking home, one time. Maybe she was fourteen years old? Thirteen? Real young like that. No one told her yet what happens for babies . . . for anything. Big joke to them, those guys."

"Germans?"

He shook his head. "From her town . . . why she come over here, after."

"She told you about it?"

"Not me," he said. "Louisa."

His wife. We'd never met, even though she and Egon shared a cottage on Bonwit's place. Never seen the cottage, either. Up in the woods somewhere.

"Louisa?" I said.

"One time," he continued, "they were maybe a little drunk together, New Year's. In the kitchen, party for the Townsends. They talk when I was on the bar. Big dance, maybe five hundred people. Olden days."

At midnight Louisa had started to cry, he told me, because she couldn't get pregnant. Tried for five years after they'd been married.

"She was still so young then, Louisa. Such a tender heart," he said. "Gerdie tells her, go adopt a child. . . ."

Gerdie confided that she'd been raped, and about the baby afterwards. How she gave him up and always hoped the parents were loving, good people. Maybe like Egon and Louisa. And how maybe some other girl was wondering that right now — if there weren't kind, honest people in the world who could love her child.

And then the schnapps had run out, and Gerdie had found a bottle of brandy, which Louisa refused because by then she was a little dizzy.

Gerdie refilled a juice glass, and admitted that she felt as though the Townsend boys were her own, sometimes.

A good thing Mr. and Mrs. were so seldom at home. She had a free hand. They would respect women, those boys. She'd made sure.

Finally Egon and Louisa had to haul her up the back stairs to her bed, Louisa with one hand clamped over Gerdie's mouth because the woman kept sobbing.

"Big she was, then," he said. "Lot of work to carry, all that way. You wouldn't know, you see her now."

I nodded, thinking of the tiny crone I

remembered — thin white braids wrapped around her head, suspicious little wet-raisin eyes.

"Was 1951, so . . ." he said, "same year was born the youngest, that one you ask about."

"Lapthorne?"

"Sure."

"You ever see her with those kids?" I asked.

"I was getting set up one time, another party. Lapthorne, maybe he was six years old. Gerdie had him, like this," he said, grabbing my upper arm so hard I felt the blood stop. "Talking nasty . . ."

"What'd she say?"

"Calling him 'filthy boy, bedwetter,' " he hissed. "Saying how she was gonna tell all the girls.

"The mother come outside on a terrace and sees," he continued, "with Gerdie still holding but now like *this*," he gave my arm a twist. "Doesn't say stop, that Mrs. Townsend. Doesn't make even one sound. Only watching."

He was pretty much killing my arm, but I wanted to keep him talking so I fought the urge to yank it out of his grip.

"You know how some people, you don't have to see them, behind you?" he continued. "Just you feel it? So with Gerdie. Mrs. Townsend comes outside, she knows . . . stops talking, like . . ."

He shuddered, melodramatic, and thank God relaxed his grip on me.

I rubbed my newly paroled biceps. "Uncle Hunt claims the ambient temperature drops any time Binty comes in a room."

Egon nodded, his little grin betraying full awareness of her Nom de Bitch.

"So . . . Gerdie turns around." He drew himself up, assuming the rigid yet utterly servile posture one rarely sees perfected outside West Point. "The mother, when she knows she has attention . . . *only* she says, 'What *has* Lappy done *now?*' "

Egon did a perfect Binty, had her nailed right down to the impeccably condescending nostril flare with which she accompanied any stressed word — nasal italics.

I shivered.

"Gerdie," he went on, "all sweet, she says, 'I'm reminding him to be on his best behavior, madame' and Mrs. Townsend answers, 'That's *wonderful,* we like to see a firm hand.' "

I was still babying my sore arm, and Egon's gaze flicked across it.

"The little boy was hurting more than that," he said, "from what she did. He was holding it, trying not to cry, but his mother turns to go without ever looking him in the eye. At her back, her son gives one moment, one face of the most pure . . . But Gerdie, he wants to please. Obedient. A little dog."

He gave his head a cunning tilt and raised his hands like paws. "A puppy."

"Did you and Louisa take Gerdie's advice, about a baby?"

He nodded. "We adopted that year Helen. Then Louisa got pregnant, after, with Julia. It happens like that a lot. We raised both girls just the same. We loved them just the same, until we lost our Helen."

"I'm so sorry. . . ."

"She died in college," he said, looking off toward the water. "She was drowned. I had to fly out . . . tell them 'Yes, my daughter.' For two days I cried, after. Only time, you know? Since I was a kid."

"Oh, Egon . . ."

He pulled a sharp breath through his teeth. "You cutting those limes too thick."

When I was back up from the cellar, placing the case of Gilbey's on top of the carton pile, Bonwit stepped into the doorway. He put his hands in his pockets and leaned against the frame, whistling.

"What you need?" asked Egon.

"Hm?" said Bonwit, looking up and batting his lashes.

He snapped his fingers a few times, as though trying to remember why he'd come.

"Oh yes . . . *that* was it . . . someone on the phone for *you,* Madeline," he said at last. "Rather an *impatient* bugger."

I darted past Bonwit for the pantry, not fast enough to miss hearing him say, "Wonder who the hell'd bother with her, eh?" behind me.

I yanked up the receiver, hopeful and breathless. "Dean?"

"No . . ." Throat-clearing on the other end. "It's, ah . . ."

There was all this murmur and clinking glassware in the background.

"Kenny?"

"Yeah," he said. "*Yes.*"

I heard him fumble the phone.

"You still there, Maddie?" he asked, sounding all worried. "I was, *Jesus* . . . I acted like a goddamn . . ."

"Sure did," I said.

"Just . . . I feel terrible. I'm sorry. Everything."

"How'd you find me?"

"Your machine," he said. "Guess you left it on there for Dean, in case?"

In case. Yeah.

Kenny coughed.

"So, ah . . . make it *up* to you," he said, "I called in a couple favors. Might've found something out."

CHAPTER 25

"Kenny told you Lapthorne was in *jail?*" asked Ellis. "Why is that good news?"

We were up on the third floor, putting on our makeshift costumes.

"It was the same night as those girls were killed," I said. "Kenny got an old cop pal to go through files, and the guy told him Lapthorne was picked up for driving drunk or something. Whatever the timing was, Kenny said it meant he couldn't have done it. He was in some holding cell all night, before the MPs took him back to Camp Drum."

"Kenny was that vague?"

"Bonwit kept picking up the phone."

She snorted. "Was he pretending to be the receptionist at the Academy of Blind Interior Decorators?"

"*Don't* you goddamn laugh," I said. "Poor Kenny . . ."

She couldn't help it. Kept snickering. "I'm sorry, he did it to me this morning. Offering discounts on Braille wallpaper . . ."

"Such a prick."

Ellis shrugged, tucking in the tails of a boiled shirt we'd found in a steamer trunk of tuxedo bits, its bib of pleats still rigid with ancient starch. She'd decided to go as F. Scott Fitzgerald, complete with spiral notepad and mini-golf scorecard pencil in the hip pocket of her dinner jacket.

I was a *Titanic* survivor in Mom's deb dress: yellowed *peau de soie,* off the shoulder with those fifties pointy-atomic-boob darts. The thing had gotten ripped to shit when I wore it to come out myself at the Junior Assemblies, its hem trod upon continually in the Plaza Hotel's ballroom murk.

Ellis looked at this tattered getup, frowning. "Your mother made you wear that? To an actual deb thing?"

"It didn't look this bad when I showed up," I said.

"So, then you got jumped by your ugly stepsisters, and . . ."

I shook my head and pulled on one long kid glove, wiggling fingers and thumb into their respective casings. I donned the second one, then started wrestling with the three tiny buttons at my left wrist.

"I mean, I made it through . . . *damn it . . .*" I said, my kid-covered fingertips slipping off the first disk, just as I'd almost got it through the microscopic buttonhole.

Ellis leaned in, gently pushing my hand aside. "Let me."

"I made it through the *receiving* line," I continued, "before this thing actually started disintegrating."

"Other hand," Ellis said.

I held my wrist out. "Just all these people stepped on it, later. Dancing. I kept hearing it tear. . . ."

"Turn around. . . . I'll do you up in the back."

"Thanks."

There were fifty-seven silk-upholstered buttons going up the bodice — no bigger than Excedrins — each needing a nimble shove through its own little silken loop. Not a dress you could get into, or out of, alone.

"Dress like this," I said, "chastity's practically guaranteed."

"Oh please," said Ellis, kneeling behind me. "Throw the skirt over your head and go to town."

"In the *fifties,* I mean, all those garters?"

She tugged at the fabric around my hips. "So after talking with Kenny, you figure it's cool? All this stuff with your cousin?"

"If Kenny thinks so? Sure," I said, smiling.

Now it was just a party.

"Breathe out," she said. "I'm at the tricky part."

I exhaled and sucked in my stomach.

"More," she said.

"Bitch," I muttered.

"More," she said.

I pushed the last quarter-cup of air from my lungs, already feeling dizzy.

Ellis stood up, her breath warm on the back of my neck.

Her fingers climbed slowly. Seemed like decades before she reached my shoulder blades.

"Okay," she said. "Inhale."

I did and my vision went all black and spotty around the edges for a second.

"Almost done," she said, but as she tucked the last button through she accidentally pulled a strand of my hair along with it, some piece that had fallen free from the bone pins holding up the rest.

I jerked my head away from that sudden pinch, felt the little hairs yank out. Stupid reaction . . . hurt like hell.

I winced and raised a gloved hand to the spot.

"Sorry," said Ellis.

"My fault," I said.

She stepped back and appraised me.

"Pearls. More the better."

I dropped half a dozen strings of them over my head — different lengths, different diameters, all fake as hell — then turned to see the effect in the closet door's long mirror.

In the reflection, I tried to catch Ellis's eye. "Darker lipstick, you think?"

She didn't answer for a second, just stared blankly at my neck, now hung with a Mardi Gras' worth of milky plastic.

"The other stuff," she said, "that doesn't still bug you?"

"What other stuff?"

"The dog tags," she said. "I mean, if he was in jail, how'd they get in the field?"

Chapter 26

The Bancrofts wore capes and berets, the Hollingses his-and-hers Groucho glasses, and Louis Toohey, fresh from a Caribbean prison after that unfortunate misunderstanding about the crates of automatic weapons in the hold of his ketch, insisted that coming in his own clothes was costume *enough*, by God.

The noise began to arc in dips and swoops, shot through with hoots of laughter.

Ellis and I went for the bar, past Bonwit holding court in a Porthault-sheet toga and a flesh-toned bathing cap fringed with black curls. Mom was still at the door, meeting and greeting. She always dressed as a witch for costume parties, teasing her hair until it looked like unruly surf, then dusting it with talcum powder.

Bobby Millhammer stood up from his crowded sofa, declaring, "Off for another drink, fellows, what may I get you?"

Down the line they answered:

"Scotch on the rocks."

"Scotch on the rocks."

"Bourbon on the rocks."

"Scotch on the rocks."

"Gin and tonic . . . I'm driving." — This last met by restrained brays all around.

Ellis jotted it down on her little notepad while we stood on line at the bar.

Egon whipped us up a pair of Southsides, rum and soda and lemonade and mint.

We thanked him, knocked those back, and asked for two more.

Ellis held up her watch. Eight-fifteen, time to meet Lapthorne at the dock.

We limboed and wiggled through the crowd, struggling toward the terrace.

Dealie Van Couvering's gang plugged the French doors.

"Don't you *think*," he was saying, "that what we all have to *do* is join Piping *Rock* and take up drink?"

Poppy Cochran blinked three times, working through a stammer. "Oughtn't we rather take up *drink* and *forget* Piping? *Hm? Hm?*"

Edwardia Crow wheezed out a cackle at that, orange lipstick smeared across her teeth and the rim of her glass and the entire filter of the cigarette in her spotty hand.

"Good *God.*" She frowned at Ellis. "That's not a *haircut,* that's *birth* control."

Ellis smiled, muttering, as we sidled through the last clot of boozehounds, "Can't *wait* to shit on her grave."

"Take a number," I said.

We finally made our way out into the cool quiet of the evening beyond. A harvest moon rose over Cooper's Bluff, scattering jewelry on the bay. The lawn was bedizened with fireflies, and cicadas thrummed in the trees around us.

We walked across the grass, sweet and newly mown, past the black-powder cannons, and down the old wooden stairs to the edge of the dock. Everything was still, though we could hear the party humming and tinkling behind us, like an orchestra warming up. It reminded me of summers at my grandparents', when I'd sleep in my mother's old room and hear the sound of crowd chatter and satiny Lester Lanin tunes wafting down from tented parties up the beach.

We strode out onto the dock, feeling it sway and dip in time to our footsteps, and both sat down cross-legged when we got to the end. Bonwit's boat was tied off to leeward, and we had an unobstructed view across the water to the town of Oyster Bay.

"Gatsby believed in the green light. . . ." said Ellis, toasting the great black hump of Long Island.

I raised my glass, but couldn't help adding, "Like a good little nouveau riche."

"Hey, better nouveau riche than no riche at all."

For that I clinked her drink with mine. When we'd drained them, we pitched the glasses out over the moonlit water, hard as we could.

For a while the only sounds were small waves collapsing rhythmic on the beach behind us, the occasional chime of halyard against aluminum mast. The 8:21 gave a lovesick moan as it pulled out of Oyster Bay, headed for Penn Station. When that died away, I could hear an outboard motor in the distance.

Despite the cushioning Southside haze, a pizzicato of dread plucked along my skin. The engine noise drew closer, and moments later we were making the bow and stern lines of Lapthorne's beautiful old Chris-Craft fast to cleats at the dock's end.

He put a foot on the rail and jumped neatly over.

"*Chère cousine,*" Lapthorne said, leaning down so he could graze my cheek with that superb mouth.

He straightened up, took his time looking us over, like he wanted to savor the visuals.

And there he goddamn was, all sly and lax in ancient whipcord breeches and polo boots, glint of buckle marking the length between ankle and knee, skin so summer-dark against the white of his shirt you ached for a taste.

No help for it. The *fact* of him generated its own pizzicato, one of an entirely different order. Everything else wiped clean away — Kenny and Dean and even fear. This moment hooked irrevocably back to the last time I'd seen him, negating all that fell between.

He grinned then. "To what do I owe the honor? Being met by a *pair* of such lovely women . . ."

"Two if by sea," said Ellis, voice all silken cool.

But her eyes glittered, taking him in — set of her jaw making its own proclamation: one for all and all for *me*.

I was stripped back so pure to lizard brain that I hated her for it.

"I'd like to introduce my friend Ellis Clark," I said.

He took her offered hand and bowed over it, Ellis licking her chops.

"Cool costume," I said.

He smiled, teeth glowing white in the moonlight. "These aren't the greatest deck shoes, though."

"They make you look charming . . . well worth the trouble," said Ellis, placing her hand through the crook of his elbow and leading him back toward the house.

The party had escalated since we'd been gone. As we came up over the lawn, we could hear echoing guffaws and gin-imbued shouting. The guests had spilled out onto the terrace, and several people greeted Lapthorne. The three of us were the only people there under sixty.

Trip Harcourt announced, "I'm taking penicillin, you see, and alcohol deteriorates it or something, so in consequence I'm drinking *lightly.*" He waved his glass for emphasis, causing its contents to slop over the rim.

"Lightly?" his companion asked, twitching back the sleeves of her Chinese imperial robes.

"*Light* rum," he assured her. "Have to stay *away* from the dark stuff. Dark stuff'll *kill* you."

We pushed onward, Lapthorne walking point. When we broke through to the bar, he leaned in and said, "I see they're keeping you busy, Egon."

"*Guten Abend,* Herr Townsend," said Egon, ducking his head.

I was reminded of Peter DeVries' observation that the German language was like dozens of steamer trunks falling down stairs.

"Six Southsides, please, my good man . . ." said Lapthorne, "and make them 'Race Committee,' won't you?"

Egon nodded, topping them off with a floater of Myers's.

When we each had a pair in hand, Lapthorne asked, "Anywhere we could go to escape our ancestral paucity of culture, so as to drink in peace?"

"The green room," I said, leading the way.

We fought our way out of the living room, across the marble floor of the formal entry and past the building's most elegant staircase. There was a buffet laid out beyond the next doorway. Here the crowd thinned considerably, WASP parties never being about food. Mom could have put out rats with the fur on and not heard a single complaint.

The three of us trekked onward into the pantry, past a second staircase, and through the empty kitchen and *bierstube.* The green room was just beyond the third staircase, but when I cracked the door we were greeted by a blast of bagpipes.

Bonwit had beaten us there.

CHAPTER 27

Bonwit was sitting alone on the sofa, his back to us, waving a bottle of ouzo in time with his favorite record, *Strathspeys, Pipes, and Reels of the Highlands.*

"He always puts that on when he wants people to leave," I said, as loudly as I could without actually yelling, "but of course they can't hear it at the other end of the house, so it doesn't work for big parties."

"I take it it's quite effective for the more intimate gatherings, though?" Lapthorne said, straining to be heard. I shut the door.

"Pretty soon he'll switch to *Railroad Whistles of the World* and Harry Lauder," explained Ellis. "Sends them home in droves."

Lapthorne smiled at her. "You've enjoyed Bonwit's hospitality before?"

"Ellis and I go way back," I said. "But this doesn't look like such a great place to hang at the moment."

"Why don't I run you out to my boat?" Lapthorne linked an arm with each of us, mindful of the Southsides, and steered toward the terrace door. "Got the old yawl moored off Seawanhaka, thought I'd sleep aboard."

"Excellent," said Ellis as we stepped out onto the dusky flagstones.

I was going right along and then I thought of the dog tags again, of Ellis's last question when we were getting dressed. She and Lapthorne were laughing, all cozy, and the glittering water beckoned, but I just had this weird little chill.

We stepped onto the grass, and I tried to tell myself I could just relax, that even Kenny thought this was about Schneider now.

But Bonwit hadn't seen the three of us together tonight. Nor had Mom. Only Egon knew we were in Lapthorne's company, and he wouldn't have a clue when we'd left or where we'd gone.

I slowed my pace, and Lapthorne turned to look at me, wondering.

"Let me just, um . . . make sure Mom doesn't need anything," I said.

I pulled my arm free and started to back away. Ellis sidled in a little closer to him.

"Meet you on the dock," I called back over my shoulder. "Only be a minute. . . ."

"*Madeline,*" my mother enthused, "*just* who I wanted to see."

"Hi, great party," I said. "Listen . . . Ellis and I are going out for a boat ride with Lapthorne."

"Wonderful. Find out if he did it. Any of you have a joint?" she asked brightly.

I shook my head. "Sorry, I —"

"You know," she said, "weren't for all of us in the sixties, life would be *totally* different —"

"Do you need anything else? Because I should —"

"Wouldn't have Chicken *McNuggets,* for instance," she continued. "Got to be stoned to think up all those little sauces. . . ."

"Absolutely, Mom," I said, patting her on the back, edging away, and generally wondering why I had bothered filling her in. I mean, like she'd really notice anything before we'd been gutted and filleted, if it came to that. "They're waiting on the dock for me. Thanks again for the party."

Mom twinkled her fingers at me and then flashed a peace sign. As I stepped back outside, I heard her call out her traditional farewell, "Talk to strangers!"

Lapthorne pulled smoothly away from the dock as soon as I'd jumped in. When we arrived at his mooring a few minutes later, we helped him grab onto the lifelines at the stern of his boat.

Beautiful. An old Herreshoff, for God's sake, the name *Stray Lamb* picked out in an arc of gold letters above us.

We climbed aboard and I watched the smaller boat coast aft, tugging on its bowline like an elephant calf on its mother's tail.

"Let's go below and grab a little ice," he said. "I'll give you the five-cent tour."

Ellis was first down the companionway to the main saloon.

"Oh my God," she said, surveying the cluttered landscape. "Madeline! We've found your spiritual homeland!"

A bottle of rum held down messily unfolded charts on the central table, alongside the silver porringer containing a spent cigar.

Dozens of books spilled crooked along one bench seat, next to an explosion of laundry.

He was my style of slob, however. All the brightwork was highly polished, little needlepoint rugs were laid along the floor, and a pair of Sargent sketches in thin gold frames — Dodie and Jake — were affixed on either side of the entrance to the galley.

Lapthorne led us forward, stopping to fill a silver bucket with cold shards chipped from a block in the icebox, and then we passed a pair of single cabins and the head. There was a double tucked into the bow, and the bunk's tangled sheets were Porthault, same pattern as Bonwit's toga.

"That's beautiful," said Ellis, ever the art history major, eyeing a small tropical seascape hung above the bed. "Winslow Homer?"

Lapthorne stayed down below, freshening drinks and selecting music. Ellis and I lounged topside like inebriated Egyptian princesses barging up the Nile.

"I could get used to this," she said, her hand making a slow balletic sweep across the vista of moonlit water.

We could see a few dark figures walking along the covered porches of Seawanhaka, backlit by the bright glow of another party inside the old wooden clubhouse. Every few minutes, someone blasted a little air horn, calling the launch so they could come in for the night.

"The wages of sin," I said.

"Don't be tiresome."

"Don't forget why we're here."

She sat up. "What, because you're so busy investigating? You haven't asked him a single goddamn thing. Opportunity practically *yawning* in front of you . . ."

I looked away.

"I mean, come on . . ." she said, "I saw Schneider, too. I was right there with you. You can't tell me you think this guy is involved . . . even if you did, we both know you'd be lying your ass off."

There was a clatter from down below.

I dropped my voice. "*You're* the one who said —"

"— You would *totally* jump his bones if he wasn't your cousin."

I didn't answer that.

"Look at you," she said. "You'd totally do it *anyway,* if I wasn't here. *That's* how come you're all pissed."

I closed my eyes.

"Oh for chrissake," she said. "Don't think for a second you can give me that Grace Kelly attitude. That Ingrid shit. I *know* you.

Not a chaste bone in your body. Not a pinkie fingernail's worth of moral fiber."

"Quit it," I said, trying not to sound petulant. Unsuccessful.

"—You'd be down there right now, mucking up those pretty sheets. . . ."

"Yeah, and Dean wouldn't mind at all."

She laughed. "Like he'd know. Like any of them ever do."

"*I'd* know."

She cut her eyes at me and smiled. "And wouldn't *that* give it an all-the-more-delicious edge . . ."

The sound of Lapthorne's steps below cut her off.

She shook her head. "How *did* you end up married? Goddamn crime against nature, all I can say."

"What's that?" asked Lapthorne, head popping up from the companionway.

"Madeline being monogamous," said Ellis. "I find it quite disturbing — my former partner in debauchery redeemed by a dashing young man. Breaks my heart. The Berkshires are still in mourning. Left rear wheels of all the cars painted black, et cetera, et cetera."

"I can see why," he said, taking a seat between us, barefoot now.

I blushed, thankful for the dark. Ella

Fitzgerald's voice swelled from speakers hidden around us.

" 'Never a Dull Moment,' " he said, "the family curse."

"Indeed," I answered.

"Your branch got off lucky," he said, "escaped to exotic California. I've often envied you."

"Well, I envied the trappings you guys had, but being a kid here always seemed like such an ordeal, never any time to just ride a bike, you know? Don't let your back touch the chair and thank-you notes and God forbid your elbow made contact with the table, because somebody'd stick a fork in it . . ."

Lapthorne chuckled at that. "Still," he said, "it sounds so dopey to whine about my childhood — oh, poor me, with my nanny and my boat and my great big house . . ."

Ella sang, "Sponges they say do it/Oysters down in Oyster Bay do it . . ."

"Synchronicity," I said.

And then we were quiet, just listening to her voice and the small waves sliding along the hull.

"Getting awfully late," said Lapthorne when the song was over. "I should run you back to Bonwit's. You both down for the weekend? Be great to meet for dinner in the city tomorrow. . . ."

"We'd love to," answered Ellis, before I could say a thing.

Ellis and I walked up the dock as Lapthorne's boat chugged off into the distance.

"Dinner?" I asked. "What are you, nuts?"

"And here I was, expecting at least a '*thank you*,' " said Ellis.

"Thank you?"

She stopped and put her hands on her hips. "If you want to find out *anything* from this guy, you'll need bait. Plus, of course, if it turns out that he's not 'your cousin, the sexual-predator-psycho,' but just 'your cousin, the single, handsome, and heterosexual owner of a boat, some art, and a no-doubt tastefully appointed brownstone on the Upper East Side . . .' "

"This doesn't strike you as a peculiar way to get dates?"

She rolled her eyes. "Marriage has made you soft in the head."

CHAPTER 28

I didn't sleep for shit that night — just lay

in my old lumpy bed up under the third-floor eaves of Bonwit's house, fretting in the darkness. Around two I got up, suddenly driven to call Kenny, thinking he'd still be at the Crown and that maybe he could coach me on what the hell I should do when we got to Lapthorne's.

I tiptoed out to the sitting room, but the ancient wall phone was gone, nothing left but cloth-wrapped wires dangling from a crooked hole.

I pictured Egon chuckling as he'd crow-barred jack-plate from plaster, Uncle Bonnie's proud lieutenant in the grand campaign to ensure our misery.

I skulked to the head of the stairs, all ready to sneak down those moon-blue treads for the pantry extension, when I froze at the twang of protesting metal.

Bedsprings.

Ellis tossing, murmuring in her sleep.

"I promise," she said, her voice tiny and sad in the darkness.

She thrashed again. "Please?"

Then she was still, her breathing soft.

I considered the stairs again, the moon-light coming weak through small panes of old glass.

Kenny would only tell me not to go.

The sky went gray, then pink, before I fell asleep.

On the way off Centre Island, I parked outside the cemetery.

Ellis sighed. "Aren't we late enough?"

I'd made her wait until Mom came home that afternoon, so I could tell someone our plans, that we'd be catching the last train back out of the city.

"I just want to bring something for Lapthorne," I said. "You don't have to come in."

She followed me anyway.

It was an acre of land, brick-walled and copper-beech–shaded, quiet and cool even on the hottest day. The cast-iron gates were always crisp with glossy black enamel, the myriad rosebushes Dodie had planted always deadheaded, pruned, watered, and artfully fed in summer, then carefully wrapped in straw and burlap to hibernate through winter.

Though it was Jake Townsend's financial acumen that gave these roots "meaning" in the eyes of most, the true family patriarch, Joseph, had lived two hundred or so years earlier. He was buried beneath a large boulder, in a nod to Gethsemanean tradition. If you stood on top of it, you could see water in both directions, which fulfilled the burial instructions in his will.

A bronze plaque atop the rock read "Joseph Townsend, 1698," his birth year in England unknown.

My own favorite headstone, however, was that of my namesake and great-great-grandmother, Madeline Ludlam Townsend. It sported an uncommonly creepy winged skull, symbolizing "the flight of the soul from mortal man," according to a gravestone iconography handbook I'd once read, and the inscription was no less horrendously dismal, reading:

Behold and see as You pass by,
As You are now, so once was I.
As I am now, You soon must be.
Prepare for Death, to follow Me.

A real ray of sunshine, that Madeline the First.

"So this is who you're named after?" asked Ellis.

"Yup," I said, scouting the rosebushes for the ones I wanted, walking past The Fairy, Cecile Brunner, Souvenir de Malmaison.

Baron Girod de l'Ain and Félicité-Perpétue were still showing a last flush of bloom. I picked a quick bouquet.

"You're bringing him *roses?*" said Ellis.

"You're just pissed because you don't have a present for him."

"Course I do," she said. *"Me."*

We caught the 5:11 to the city. As the old diesel pulled wearily away from the station house, the conductor came into the car.

"*Oy*stuh Bay train, this is the *Oy*stuh Bay train," he chanted like an auctioneer, "making station stops at Locust Valley*Glen*Cove *Glen*Street*Sea*Cliff*Glen*Head*Green*vale*Ros*lyn*East*Williston*Mine*ola*Jamaica*Wood*side *and* Penn Station. *Change* at Jamaica for *Rock*away, *Long* Beach, *Mon*tauk, and *Baby*lon."

He punched our slips and stuck them under the clip on the seatback's rounded maroon shoulder, then swayed down the aisle to the next car.

I looked out the window and thought about all the times I'd ridden this train with no money for a ticket — every pathetic episode of crying on cue for the conductor, and each heartfelt promise to send a check or money order, later, to the Long Island Railroad.

Water and trees and people's backyards flashed by. We jumped off and caught a subway at Woodside.

Ellis was chatting away but I couldn't focus long enough to contribute more than an occasional nod or "Really?" I kept getting distracted, reading the long ad-cards posted along the curving edges of the car's ceiling, over and over.

"Anal Fissures?" proclaimed one. "Genital Warts? Dr. Suleiman Understands! Fast Laser Outpatient Surgery!"

And then there was my perennial favorite, the Spanish ad for Roach Motels: *Las cucarachas entran, pero no pueden salir!* — which had become something of a motto during college: "The roaches go in, but they no can leave."

The train squealed around a corner, and after the noise died away Ellis was saying, ". . . time Rizzo came back from the Cape, and finally figured out that mechanic had been breaking things on your car, because he knew he'd get paid in coke?

"I mean," she said, "what were we thinking? Right there on Spring Street, in front of King's Liquors . . ."

I smiled at her, nodding. Thought about Lapthorne, wondered whether or not he'd recognize the dying blossoms gripped in my thorn-weary hand . . . whether it had been his elegant fingers that had twined roses exactly like them, red and white, into the tresses of those long-dead girls. I'd have to concentrate, watch his face when I handed them over.

"That horrible coat you had," Ellis said, "nasty pile of tweed, so scratchy it looked like you'd stolen it off some passed-out old homeless guy in Ireland . . ."

"Cruel of you to remember that," I said, and her answering laugh was drowned out by an eastbound string of red cars, in the buffeting rush of its backwash wind.

I thought about all the questions I hadn't had the wit to formulate, or the balls to ask Lapthorne, the night before. Once again I'd been overwhelmed by how pretty he was, how beautiful were all the trappings of my lost heritage. And then, of course, I was stricken by how little hope there was that I might ever earn the slightest of those luxuries back for myself, or prove worthy of their enjoyment, even if I could.

The subway hurtled downward, into the dark.

Ellis's voice, luring me back, ". . . typing up that paper, about 'My Life, by Somebody Else,' only you called it . . ."

The lights went out. Flashed again, once, making the darkness more hollow and complete . . . struggled back on, gaining strength with each flicker.

"And Mimi," she was saying, "with that disgusting bird crapping all over her dorm room . . ."

I thought about Schneider, about how maybe all I had to find out about was the dog tags. Just ask Lapthorne how they'd ended up with the bodies in that field.

Kenny said so, and Kenny was a pro.

". . . claws mutilating that perch. Big-ass white thing," she went on, "straight out of *Baretta*."

Find that out, I told myself, and then I was off the hook. Piece of goddamn cake. Something even *I* couldn't fuck up, because how hard could it be? Just wing it . . . open my mouth and allow one phrase to tumble out, no more than thirty seconds over cocktails, or dinner.

But I didn't unclench my fists, except to shift the pathetic bouquet to my as-yet-unpricked palm, until we braked screaming into the nether-belly of Grand Central.

"Chatty bitch," said Ellis, standing up as everyone else bolted past us. "What's the matter? Thinking about Dean?"

Dean.

Of whom I was least worthy, beyond everything else I'd never deserve.

"Yeah," I lied, dropping my eyes to the scummy floor. "Exactly. That fight we had, right before he left . . ."

When I looked again she was gone, half-way onto the platform already, so I shoved off after her, catching glimpses of her neat dark head as I climbed a broken escalator, an echoing staircase. Up and up, along tiled hallways and past a thousand yards of beige marble, until we burst out onto the con-course and the crowd thinned, spreading across the expanse beneath the great barrel arch painted with constellations, half the bulbs burned out. And still I didn't fall into step until just before we reached the stench and clamor of the street.

"Don't worry." She touched my arm. "He'll call. Probably trying right now, Bon-wit giving him no end of shit . . ."

"Sure," I said.

"Dean loves you."

"Can't imagine why."

She shook her head and laughed again and we began to make our way along the blocks, north and east, north and east, toward the river and the quiet little stretch of East End Avenue fronting on that gem of park containing the mayor's place.

I slowed my pace so Ellis could mount the worn limestone stairs to Lapthorne's entry first, stopping one tread short of the landing so I wouldn't crowd her.

Centered on the door's black gloss was the face of a gilt-bronze lion, big as a headlight.

Resting my hip against the stair rail, I watched her lift the hoop caught in its snarl-bared teeth. Not to bang the thing, announcing our arrival, just to get it out of the way for a curtsied lipstick-check in the strikeplate's golden mirror.

Satisfied, she caught my eye in the reflection and threw me a wink before drawing herself up, tall as she could go. Then she inhaled, threw her shoulders back, and rapped the ring's heft smartly, twice, against the answering metal.

As though he'd been standing at the ready, Lapthorne swung the door wide, and I saw how the corners of his eyes crinkled with pleasure at the sight of Ellis. In a clean arc of kiss and compliment, he'd passed her inside, not even shifting his weight.

So then it was just me, hesitating still, one step shy of the landing — fistful of roses head-down behind my back.

Now I could see him in full: the pink Brooks Brothers shirt with a couple of buttons missing, the ratty khakis that hung perfectly off his narrow hips, revealing an inch of sockless ankle above each patent-leather tuxedo pump — shoes so old the finish was veined and cracked at the balls of his feet.

Proffering the roses, I stepped forward, presenting a cheek for the expected kiss. He went for my mouth instead, dragging it out for a second, which just about killed me. I had to grip the cast-iron railing to keep from leaning into him.

When he pulled back, I willed myself to keep my eyes on his face, watching for any reaction to the bouquet.

Still looking at me, he wrapped his hand around the stems loosely, just above my own grip, letting my fingers slip away beneath before he tightened his own.

I could still feel the nick of each thorn in my palm, but Lapthorne didn't flinch, only smiled down at the red and white blooms nodding, heavy, over his hand. He nudged a fingertip beneath one sulky crimson flower, tilting it upwards, then let it sag back against its brethren before lifting them all to his face.

He closed his eyes as he inhaled the perfume.

"Magnificent," he said, raising his head at last. "Thank you so awfully much."

Lapthorne and Ellis had gone farther inside, but I'd hesitated before a mirror hung in the dull red front hall. My attention was caught not by my reflection, but by the black spots eating into the glass's silvery backing. I had no idea I'd ever been in this place before, but I must once have been made to wait, in this exact location, long enough to decide that the dark patch nearest the bottom left-hand corner looked like a tugboat.

There it was, the stubby little craft plowing through waves, complete with cartoon puff of smoke trailing from its crooked rooftop stack. While I considered the shape, another fragment of memory surfaced — a glimpse of my own earnest little face, reflected in the glass back when I was small enough to have been eye level with the bottom edge of its frame. Then as now, I'd held my breath so I wouldn't fog the surface.

Underneath the mirror was a spindly table, originally positioned there for the receipt of calling cards. I opened its single drawer, knowing it would contain two golf tees, a palm-sized bronze medal commemorating Hoover's inauguration ("Engineer, Scholar, Statesman, Humanist . . ."), and a spent book of matches from the Stork Club.

Then I had to wonder who the hell had left three-foot-tall me standing alone in a

New York City hallway long enough that I not only started looking through drawers, but memorized their contents.

The only object new to me was a fossilized lipstick, the coral shade of which dated to the cusp of Mayors Lindsay and Beame. I found this thing's presence offensive, an upset to the natural order, and so dropped it into a handy umbrella stand.

Just as I started walking toward the doorway Lapthorne and Ellis had gone through, he peeked his head out into the hall.

"You okay?" he asked.

"Yeah, I'm . . . I didn't think I'd ever been here, but I totally remember . . ." I didn't know how to finish the thought, so I just shrugged in an attempt to indicate the hallway generally.

Lapthorne put his hands in his pockets. "Used to be Dodie's place."

"Yeah," I said, "right . . ."

Dodie the junkie matriarch, blood connection of our second-cousin-hood.

He looked sheepish. "She couldn't keep up . . . taxes, you know? I paid the, ah, fair market —"

"Did I come here, when I was little?"

He smiled. "Madeline, you were *born* two blocks away."

"Oh."

"Doctors' Hospital?"

I nodded, embarrassed. "Well . . . so this is still her stuff?" I said, glancing again at the mirror, its thin gold frame bright against the tomato-soup wall. How many years later, and here I was, out here alone. Waiting.

"Sure you're okay?" he asked, sounding genuinely concerned. "Come on in the library . . . have a glass of wine."

My cousin was leaning against the doorframe, holding out a hand like I needed help reaching shore.

"Hey," he said, "welcome back."

"Now, what can I get you? I have the usual complement of the hard stuff, if you don't want wine. . . ."

Lapthorne was standing in front of a little copper sink and a bar hidden behind a door full of fake books in the library. Booze masquerading as literature, how too-too perfect.

"Wine sounds wonderful," I said. "Whatever you two are having."

He reached up to the shelf above his head and plucked down another glass. "I've got a nice backstrap of venison, so we could segue this right into dinner."

Ellis was holding up an old black-and-

291

white shot in a silver frame. "Is this you, Maddie?" she said, pointing.

I stepped up to see what she held: the big family shot of Dodie and progeny, on the lawn in front of her house on Centre Island . . . two generations of handsome men and their slender wives, then all the great-grandchildren — shining teenagers in madras jackets or Lilly shifts and the youngest in button shoes and smocked dresses, or gray flannel shorts and Peter Pan collars.

Lapthorne at thirteen and even me, just above the tip of Ellis's finger. I was almost a year old and sitting on my mother's lap, my father standing behind her with a hand gently on her shoulder, both of them beaming. That was when I was still the youngest in the whole family. There was never another portrait of us all together.

"You can see where they grafted us onto the group," said Lapthorne. "We were fogged in on Nantucket the day they shot everyone else."

I leaned in closer and realized there was indeed a thin line separating Bat, Binty, and their four boys from everyone else, and that a touch of tree branch repeated, just above their heads.

Binty was looking pissed.

Lapthorne gave me the glass of wine. "I

made up a plate of cheese," he said, "but I left it in the kitchen, which is of course in the basement. Should we head down and I'll finish dinner?"

We followed him down a narrow staircase — the architect having wasted no space or detail on what would have been used exclusively by servants.

The kitchen was low and wide, with dark beams across the ceiling. Lapthorne set a double-boiler to simmer on an old eight-burner Garland stove. Through French doors at the back, I could see the evening darkening a small garden.

A sweet fragrance started to float atop the deep scent of meat roasting in the oven.

"Give this a taste," said Lapthorne, proffering a spoon coated with clear and deep golden red. "Little bit of port for the venison."

Ellis first blew on it, then touched her tongue to the liquid. "Oh my God," she said, grinning.

"I think we're good to go, then," said Lapthorne. He moved the browned backstrap of deer to a platter and poured his sauce over it, then loaded it into the dumbwaiter. "Why don't you two head up to the dining room. I'll send this aloft. . . ."

When we were out of earshot, she said, "I

really want him not to have done it, Madeline. I just think he's so cool."

"It's not like I *want* it to be him," I said. "Not like I even think it, now, after what Kenny said. All I want to know about is the dog tags."

"Good woman," she said.

We turned to the next set of stairs and went on climbing.

I took a bite of the venison, which was perfect, the sweet, tangy sauce a magnificent counterpoint. The dining room walls were a soft gray and Lapthorne had lit candles all around, tapers glowing from wall sconces and from the branches of some heavy Georgian sterling numbers on the table.

How to start? Just say, *So those dead chicks . . . you were in jail, but your dog tags weren't?*

Ellis was no help, she was practically lying in Lapthorne's lap asking if she could peel him a grape.

God, I just suck at this.

Lapthorne kept refilling our glasses, and as I got a little hazy with the wine it all started to seem ridiculous.

"You look pensive, Madeline," he said to me, an edge of concern to his voice.

"Just thinking how nice to sit down for a

meal without Bonwit pecking at me," I said.

"That man's a piece of work," he said, smiling at me. "I remember he told me once that his daughter had served him her scabs on toast that morning. Said they'd been rather tasty, considering."

"Typical," I said.

"I love your mother, though . . . one of the few people I ever wanted to emulate on Centre Island."

I took a sip of wine.

"How's your father these days?" he asked. "Haven't seen him in years. . . ."

I explained about him living behind the gas station, and how he thought the KGB was reading his mail, and how strange it was to look so much like him and yet not know him at all.

"I'm Hamlet Plus — instead of meeting my father's ghost, I *am* his ghost. . . ."

This was met with silence.

"Sorry . . ." I said. "Don't mean to get all maudlin."

Lapthorne laid his hand over mine. "Not at all. That sounds . . ." he said, "well, that sounds as though it must be really awful. I'm sorry. But you were always cool yourself, Madeline. You knocked me out, even when you were a little kid. I remember asking you once when you were about seven what you wanted to be when you grew up, and you thought about it for a minute and said 'Myself,' in this really serious little voice. Never forgotten that."

"Not really an aspiration one can fail to achieve," I said.

"Don't be ridiculous . . . look at the rest of the damn family. Utterly bloodless by the time they were twelve, most of them."

I laughed.

"You're a credit to the race," he continued, "and God knows to the family at large. It's a rare occasion I actually get to enjoy my relatives — I should be breaking out champagne."

I had a rush of affection for him. Just because it had been so damn long since a member of my own family had been happy to see me, had smiled when I came into a room.

Here I was, made welcome in this beautiful place — as if I belonged, once again. As if, just maybe, the hubris of my parents and my own failures hadn't managed to cut me off from home and clan forever.

"Thank you," I said.

He poured more wine into my glass.

"In fact, though," I said, "I think I may have had enough already. Where's the bathroom?"

"Go up another flight and through my office," he said.

I stood up, light-headed. The stairs were dimly lit, and the dark banister felt satiny and cool under my hand as I started for the third floor. I got to the top and fumbled inside the door for the light button. The sconces over an old desk lit up, and I glanced over the wall, admiring a jumble of pictures hung between a pair of bookshelves.

The room was papered in a green and white toile, a pattern of walleyed peacocks, again familiar. I ran my finger down the line of the repeat, but I really had to go to the bathroom.

I peed, washed up, looked in the mirror, played with my hair, put on lipstick. My cheeks were too red from the wine.

I came back out. Music from downstairs: Django. "Sweet Georgia Brown."

"Oh *fuck*," I said.

Four frames hung in a row alongside the door. In each was a silhouette. There were two crewcut men, one of them perfectly Lapthorne. Above them were two women: one with her hair in a thick braid over the top of her head, the second wearing a high Spanish comb.

Sphincter chill.

CHAPTER 29

I walked slowly back into the dining room, silhouettes in my hand. Lapthorne had indeed broken out a bottle of champagne.

"So I knew I had to break up with him," Ellis was saying, "when I went home to his family's for Thanksgiving and his mother broke out a set of sterling *grape* scissors. . . ."

She looked up at me and stopped talking.

I laid the silhouettes down on the table.

"Change of subject," I said.

Lapthorne's face went pale in the soft light. "I've been waiting for you to —"

"You've been *waiting?* You *knew?*" I was shaking, hands clenched.

He dropped his eyes. "Those exact roses, Madeline? You live in the same city . . ."

Ellis was silent.

"So you just figured, what," I said to him, "act all charming and shit, maybe I wouldn't ask if you killed those girls?"

"You think *I* —"

"Your dog tags were found at the scene," I said.

"Because I *gave* them to Delphine, and she wouldn't come with us anyway . . ." he said, then just shook his head and stopped talking — like it hurt too much, producing words.

I watched the black silk of his eyepatch darken. Seconds later, a fat teardrop crawled down his other cheek.

"All right," Lapthorne said finally, "why *wouldn't* you believe that I was responsible? I was such a useless piece of shit I let them go. . . . But if I'd *known?* If I could have *stopped* it?"

Ellis stood up, grave for once.

She gripped his shoulder and said, "Bourbon."

We hoisted him up and propelled him down the stairs, back to the library.

Ellis was pouring Lapthorne an ungodly amount of Jim Beam. We'd settled him into an old leather club chair in the library. I took the one across the butler's table.

"All right," I said. "I've gotten bits and pieces. You were drafted, you were based at Fort Drum —"

The guy was broken, all hunched in on himself like some beat-up doll from a thrift-store nickel bin.

Ellis set the glass in front of him. He wrapped both hands around the vessel but didn't try to lift it.

"How did you get into all this?" he asked,

not looking at me.

"The dog tags," I said. "I've held them in my hand."

"I take it you know the date in question?" he asked.

I nodded. "Let's hear your version. Start with who the hell the girls were, since no one up in Syracuse has ever figured that out."

He fell back in the chair.

When he didn't say anything, I pushed his glass closer to him and said, "Where were they from?"

"France."

"How'd they end up at the fair?"

"They'd been in Buffalo for the summer. Au pairs. Wanted to see a little more of the country before they went home. Chris and I had a pass. . . ."

Ellis leaned against the back of my chair. "Chris?"

The silhouettes were laid on the low table before Lapthorne. He tapped the fourth profile. Bottom right. "He was in my unit. I knew him from St. Paul's."

"Tell me about the girls."

He drank before speaking, then cleared his throat. "I had a little Porsche, an old 356C. . . . It was beautiful out and we put the top down. Chris saw the girls walking along, near that rose garden downtown. . . ."

"The E. M. Mills Memorial," I said, "in Thornden Park."

"Just so."

He leaned forward, resting his elbows on his knees and letting his hands hang loose between them, patrician ankles crossed below.

"You made the garlands?" I asked.

He nodded. "It was beautiful. The moon, fireflies — heady scent of that last flush of bloom, but just enough breeze. I made them each a crown of blossoms. We'd paired off by then. . . ."

"What were their names?" I asked.

"Sophie and Delphine," he said. "Last name was Descognets. Sisters."

"You wouldn't know it," I said, "from the photographs. They didn't look alike."

"Photos?" he asked. "Where did you . . . ?"

"One of those strips from a booth at the fair," I said. "They found it on the bodies."

"Don't remember when the girls did that. Must have been when Chris and I were buying beers or something, which was why they wouldn't leave with us."

"Why not?" asked Ellis.

"We were just so hammered," he said. "Chris and I'd been drinking all afternoon. There was a full moon, did I tell you that? I turned off the headlights when we were driving to the fairgrounds. The girls didn't like it . . . later they didn't want to get back in the car with us. . . ."

He reached for the bourbon and knocked it back.

"We were just . . . young," he said. "Didn't know what the hell was going to happen when they shipped us out, so we were rowdy and stupid. Having so goddamn much *fun,* but . . . Last time I ever . . ."

Ellis refilled his glass.

"I should have *made* them get in the car," he said. "We should have stayed with them . . . if I hadn't been so —" He went silent again.

"Where's this Chris guy now?" asked Ellis.

"Blown up about three weeks after we'd been shipped to Asia," he said. "A little kid with a grenade taped to him came running up and Chris knew we'd all be . . . ."

Lapthorne swilled bourbon and leaned back. "I remember pelting toward him, yelling at him to stop, to turn away. Caught a piece of shrapnel." He touched the patch. "So my mouth was open when he . . . there was —"

"Please," I said, dinner shifting nastily in my stomach. "Just tell us about the fair."

"We were trying to talk the girls into leaving with us, a motel or something, and they wouldn't. It was still early, and Chris and I were begging them, finally . . . ridiculous. We were so drunk, and Delphine said she'd kiss me if I gave her the dog tags, a souvenir to bring home, and when I did they danced away from us, laughing."

He stopped again, covering his eye and the patch with one hand.

"So then . . ." coaxed Ellis.

"So then we called after them," he said, "and told them we'd leave. We were right near my car. I guess we thought that would make them follow us . . . pique their interest. We were going to come back. Just drive around the block . . ."

I almost asked if that was when he got arrested, but I wanted to hear it from him. A test. See if his version matched Kenny's.

"I peeled out of the lot," he said. "Wanted to make some noise and get their attention. Didn't get very far and then I hit a van, sideswiped it, and the guy got out and Chris was pissy to him, took a swing or two and then there was a cop car and we were . . . belligerent. Out of hand."

"Did you find the girls again?" asked Ellis.

"If I hadn't told the one cop he was a

fucking asshole townie and to get his fucking hands off my car, maybe they wouldn't have cuffed us. And then when he had me up against the car I told him they had to let us go, because we had these French girls decked in roses who were hot for us, all ready to get down and . . . Girls who'd never look at his sorry ass twice, so he slammed my head against the door a couple of times. I started puking, and after that . . ."

He dropped the hand from his face and looked at me, then turned his head away. "I came to in the holding cell with a rib busted," he said, "stinking of vomit."

"And the girls were killed," I said.

"Yes," he said, "and the girls were killed. And the cop made sure I knew it before he let us go. End of his shift, and they'd just found them . . . the bodies. He heard it when someone radioed in, told us all about it, how they were still wearing the roses. Took me out of the cell . . ."

"Oh my God," said Ellis.

"I can't tell you how badly I wanted to . . . when he told me that, like he was gloating, rubbing it in . . ." said Lapthorne. "He said I'd have to live with knowing, bad as if I'd done it myself."

"What did you do?" I asked.

"Nothing. I just . . . He let us go and I

couldn't even tell Chris, not until the day after, when we shipped out."

"But at the station, they never asked you . . ." said Ellis. "I mean, if no one knew who the girls were, didn't he want to . . ."

I cut her off. "The cop," I said. "Tell me his name."

"It doesn't matter," he said, looking like he was going to cry again. "He was right. I'm the one who has to live with it. It wasn't until we got back to base that I realized I still had the silhouettes, all smashed in my pocket. I've kept them, ever since. . . ."

"Hey, Lapthorne," I said, leaning across the table, right in his face. "Stop feeling sorry for yourself and tell me his name."

He flinched, then quietly answered, "Schneider. Officer Jack."

"Schneider?" said Ellis. "We *saw* him and Madeline thinks he's —"

"You *what?*" said Lapthorne, snapping his head around to look at me. "Goddamnit, Maddie, you *saw* Schneider? What the hell does that mean?"

"It means," I said, "that I never believed you killed them."

CHAPTER 30

"So all this time you just let me go on think-ing . . ." Lapthorne was now totally ticked off at me, which I chalked up to the fact that he'd been acting like, well, kind of a pussy, frankly.

"I'm sorry. I didn't *believe* you had done it," I said, "but I didn't know for sure. I mean, what would you have done? You get told about a double murder and then right away your cousin's name turns up?"

He thought about that. "Of course you're right. You had no way of knowing whether or not I was . . . my God, someone *danger-ous.*"

"Well then," I said.

"In fact," he said, rather sheepish, "as your favorite cousin, I forbid you to *ever* do anything like this again. What the hell were you thinking?"

"I was thinking I had to know," I said. "Those girls . . . I saw the pictures. Not just the ones from the fair, the ones of them after. They were killed in a strange town and no one knows how it happened, no one even knew who they were."

"But now we do," said Ellis. "Now they have names, and now you know Lapthorne wasn't involved."

"Now I want to know who was," I said.

"As do I," said Lapthorne. "Your money's on Schneider, Madeline?"

"Yes."

"I don't know how to ask," he said, "but if you want to do this . . . it would mean a great deal to me."

"Of course we want to do this," said Ellis.

I nodded.

He looked down at the silhouettes. "I've kept these for a long time," he said. "Mostly because I felt responsible. But also because I miss what it was like, before the war, before Delphine and Sophie were . . . I wanted to remember how that felt."

He looked up at the two of us. "Thank you."

"Our pleasure," said Ellis.

They smiled at each other, all sappy. I looked at a clock on the mantel.

"Sadly, Ellis and I have a train to catch," I said. "So if we want to figure out what to do next . . ."

"Won't you stay?" asked Lapthorne. "Plenty of room, and it would be my pleasure to cook breakfast."

"Thank you, but I've got to go back to Syracuse tomorrow, early," I said.

"So be it, then," he said. "Let's get started."

"All right," I began, "here's what I know so far," and I explained about meeting up with Sembles at the fair, and our run-in with Schneider and Vomit Girl. I told Lapthorne about Kenny, to let him know I had someone formidable on my side, someone who'd know if I was getting into dangerous territory.

"What next?" asked Ellis.

"Have you been to the, ah, crime scene?" asked Lapthorne.

"I should," I said. "Maybe I can go from work. Take an hour or something."

I checked the mantel clock again . . . time to leave.

"We'd better hit it," I said to Ellis.

She looked twitchy.

"What?" I asked.

"I'm going to stay," she said.

I just stared at her.

Lapthorne threaded his fingers through hers and put their hands on his knee.

Ellis looked at me, a satisfied little smile tipping up one corner of her mouth. "You'll miss your train."

Lapthorne stood up and walked out onto the quiet street with me. He hailed a cab and opened the door, his fingertips just barely trailing along the curve of my lower back as he ushered me in.

I turned to say goodbye. He kissed me on the mouth again.

PART III
SYRACUSE

A photograph is a secret about a secret. The more it tells you, the less you know.

— Diane Arbus

CHAPTER 31

It was after nine Sunday night when I reached Green Street. I couldn't remember when the six-hour drive had ever been so exhausting. Maybe it had been this time because I'd spent mile after mile rehashing every word Lapthorne had said over the last two nights. Or maybe I just didn't want to face my Dean-free apartment.

I'd fought sleep since Saugerties, blasting Hendrix and Callas-as-Carmen with the windows down. By Whitney Point, my resistance to the lure of a nap in the break-down lane was so weak it took sucking back three tragic gas-station coffees before I could soldier on.

And for what, ultimately? Here I was in my own driveway, not feeling a damn thing but sorry.

It was just so ugly, after lush downstate. Made me want to shoot out every streetlight on the block.

Instead I dropped my forehead to the steering wheel, drifting off to sleep while crickets bitched from the dead grass out back.

I was totally under, right up until someone crunched onto the driveway's gravel.

Two steps . . . heavy . . . then a hesitation before the guy's next stride brought him smack against my still-open window.

I didn't flinch, not even when he put a hand on the sill to steady himself into a crouch, down so close I could hear him breathe.

My keys were hanging out of the ignition. I reached for them slowly, wondering if I could yank fast enough to jam a fistful of Medecos into his eye socket.

Then he cleared his throat and said, "Hey, Bunny, want me to carry your backpack up?"

"Dean? Shit!" I snapped my head up. "Why the hell aren't you in Canada?"

"Nice to see you, too."

"Oh my God! I am *so* sorry. I thought you were . . . Jesus, Dean . . . I was about to stab you in the eye with my keys."

He laughed and opened my door. "I'm a sucker for feisty, but that would have been pushing it."

I jumped up and threw my arms around

his neck, mumbling more about Canada into his shoulder.

"Couldn't stand it," he said. "Had to know you were okay. I was going to fly down to Long Island, but when I called Bonwit's he kept saying it was an obstetrician's office and hanging up. Your mom finally answered, after you'd left. Came here instead. . . . Got in a couple of hours ago."

"How long can you stay?"

"Tonight," he said. "Don't get back first thing tomorrow, I miss the crew. Six a.m. flight and Al's picking me up on the other end. Then we're out in the real woods."

"Couldn't you just . . . ?"

Dean shook his head, reached into the car for my pack.

"Made your favorite dinner," he said, throwing it onto one shoulder, "Wafers of Splendor, Nuggets of Glory. In the oven all toasty, ready to go."

I followed him down our beautiful side-walk, up onto the stately front porch of the classically handsome building we lived in.

I loved everything, right down to the cracked and dented paneling along the splendid staircase, and the painted-over frieze of crowbar marks with which some long-forgotten burglar had once adorned our front door.

All the lights were on, inside, the Weavers crooning old pinko ballads from the stereo in my honor.

Dean got out two plates and dished up his wafers and nuggets — zucchini slices and mushrooms, respectively, dipped in cornbread batter and fried. Only thing he knew how to cook, but always killer delicious.

We didn't eat them. Didn't sleep, either. Too busy messing around, except for occasional intermissions spent apologizing about having been such shits to each other, last time we'd both been home.

By the time the sky started inching toward bright, we were crumpled and useless, sheets all twisted around our legs.

"Last round almost finished me off," he said. "Definitely got the poisons out."

"Should hope so. Any more, I'd be on crutches *past* Thanksgiving."

He rolled toward me, twining fingers into my hair. "Just enough light to see you by," he said. "Have to stock up for the road."

"Same," I said.

We just looked, not moving, while the room went from pale blue to lavender, pink to apricot.

"So," he said.

"So."

"You find out what you needed, down-state?"

"I think."

"He's in the clear, your guy? Spent that year in Zurich or something?"

I closed my eyes.

"What?"

"Spent part of it at Camp Drum," I said. "Then Asia."

"He go to the fair, meet some girls?"

I nodded.

Dean sighed. "You don't seem too upset, or whatever."

"Because I know he didn't do it."

"For real?"

"For real." I opened my eyes, looked at him as hard and true as I could. "Not just because of what Lapthorne said, down there . . . there's stuff Kenny found out."

"Kenny's on board with this?"

"Very."

"Shit."

"It's okay," I said.

"What comes next?"

"I don't know."

He touched my hair again. "Ballpark ideas?"

"Like talking to the cops and stuff?"

"Sure . . ."

"It's still really tricky. Schneider and

everything . . . ."

"There's no hurry, seems like. You can take your time, right?"

"Exactly."

"Make sure of it . . . every detail . . . don't decide anything until I get back. Don't *do* anything, okay? Just be really, really careful."

"Really, really, *really* careful. I promise."

"Because, no offense, Bunny, but, like, that keys-in-the-eyeball thing?"

"Yeah?"

"Some guy wants to hurt you, that's not gonna stop him for shit."

"I know."

He framed my face in his hands. "Don't just say 'I know' to make me lighten up. I'm not fucking around. I want you to tell me you understand me and *mean* it."

"I understand you. I mean it."

"You sure?"

I nodded.

"Are you in any danger, the way things are right now?"

"No," I said. "Nobody else knows about this. The dog tags, all that. It can wait until you get home again. Kenny will make sure."

"Nothing with Schneider?"

"Nothing. He doesn't know my name. Never saw my car."

"Promise me."

"I promise."

"Because I won't leave, otherwise," he said. "If there's any chance you're in danger."

"There isn't."

"I'll quit everything with the grinder," he said, "and follow you to work every day instead, all you have to do is say the word. I don't care if it means I end up working for Wimpy my whole damn life."

"It's okay. I promise."

Dean shivered. "Makes me crazy . . ."

"So . . . want me to reheat those Nuggets of Glory, for the road?"

He grinned at me, and right then his alarm clock started buzzing: 4:37.

When he rolled over to turn it off, I gave him a solid swat on the ass.

"G'wan," I said, "you're burnin' daylight."

I took him to the airport, walked him as far as security.

"I'll call tonight," he said. "Don't know when I'll be able to again, off in the Yukon or whatever . . ."

"I'll be home."

He kissed me and went on through.

I watched him go, duffel bag hoisted over his shoulder.

I stood there until long after I couldn't see him anymore. Just to remember how he'd looked.

When I turned to go, Syracuse was ugly again.

I stopped in at work and told Ted I wanted to return to the scene of the crime, as it were, then talked Simon into giving me the manila folder jammed with prints.

There wasn't much traffic, so I was out of the city fast. I pulled onto Collamer Road and was soon away from the tidy stretch of ranch houses with well-kept lawns and sparkling Methodist blue American sedans. After the farm stand, you had to run through the flat, barren crossroads where the skanky bar with the mud-wrestler chicks was, and then there was nothing for a while but stunted trees and swamp around old fucked-up houses sagging into the dirt with "in-law" trailers out back.

In front of most were snowmobiles up on blocks, next to either a plywood fat-lady-leaning-over-to-expose-dotted-bloomers cutout or a knee-high Madonna sheltered by one of those things that always looked to me like a plaster bathtub upended, half-buried, with the interior painted turquoise.

I couldn't find crap to listen to on the

radio, just endless Supremes and bad skinny-tie hair bands, but I kept punching buttons until I was nearing the cornfield in question. I slowed down, then pulled across the narrow lanes and thunked off the asphalt onto a runoff-corrugated shoulder of hard, pale dirt.

I got the folder containing all the photos out of the back, and opened it carefully on the roof of the car.

I flipped through the prints and picked a couple of distance shots in which the bodies figured. Then I started to read from my Xerox of Wilt's piece, " '. . . Two girls lay side by side in a tiny grove along the *western* edge of Johnston's acreage . . .' "

I looked up. The sun was directly overhead, so that was no help. Where the hell was west? I could never tell directions around here — too damn flat and no ocean.

I started looking at the trees in each photo, finding a maple with a peculiar fork, right next to a pair of firs. When I looked up, all the trees were a lot taller and more filled out, but those three were recognizable. I headed into the gap between two rows of tall corn. It was close to noon, and the sun was strong enough to make me squint at the deep green all around me. It felt like the light would tint anything pale with a glowing aura of lime chiffon.

There was no breeze, so the only sound was the occasional rush of a car and my footsteps in the dirt. When I stopped for a second, though, there was a strange squeaky popping noise all around.

I'd been up here long enough to recognize the sound of corn growing, the broad green leaves dragging against one another as they sought sunlight and altitude.

Then I was at the end of the stately tasseled plants, my identified clutch of trees thirty feet beyond. Looking from the photographs to the grove and back a couple of times, I figured out the placement of the bodies, roughly fifty feet into the woods.

One photo showed the spot after the cops had left — Simon's shot. Another, one of the official pictures, was framed about the same, only with the girls still lying on the ground.

I looked at both again, then walked forward toward the grove, passing out of the bright sun and into cool shade. For a moment I couldn't really see, until my pupils dilated enough. Something was tugging at the edge of my consciousness. I walked in a circle, then stopped, backing slowly away from the tree under which the girls had lain.

I looked at the ground. Although some

sunlight was coming through the branches overhead, I cast no shadow in the dappled light.

I squatted down and put the same two photos on top of Simon's folder.

They were taken from roughly where I was positioned, but one didn't match . . . the one that showed the girls' bodies still on the ground.

I looked at Wilt's article again. There it was, the statement about when the police had arrived — eleven a.m.

If that were true — and it probably took some time to set up — the photographer would have been shooting around the time it was now. Almost noon.

But the police photographer's long shadow was captured in the shot, spilling past the bodies. He'd been standing in just about exactly the spot on which I was now hunkered down, me casting no shade at all. Impossible.

I closed my eyes and tried to orient myself . . . had to be facing west, so the "police" shots must have been taken just after dawn, hours before the cops officially showed up.

I looked again at the photo. Both girls' eyes were open, staring up at nothing.

Back at the paper, I spread the photos out

over the big round table in Ted's office and showed him, Wilt, and Simon the deal with the shadows.

"Jesus," said stubby Simon, shaking his head. He jammed his fists into the pockets of his jacket, bracketing his friar's belly. "It never occurred to me. Of *course* those had to be taken in the early morning. I think mine were done around noon the next day, so that's the lighting these *should* have."

"But not all the police photos were taken that early," said Wilt, perching on the edge of the table, stretching out his long legs and smoothing down the rumpled pant legs of his brown suit. "It's just these four, here." He drew those shots off to the side. "The rest look about right."

"The quality's different, too," I said. "These four are almost as good as yours, Simon — sharp focus, very high contrast, really *black* blacks. The rest of them are a little muddy."

"Holy shit," said Wilt.

"Huh," said Ted.

You could tell he was getting excited — he kept raking his fingers back over his head, freeing long strands of his red hair from the rubber band at the nape of his neck so that they flew haphazardly around his olive face.

He turned his back on me and threw an arm loosely around Wilt's shoulders. "You know, Wilt, maybe you'd better look into this —"

"Uh, Ted?" I said. "I'm on it."

"— because this could be a real scoop, you know?" he continued, not even turning his head toward me, and Wilt nodded.

"Oh, come *on*," I said. "First you made me take the assignment, and then the minute I tell you I found something, you give it to Wilt?"

His head snapped around. "That's just it, Madeline. I had to badger you into taking it on at all. It's not like you were overjoyed about it," he said, lips pulled back in full Angst Lizard sneer. "You're not into hard news, and Wilt's got the experience to do this right."

"Look . . . I just . . . I think it would be a mistake," I said. "I have some other information about what went on, aside from this."

"Okay, so sell me on it. Why should I let you be the lead on this? Why is this the moment you should break out from, what was it, 'green bean casseroles with mushroom soup and canned fried onions on top'? This is potentially huge for us, and I don't know if I trust you with the responsibility, frankly,"

Ted said. "I mean, we're not talking about Jell-O recipes."

"First of all," I said, "who's the one who noticed what was up with the photos you've had lying around for twenty years? It took your food-and-whatever writer to catch something that should have been obvious from the outset."

He pursed his lips at me.

"And second, there's *this*," I said, pulling the folded-up dog tag rubbing from out of my wallet. I yanked it open and slammed it on the table in front of him.

"Yeah?" asked Ted, looking unimpressed. His lips made a pressed smirk. Simon went pale behind him.

"The girls were last seen with two soldiers, right?" I said, my voice getting a shrill edge. "That's a set of dog tags Dean's father plowed up in the field where their bodies were found."

That wiped his smirk right the hell off.

"Plus which, I know who the owner of those tags is," I said. "I just spent the weekend with him, and I found the silhouettes from the fair at his house, so I made him tell me what happened, and now I know *he* didn't do it."

Now he just looked confused. He probably hadn't read Wilt's article since it first came out, and I could tell he wasn't completely following what I was talking about, but Wilt and Simon were zeroed right in.

"Well," said Simon shyly. "I guess the next question is who that man is . . . the guy on the dog tags . . ."

I fumbled, and the three of them stared at me. "It's not about him," I said, finally.

Wilt brushed his long bangs out of his eyes and focused on me. He spoke slowly. "I think you'll find, Maddie, that it's going to be very much about him . . . sooner or later —"

"Sooner being a lot fucking better, if you have any hope of getting your byline anywhere near this piece," snapped Ted.

"It's not the byline." The words *you reptile asshole* hanging unsaid between us.

" *'It's not the byline,'* " he mimicked, in a smarmy mincing singsong.

Flaming reptile asshole.

"Why would I tell you," I said, "if I don't have the assignment?"

"Why would I ask you," said Ted, "if you were no longer employed here?"

Wilt stood up from the table. "Hey, man . . . lay the hell off her," he said, hooking his thumbs in his belt and glaring down at Ted. Mr. Natural to the rescue.

"That's right," said Simon, Wilt's Sancho

Panza, taking a step closer to him and crossing his arms, staring up at Ted. I'd never seen Simon defiant, and even the fluorescent light seemed to glint off the top of his head more sharply, the dark curls over his ears to bristle — the man was a pissed-off hedgehog.

I turned toward the two of them. "You guys know the players in this. I've already talked to Archie Sembles, and I know he was threatened, told to keep quiet after he spoke to Wilt."

The three of them stood silent for a second, and I was shaking. But instead of getting further ticked off at me, Ted did an emotional one-eighty, slapped me on the back, and said, "Well, it's about damn *time* you got serious. We might make something of you yet."

Sure, he did it more for them than for me, but I'd take what I could get, and I'd managed to avoid telling any of them why I knew the guy whose name was on those tags.

CHAPTER 32

Ted finally said he was glad to have me continue with the article, and I told him I'd be happy as hell to have whatever input Wilt could give me, so Wilt dragged me over to his desk.

I was holding Simon's file on the Rose Girls, but couldn't find a clear spot on which to set it down, so Wilt leaned across to pluck the photocopy of his original article out from the side.

"So what's your next step on this?" he asked.

"Hell if I know. What would you do?"

"Well, let's look this over, Madeline," he said, "see who you've talked to out of my old sources. . . . Who was the cop? Have you talked with him?"

"He wasn't forthcoming with the sound bites," I said. "Nobody was, to tell you the truth. Sembles was convinced that if he talked to me he was going to be seriously messed up, so even when he wasn't nodding out he wasn't exactly psyched."

"I'm hip. But Sembles, he's a local dude, right? Any idea where he lives?"

"Marcellus or Bridgeport or something, but there's no way he'd talk to me again," I said.

"They'll all talk, Maddie, you just have to find the right motivation."

"Oh, what, like offer to buy him a bulletproof vest? I'm serious, Wilt, the guy was terrified. I really think he's a dead end."

"So get in his face, Maddie. If he's getting wiggy on you it's because he's close to the stuff you need to know," said Wilt. "You've just gotta hammer him until he talks to you. Find a lever . . ."

I must have looked freaked, because he just gave me a little punch in the shoulder and said, "It sounds like you might need a little *negative* incentive for this guy. If there's nothing he wants, figure out what he *doesn't* want. What's he scared *of?*"

"He's scared somebody's going to find out he talked to me, but I don't even know who. I think it's the cop, but maybe he's just the heavy for somebody else. I don't have any goddamn idea who's behind the threat."

"Who's the cop? You haven't said."

I shifted my weight from one foot to the other.

Wilt raised an eyebrow, but then shrugged and let my lack of an answer go unchallenged.

He probably thought I was making sure he couldn't scoop me, but that wasn't it. I just didn't want to show all my cards yet. I didn't want anyone else following up on what I was pursuing, or hounding me further. I was too scared of screwing things up if I were to face more pressure.

He leaned back in his chair. "If Sembles doesn't want to talk because he's afraid someone's gonna find out," he said, "all you have to do is tell him you'll make it known he told you everything, whether he does or not. Tell him you know perfectly well who 'they' are. Make it sound like it's an even bigger conspiracy than he suspected, what the hell?"

"And what if it really is? What if I coerce him to talk and he *does* get fucked up for it?"

"What, by the second gunman on the grassy knoll? It doesn't work like that, Madeline. Bad guys are like roaches, the worst thing you can do to them is turn on the lights. They want to stay in the dark, where it's safe and they seem bigger and nastier than they really are."

Wilt pulled a phone book from under a pile of old grocery bags. He flipped through the pages. "Here he is," he said, "Archibald Sembles. Tell him you want to meet tonight."

He turned the book toward me and shoved his phone across the desk.

"I can't," I said.

"Can't what?"

"Tonight. Dean is calling from Canada . . . he might not be near a phone again for

331

weeks, there's no way to get him on the road. . . ."

Wilt rolled his eyes.

"Any other night," I said. "Honest to God."

"Dial the phone," he said. "Meet him for goddamn brunch, all I care."

My stomach went into a nifty little helix. "Aw, Wilt, you're going to make me do this with an audience?" I said.

"We can sit here all day, Madeline. I don't have no stinking deadlines. My piece for the week's already in."

"Jesus Christ," I said, reaching for the receiver.

"Yeah, yeah, yeah . . ." he said. "Just dial."

By the middle of the phone call with Sembles, just to add to my misery, Ted came over to lean on the back of my chair and listen in, and Simon was standing quietly on Wilt's side of the desk. I was so nervous the soles of my feet were wet, slicking up the lining of my old black loafers as I scrunched my toes in embarrassed misery.

"So I'm coming to your house at eleven tomorrow morning, Archie, and I'm not leaving until you talk to me," I said, trying to sound like I even half believed the whole line of hooey myself, much less meant any of it.

But after a while I had him, I could tell, even though I sounded like the lamest-ever guest bad guy from some cheesy *Starsky and Hutch* episode. Sembles just kept mumbling "Oh God oh God oh God" between every rasping intake of breath.

Wilt was making hand gestures at me, holding his hands out palms-up and pushing them toward the ceiling . . . *ramp it higher.*

"They know me," I said, looking away from him and trying to sound menacing. "They know my car. And all they need is to see me there, Archie. Even if you don't say a word to me, even if you're not home, Archie, you're fucked. Tell me what you know, and I'm your best friend. Don't tell me, and you have no protection at all." Then I couldn't think of another word to say, so after a minute of silence on my end and whimpering on his, I just laid the phone back in its cradle.

Ted said, "Attagirl!" and gave me a clap on the back, which was a relief, but threatening Sembles just felt wrong, especially if I *was* really putting him in danger.

"And you do that all the time?" I asked Wilt, after Ted went back into his office.

"The poor guy's terrified, and I just lied my ass off. I feel like I should wash my mouth out with Ajax."

"You were great," said Wilt.

Simon just gave me a shy smile.

"No, really, Wilt. I mean, I want to be all, like, 'Madeline Dare, Cub Reporter,' and do you proud, but that was kind of . . . *slimy.*"

"Fight slime with slime," he said.

Simon sighed. "I know how you feel, Maddie," he said quietly. "I'm always more comfortable with a camera in front of me than talking, but I think you're doing the right thing."

"It'll get easier," said Wilt. "Don't worry. And besides, you're using your powers for the forces of good, here, remember? It's one of those ends-justifying-the-means things. No big deal."

Yeah, sure, I thought — that's probably just what Kissinger told Nixon after they bombed Cambodia.

When I got home, the little red light on the answering machine was blinking. I hit Play and heard the mousy hiss of the micro-tape, rewinding on its micro-spools.

"One . . . new . . . message . . ." said the little lady who lived inside the plastic box.

I sucked in my breath and willed it to be Mom on the tape. Or Kenny.

Not Dean.

"Hi, Bunny!" Dean's recorded voice was tinny, with waves of static crashing all around like he was standing under a tin awning during a hurricane. In Finland.

"I'm so sorry I missed you. I wish you were there so I could tell you how much I already miss you in person. I am so sick of bunk beds. I am so sick of steak and eggs. I wish I had some tabouleh, and that you were right here. I'd rather have you than the tabouleh. If I'm anywhere near a phone tomorrow morning, I'll try again, but it's pretty —"

Click.

I hit Rewind.

I hit Rewind a few more times after that, just staring into the little speaker grille on the machine's beige plastic, as if I could see him in there if I really tried hard enough. I'd started pacing, waiting for the phone to ring, so I put a sweater on and wandered out to sit on the porch. I sat out there shivering — arms wrapped tight around my knees, legs still jiggling like crazy — but knew that it might be ten months before I got the chance to be out here again at the rate the evenings were cooling, this late in

September.

The night was clear and still. There was no traffic on Green Street, and I could hear a dog whining from somebody's backyard up the hill.

I wondered what my friends from college were doing. Probably attending splendidly witty literary parties in New York where iceberg lettuce was only admitted as performance art.

Lapthorne would be lounging in his lapidary library. Ellis was probably frolicking in some Berkshire steel-sculptor's meadow with a rowdy gang of itinerant poets and a gallon of Chianti. And here I was, freezing in the dark, life blowing past me like a limo bombing down the thruway: close enough to whip your hair back, impossible to touch.

I had to admit that the worst of it was how whiny I'd become. Maybe Dean was right — the city of Sore Excuse was perfectly fine and all the trouble with it resided in me, in the weak and raddled Swiss cheese of my soul. I'd practiced fear and self-loathing in some of the world's most renowned locations: been crestfallen in Carmel, morose in Manhattan, a "Nattering Nabob of Negativity" in Nepal. The only place I'd ever really been happy was boarding school, probably only because everyone around me was so miserable that my usual state seemed, for the first time, normal. Maybe I *was* deluding myself when I thought that leaving this town would make things any different.

Then I thought, no — it *was* really different out there. Lapthorne's house . . .

The phone rang.

I raced into the kitchen, my "Dean?" into the phone breathless.

The response was Lapthorne's deep voice saying *"Chère cousine?"*

I was disappointed. Relieved. Fucked in the head.

"Oh," I said, "hey there. I'm just sitting here bemoaning the lack of civilization in my general vicinity."

"Well, how about that marvelous husband of yours? He sounds more than civilized."

"He is," I said, looking out toward the sofa, "but sadly he's still in Canada, busy inventing . . ." I glanced at the stove clock — just after ten.

"More power to him," he said.

"Yeah, well," I said, and proceeded to tell him the story of the shadows and photographs. When I moved on to the proposed meeting with Sembles, however, he seemed alarmed.

"Madeline, I don't want you to think that I doubt your abilities, but please understand that I'm leery of putting another young woman in danger, in light of my past failings to safeguard my friends," he said. "Are you sure you wouldn't like to postpone that meeting? Let me go with you. . . ."

"I think this is a limited-time offer," I said. "We've got Sembles believing he's over a barrel, and if we told him to get up so we could move it, I'm not sure he'd still believe us when we told him to lie back down across the damn thing."

"Point taken, my dear. But I want to know when you expect to be done."

"An hour? Not long."

"Will you go back to your office?"

"Yeah, tons of stuff to do."

"Ellis has the number? We'll be out and around, so I'm going to call you there. Make sure you're all right. I'm not prepared to lose my favorite cousin, just when I'm really getting to know her."

So Ellis had gotten lucky. Maybe I should have been surprised — even happy, but all I felt was tired.

"I'm flattered," I said. "Aside from all the drama of this past weekend, I greatly enjoyed your company. And Ellis . . ."

"She's right here. Would you like to exchange confidences?" he asked with a rumbling laugh.

"No," I said. I was too lonely to listen to her being all happy about a new guy. "I'm . . . hoping Dean will phone, actually. I missed him earlier, but his message said he'd try again. . . ."

"Let you go then," said Lapthorne. "Don't forget I'll be calling tomorrow."

"Promise," I said.

I replaced the receiver. By one o'clock, I had to admit the phone wasn't going to ring again.

CHAPTER 33

Dean called the next morning. I croaked a hello into the receiver while trying to undo the jammed espresso handle, almost dropping it and the phone into the sink.

"Bunny . . ."

"Oh, it's good to hear your voice. . . ."

Forget the coffee, I thought. I just wanted to soak him up through the phone line.

"I'm sorry I didn't get you last night."

"It's fine," I said. "I was thinking about you, but you probably couldn't find a town again?"

There was a burst of static on his end, then ". . . tried to . . . but we were . . . freaking Yukon . . ." then silence for a moment too long.

"Dean?"

". . . nothing but trees . . . did you?"

"Did I what?"

Static again. A burst of it like big surf.

"— chance? . . ." his voice burst through, then another crush of static.

"Chance? What?"

". . . find you? . . ." said Dean. ". . . god-damn get on a plane for home right . . . I can't believe I left, because if anything happens to you, Bunny . . ."

"It's okay . . ."

"I mean, I'm up here and you can't call me if you need help, and the whole thing's scaring the goddamn pants off me. I *have* to know you're okay. Nothing else matters. Say the word, I'll commandeer a pickup and get my ass to an airport, soon as I hang up the phone."

"Dean," I said, "*fuck* that. I would never forgive myself. Your grinder . . . all the work —"

Another rattling scrimmage of electrons blotted him out for a second. I pressed a hip against the kitchen sink, twisting my fingers hard into the phone cord so I wouldn't start bashing the receiver against the countertop.

". . . here in the bunks at night," he continued, "and over every meal, and the whole . . . guys are bitching about women. Ex-wives who screwed them over. Girl-friends who constantly whine and pout because they want more . . . someplace fancy. Custody . . . and I don't . . . so god-damn lucky I can't let on, because they'd pitch me out the . . ."

Silence.

"Dean?" I turned sideways and braced my back against the counter's edge, like that might change the reception.

"Can you . . . ?" he said.

"What?"

"Promise me you're . . . if I know . . . safe."

"I promise," I said, scrunching my toes. "I promise I'm safe."

Another ping. ". . . you, Bunny, *so* much . . ."

The tone of his voice filled in the blanks enough so my knees gave and I slid down the base cabinet. When my butt reached the floor, I clenched my eyes shut and said, "Oh, man, I miss you like hell. . . ."

The phone spat some Emergency Broadcast System sound effects, and then Dean's voice came through perfectly again, just for a second.

". . . clothes off," he was whispering, "soon as . . ."

One more crackle, two gargling pops, and then it was nothing but dial tone.

I sat there holding the phone to my ear for so long that even the woman who comes on and says "moo Mee MEEEEEE . . . please hang up and try your call again" finally packed it in.

Of course like three seconds after I'd managed to go back to sleep, the phone rang again. I peeled an eye and checked the alarm clock. Five of nine.

It wouldn't be Dean again, so I didn't hurry. Picked up on the fifth ring, right before the machine would've taken it.

"Madwoman!" said Ellis, sounding entirely too perky.

"Don't tell me, you just had to wake me up to tell me how magnificent my cousin is in the sack," I said, yawning.

"Well, he's finally in the kitchen, making breakfast, so I have a minute to gush detail. He's taking another day off work, which must be a good sign. Anyway, it's not like I could tell you last night . . ."

I growled while yanking on the still-jammed espresso thing.

"Hell is that?" she said. "You have a dog there?"

"Sorry," I said, just as the handle gave way. The puck of grounds flew out, bouncing once before it smashed into powder and chunks by the pantry door.

"Fucking piece of goddamn fascistic garbage *crap,"* I said to the implement in my hand.

"Have your hideous coffee yet?" she asked.

"Trying," I said. "Damn machine . . ."

"All right, don't try talking yet. Just sit back and let me overwhelm you with endless detail before he gets back."

"I have to?" I said, trying to smash a kilo of French Market into the wimpy-ass strainer thing.

"Oh, come on, when was the last time I subjected you to endlessly annoying new-crush babble?"

"Memorial Day weekend . . ." I said, measuring water into the wretched machine. "Most of July . . . That *entire* Tuesday afternoon about six weeks ago, which was during *work* . . ."

"Rot in hell," she said.

"Ungrateful bitch."

"Rot in hell double."

"Slut."

"Slut."

"Really?" I said. "I can still be a slut?"

"What, get married and suddenly your legs fuse?"

"Minute you finish the vows," I said. "*Swock!* Virtual mermaid."

"Drink your goddamn coffee."

I pushed the On button. Wondered if I could cram my head in there far enough to get my mouth right under the little spout. Cut out the middleman.

"Can I talk about all the astonishing sex now?" she said.

"Like I could stem the tide."

"Okay, so he's amazing, and thank you very, very, very much for being related to him, and for believing he didn't do it, because believe me there's no way he could have done it. I mean, how could he have done it and be so amazing? It's just not possible. Really."

"Got it bad," I said.

"Worst ever," she agreed. "I'm eternally in your debt. I mean, the man is a genius with an ice cube —"

"Ewwww."

"Drink your damn coffee so you can actually converse. I hate it when you just grunt at me in the morning, especially when I can't throw stuff at your head, in person."

"I'm not grunting," I said, pouring the

now-finished atomic caffeine splendor into my habitual glass. "That was an 'eww-www.' "

"Why didn't you and Lapthorne ever . . ."

I reached for the sugar. "We just didn't."

"Should've."

"Would've," I said. "*Probably.* Not like an invitation was forthcoming."

"Through no fault of yours . . ."

"I guess. Sure." Soon as I poured in the milk, I drank half the Crude right down.

"No, I mean I think he feels too . . . protective? Not like the guy doesn't dig you."

"Whatever."

"Serious," she said. "How he checks you out when he thinks nobody's looking? *Covetous* as hell. Pissed me right off."

"Really?" I said.

"Oh please, he *so* wants to nail you. . . ."

"Thanks. Means a lot."

"I'm sorry I . . . well, since you didn't ever get to."

"Don't be. Live it up. *Mi* cousin *es su* cousin. I'm overjoyed for you both."

"Yeah. You're just *dripping* with overjoyed."

"*Not* about this — you guys — really really really," I said.

She waited.

"Dean called earlier," I said. "First time in forever, and it's hard, you know? We had this huge fight before he left, but on the phone this morning he was so great and that's even worse. Because he's still away and now I'm not pissed at him or worried he's pissed at me . . . so . . ."

That made her fidget. Too real and private, or maybe coming off like an attempt to trump her new guy with a spouse card.

I could practically hear her plucking at Lapthorne's Porthault sheets. Which I didn't envy. At all. Not for a second.

Because I would have done things exactly the same, even if I'd known Lapthorne was still single, all this time. Even if I'd known he was interested in me the tiniest bit, that I could have invited him to a party years ago, and that he'd have picked up the phone all happy to hear from me, there in his perfect house in the *real* city, with all that beautiful silver and the stupid library, not to mention the fucking boat with the fucking Winslow Homer watercolor — not a print but the genuine goddamn article — hanging in it as an *afterthought,* for chrissake, since there was so much more to go around.

I would have done things exactly the same.

I would have married Dean, who was worth more than all the world's sublime boats and magnificent sheets and chilled salad forks and heartbreakingly beautiful loafers and exquisitely delicious cousins put together, damn it.

"I *love* Dean," I said. "Just the sound of his voice is . . . I'm so happy. It's only when I look out the window and it's still . . . Syracuse, you know? Being here alone? I mean, Dean's my whole *raison d'upstate* . . . I *miss* him."

"Cha," she said. "I guess *so.*"

"Sorry, I'm *totally* boring you."

"No!" she protested too much. "You just sound really, um . . . Maybe you should go to bed earlier? Makes such a huge difference. I slept like the proverbial baby last night, can't recommend it highly enough."

Then she sighed, grotesquely content and happy.

"You *slept?* Talk about letting down the side," I said.

"Well, not at *first* . . ."

"Okay. Start with the ice cube, go from there," I said. "Inquiring matrons want to know."

I finished my coffee while she babbled on. God knows I owed her a patient ear — she'd had to hear me talk my way through the first flushes of lust often enough, most egregiously when I first met Dean, and besides, listening allowed me to think about what the hell I should say to Sembles.

I knew the only hope on that score was to just show up there, open my mouth, and hope for the best. So as a palliative measure I egged Ellis on until it was about five minutes before I had to leave, having pulled on my clothes while she yammered happily away. Thank God for long phone cords.

CHAPTER 34

There was a note thumbtacked to Sembles's front door: "Madeline come on in back in a few minutes."

I was late. It'd taken me a while to find his house amidst the warren of tiny bungalows near the train yard.

The neighborhood was primly neat, down to the green precision of each handkerchief front lawn, the tidy rows of children's bikes. All the streets were named for presidents. I couldn't imagine a junkie here.

I looked at the note again.

Despite the fact that *I'd* threatened Sembles with the idea some bad guys would recognize my car — or perhaps because of it — seeing my name broadcast on his door gave me the willies.

I took the paper down, shoving it in my pocket, and the motion made the door swing inward a few inches. Even this slight gap in the entrance let out a gust of foul air. The place stank — a musky, invasive reek that smelled like someone had left a fridge door open for days in July. I grabbed the handle, keeping the thing from opening wider, then knocked and called out "Mr. Sembles?" a few times before I got up the nerve to cross the threshold.

The smell was immediately stronger. I could feel it coating my throat and nostrils, and reflexively started taking shallow breaths through my mouth alone, but it was so powerful I could literally taste the stench.

When my eyes adjusted to the dim light, the first thing I saw was the edge of a pale, liver-spotted hand flopped over the arm of a sofa, just beyond the doorframe at the end of the microscopic front hall. There was a low hum, like a TV was on with the sound turned way down.

I wondered if Sembles had shot up and nodded out, forgetting our appointment, but then he wouldn't have left a note. I stopped and cleared my throat ostentatiously in the hope that he'd wake up without me having to roust him.

The hand didn't move, so I took another step forward and said "Oh, *great*" out loud as I saw more of the forearm, including the bloodspattered shirt cuff.

I took a deep breath, held it, and moved forward until I had a full view. The hum was flies. They were everywhere — circling his head, at the corners of his eyes, and clustered especially thick and blue-black around his neck.

His limbs were angled oddly. Left knee bent and turned outward, right leg resting on the seat, as though arrested mid-kick. His right arm was parallel to that, high along the sofa's back. Both his toes were pointed like he was doing a little jig.

Struwwelpeter. I would have recognized the posture even without the pair of thumbs sticking out of Sembles's mouth, the long scissors stuck in his neck.

I swallowed down bile.

Sembles's clothes, from his neck to his knees, were blood-saturated — the stuff thick and gummy now so the fabric looked like reddish-brown leather, but there wasn't a spot on the pastel afghan used for a slip-cover.

Too clean, all around. He hadn't been killed there.

I stood there, unable to shut my eyes but

unable to focus on him — just stunned for a dragging moment.

I could see in the kitchen, just a corner of it through an open doorway, and it occurred to me I might not be alone with what was left of Sembles.

I stepped slowly toward the aperture, edging toward a view of the whole room — dishes and a Coke can by the sink, a glimpse of dull avocado stove rimed with grease and dust, a light panel in the ceiling still on and buzzing, though midday glare spilled into the room. Another step forward, easing onto a floorboard I willed not to creak — nothing, the room was empty.

I looked up. One of the padded chairs was yanked back from a card table, tipped against the wall with its splayed-and-chromed front legs rearing in protest.

On the table itself, a juice glass had tipped and rolled, spilling brown liquid, maybe the Coke? It looked sticky, drying to a stain from the outside in.

A single fly walked around the edge, noodling for sugar, missing the feast in the living room.

So whoever'd done this wasn't a guest Sembles would sit with companionably over a couple of sodas — he'd jumped or been dragged out of his seat.

There were two more doors behind the table, both ajar. I stepped closer — broom closet, empty bedroom. I was keyed so high that when I let my breath go I got smacked with a headrush and had to reach for the counter.

I turned around and walked slowly-slowly back into the room with Sembles. One more door.

"Bachelor number two," I whispered, and threw it open. Nothing — a pink and gray fifties bathroom, like Band-Aids on an elephant. I made it to the toilet just in time to puke forth that morning's coffee, then walked out to the living room and picked up the dead guy's phone.

When the 911 operator answered, I said, "I want to report a murder."

"May I have your location, ma'am?"

"I'm in his house. I was supposed to meet him here but he's, you know, dead —"

"Ma'am, I need the *address* of your location."

I looked down, it was inked on the inside of my wrist. "It's 1913 Fillmore, by the rail yard."

"I'll dispatch emergency services."

"Could you just send the cops? It's not a CPR situation or anything."

Maybe it could have been. Maybe it could

have been no situation at all if I hadn't fucked with this — pushed him into talking to me. All very well for me to think I could gad about, playing parlor sleuth, tra la. Without me, Sembles wouldn't be rotting in the heat, rapidly becoming a pool of slop — meat soup. I'd known it wasn't right, but still blew off that tinny little voice as fear, not conscience.

I took a deep breath and gagged again.

"Ma'am?" interrupted the voice.

"Um, yeah?"

"Why don't you go outside and sit down. Get some air. That way you can direct the police and EMTs to the location when they arrive."

"Good," I said, light-headed. "Okay, good. I'll do that. Thank you so much. You've been so helpful."

And just as I'd done the day before when I finished with talking with Sembles, I placed the handset back in its cradle without a goodbye.

I walked shakily back outside and stood on the front stoop, waiting for the cops, biting the inside of my cheek and feeling the enormous and wretched certainty that I'd caused someone to die.

I started to black out, swaying a little, so I edged down one step and let my knees give, hands wide for balance, full dead weight plummeting. Landed so hard I heard my tailbone smack the top step's concrete edge.

It hurt worse than shit and then kept building, like the shock of water so hot you think it's cold, pain rising in pitch until my ass and my teeth and my ribs and my eye sockets sang with it. All I could do was hang on to my knees and ride it out.

It peaked, finally, then started to let me go, slower than it came on, of course, but still every inch a blessing as the tide of hurt ebbed, dying back until it was just a keen pulse in my coccyx.

Everything was clear and sharp again. I could breathe. I was alive. I was grateful.

I could think.

I started wondering about the note on the door. The interior of the house had been fussily immaculate, except the spilled Coke. If Sembles hadn't been killed here, he was brought back dead and couldn't have posted the message himself.

The killer knew my name. Knew I was expected.

How many people had I told? *Think.*

Of course Lapthorne, but Ellis was with him in New York all night.

Ted. Wilt. Simon.

I'd made the appointment with Sembles

last night around eight o'clock, so I knew he'd been alive then. The clock in the car had just read quarter past eleven, when I parked.

It was six hours from the city to here, so thankfully Lapthorne really *was* an impossibility — I'd talked to him last night at ten and Ellis had said he was in the kitchen when she called this morning at nineish — no time to drive up and back.

The blood was thick and coagulated, so Sembles had been dead for a while. How long did blood stay wet? The cops would know stuff like that.

My brain was stammering. How would someone get the body inside? They'd have to have done it at night — there was no attached garage to drive into and the houses were too closely packed to get away with humping a corpse up the front or even back steps in daylight. Plus it was a blue-collar neighborhood, so people left early for work. You'd have to have had Sembles inside before five, say, to be safe.

The first patrol car screeched to the curb and I tried to stand up. When I realized my legs wouldn't work, I burst into tears.

Two cops got out: one older and kind of stumpy looking, with a gray crewcut, and a red-haired kid who looked like he should be yawning through fourth-grade math instead of riding shotgun in a blue uniform and heavy black brogues.

They slammed the doors and started coming up the flagstones. The engine ticked slowly. Cold out.

"The dead guy's inside," I said, sniffling and all shaky. "His name is Archie Sembles. I was supposed to meet him to talk about a newspaper article."

Another cop car pulled up, and then a fire truck and two minutes later an ambulance. People started leaking out of the houses along the street.

I brushed a fly away from my face, thought about where else it might have landed recently, and felt distinctly unwell.

The older cop and the two guys from the second patrol car talked to the EMTs and then went inside. The fourth-grader sat by me, one step down.

He pulled out a steno pad. "Ma'am? Can you tell me your name and address?"

I looked at him. Younger than me. Face guileless and nearly Osmond-sweet.

"Madeline Dare," I said, "Two-oh-six Green Street. Down-city."

The name-plaque thing on his shirt pocket read "Franklin."

"Okay, Miss Dare? Can you tell me a little

bit about what happened here today? You stated you were going to talk about a newspaper with the deceased?"

"Not *about* . . ."

The fly came back. Looping around slow and loose, like it was drunk now. Satiated.

"I mean not, like, his *subscription* . . ."

The fly wheeled toward my face. Jonathan Livingston Carrion-Swiller.

I lifted my hand to bat it away, feeble and jittery. Closed my throat against a surge of acid.

"Miss Dare?" Franklin sounded all worried.

I dug into a pocket for my card from the *Weekly*. Handed it to him and shut my eyes.

"Madeline? You okay?"

I shook my head. Very. Slowly.

Got all sweaty, then, like the bad juice in my belly had to leach out through my skin if I wouldn't let it flood my throat.

"Feel faint?" he asked.

"Pukey."

"Tell you a secret," he whispered. "Me too."

I opened my eyes. "Thank you."

Ten years old if he was a day. I swear.

"Hey," I said. "What's your name? I mean, aside from Officer Franklin."

"Grant."

"Okay," I said. "Grant."

"Want to try leaning forward? Sometimes it helps, just letting your head rest between your knees."

"Maybe we both should?"

He looked away, a little embarrassed.

"No offense," I said.

The older cops turned toward us, a phalanx of grim purpose.

He stood up.

I didn't want him to leave. "Grant?"

He looked down at me.

"Don't go in there," I said. "It's really gross."

They loaded me gently into the patrol car. Its back seat was composed entirely of hard black plastic.

CHAPTER 35

Officers Sully and Franklin were, I have to say, terrific. They pulled right over when I said I thought I was going to throw up, and Franklin — Grant — kindly gave me a stick of Doublemint after my final toss of bright yellow bile by the side of the road.

I apologized profusely, and Sully said there was nothing to be embarrassed about at all, that you never knew how it was going to take you, and some of the toughest guys he knew had had their stomachs go all delicate on them all of a sudden, like, and he was just happy I'd made it out of the car.

I felt better, but everything seemed as though it was happening in the next room. Even when I was throwing up, I was not so much experiencing it as remembering it while it was still happening — *vujà dé*. It was strange, because right after I'd found Sembles's body, everything had seemed hyper-real for a while, as though I were more there than there, but now everything was soft and wobbly around the edges like God was hitting the wa-wa pedal.

The police station was only five minutes away from Sembles's house, and when they brought me inside they said the detective would just want to talk to me about what I'd seen and everything, that it was what they did when something like this happened, just talk to everybody so they could get their bearings, and did I want to call someone and maybe have a soda to settle my stomach?

I welcomed the soda idea, and said I probably should call somebody but wasn't sure who yet. Maybe somebody at work, because my husband was in Canada, and was it okay that my car was still there at the house, I might need to ask for a ride but maybe I could just walk back, it didn't seem that far, really.

But I was thinking that they hadn't given me any Miranda warning, so maybe it meant I wasn't a suspect.

I was being treated with kindness and pity and solicitude, not suspicion, but maybe that's what they did when they really did suspect you? I didn't know.

My only exposure to cops, outside Schneider and Kenny, was a couple of speeding tickets and a tsk-tsk when I'd crashed my moped. Maybe these guys were just doing a "good cop/good cop" routine — a new twist.

Sully asked if I didn't want to sit down, because I was looking pale again, and said I didn't have to decide who to call right away, to take all the time I needed, nobody was in any hurry and I might have to wait a while for the detective to come back from the scene anyway. Franklin left the room and returned with the soda, which I thanked him for and sipped gratefully, if only because it made me shut up.

Despite my reservations, I had a bad case of the post-shock chatties, and thought I'd better take a minute to figure out what the hell I was going to say to a detective, anyway, before I blathered the whole thing out. I didn't know how the local jurisdictions were organized, and although I was pretty sure this would be a different outfit than the one that had handled the original Rose Girls case, maybe these guys were all old friends or even enemies of Schneider's and *he* might not be the most politic person to mention, no matter which.

I mean, for all I knew, these guys still invited Schneider over for barbecues and horseshoe tournaments, and God knows the case had been open long enough that they might want to pin it on anyone handy. I sure as shit didn't want to get Lapthorne and maybe even Ellis dragged into it, especially now that his innocence seemed truly verifiable to the greater world.

I latched onto the idea that I just shouldn't bring up anything I wasn't asked about specifically, and then realized that the best person to call was Wilt. First because I wanted him to know that I'd been right, that we'd set up Sembles in the worst possible way, and second because out of everybody he was the only one who couldn't really say "I told you so," which was the last thing I wanted to be told right then.

Sully let me use the phone on his desk.

When the call was put through to Wilt, he said, "Hey, Maddie! So how'd your first big interview go?"

"It didn't. Sembles is dead."

"Aw, Jesus," he said. "Jesus Christ. And I'm guessing it wasn't something nice and simple like a heart attack?"

"He was . . . no, it wasn't something simple," I said.

"Aw, Jesus . . . *Aw.* You okay? Where are you?"

"I'm at the police station. Bridgeport. I need to talk to the detective, when he gets here, but I might need a ride later?"

"I'm on it. I'll stay right here by the phone until you call back. Just be cool. Polite, but, you know, *keep the faith.* Know what I mean?"

"That's right," I said. "I was feeling a little sick earlier, but now I think I'm okay. These guys have been great." I gave Sully and Franklin the best smile I could manage.

"Right on," said Wilt. "Power to the people."

Hippies. Jesus Christ.

The stuff with the detective wasn't that big a deal. His name was Fritz Huber, he looked exactly like Captain Kangaroo, and he shook my hand with a dry meaty paw before leading me over to his desk. It was in the corner of the main room — walls painted mint-green halfway up, faded beige above — with a couple of battered olive chairs hunched around it. His had wheels.

"You know this guy outside work?" asked Huber, hitching up the belt his gun hung off and easing his considerable bulk into his chair.

The desk looked like something army-issue, sooty green and massive enough to support the groaning weight of government work. He leaned on his elbows, forearms like tapered Smithfield hams, and flipped up the cover from a spiral pad of mint-toned paper.

"I met him at the state fair," I said. "Seemed like a good guy to do an article on. He cut those old silhouettes . . . knew a lot about the history. Local character, y' know? People like that stuff."

Huber leaned back in his seat and spun slowly toward me, looking skeptically down his nose.

Here it comes, I thought, the cough and squawk of a dispatch radio filling the silence while he considered me, but he dropped his eyes and only asked when I'd last spoken to Sembles, where I'd been the previous night, and whether or not I'd seen anyone else in the vicinity before or after I'd found the body. Not "So how'd you get this guy killed?" or "What the hell did you think you were doing?"

He put down his ballpoint, coughed into a fist, and then started feeding thickly triplicate forms into his old green Underwood manual. Everything was green — the color they choose for mental hospitals to calm down the patients.

I gave him my address, which got me a raised eyebrow — down-city. One o' them liberals — then my work and home phone numbers.

"We'll wanna get your prints, if you don't mind," he said. "Exclude you from any found in the house."

All I could think of was that that pretty much ruled out any second career as an international jewel thief, which was first strangely upsetting to me and then made me feel guilty as hell considering I wasn't dead and Sembles was and it seemed like a stupid and petty thing to fixate on under the circumstances.

Franklin-the-kid was given the intimate task of rolling each of my fingertips sideways across a damp black pad and then an index card. My hands trembled in his. A test? He handed me a Wash'n Dri wet nap, but it didn't get the ink off.

I assured Huber that I'd be in town for the full extent of the foreseeable future, and would be happy to answer any further questions he might have. He gave me his card, and asked me to call him if anything else came to mind, whether or not it seemed important.

I thanked him, shook his hand carefully with my sooty fingers, and promised I would.

I shoved my fists in my pockets as I walked outside, and only then realized that the note from Sembles's door was still in my pocket.

I stood outside waiting for Wilt and started to second-guess myself. Maybe now was the time to bust back into the station, hand the piece of paper over, and start telling them about the connection with the Rose Girls. But did I want them to know that the murderer knew me? Knew I was coming?

Then I thought maybe I should wash my hands of the whole thing, get back to writing about what I was comfortable confronting — green beans and Jell-O, if it came to that.

I mean, Lapthorne had a credible alibi, and for all I knew they'd find a kilo of slam and Sembles's works under the kitchen sink and think I was there to tie off and fix.

Worse, they might think I was making a delivery.

My paranoia was not helped by the fact that Wilt's trusty blue Gremlin reeked of dope. He got out from behind the wheel, unfolding his long legs to tower over the car.

The knot of his wide paisley tie was pulled down to rest all scrunched at the third button of his shirt, his suit looking like it had been wadded up in a wet towel for a week. Simon got out of the passenger seat and moved to the back.

"You buying air freshener from Cheech and Chong?" I asked.

I shut the door quickly, in the hope that more of the atmosphere wouldn't leak out and rouse the K-9 unit or set off smoke alarms in the station house. "Man, I'm glad you didn't drive me over here. I'd be asking you for bail instead of a ride."

"Want me to roll down the windows?" Wilt asked, throwing the car into gear and pulling back onto the road.

"Not until we're over the border," I said, "and thank you for coming to get me."

"Least I could do, considering I pushed you into it," he said. "How was the detective?"

"The questions were routine, I guess —

where I was last night, what I was supposed to be doing with Sembles today, did I see anybody. When I left I had a sudden urge to go back in and tell them everything I know, not that I really know all that much."

"In my experience, you can always go back and tell more, but you never get the opportunity to take it back once you've started. I think you should hang on to what you know and see where it takes you, at least for a couple of days . . . not that you're going to be listening to me for a while, if you've got any sense."

Wilt got quiet for a minute, then blurted out, "Listen, Maddie, I'm sorry as hell about this. I thought you were just jittery because you were a novice, and I didn't respect the fact that you had what were legitimate reservations about pushing this guy to talk."

"Wilt, I didn't listen to myself either. I was too pissed at Ted for suggesting I couldn't handle it, when I knew I had no idea what I was doing. Don't worry about it. You know where we're supposed to be going?"

"Got the address right here . . . Simon looked it up for me," said Wilt.

Simon turtled his head forward between the seats. "Figured I'd come along for the ride, get shots of the place in case we need them later," he said. "How're you feeling, Madeline? It must have been pretty awful to walk in there and find him like that."

I caught his eye in the rearview mirror. He looked even more pale, haggard, and concerned than usual, his round cheeks and bald head with its tonsure of dark curls giving him the air of a once-jolly-but-now-clinically-depressed monk who spent all his waking hours in a dim scriptorium. All he needed was a little brown hooded robe with the rope belt and sandals. The hair shirt went without saying.

"I've had better mornings," I said. "But so did Sembles, poor guy."

We pulled up right behind my car in front of the dead man's little house and all got out.

Chapter 36

The two guys tailed me back, so we all got to the parking lot at work around the same time. Wilt and Simon started to head toward the *Weekly,* but I hesitated.

"You know, guys," I said finally, while we waited to cross the street, "I don't think I want to go back in right now. I'd like to talk to my pal Kenny up at the Crown, if that's cool. He used to be a cop, and he's been talking me through this whole thing. I should tell him about all this shit today."

"You could probably use a beer, Madeline," said Wilt. "Promise me you'll eat something first, though, okay? And stay away from those damn pickled eggs."

"Pig knuckles it is, then," I said, and Wilt patted me on the back.

"You take care, Madeline," said Simon, and the two of them walked toward the *Weekly*'s narrow glass door.

Kenny was busy taping a much-photocopied sheet of paper up over the bar when I walked in. There were a bunch of buttocks with wings on them zooming around the page, with the legend "If assholes could fly, this place would be an airport!" in the center.

"Charming," I said, and he looked back over his shoulder at me with a big smile.

"You would know, Madeline," he said. "Set you up with a Shirley Temple?"

"I'd prefer a boilermaker," I said.

"It's too early for you to be drinking something like that," he said.

"I got somebody killed. I'm here to get the 'I told you so' part over with."

"I *never* say I told you so. Best way to increase your life expectancy."

"That and avoiding my company," I said.

He nodded, pulling a tall narrow glass out from under the bar and proceeding, in fact, to construct a Shirley Temple.

"How old's that grenadine?" I asked, before taking a sip.

"I'd worry more about the cherry. Jar's been here since I was in short pants."

I lifted the glass and swallowed some of the sweet, syrupy pinkness. "Hey, that's actually good," I said.

"I can mix a drink. Surprise. You eaten anything since you threw up?"

I blushed. "What's it, on my shirt?"

"Let's just say I've smelled better breath. Not lately, of course," he said, tipping his head toward the two old guys at the other end of the bar. "So. Who was it?"

"Sembles," I said.

"You find him?"

I nodded.

"Nasty?"

I was going to tell him about the thumbs and the scissors and the flies, but my stomach went all acid and my eyelids started to sting and I didn't want to start crying in front of him again, so I just shrugged and dropped my head like there was something really interesting in the bottom of my glass.

Kenny was quiet for a minute. He took one of my hands, held it palm-up in both of his, and looked over my still-darkened fingertips.

"So you called the cops," he said finally, giving it the local pronunciation: *caps*. "And they took you down to the station. Did you fill them in on all the background? Family ties and whatnot?"

"I wanted to talk to you first." I took my hand back gently and stirred my kiddie cocktail with the straw, miserable.

"Finish that," he said, "then wash your hands and I'll bring you toast."

I went to the Ladies, thinking about my promise to call Lapthorne. Wishing I could call Dean instead.

I should've gone back to work to talk things over with Ted, to thank Wilt again for coming to my rescue and Simon for being so reassuringly Simon-like. I knew that I wasn't about to do any of that. The après-adrenaline exhaustion was going to keep my butt glued to the barstool. I only wished Kenny had a cot in the place, the kind they have for naps in kindergarten.

I scrubbed my hands in the skanky little chamber with some wetted rough brown paper towels and syrupy pink soap, which didn't really help, then pumped some extra into my palm and got it into my mouth, tipping my head under the hot faucet so I could swish it through my teeth and spit.

By the time I wandered bandy-legged back to my stool, Kenny had produced a plate of buttered toast.

"Thank you," I said.

"Don't talk. Eat." He stood over me with his arms crossed, waiting until I'd finished the last bite — slow going. For once in my life I had a complete absence of appetite.

"So," began Kenny.

I looked down at the glossy surface of the bar and nodded, expecting that now I'd get my lecture.

"I take it you have concrete evidence of Lapthorne's whereabouts for last night?" he said.

"How'd you know?" I asked.

"Because otherwise that's the first thing you would have told me when you walked in here — I understand you that well, at least, Maddie. You think you're a softie, but in the clinch you see things black and white. If the guy didn't have an alibi, you would have ratted him out the minute they got you down to the station. Even with what I told you, how he was in jail and all of that. So why don't we start with what that alibi is, proceed to the events of the day, and see where we can go from there."

So I told him about the phone calls from Ellis and Lapthorne, that morning and the night before. He nodded when I described how clean the sofa was under Sembles, and after asking me whether I'd checked to see if the house had a basement or an outbuilding, agreed that he had to have been killed elsewhere.

"If I was still on the force, I'd get the phone records, see if anyone else called Sembles last night," said Kenny, "but whoever it was could just as well have shown up at the house, so that's not necessarily important. Tell me more about how he looked when you found him."

I described the whole deal with Sembles's thumbs, the scissors stuck in his neck, how his body seemed to be laid out for presentation. Kenny asked me about the whole *Struwwelpeter* reference, and I explained that Sembles had mentioned it the night of the fair.

"So this is the second one with a story behind it — some kiddie thing, am I right?" he asked.

"Yeah," I said.

"That's messed up," he said.

"It's *all* messed up."

"Even more so."

"Oh," I said, "and there was a note on the front door. I figure he couldn't have written it, but it had my name on it, and it's why I went into the house even though he didn't answer the door."

Kenny was silent for a minute, digesting that. "Okay," he said finally. "That's the most important piece of information we have, Maddie."

"The creepiest, anyway."

"Madeline, the note means that whoever did it is aware of you . . . of your appointment, your involvement. How many people knew you were gonna be up to Sembles's?"

"Well, I told Lapthorne last night. Other than that, there were just people at work . . . Ted, Wilt, and Simon."

I explained about the deal with the shadows in the photographs, then ran the whole meeting at work by him, plus my phone call to harass Sembles.

"And nobody else was in the room with you? Just those three?"

I nodded.

"Did you tell them about the thing with the thumbs? How Sembles had been threatened with that?"

I shut my eyes and thought about it, running back over the conversation in Ted's office, sitting at Wilt's desk.

"No," I said. "I didn't even tell them today, after it all happened. I haven't told Lapthorne about it, either."

"Do those three at work know you didn't talk to anyone else about going to see Sembles?"

"No."

"Tell them you did. Tell them you talked to everybody and your mother about it after you got home last night."

"Why?" I asked.

"Because the information that you were going to have this meeting today had to come from one of those three people, Madeline, and we don't want to confirm that for them."

"And if I didn't tell them about the thing with the thumbs, either one of them knew it already, or he told someone who did," I said. "Like Schneider."

Kenny cocked his finger like a pistol and clucked his tongue.

"So what do I do now?" I asked.

"I think you go back to work and make a point of convincing those three that you don't know shit. Tell them you were on the phone all night with everyone you know. If there's any way you can find out what they were doing last night, great, but don't ask specifically. Especially Simon."

"Simon?"

"I don't like the sound of those 'extra' photographs he had, Maddie. And think about his hands. The killer's a lefty, remember? Those guys have all been in here for drinks after work, over the years. He's got those black fingernails on his left hand, am I right? Some kind of chemical?"

"Amitol," I said, trying to remember which of Simon's hands it was and feeling awful about it.

Kenny sighed. "I know. He seems like a perfectly nice guy. But you can't rule anybody out as the conduit for this, or the suspect. . . ."

"Like *Schneider,*" I said.

"Like even your cousin."

"C'mon, Kenny . . ."

"Just saying."

The front door of the Crown banged open.

"Madeline! Thank God you're all right!" Lapthorne said, rushing over to me.

"Speak of the devil," said Kenny, as Ellis pounded in behind.

CHAPTER 37

"Lapthorne Townsend. Damn glad to meet

you," said my cousin, reaching across the bar and giving Kenny a solid handshake. "It's good to know Madeline's with someone who can be trusted."

"The famous cousin," Kenny said. "The lovely Ellis. *Willkommen. Bienvenue. Céad míle fáilte.*" He took a few steps back, grabbed a Labatt's Blue out of the cooler, and slid it toward us.

Lapthorne, at the corner of the bar's L, snapped the bottle up neatly with his right hand.

"Thank you, sir," he said, smiling.

A test to see which hand he'd use. I rolled my eyes at Kenny, who gave me an infinitesimal shrug before leaning an elbow on the bar and pursing his lips at the sight of Lapthorne's splendid tweed jacket and Guccis.

"How'd you guys track me down?" I asked Lapthorne.

"I tried reaching your office. They kept saying they expected you back at any moment, so I finally gave up and we jumped in the car."

"We hit the *Weekly* first," said Ellis. "They sent us here. What happened? Excuse me for saying so, but you look like shit."

"You should see the other guy," I said.

"Good *Lord!*" said Lapthorne. "He actually threatened you?"

"That would have been tough," said Kenny, polishing a glass and then holding it up to the light, "seeing as how he was already dead."

"Good *Lord!*" Lapthorne said again, shaking his head and grabbing my shoulder. "I wish to hell you had waited for me to come up, Madeline. If anything had happened to you —"

"Our Maddie can think on her feet," Kenny cut him off. "Don't get your panties in a knot."

When worlds collide, I thought, fully expecting one of them to whip it out and piss on me to entrench his territory.

Ellis shot me a look of sympathy. "Let's get you home," she said.

Lapthorne looked at me. "May I extend the invitation to Kenny?"

"Thanks, but I'm a working stiff," he said, looking at his sorry customers down the bar. "Somebody's got to keep an eye on these boys."

"You'll be missed," replied Lapthorne, ticking the moisture-beaded neck of his Labatt's with an immaculate fingernail. "Madeline's been filling me in on your many talents."

Kenny's lips curled back into a rictus of

contempt only the career drunk could confuse with a smile.

"Excuse me while I visit the head," said Lapthorne.

Once the men's room door, such as it was, had closed behind him, Kenny leaned across the bar and caught my elbow.

"This guy, Maddie," he said, "I know he's family, and I'm sorry for the disrespect, but Jesus Christ, *Lappy?* Kind of name is that?"

Ellis smiled, then walked over to the jukebox so Kenny could insult her paramour in private.

It pissed me off. I mean, okay, Lapthorne was wearing the tribal uniform: the pink Brooks shirt with the tiny monogram stitched on the cuff, the shoes no more durable than giftwrap. Fuck-you clothes. I-needn't-dirty-my-hands-with-employment clothes — the kind that quietly let you know the wearer's dividends roll in like clockwork and he lives damn high on a hog you'll never make the acquaintance of.

But as much as his ensemble spelled "useless pussy" to Kenny, so Kenny's white-on-white short-sleeved dress number with the built-in collar tabs sealed his fate as a peasant according to Lapthorne. The thing was all synthetic, see-through enough that one could trace the outline of the big man's sleeveless undershirt — both tops tucked into a pair of black slacks a little too shiny, a little too meticulously pressed. One didn't need X-ray vision through the bar to know he wore heavy black cop shoes, spit-shined wingtips built to last through the next hundred-year flood.

That Lapthorne's jacket was a good twenty years old, that his cuffs were frayed and his shoes scuffed just enough to show what he supposed was a proper masculine disdain for the dictates of fashion, would do as little to bridge the sartorial divide as his knowing Kenny arose each morning at six to achieve that Marine Corps crease running perfectly down the front of each trouser leg. There wasn't going to be any clasping of hands for a chorus of "This Land Is Your Land, This Land Is My Land."

And then I just thought, *You are really sick. You got someone killed and you're thinking about shoes.* But it wasn't fair of Kenny to dismiss Lapthorne. That mattered.

"Yeah," I said, "you hide your disdain *so* well."

"Oh, like I give a shit what the rich boy thinks of me. . . . I need to talk to you about some other, uh, *information.* Can you get back here tonight? By yourself?"

"I'm so tired, Kenny."

"It's important."

"Tomorrow morning?" I said. "You're open at ten, right?"

"Eight."

"Eight?"

He looked down the bar and shrugged. Keep the customers satisfied.

Lapthorne came out of the bathroom. Kenny looked over at him, then back at me. "Didn't even wash his hands," he said under his breath.

"Oh for Christ's sake, he was only in there five seconds. Probably too appalled to piss."

"Faggot," said Kenny.

"Nice little man," said Lapthorne, as we came onto the sidewalk outside the Crown. I smiled — what a Long Island thing to say.

Kenny had fifty pounds on Lapthorne, and they were roughly the same height, but "little" was the epithet applied to tradesmen who'd performed nicely for a reasonable fee — in this case, the ten bucks Lappy had lain on the bar as we said good night. Y chromosomes, what a pain.

"I'm just up here," said Lapthorne, waving to a black Porsche Carrera halfway up the block. "Shall I drive you home?"

It was the acme of automobiles: black with

a red interior, smooth and fast. A perfect scarab.

There was something reassuring to me about Lapthorne's whole aesthetic. Like it would make the ugly stuff go away, the scary stuff. I wanted an anchor. Anything.

I closed my eyes and saw Sembles and all those flies. Felt sick again. Took a stumbling step forward.

Lapthorne wrapped his arms around me, putting my head on his shoulder. "You have to take it easy," he said. "You've seen terrible things today."

"Don't think about anything," said Ellis, and I felt her hand on the back of my head, stroking my hair.

Lapthorne smelled good, and I just wanted to let my whole weight liquefy against him, to relax and let somebody else take the helm for a while.

I stiffened and pulled away. "It was my fault," I said. "The whole thing."

His hands were still on my shoulders. "Let's just get you home. I have some things to eat in the car. Some port. You just need to be someplace safe and warm and have a drink and stop thinking about it. I'll drive you. Everything will be all right."

So Ellis got in back and I curled up sideways on the passenger seat, knees tucked up under my chin, and the sound of the car and the way the seats smelled was just like in my dad's 911 when I was a little kid, when everything was still okay and we were still a family and I hadn't done anything wrong yet, and that made me want to start crying but I stopped myself and just gave directions, and they were both thankfully quiet other than that and I didn't have to say an extraneous word.

As soon as I walked into the apartment, Dean's absence hit me so hard I did start to cry, and the next thing I knew they'd wrapped me in a blanket with the greatest kindness and propped me against a couple of pillows on the sofa, Lapthorne giving me an honest-to-God handkerchief.

He and Ellis conferred quietly in the kitchen while I just rested there with my eyes closed.

I could hear snatches of the conversation, Lapthorne saying "a terrible shock, of course," and Ellis, in counterpoint to Lapthorne's bass, emphasizing the word "concern" a few times.

While he went back down for the port and some Stilton, she found three of Grandmama Dare's small glasses, the ones etched with a thin line of tiny leaves that they used to use for orange juice.

Ellis sat next to me and Lapthorne poured a dollop for each of us.

It was a tawny, not the deep ruby I was expecting.

It started out tasting like a syrup distilled from golden raisins, but then it was reincarnated as butterscotch, and finally metempsychosed to hazelnuts. I swallowed, and it made my throat feel like it was being warmed by the hot sun in some rocky and treeless country bordering the sea. "Jesus," I said.

Ellis swallowed her own taste. "Outstanding," she concurred.

"Do you have any apples?" asked Lapthorne, and I pointed him to a pair of Granny Smiths in a basket on top of the icebox. He pulled a Swiss Army knife from his pocket and cut them into wedges, then sliced the thin strip of core from each.

"Okay," he said, handing a piece to me and to Ellis. "Take a bite of this and then another sip after you've swallowed it."

Now the port tasted smoky: an inhalation in the woods outside Salzburg on the kind of October afternoon which, as Cheever once remarked, made you "realize your sweater was thin."

"Like truffles," said Ellis, "or what truffles *should* taste like."

We tried the Stilton, then more tawny — now it was caramel, clear as a bell, with a finish like cider boiled down to an intensity of fruit.

"Feel a little better?" asked Lapthorne, while Ellis held my hand.

I shivered. "I just want to rewind everything. Make it not have happened."

"You're not allowed to talk about it tonight," he said. "Family tradition. Tonight let's just have a drink and talk about anything else . . . furniture."

Lapthorne kicked off his shoes and sat Indian style, looking around the room. "This place is a perfect setting for the two of you . . . completely unexpected but totally right, somehow. You were always a cool little kid, *chère cousine.* I'm glad you grew up so well, and from what dear Ellis tells me, I very much approve of your taste in spouses."

He clinked his glass against both of ours, looking each of us in the eye as he did so.

We just talked about nothing for a while, and the port and cheese mellowed everything. I felt safe and warm and tired, listening to Lapthorne ask about Dean's railgrinder, and how we'd found the apartment, which he liked so much, and Ellis took over, explaining things when I faltered, charming Lappy with tales of our college adventures.

"You guys should sleep in our room," I said at one point, and Ellis said she'd go deal with the bed.

Lapthorne topped off my glass. As he handed it to me, he asked, "Are you really happy?"

"Today?" I took a deep sip.

"Not today. Generally. It seems like you're happy . . . you have a husband who adores you, so I'm told . . . you live in a wonderful place . . ."

"Here?" I looked around the room, comparing it with the elegance of his own digs.

"Yes, here. It's quite handsome, with some wit to it. You've made it your own."

"With the Naugahyde?"

"I'm enjoying the fact that you haven't succumbed to the tyranny of chintz."

"Too broke."

"You make it seem okay. Enviable. I've always wondered what I'd do without money. Don't really think I would have survived it with your style."

"I don't think I could survive being rich," I said.

He laughed.

I put a hand over my mouth so I could suck in a yawn through clenched teeth. "Not kidding," I said. "I don't have the moral fiber for wealth. I'd start taking Ayn

Rand literally and implode with a noxious bang. Too self-centered."

Lapthorne's smile glittered on the edge of laughter, and he refilled my glass.

"Now, see?" I said, taking another sip. "You make a much better rich person. So elegant, to make sure someone else has enough — very Japanese. I haven't poured you anything all night."

"You don't, ah . . . miss it?"

"Money?"

He nodded.

"Always wanted a pony. Didn't get one. Porsche would be nice. Other than that, it's pretty much okay. Long as you've got enough for gas . . . the occasional bridge toll."

"You look exhausted," he said.

It was eleven, and Ellis made me get up so she could make me a little nest on the Naugahyde. She carried out sheets, a great pile of pillows, and an old leaky down puff.

They tucked me in and turned off the lights.

The minute I closed my eyes, I felt as though a dark velvet canopy was being pulled over me, while I fell backwards into a whirling spiral of black on black.

I woke up groggy, standing up slowly before

I slumped into the kitchen to start the espresso. Lapthorne came out of the bedroom, looking remarkably alert. He was bare-chested, dressed in a pair of those handsome old boxers from Brooks Brothers that button up the front and have a little bow from the drawstring in the back.

"Oh God," I croaked. "Don't tell me you're one of those damn people who are perky in the morning. Ellis is perky in the morning. Drives me crazy."

I twisted open the espresso handle and dumped the grounds into the garbage, then gave up and decided to shift my attention to the "big coffee" side of the machine. We were looking like we needed at least a carafe of the stuff.

"If it helps to set your mind at ease, I feel like utter shit," he said, raising his arms and yawning.

I snuck a look at his belly and had myself a little nonmarital moment, then got busy with the coffee. I put eight slices of wheat bread in the broiler and set up a tray with sweet butter and a jar of Rose's Lime Marmalade, flipped the bread, grabbed three small plates and butter knives, and brought it all out to the table.

I went into the bathroom and set about looking for toothpaste. We had pressed our tube of Crest down to the last molecule, but then I spied Lappy's toilet kit, saddle leather with a tiny "LST" embossed in gold, and figured he wouldn't mind spotting me some dentifrice.

I unzipped the thing and rummaged around, taking out his shaving brush and little wooden tub of soap, his wicker-wrapped flask of lime aftershave from the Bahamas, and some small brown dropper bottles with hand-lettered labels on the side. One said "elder flower (eyes)," one was marked "Mouthwash (C.H.)," one said "antiseptic," and then there was a peppermint oil.

When I came back out, Lapthorne was wearing his khakis and folding up my bedding. He shook out the down puff with his back to me, long ridges of muscle tightening alongside his spine. Lucky Ellis.

"Coffee?"

Ellis wandered out amongst the living. "My God," she said, "dreaming is like cubist television."

I cued up a few Brandenburg concerti and the three of us tucked into breakfast, finishing off two pots of coffee, all of the marmalade, and lots more toast. When we were done, I dressed for work — cold enough out that I grabbed my old Red Sox cap and shoved it in my back pocket.

The day was clear with an achingly blue fall sky, and they dropped me off at the door of the Crown.

Chapter 38

Daylight spilled into the bar with me, making the three old guys already at the bar squint in pain and Kenny pause the swirl of his string mop. I wanted to thank him for the toast, for the Shirley Temple, and all his kindness the day before, but he started in first.

"Little Lord Fag-leroy left town yet?"

What the hell do you say to a greeting like that? I didn't answer him, just moved over to the jukebox and fumbled in my pocket for a couple of quarters. I thumbed the dial in the glowing machine's dashboard, making the heavy-paged song list flip to the left.

"Got some real hokey crap here, Kenny," I said. "You put any new 45s in this thing since 'Ballad of the Green Berets'?"

"Don't go knocking that Staff Sgt. Barry Sadler. Man's a fine musician and true patriot."

"Oh please."

"Like your pinko ass knows the first thing

about music."

"My pinko ass will *forget* more about music than you'll ever know."

He smiled. "Oh, g'waaan . . . punch me up some Ray Charles. 'America the Beautiful.' Might learn something."

"I will not play cheesy-travesty Ray with my last two quarters. You want to hear Mr. Charles, you get something decent of his in this thing, something without that damn Mormon-Mantovani string section."

He reached into his pocket and pulled out a quarter, tossing it toward me in so fine an arc that it spun, winking silver, and seemed to hang in the air. I snapped it down in a quick fist.

"Good eye," he said.

I ignored him, pushed in his coin, and kept looking through the list. "Some night I'm going to sneak in here and fill this thing up with Joni Mitchell and Hendrix. Fifty-fifty because I wanna make sure to piss you off and I don't know which one you'd hate more."

"Just push that B-17," he said.

"In your dreams."

"C'mon . . . it's my all-time favorite."

I punched two buttons and Merle Haggard came on, saying how he was tired of this dirty old city, was gonna walk off his steady job today.

"Truce," I said.

Kenny jumped in with a smooth baritone on "and your *so*-called Social Se-*cur*-ity . . ." singing on to the end while he mopped.

I didn't comment.

"Aw, honey," he said, putting the mop back in its holder-bucket, "there's hope for you yet."

"Stop insulting my relatives, I might even play 'Muskogee' for you." I queued up some nice twangy old Bob Wills and took a seat at the bar.

"Didn't mean any disrespect, Maddie."

"So the whole preppy-boy thing gives you a pain — I can understand that — but he's an okay guy despite the trappings," I said. "Now what'd you want to tell me?"

He didn't answer, just stood there wiping the bar.

"Bar's clean already, Kenny."

He leaned in, conspiratorial, point of his elbow touching down in the moisture webbing up across the wood. "Night Sembles was killed?"

I waited.

"I know where Schneider was," Kenny said, "and he couldn't have done it."

"That's not what you were going to tell me," I said. "Not what you wanted me to

392

come back for, last night."

"Says who?"

"Don't jerk me around, Kenny," I said. "I brought up his name what, twice? Three times? If you already knew, you would have told me then. Before Lapthorne and Ellis showed up."

"I wasn't sure of it. By the time you'd have come back, I knew."

"Knew what?"

"Big party at the Hotel Syracuse . . . the Benevolent Association throws it every year. Schneider was there the whole damn time, like always. And I mean until *late*."

Sure, I thought, because he was no doubt blowing rails of coke with Vomit Girl every other second. Probably danced up a god-damn storm, the two of them.

"So it's not him," I said, deflated.

"Cheer up," he said. "Doesn't rule him out, entirely . . . I think he's got a finger in the pie."

"Like what?"

"I've been asking around," he said. "Something's up with the guy. Has been for a long time. Not married. Family's got no money . . . too young for a government check, but he's living awful high for a guy who hasn't done a lick of work since before your ass-hole buddy Jimmy Carter was running the country down. Snowmobiles and a couple of new Harleys. Big-screen TVs."

"Cracker heaven," I said.

"Got his house all paid for, I hear."

We'd danced around the purpose of my being there for long enough, my own fault, but I was late for work and started to get pissy. "So maybe he's dealing coke," I said. "If his girlfriend's anything to go by, the guy does so much of it, it's amazing they've got a nostril left between them."

"Listen, way things go around here, if he's dealing anything, one of my old boys would know by now. Can't be a regular thing for this long and him not busted. Cops around here aren't perfect, but we don't stand by for that shit. Not from another cop, specially."

Bob Wills started up on "Twin Guitar Boogie," crowing "*Awwwww* take it away, Leon, *take* it away . . ."

"What's it got to do with the Rose Girls?" I scrubbed my hand through the air, impatient, like I could clear away the small talk.

"You heard he was fired, am I right?" said Kenny, leaning in even closer. "Heard he was maybe getting a little heavy-handed with the, uh, the *brothers?*"

"You know that's what I heard. We talked

about it in here with Dean when this all started."

"Well, now I hear he *retired.* Told 'em they could all go to hell. Didn't give a reason, officially. Friend of mine saw him drunk one night later on and Schneider laughed and said he didn't need to work 'cause he'd be getting regular infusions of cash for the rest of his born days. Sitting pretty in the cat-bird seat, he said, just like winning the Lotto."

"So?"

"So he went his merry way about three months after your Rose Girls, right when they were pressing him hardest to sew it up. He just walked off that case and never looked back. . . ."

I stared him down, not liking the sneaky little smile in one corner of his mouth, how he was so obviously savoring the best-for-last detail before letting it go.

"Don't be a tease, Kenny. It's not becoming."

"Last night I asked around some more, after I talked with you. My boy tells me some of the evidence maybe went missing, when they tried to hand everything over to the guy who stepped in as primary."

"What kind of evidence?"

"Photos, Maddie. The pictures and the

negatives, too. Not a one left in the file. Never signed out. Just *poof* — he snapped his fingers — "and they're gone."

He slapped a quarter onto the bar and slid it toward me, smiling and batting his eyelashes. "Now get your little butt off that barstool and play me some *got*-damn Ray Charles, why don'tcha."

I stared at him, trying to get my head around that — what it could mean.

Was Simon's file the stuff that had been lifted from the evidence room? Did he take them? Did Schneider? Were they hooked up somehow?

I poked at the idea of shy, rotund Simon as a criminal mastermind, which seemed about as likely as Maria Callas joining the Symbionese Liberation Army.

I mean, first of all, why the hell would he *show* me the pictures if he'd stolen them? Why would he keep the file at the *Weekly*? It made no sense.

I slogged my feet toward the jukebox, punched in Kenny's B-17. There was a martial little snare drum, then sappy trumpets, then Ray's rasp over some organ chords that would have made a perfectly serviceable roller-rink background tune. All-skate music.

I shuffled back over to the bar and climbed

back up on the stool. "I don't get it."

Kenny set up a couple of Rock 'n' Ryes for the guys down the bar. "What's not to get?"

"Well, Simon's file . . . it's supposedly copies of all the police photos from the crime scene. He said they came from a friend of his, the evidence room guy — that he got to make prints from all the negatives."

"So maybe he's lying."

"Well, yeah, but then why would he show me everything? Because he's some gloating sociopath daring me to catch him? I mean, especially since he let me take the whole file out of the morgue. He never does that. He's like a total maniac about allowing anything out of that room. If he's not there, it's double-locked, with bars over the windows. No one else has keys."

"So it's already completely out of character for him to let you take his precious eight-by-ten glossies on a field trip?"

I thought about that.

"And if this 'evidence guy' knew Simon had copies," continued Kenny, "why didn't he ask for them back? Cover his tracks when the shit turned up missing?"

"Oh," I said. "Right."

"Doesn't add up."

"Doesn't point us in any plausible direction, either."

"Never does," he said. "You just go over the shit until something comes up wonky. Then you hustle and dig until you can play connect the dots."

"Well, you're the cop . . . hustle and dig *where?*"

"Where I'd start?" he said. "I'd try finding out whether Simon had any dough."

"He works at a second-rate newspaper, Kenny. None of us can afford soft toilet paper, for God's sake."

"So find out how much he makes . . . does he get any outside work like weddings or something . . . maybe some inheritance — you want to know how he's set for cash and how he spends it."

"Why?"

"Because somebody's paying off Schneider, Maddie. Somebody put him in that damn catbird seat with the snowmobiles and all. And when you find out who that somebody is, you've probably fingered your killer. You wanna know why I don't like your cousin? It's not because he acts like a homo — I could give a shit if he wears sequined lavender jumpsuits and walks around singing show tunes with five gerbils shoved up his ass."

"Now *there's* an image," I said.

Kenny wrapped a hand around mine and squeezed. Hard. "I'm not messing around here, Maddie. You're in danger, and you're in danger from somebody with ready cash. If that doesn't sound like Little Lappy Loafers, I don't know what does."

"Let go of me," I said.

He didn't.

"Okay, so if I'm in so much danger, how come I'm not dead?"

He dropped my hand.

"Look, Kenny, I'm a complete chickenshit and I don't have a death wish — but think about it. If whoever killed Sembles was scared of me, they'd have stuck around his house and finished the job when I showed up, not left me a cheery little personalized note on the front door and taken off."

He looked down and started wiping the bar again.

"Let's say it *was* Lapthorne," I said, "even though there's no way he could have driven the six hours from New York and back in between those two phone calls, and even though he spent the night with Ellis — why not off me if he's worried I'll nail him?"

He didn't answer.

"Why kill Sembles at all?" I said. "The guy hadn't talked in twenty years, and he wasn't about to start. All he wanted to do if he even thought about it was shoot up and nod out. So why not just get to the point and kill *me?* Lapthorne knows where I live, and so does Simon. For chrissake, *Schneider* probably does, if he's connected to either of them."

"Must be," Kenny said slowly, "that keeping you alive means you'll be doing somebody a favor."

"What the hell is *that* supposed to mean?"

"It means that whatever you're digging up is something the killer wants to know."

My turn to stand there, all "no comment."

"When you've turned that last shovel of dirt," he said, "when you see the little glint at your feet . . . seems to me you'll find yourself in one of those shoot-the-messenger type of situations. And given everything else that's gone on with this damn program, they'll find your body all dressed up like Little Bo got-damn Peep."

He leaned back and crossed his meaty arms across his chest. "So unless you'd like to meet your maker in a hoopskirt, frilly pantaloons, and a big poke bonnet, I'd suggest you watch your back."

CHAPTER 39

Hoopskirts never having been a look for me — much less, you know, being dead — I left the Crown shaken. It was starting to get cold. I put the Red Sox cap on my head, shoved my fists in my pockets, and stalked down the sidewalk toward work. Kenny's parting words had chilled me enough that my shoulders went tight and my weight shifted to the balls of my feet every time I heard a car coming up behind me.

Simon was the key. He might not be the killer — in fact I couldn't picture him in that role at all — but what with this new crap about missing photos, he was, at the very least, central to finding out who was.

And Kenny was right. I had to see if I could follow the money from Schneider toward whoever was willing to pay him for shutting up and walking off his steady job all those years ago. I couldn't blame my bartender friend for thinking that cash automatically meant Lapthorne, but it didn't have to be him, either.

I mean, how much could it possibly cost to keep somebody in snowmobiles and Genny Cream Ale down near the Rez? We weren't talking a lifetime of polo with constant bumpers of Veuve Clicquot all around, for God's sake.

In upstate dollars, the Schneider lifestyle was costing somebody maybe twenty grand a year, tops. Not the kind of cash I had lying around, but not an amount that really ruled anybody out as the asshole's benefactor. In fact, that kind of money might even leave Ted or Wilt or Simon himself wide open.

I didn't make shit for pay, but I was a flunky peon. Those guys had been on the staff for tons longer. Maybe they cleaned up.

It all joggled around in my head like a couple of dozen Super Balls — bouncing everywhere, no tracking a single one, no cohesion. I couldn't imagine where I'd start once I got upstairs, so I just stopped on the sidewalk for a second, eyes clenched and head down, in front of the door to the office.

It swung open and almost hit me, but the hydraulic noise of the auto-close arm along the top made me jump back. Someone clomped out, moving so fast they didn't even see me. It was a woman in big sunglasses, unsteady in cheap, white, and stupidly tall high heels that looked especially nasty against a pair of "suntan" pantyhose.

Vomit Girl.

I watched her from behind as she toddled toward the parking lot, her Moby Dick of a purse — tsk-tsk, white after Labor Day — swinging across a patchwork rabbit fur jacket to hit her squarish and stretch-acid-washed-denim miniskirted butt. Her red hair was still permed to a frizzle, the short pieces up top shellacked into a mall-goers' coxcomb that didn't move despite her haste.

As she turned to unlock her car, brussel-sprout–sized fake pearl earrings bobbled and pulled at her lobes, while her jaws smacked wetly over a defenseless wad of gum.

No rest for the tacky.

My view of the old sedan's passenger seat was blocked by another car, so it wasn't until she started talking that I realized she hadn't come alone.

"Said he didn't have it," she said, before a hand grabbed her forearm and dragged her inside the car.

Vomit Girl grimaced as she went down, but tried to compose herself on the seat, taking off her sunglasses to reveal a fat shiner. She shut the door behind her, then flinched toward it as though being yelled at.

My disdain for her fashion sense turned to dirt in my mouth. I couldn't stand it.

The darkened pale skin swollen around the delicate frame of her eye, the way her face scrunched up like a little kid's who'd just taken a bad fall but was too stunned to make a sound, the way she cowered against the inside of her door, like it could help her somehow, that tiny amount of distance.

She started the car, grinding the gears before she reversed out of her spot, then peeled out of the lot. She turned right and I got a brief glimpse of the passenger side. There was a little redheaded girl in the back seat. Had to be Tiffy.

Up front, the window framed an oleaginous pompadour, a too-carefully trimmed beard, a grim and utter absence of lips — Schneider.

Just before they turned the corner, his eyes flicked over me.

I hunched my shoulders and exhaled as though I'd just taken a punch to the gut.

Had to go inside, couldn't have wanted to get off that sidewalk any more than if it were being strafed by Jap Zeros as I stood there, but I just lacked the ability to make my feet move.

Had he *seen* me? Could he tell who it was in the bulky jacket and the baseball cap? Yes and yes.

Move, goddamnit.

I ducked inside and into a recessed corner of the vestibule, a foot from the doorframe. Would they come back? I turned off the stairwell lights, knowing that in the glare of the overcast day they wouldn't be able to see in the glass, while I could eyeball a good slice of the street from behind the reflection. I stood there, heart chattering, for a solid five minutes.

Only one car came past, turning into the lot. Wilt's Gremlin, the interior blue with smoke, and out of it he telescoped, with Ted spilling from the other side. So it hadn't been either of them Vomit Girl talked to.

I took the stairs two at a time and screeched to a halt in front of the reception desk. The new chick was there, Amy from Utica.

"Did a woman just come up here?" I asked. "I wanted to catch her before she left . . . big hair? Furry jacket?"

"Didn't see one," she said. "Only people in so far are Marion and Beth and Lorraine. And the advertising guys, but they had an early meeting. You okay? You're shaking."

"Exercise," I said. "Crap just doesn't agree with me."

She nodded.

"Simon down in the morgue?" I asked.

"As always," she said, feeding a classified

form into her typewriter. "Came up for coffee about an hour ago — I've routed a couple of calls down to him. Guy should get some sun while there's still a little left, you know?"

"You bet. Thanks . . ." I started walking toward Editorial, legs not working quite right.

"You wanna watch that exercise," she called after me. "Stuff'll kill ya."

So, Vomit Girl must have been here to see Simon. He was the only person in the building you didn't have to walk past Amy to get to, the only one downstairs — and I couldn't believe Amy'd have missed seeing her.

Said he didn't have it . . . what had she meant by that? What did Schneider want from him? The photos? More money? Like I had a clue.

I thought about everything Kenny had said, both the night before and that morning. And, yes, despite my lame excuses to him, at the minimal privacy of my desk I could admit that I was scared.

I thought about calling that detective in Bridgeport back, telling him everything I knew and hoping he could deflect any danger from me, from everybody else.

But even Kenny had said I was right not

to go to the cops, that he couldn't tell who was on the level, and if *he* couldn't tell, what the hell hope did I have of navigating the morass without making it all worse?

The one thing I could focus on was Kenny having told me to figure out whether or not Ted, Wilt, and Simon had alibis for the time of Sembles's death.

Ted wandered in just then, his eyes redder than his hair, a self-satisfied lizardy grin playing across his lips. He stopped about ten feet away from me and crossed his skinny forearms, tapping an index finger against his wrist.

"Well," he said, looking me up and down, "if it isn't Little Nellie Bly, star reporter. Guess you screwed up that interview pretty well, huh? Didn't they teach you in Journalism 101 not to get your sources knocked off?"

Prick.

When I offered no answer, he made a hugely unattractive lip noise and stalked away, slamming his office door behind him.

Wilt loped in and came right over to my chair, putting a big hand on my shoulder. "How you holding up? I was worried about you last night."

He pulled up a chair next to me and pushed the too-long bangs from his eyes, looking all worried and freaked. He was wearing the same rumpled suit as yesterday — different shirt on underneath, but there was a small white feather tucked through the weave of his jacket's shoulder.

"You sleep in this?" I asked, pulling on the little quill to get it out.

"Oh, man. What sleep I *did* get. I've been sitting up with Ted every night since Saturday. Wife left him and the dude's a goddamn mess. Won't go home. All he does is mutter and pace."

"My heart *bleeds*," I said, but I was thinking that the two of them could then cover for each other, alibi-wise, leaving Simon the only one of the three who might have been free the night of Sembles's death.

"Trying to get him to talk it out," Wilt continued. "I'm afraid he's not . . . uh . . . acting too rational with members of the fairer sex. I mean, don't take it personally if he's acting hostile — you dig?"

"Like that would be so *markedly* different from normal."

"You shouldn't think that. He's got a real soft spot for you, actually."

"Yeah, right," I said. The only difference in Ted's treatment of me now was that now he wasn't as careful about avoiding witnesses.

"So what was she pissed about, the wife — money? I mean, that's pretty common. I don't know what you guys make. More than me, I figure, but enough?"

"This year Ted'll get about forty grand. Told her it wasn't enough to have kids on. She thought it was."

Forty grand? And my W-2 had read a neat $6,382 gross for a year of full-time work, no benefits. Fuck Ted.

"Simon pulls down the most, actually," Wilt said. "And he's the biggest tightwad I've ever met. Dude's wiggy. You'd think it would kill him to pick up a bar tab, and he packs his own lunch every day. Lives in the tiniest apartment I've ever seen. Beyond 'efficiency.' I dunno — maybe he gives it all to Save the Children."

A single guy packing his own lunch in Syracuse and living in a studio, even on forty grand, could bank about thirty of it — and that was with two-pound lobsters and drawn butter for dinner every night.

"Huh," I said. "No shit."

CHAPTER 40

With Lapthorne out of the equation and Ted and Wilt covering each other, Simon was the only one with foreknowledge of my interview whose opportunity hadn't been ruled out for the night Sembles was killed. Kenny'd said to look for something wonky, and Simon was looking wonky as a heifer for Uncle Weasel.

Wilt looked up over my shoulder, giving out a cheery "Simon!"

I flinched so hard my chair squealed back across the floor, banging straight into the object of my speculation's shins.

He yelped and I jumped to my feet.

"Sorry! Jesus, Simon!" I said, my heart going so fast I could feel it in my throat, and he was apologizing at the same time so everything was all garbled, but he wouldn't look me in the face even after we'd both shut up.

I just stared. The man was a mere shadow of his former mere shadow — his round little face literally a whiter shade of pale — eyes raw-looking above purple-green bruises of sleeplessness so profound that they were dents rather than bags.

His arms clasped across his middle as though to guard his little belly, and all the dark curls edging his baldness were rubbed into a lopsided halo of frizz. The man was a veritable *New Yorker* cartoon of nerves.

"Hey, man," Wilt said to him, "you all

right? Look like hell."

"Oh, all right. I'm all right. Sure," said Simon.

His vision was focused on some obscure distance between Wilt and me, and a little arched muscle just above his left eye started to tic. He wove his fingers together and pumped his now-facing palms in and out like a tiny bellows, worrying the knuckles of each hand with the fingertips of the other.

Wilt touched his shoulder. "No, I'm serious, man. Never seen you like this. . . . You should sit down."

"Hmm?" Simon tilted his head back to look up at Wilt's face, as though noticing for the first time that he wasn't alone in the room.

Wilt turned my chair toward him, face limned with concern. "Sit."

Simon looked down at his hands and complied. The weird dance of his fingers seemed to fascinate him, but after a glance at Wilt he pulled them apart and shoved a fist under each thigh.

That worked to keep him still for a few seconds, until the heel of one shoe started jitterbugging against the floor.

"Hell's wrong with you, man?" asked Wilt gently, squatting down next to him protectively. "Everything okay?"

It seemed like the very solicitude in Wilt's tone made Simon snap. The little man jumped to his feet, a flood of red suffusing his face, even the shiny crown of his head.

"I don't have to *take* this!" he rasped, shaking a short thick finger down into Wilt's face. "You just lay *off* me, you sonofabitch!"

Simon pushed out of the chair and stomped away, hands bunched in chubby fists.

Wilt and I gawped in his wake.

So Simon had a temper — surprise, surprise.

"Jeez, man, you know?" said Wilt, placing his hands on his thighs before rising, with a resounding click from each kneecap. "What the hell's eating the little dude?"

Oh, I dunno — guilt?

I shrugged. "Doesn't look like he's been getting a whole lot of sleep."

Wilt waggled his shaggy head back and forth. "Poor little guy."

"How long have you known him?" I asked.

"Like, forever," said Wilt. "I mean, since when he still had a crewcut, you know? High school."

"And you've never seen him like this?"

"S'what I said, right? Seriously . . . never."

I briefly considered asking him what he thought of the idea that Simon was somehow involved in the Rose Girl thing, that he'd at the very least have to have set up Sembles to be killed by warning Schneider or somebody else, but then it seemed like a better idea to keep that cat shoved deep in the bag.

The rest of the morning crawled by on its knees over broken glass. I spent most of it with Harvey Kaiser's *Great Camps of the Adirondacks* open on my desk, making what I hoped appeared to be relevant notes on a steno pad. Mostly, though, I just skimmed the chapter on Dodie's family camp — its pristine "pond" the spoils for ruining Lake Oncas here in Syracuse — then started jotting down ideas about Sembles, Simon, Schneider, and the whole rest of the minstrel show.

My handwriting is so bad I didn't even need to encode anything.

I was leaning back in my chair, considering what I'd jotted down, when Ted slimed over and leaned against the wall by my desk, his lips peeled back in reptilian glee.

"Oh, don't get to work on account of me," said Ted. "It's not like we're running a business here or anything." He turned his hand and examined his nails. "I'm just wondering how you're coming on that Adirondack piece."

"Fine," I said, patting the Kaiser book.

"Bullshit."

"Even if I *was* working on the Rose Girls . . . which I'm not . . . Adirondacks aren't, like, *going* anywhere, Ted."

"Gotta learn to keep more than one ball in the air."

His tone was so nasty I gave up my pretense. "I find a dead guy yesterday, I'm working on tracking down a killer, and you want me to crank out some travel-puff crap? I mean, I'm sorry your wife left, but there's no need to shit all over me. I'm pulling my weight."

"The hell you *are* . . ."

"Jesus, Ted," said Wilt from across the room, "lighten *up*."

"You can screw around with this other bullshit all . . . you . . . want," said Ted, turning his back on Wilt and stabbing his finger into the surface of my desk with each word, "but I expect that Adirondacks piece on my desk Tuesday. You took it on, you goddamn well *finish* it on deadline."

I tilted my head back so I could consult the ceiling tiles, and he stormed back into his office.

"Place is a nuthouse, man," said Wilt.

"Goddamn cacophony. The *Eagle* has landed."

"How the hell did his wife last this long?"

"Guy's hurting, man."

"Shit flows downhill?"

"Doesn't give him the right to come down on you. Stick to your guns."

"Big hill," I said. "No shortage of shit."

The extension on my desk bleated like Wodehouse's sheep with a secret sorrow.

Wilt gave me a floppy salute as I picked up the receiver.

"Madeline Dare . . ."

"How's things down-city with all them pinkos?"

Wimpy? "Scott?"

"Yup."

What the *hell* . . . he had never called Dean at the apartment, much less me at work.

Had to be some horrible news. "Everybody okay? Your parents?"

"Hunky-dory," he said.

"So, ah, you just calling to chat?"

"Some guy called for you, here at the shop."

"Some guy?"

"Might've been one of your kike buddies."

"Yeah?"

"Guess so," he said.

"You know, Scott, I'm kind of having a

day, down here. Me and the pinkos."

"No kidding?"

"Wouldn't kid a guy like you."

"Huh," he said, volunteering nothing.

"Well, Scott, I guess I need your help with this."

"That a fact?"

"See, it's just that I have so *many* kike buddies . . ."

He chuckled.

". . . that I'm just sitting here, wondering whether you can possibly get your head out of your ass long enough to tell me which one this was."

"*Hell* you say?"

"Now, Scott, I think you should keep in mind that even though Dean's in Canada, it's not like he won't kick your teeth in the minute he gets back. All I have to do is say the word."

That shut him up. Now I could hear him breathing.

"Look, like I said?" I continued. "I'm pretty busy today. So why don't you just tell me who called and what the hell they wanted."

"Izzy Fleischmann's coming here. Five o'clock."

I heard him mutter "bitch" as he dropped the phone.

CHAPTER 41

Ted's office door was shut for the rest of
the day, his voice alternately rumbling and
shrilling, depending on whether he was on
the phone with his lawyer or his wife. Wilt
was off eating ziti at another failing campaign headquarters — the Republicans
seemed to be cornering the market on soon-
to-be-landslide-winner shrimp buffets. Simon was nowhere to be seen, which was
just fine by me.

I was exhausted, and the hours between
two and five seemed countable in dozens.
My head hurt so much it was like I could
actually *hear* the whining frequency of the
fluorescent tubes.

I pounded Excedrin and kept slogging
until 4:37, when I crept to the parking lot,
head low, and raced out to the Bauer farm.

Wimpy was nowhere in sight.

I waited outside the shop, trying to keep
out of a chill wind coming off the rows of
corn. I stayed out of sight, ducking my head
around the corner of the cinder blocks to
check the road, feeling like Lucy Ricardo
meets *Clockwork Orange*.

There was a sudden little gust of cold air,
filled with dirt and tiny bits of dead leaves,

417

one of which I caught in the eye. I rubbed at it with my fist to get it out, and when I looked up, there was Izzy Fleischmann's theory-of-relativity hair and broad ruddy face.

He grasped both my hands and bussed my cheek. "You don't mind I give a little kiss, *hein?* Make an old man happy?" he twinkled.

"How's business?"

"Business . . ." Izzy waggled his eyebrows, shrugged. "Ah, you know, selling heifers . . . today we get too many little beauties with no calf to freshen them, the kind you have to say, '*Take* her home and *breed* her to your *fave*-orite sire.' Maybe I sell a few to your uncle-in-law, hm?"

"God forbid," I said, and Izzy cackled.

"And you?" he asked. "How is your business?"

"Scary," I said.

"So I am hearing."

I shivered. "Hearing? What do you mean?"

"I think you are finding things out? Small towns, this does not go unnoticed. . . ."

"You know what I want to find out?"

"I remember about those girls. Long time ago, now, when it happened."

I nodded.

"The police, I think . . ." He paused, looking out toward the far trees. "Maybe not so interested in the solution, back then?"

"Maybe not so interested in the solution now," I said. "Maybe they are. Some of them."

"Ah, but which 'some'? Always, that is the *most* important question."

"I would say *not* Schneider," I said. "You ever run across him?"

Izzy's lips twisted into a moue of distaste.

"Guess you have," I said.

He leaned around the corner of the shop, checking for traffic on the narrow road.

"So, just now you and me," Izzy said, tucking my arm through his, "I think we need to have a little talk. It is concerning things I overheard when I was at Johnston's farm yesterday, settling accounts from the auction. I am not sure what-all to which it pertains, you understand, but I am thinking perhaps it has to do with your mysterious undertakings."

I got hit with a wave of exhaustion as we moved slowly across the shop yard. Jesus, I needed sleep. Speed. An eight ball of John-the-Conqueror root.

Izzy steered me out beyond the pole barn, hidden from the road and even from the Bauers, should Wimpy or Weasel decide to visit the shop.

"You should know that your husband, I saw him again after we met. He told me some of what is concerning you," he said. "He asked me to pay attention, see if I heard anything while I was around the town."

"He did?"

"I know these people, around here," he said. "Over the years, I've become, well, maybe a good word is 'cautious.' I pay attention, just in case something should start to . . . occur. Again."

"I understand," I said.

Izzy sighed.

"Nu," he said, "so what you are mixed up in, it is coming as they say 'to a head' perhaps?"

"I get that feeling."

"It is ugly business, whatever is going on. That *oisvarf* Schneider figures in the picture. Johnston is in it, also, from a long time ago."

"Johnston?"

He looked at the ground for a moment as we walked, then, patting my hand, back at me. "I think that you may be in some danger."

I stopped dead. "Why, specifically?"

"Because, my dear, what I heard them talking about was you."

"Talking about me?" I pulled my hand

420

back out of the crook of Fleischmann's elbow. "Who's 'they'?"

The wind stirred distant tree branches into clattering black *kanji* against the sky. Shifting haiku. Indecipherable.

"Johnston and his son-in-law," Izzy said, "just when I was coming into the barn. They were discussing, please pardon how I am saying, the day of the 'sweetheart auction,' then mentioned 'that nosy little bitch from downstate.' And also, shortly after that, how 'Schneider wouldn't like anybody messing with his livelihood, nosiree Bob.' At least that's how I remember exactly the wording. Of course, it is not just you they are insulting. Me, I am apparently 'that goddamn little hunchback Hebe who's never on time.' "

"I'm sorry you had to hear that."

He crossed his arms and rubbed his hands briskly along his biceps, his slick windbreaker squeaking at the friction. "Is getting cold already. Too early in the year."

"Did they say anything else?"

"It made no sense to me . . . maybe for you there will be some meaning. The father said something like, 'I told him when he brought that little fruit out here it wasn't no good. Guess he lived all right off it for quite a while but everything comes to an end.'

And the son said, 'Won't come to an end if Schneider shuts that girl up.' And I am afraid that once again, Madeline, he was speaking of you."

"Wait, 'the little fruit'?"

"Oh yes, hardly an agricultural product," said Izzy. "Someone named Simon."

Well, there you go.

Izzy peered at me with concern. "You look as though this confirms your suspicions," he said.

"You could say that."

"Your face has changed since last we met. You are less . . . innocent. It is the eyes, I think. You have been seeing things that are very painful. Very troubling to you. And, *nu,* maybe you are feeling a bit responsible for these things?"

"Are you fortune-telling again?"

"Oh yes indeed, my dear, and do believe me when I say you must be extremely careful," he said.

"Are your predictions always very accurate?"

"Accurate? Oh yes. Sadly, I have been cursed with a great deal of accuracy."

Of course, when I got home, there was a message from Dean. If I hadn't met with Izzy, I would have been there in time, could have told him about Sembles, and how everything was closing in.

I paced around the apartment, pissed at Dean for being gone and not calling back, pissed at myself for being pissed at him. I wanted to talk to someone. Mom didn't answer her phone. Ellis was no doubt with Lapthorne, though neither of them picked up.

Finally, I dialed the Crown.

"Kenny," I said, "I should have told you right off the bat this morning how grateful I am for your kindness yesterday . . . I mean, not just the toast and the Shirley Temple, but all the work you've done, trying to help me figure this thing out."

"My pleasure. Anything new?"

So I started to tell him about the morning's events, about how it was now obvious that Schneider knew Simon, obvious that there was some question over what Simon did with all the money he was earning.

I said how I'd been thinking it didn't look like too much of a stretch that the photographer and the ex-cop had at the very least shared observations on the poor silhouettist before his untimely demise.

"But Kenny, I just can't picture Simon as a killer," I said. "I mean, again, why would he show me the photographs?"

And then I related what Izzy had told me, out at the farm.

"What the hell does that mean," he asked, " 'the little fruit'?"

"I don't know. Maybe Simon's gay. Maybe they just wanted to insult him."

Kenny sighed. "Something about that just . . . it's like it's ticking somewhere. A clock in another room when you can't sleep, you know? It's right at the edge and I can't quite remember . . ."

"I'm just not getting a bead on anything, here," I finished lamely.

"You're still *sure* you want to pursue this?"

"No one else will. I just keep seeing those poor girls' faces, and now Sembles."

And as I said that, I really did flash on the images of Sophie and Delphine Descognets, whom I'd never met.

What was it about them that had such a hold on me? Sophisticated young women, near my age, lost forever in Syracuse, a town that seemed completely uninterested in them, in what their presence here had ultimately cost them.

Oh . . . right. I'm afraid they're me.

"Houston . . ." said Kenny, "we've lost contact —"

The sound of his voice yanked me whizzing back out of the ether.

424

"What's with your family?" he asked. "You're a good kid, and it doesn't seem like there's anybody looking out for you in all of this. My parents . . . every day I was a cop, they worried. Said they didn't leave the old country so I could get myself killed in the new one. The only son. My mother said, 'Already you go Vietnam. Now is time for your opportunity. Milk and honey . . . no more the guns.' "

I looked out the window.

Kenny paused for a minute. "I guess what I want to say is, and no offense, where's your parents? Your father? Doesn't he worry about you? His daughter's up here, chasing murderers around?"

I looked up at the clock on the stove — 6:37, three hours earlier in Malibu. Well, Dad would be doing his ninety-fifth bong hit of the day over his I Ching in the VW overlooking the Pacific, and Mom was probably ladling dented-can pork and beans into a pair of exquisitely rendered soup plates while threatening Bonwit with the cricket bat.

The usual.

"I dunno," I said. "I guess it's different. America *is* my old country. My parents aren't exactly looking to me for the milk and honey. They figure it's all used up."

"But this country . . . there's opportunity enough for everybody. It's just a question of attitude."

"Yeah," I said, and he had no answer to that.

"I just want you to know," he said at last, "that *I* worry about you. I don't mean that to undermine what you're doing — but I want you to know I've got your back if anything comes up. I mean it . . . anything at all."

He'd spoken with a slow dignity — an ancient senator's gravitas.

"Really?" I said. "That means a lot."

"You're a good kid," he said. "You're going to make your own opportunities. No one can take that from you. Why don't you come down to the bar for breakfast?"

"I will," I said. "Thanks."

Sleep wouldn't settle in with me that night. Maybe it was Kenny's observation about the ticking clock, but every little noise from up and down the street seemed to rattle around in my head whenever I shut my eyes. The house creaking, the wind coming through increasingly bare branches, making them clatter — even the halting progress of every last car.

CHAPTER 42

The next morning I drove downtown, exhausted despite a full night's sleep. I left my car in the *Weekly*'s lot, then walked back up to the Crown.

I thought Kenny had stood me up. There were no lights on inside, nothing visible through the door's tiny window.

I pushed against the scarred wood, expecting to find it locked. Instead it swung inward, easily, so I stepped into the darkness.

The door closed behind me.

I couldn't see. I blinked.

There was no sound, only a smell.

Thick and rancid. Sweet.

The same fetor I'd choked on at Sembles's house.

I was alone in the dark with something dead.

I backed toward the door. Didn't want to see, didn't want my pupils to dilate in the gloom.

Too late. Shapes emerged, sharpening.

The walls . . . the bar's solid length . . . the mass laid out along it . . .

Kenny.

On his back. On top of the polished wood.

I couldn't move. Couldn't leave. Couldn't breathe.

I could only stand, frozen, watching the details bloom, slow as an image on photographic paper, conjured forth beneath the surface of a chemical bath.

The pallor of his skin.

The worn soles of his shoes.

His shirt, once white, now dark to the waist.

His throat, slashed deep as the Rose Girls' had been.

The blood, so thick it had dried in stalactites off the edge of the bar.

And there were more details. Little touches, to set the scene.

The broad arc of silver coins glittering around his head. How one hand clutched something to his chest. Only I couldn't see what it was.

He would have forced himself to go over there and look, if it had been me laid out in his place. He would've been brave enough to do that, because if he could see everything, he'd know what happened. What it meant.

He'd have had every right to ask the same of me.

I started shaking. Everything so cold.

"Kenny?" I said. "I can't."

But I had to. Because it was my fault. I knew that even before I could inch one foot ahead of me, rasping against the floor because I didn't have the strength to lift it.

I'd done this. I'd made it happen. And the flourishes were intended to let me know, rubbing in the guilt of it just like the note on Sembles's door.

"I'm so sorry."

I pushed my other foot forward, trying not to close my eyes. I didn't deserve not to see it all — how pale he was. How his face still looked so kind.

Another sliding step. Another. Still so far from him, like he was drifting away at the end of some narrow cave and it would take me days to reach him, longer and longer no matter how much distance I could cover.

I shuddered again and wanted to throw up. Kept swallowing against it, moving my feet by inches, wanting to bring him back, wanting to be dead myself.

Shuffling, weak, gaining tiny increments of ground, until I was there beside him, long after I thought I'd given up hope of reaching his body.

His eyes were open, turning milky. I closed them as gently as I could.

I made myself examine him, move my eyes slowly down past the horror of his neck, to the split pomegranate he held to his chest, then the other hand, lying alongside his body, palm open.

At its center, six of the broken fruit's seeds glowed red, ruby kernels laid out in a crooked row.

For Persephone. For me.

I bit down on the inside of my cheek, trying to hang on.

Persephone had to live among the dead every winter, because the ruler of Hades had pulled her down to his kingdom and she'd eaten six seeds from the pomegranate he tried to console her with. After that, she was bound to him forever. Married to the lord of ghosts.

I felt a rush of hot acid coming up my throat. Blanked out because my skull couldn't contain the enormity of what I had caused. Too painful. Too huge. Too much to bear.

Everything was sucked away — substance and perspective, the *realness* of it.

There was only cold, and silence, and this stupid girl standing next to a dead man, shaking, until she kissed both his cheeks and pulled a quarter from her pocket and headed for the jukebox. It took her ages and eons to walk that far, and two hands to steady the coin into the slot.

She didn't need to flip through the rack of stiff pages to find what she wanted, just pushed B and then 17, because that was Kenny's favorite, that was Ray Charles doing "America the Beautiful."

And then it was me again.

I could hear the mechanism pick up the 45 and drop it, the rasp when the needle bit vinyl.

I leaned against the machine, closing my eyes at last. There was the snare drum, then the trumpets, and the touch of Wurlitzer, and, finally, that voice:

O beautiful for heroes prov'd in liberating
    strife
Who more than self their country loved,
    and mercy more than life
America, America, may God thy gold refine
Till all success be nobleness, and every
    gain divine.

It made my eyes hurt, thinking about what kind of man Kenny was to have loved those words so dearly.

Not some flip asshole like me. Not some cheap pompous cynic who should have been killed in his place.

I stood up straight and forced myself to look at him again, at the damage I'd done.

And then whispered, "God shed his grace on thee. . . ."

There was one more quarter in my pocket.

I used it to call 911.

Didn't give my name.

I took one last look around the room.

The doors to the back stairs were jammed shut — Kenny's mop run through their looping handles. I left it in place so the cops would know this wasn't done by the guys upstairs.

Ray was finished, so I pulled the street door toward me, spilling light onto linoleum worn down to black by decades of weary boots.

My vision got all blurry with leaking salty wet and I caved against the aperture's frame, knowing the wrong person was alive. Knowing I had to make it right.

I pulled myself up, walked out onto the sidewalk, into the glare.

A front was rolling in. Snow.

Fall had lasted all of two days this year.

"*You're* goddamn late," Ted snapped from his office doorway.

I walked to my desk, rising howl of sirens as fanfare. "I just found another . . . some-one. Dead."

"That supposed to be funny?"

"My friend. Kenny."

He listened, quiet but pissed, as the sirens slowed and stopped — one at a time and quite nearby.

Ted pointed at me, snarling, "Beginner's *luck.*"

I spat, "Syphilitic *psychosis,*" and pointed right back.

He slammed the door. Good.

I turned sideways in my chair, hugged my knees up to my chest, shut my eyes, and worked really hard at not crying. I had to think. I wasn't sure about Sembles, but Kenny's death was laid squarely at my feet.

I felt a pair of hands come to rest gently on my shoulders. Wilt's voice, quiet. "You were close to that guy, weren't you?"

I nodded, couldn't talk.

"Must have been horrible, finding him like that. Can I do anything for you? Get you coffee? Call Dean? I'm sorry, I feel so damn useless. . . ."

"You're not useless. You didn't get people killed," I said, and then lost it.

He squatted down, wrapping me tight in his arms.

"Shhhh . . ." he said, while I sobbed into his tie. "You didn't kill them, honey. Whoever did is sick . . . he hurts people because he *wants* to. This started practically before you were born. You're not the reason, or the cause, you hip?"

"Maybe for Sembles. But Kenny . . . if he didn't know me, he'd be alive."

"And you always drop by the bar before work?" he asked.

I shook my head.

"Guy was a cop," Wilt said. "Knew what he was getting into."

"But —"

" 'But' my ass. You want to do something for Kenny? Get angry. Get righteously pissed and find out who did this to him, and to *you*. Nail the fucker."

I blew my nose. "Can I give Ted a good kick in the balls first?"

He curled his lip like Elvis. "Be my guest. When you're done, Simon wants to talk to you."

I shivered. "Come with me?"

"Course I will," he said.

Simon had eight-by-tens spread out all over the big table. He looked up when Wilt and I came in. I tried not to think about what he might have had to do with Kenny's death.

I needed him to believe I didn't suspect him of that. Of anything.

The phone rang. Simon picked up, listened, said, "Yes, Amy . . . Maddie's right here."

He handed me the receiver. "Your mother. Line two."

I pushed the blinking cube of Lucite, right below the dial.

"Mom?"

"Madeline. Dodie's dead."

CHAPTER 43

I collapsed into the nearest chair.

Mom's voice came through the line brisk and efficient. "Maria found her this morning. She died in her sleep."

"Jesus."

"Of course she wanted to be cremated, and not in the cemetery since Jake isn't there. There's a lunch at her place tomorrow and then Saturday we'll scatter the ashes on the lake at Camp, so I guess we'll all head up. It's not far from you, so that's easy. Or do you want to come down for the thing here? It's mostly everybody local, but Julie and Bill are coming from Boston."

She could have been talking about pillowcases, or demitasse spoons. Offhand, if breathless, logistics.

"Sure," I said, "I'll drive down there first."

"Then Friday, June and Ogden will fly in to Albany and rent a car. It's about halfway between Albany and Montreal, so flying never makes sense to me, because of course by the time you get through the airport on both ends you might as well just have driven straight through and then there's the parking and everything so I'd *rather* drive —"

"Mom, I'm at work and there's kind of stuff going on —"

"Well," she rattled on, "we're not sure yet whether Alice and Godfrey will come in from Northeast Harbor. Binty's just home from Europe with Kit but *they'll* go. I haven't called the other kids yet. Of course it doesn't make sense for your sister to come home from Florence, but since I knew you'd go I thought you should know first. Will you bring Dean? Do you want her shoes?"

"Her *shoes?*" I said. Simon and Wilt were staring at me.

"Must be a dozen pairs of Belgians in Dodie's closet. You're the only one with feet that big."

"Jesus, Mom, she's not even cold yet."

"Oh, she was. Absolutely. Stiff as a board, too."

"You *touched* her?"

"Sure, you know, just before they wheeled

her out to the hearse. Never felt anybody dead before. Always wondered."

I didn't want to compare notes.

"Well, do you *want* the Belgians?"

"Fine," I said, giving up.

"And Dean?" asked Mom, moving down her list of priorities.

I looked at Simon. Didn't want him to know I was in town alone. "Don't think so."

"Oh well, good-oh anyway. Be at Dodie's by eleven. Help with the chairs. Told you there's lunch afterwards? Turkey Tetrazzini from Piping. Typical."

"Mom? I'll come tonight."

"Must go," she said, and the line clicked dead.

I hung up and pushed the accursed implement back toward Simon.

"Bad news?" asked Wilt.

"My great-grandmother died, which makes her my third dead person in the last forty-eight hours."

I slouched down in the chair. "Can't believe this."

"Your *third?*" asked Simon.

Like he didn't know.

Wilt said, "She found Kenny this morning."

"That guy from the Crown?"

I nodded.

Simon moved closer and it was all I could do not to scoot the chair back against the wall, to get away from him.

"Um, Maddie?" said Wilt.

"What?"

"Don't you think you should, like, go home now?"

"Why, so the guy can kill *me?*"

"Oh, man," said Simon.

Yeah, right.

"Have you told Dean?" asked Wilt.

I drew my knees up again. Didn't answer.

It was cold — like Simon'd turned up the air conditioning even higher than usual down in his little crypt.

There was a short, wide window at the edge of the ceiling. It opened into a well, just below street level. There was an inch of snow piled against the glass, with more blowing in.

"I *hate* this town," I said.

"Want me to call Dean?" asked Wilt. "I can drive you out . . ."

I said I had to let him know in person. I didn't want them to know where he was, and I wanted my gun.

"I have to go to the Adirondacks," I said. "Will you guys tell Ted?"

From behind me, Ted said, "Tell him yourself."

I turned around to find him leaning against the doorway.

"Fine," I said. "Ted, I have to go to the Adirondacks."

"What, *now* you're going to work on the piece?"

"No. Now I'm going to attend a funeral."

"Always *something*," he said.

"What the hell's wrong with you, man?" said Wilt. "The poor kid . . ."

Ted pursed his lips. "Take Simon."

Even for him that was bullshit. Even if I didn't suspect Simon of anything. "To my great-grandmother's *funeral?* You're fucking kidding."

"So, he can meet you up there," he said, "get some shots afterwards."

"Ted, that's appalling," said Simon. "I can't believe you're asking her to do that. I can't believe you're asking *me*."

"The camp doesn't belong to me, Ted," I said. "I'm going to be there on my relatives' sufferance."

"And you work here on my sufferance," he said. "I want those damn pictures."

He stomped up the stairs.

"Ignore him," said Wilt. "Just get the hell out of here. Do what you need."

Simon nodded in agreement. "We'll talk to him."

He seemed so mellow, so sympathetic. Not the raver of yesterday, but he had to be the killer or the killer's little helper. He laid a hand on my shoulder and I flinched.

"Okay," I said, desperate to start driving downstate, away from him, from this shit. But first I wanted to run home and throw my gun in the back of the Volkswagen.

I wished to hell Dean were there, so I could tell him he'd been right, and that Kenny was dead because I hadn't listened.

I walked outside. All the leaves were brown, and the sky was gray.

■ ■ ■ ■

PART IV
CENTRE ISLAND

■ ■ ■ ■

You are a poor girl . . . and if you can't make up your mind to being that, you'll become one of those terrible girls that don't know whether they are million-airesses or paupers.

— F. Scott Fitzgerald,
in a letter to his daughter Scottie

CHAPTER 44

The next morning I left Bonwit's and walked up to Dodie's through the woods, following an old path that wound between archipelagoes of Queen Anne's lace and thickets of wineberry. The trees thinned, and I was at the top of Dodie's driveway.

They must have sent Egon up to cut the grass out front for the occasion. As I came inside the final pale brick bulwark, it looked as though each blade had been scythed to perfect bluntness, scattered drops of water prisming fall sunlight into flaming bijou points of intense orange, lemon, scarlet, gas-blue.

The trimmed lawn was a last-minute attempt to conceal massive and catastrophic entropy, ineffectual trompe l'oeil. There wasn't the time or inclination to pull the thick beard of ivy from the twenty visible window sashes, to replace the broken, coffin-shaped panes of glass in the great bronze lantern. It was just another rotting pre-FDR palace that had started as an homage to Monticello and ended as a second-act *Gone With the Wind* set — forty acres, no mule.

I stepped through an arched doorframe and into the cool, boxwood-scented darkness of the arcade leading to the front door. There were no sounds but the last of the Canada geese, honking as they abandoned the place, and the heels of my loafers ringing off slate in the few spots that weren't choked with fallen leaves.

More leaves had blown inside, skirling around the thirty-foot diameter of dark marble floor as I came through the front door. The entry was a circular, gossamer-railed staircase sweeping up to a viewing balcony, light slanting in through high windows.

Bronzes of my great-grandparents' heads rested in a niche halfway up the stairs. Dodie's hair was shingled flapper-style. Jake's brilliantined straight back off his forehead. The room would have been imposing, had the pale-mint wallpaper not been hanging down in broad sheets, only occasionally stuck back up to the plaster with ragged lengths of packing tape.

Considering how badly I'd fucked things

up in the last week, it seemed entirely appropriate that I was back here at Chateau Failure to mark the occasion.

"Hello?" I said, my voice echoing until a pair of yipping, rheumy-eyed shih tzus came barreling around the corner, nails clattering on stone, yellowed hair held off their faces with tiny pink and blue plastic barrettes.

I waded through the dogs and into the dining room, where the table was set for twenty. Dodie's portrait condescended from above the sideboard, emeralds sparkling from her cocked hip.

I touched the bottom of the frame, thought of the painting's nickname and whispered, "Nice to see your back again," then ducked through the pantry and into the kitchen itself.

Maria the cook, in jeans and a big plaid flannel shirt, looked up from the broad black stove and grinned at me, gold tooth flashing.

"*Hola,* Madalena! *Cerveza?*"

She wouldn't take no for an answer, pulling a chair out from the table, clapping me on the back, and handing me a cold can from her personal stash of Budweiser in what seemed like one bustling motion, her long black braids swinging in the wake of her perfectly square body.

"Is good to see you. You doin' okay?" she said, sitting down next to me and patting my arm.

"Shitty week," I said, looking around the kitchen, more deeply familiar to me than the front rooms. Children were raised in purdah, here, sequestered with the help. "How are you?"

"Two nights ago, I have a dream about a dog digging a hole," she said. "So I know this is coming. In Bolivia, that is a dream for death. I am packed everything, next morning."

"What will you do?" I asked, worried for her here with no papers, and now no job.

"Well, now you great-grandmommy is dead, I go home — one more month. Is okay, you know? I save some money, so now I see my family. Life is good for me. Death is not good, but *okay,* it happens. Everybody go with God someday."

"That's right," I said, taking a *vaya-con-Dios* pull of the beer.

"You look tired," Maria said. "You come see me before I go home. We party!" She shimmied her shoulders like Charo, threw her head back, and cackled.

"Sounds perfect," I said, smiling for the first time in days. When I finished the beer, we moved several dozen chairs into the living room, cleaned the fireplace, and swept out leaves from everywhere while the caterers brought in tubs of Tetrazzini and Egon set up the bar.

When the first of my relatives began to trickle in the front door, Maria took me aside. "When you pray for you great-grandmommy today, ask her you wish, and she *must* do. Promise you no forget, okay?"

"Okay," I said, "thank you."

She looked both ways and then hugged me, hard. "You good girl. No forget this also," she whispered, then pushed me out into the fray and vanished back to the kitchen.

As I started off toward the living room, I realized she'd stuffed a twenty-dollar bill into my jacket pocket, which just killed me.

Wasn't the first time. I'd tried refusing, tried handing back whichever bill she'd palmed on me, even tried sneaking them into her purse when she wasn't looking, but nothing worked. She'd just hide them in my car — tucked into the glove compartment, the ashtray, up under the visor.

When I asked her to stop, she said, "They give me money, they give you nothing. No problem — I give you instead."

"You *work* for them."

"Same they make you work. Just they

don't pay you."

It was still crazy.

Kit and Binty were the first people to see me. He shook my hand heartily with both of his while peering over my head.

Binty stepped forward, placed her feet in third position, touched my elbow. She looked deep into my eyes, as though steadying herself before imparting great wisdom.

"Madeline," she said, smiling, seeking the pearls at her throat with a narrow hand, *"dear . . ."*

"Yes?" I gazed back at her — awed by her flawless chignon of Peronista-blonde hair, her navy bouclé suit crisply trimmed in white — hoping desperately she couldn't see the nail polish dabbed on the runs in my stockings.

She took a little sip of air, whispered, ". . . there's *dirt* on your face," and then blushed for me, becomingly. *Innagadda d'Evita.*

I backed away and snuck out to the downstairs guest-room bath. I scrubbed the offending smear of what turned out to be ashes off my cheek, surrounded by a Deco mural of ocelots, vines, and tropical birds.

"Jungle Bunny," I said to my reflection.

Lapthorne slipped into the bedroom just as I was walking back out.

"Maddie," he said, "your mother told me

someone else was killed. Who was it? How are you?"

"It was Kenny," I said, "the guy you met at the bar."

"Shit," he said. "I am so sorry —"

His father walked in. "Christ, Lapthorne, they're starting. Get a damn move on," he said, and strode out, expecting us both to follow.

Lapthorne did a little soft-shoe on the gray rug, offered me his arm. "Okay, *chère cousine,* ready to shuck and jive?"

We had to grab the last seats, on opposite sides of the room from each other. I was stuck behind a clot of uncles with my shoulder wedged into the curtains, and couldn't see Reverend Pettit, so I just listened to him intoning Episcopalian niceties with an exquisite lack of passion, the hallmark of our Protestant descendancy, and looked out the window toward the gunmetal water.

I tried to concentrate on my memories of Dodie, to give her some due as matriarch. My throat tightened and I could sense tears coming on, gave myself shit about not having had the foresight to grab a fistful of toilet paper. But it wasn't memories of Dodie herself that got me worked up.

After all, had she been there in person,

she would at best have smiled at me and said, "Hello, Skippy, how is New Haven this year?" The only affection of hers I'd ever basked in had been bestowed through breakdowns of her visual or mental acuity.

It was this absence of memory that got me going: the warmth of other people's families, and of people like Maria and Kenny, who allowed me glimpses of what it must be like to belong to one, that made me cry. And when I looked away from the window and back around the room, at that gathering of utterly beautiful, exquisitely mannered progeny Dodie was responsible for bringing into the world, it became apparent that not a single one of them would be joining me. I still don't know whether the flaw in the scenario rested with her, with them, or with me.

As Pettit intoned a final prayer, I remembered what Maria had said, closed my eyes, and asked Dodie to help me find justice for Kenny, so that I could at least begin to repay my staggering debt to the kindness of strangers.

CHAPTER 45

"You were very sweet to cry," said

Lapthorne, when we sat down with our plates of turkey slop in the kitchen, no places having been set for us in the land of the grownups.

"Oh please," I said, "all I've done this week is cry and puke. My father would be proud. I've become the poster child for Primal Therapy."

"Your father's only problem is that his daddy was rich and his ma was good lookin'. You've had actual reasons to cry and puke — not least him."

"It's not like I was crying *for* Dodie, and that seems shitty, too. It's just . . . Kenny, and all the lost opportunity, and I'm sad I never knew her."

"Not knowing her is why you were the only person in that room who isn't grateful she's dead," he said.

"It's not even Dodie," I said, "it's all of them. I mean, don't you look around and wonder what happened? They had everything — the best education, connections — they were handsome and smart and charming and war heroes and they frittered it all away. The reverse Midas touch . . . it's like looking at a herd of failed Kennedys."

"Maddie, they wouldn't stoop to accept a blowjob from a Kennedy."

"And I'm sure that keeps Caroline and

Teddy lying awake nights," I said.

He laughed. "I'm just saying that they don't even know they failed. They're all too busy thinking how great it is that they can dump this place while there's still just enough money to pay the taxes on it. Do you know it took forty grand just to heat it, every winter? For one old woman who hasn't known what year it was since Truman. As far as they're concerned, Dodie should've died with Jake. It's all they can do not to break out the champagne."

I thought about that for a minute. "So that's how come we're the only cousins here? Not even Skippy?"

"I don't know about the rest of them," he said. "I came for you."

And before I could answer that, the pantry door swung open and Aunt Julie came in.

"Come upstairs with your fairy godmother, Madeline," she said, twinkling her fingers and smiling at me. "I have *shoes* for you!"

Lapthorne stood, well trained, and they kissed cheeks.

"Hullo, Lappy, dear — your mother is wondering what *became* of you," she said.

"Must go dance attendance, then," he said, clicking his heels and bowing. "Maddie, you'll be at Bonwit's? I want to get caught up on everything else and share some thoughts. Lovely to see you, Cousin Julie," and he was gone.

"So that's *nice* you're getting to know your cousin," said Julie, as we walked into Dodie's dove-gray bedroom. "Have you been having *fun?*"

Mom and Julie were not the closest of siblings, perhaps because Julie stayed married to a guy with a job, so there wasn't a lot they had in common. At any rate, I didn't expect her to know what had been going on in my life lately. Of all the relatives in Mom's generation, though, she had taken the most interest in me, besides which she was fun to party with and was in fact my godmother.

"I think Lapthorne is great," I said. "I just can't figure out what his parents did to deserve him. Binty couldn't wait to tell me I looked like shit."

"Oh, Kit and Binty are fine, Maddie, for goodness' sakes. *Very* nice. You probably call her that awful name behind her back, like your Uncle Hunt? It's just too ooky . . . I can't even *say* it."

"Ice Cunt?" I said, grinning at her.

"How can you even let that word out of your *mouth,* you awful child!" she said, but I'd made her laugh.

Julie opened the door to Dodie's dressing room, then pushed one of the old light buttons — black for off, mother-of-pearl for on — and led me into her closet.

"Your feet are *really* this big?" she said, looking at the dozen pairs of slippers on the shelves.

"Tens," I answered.

"My God, bigger than Clementine's. Well, I guess you even *look* like Dodie, don't you, in a certain way? You're the only one who does, of the girls. Her cheekbones, lucky you," she said, sucking her face in and making fish lips at me.

"*That's* attractive," I said.

"Well, you lucked out in the footwear department, my dear niece," she said, waving her hand at the shoes. They were in every color, with piping and little bows to contrast — navy with green, red with black, white with baby blue, a rainbowed silk with lavender, and even black patent, pressed into mock crocodile. I reached for the latter and tried them on.

"Like a glove," I said. The soles felt amazing — full of Marshmallow Fluff.

"A very expensive glove," she said. "I'm sorry they don't fit your old aunt."

"Oh for God's sake, Julie, why don't you buy yourself a pair? You guys are rich."

"You must be in *sorry* shape to think we're rich," she said, laughing.

"Okay, maybe not the Sultan of Brunei or anything, but you're, like, *normal.*"

At that, she started laughing so hard I had to help her into a chair. When she'd wiped the tears from her eyes, she asked me what I planned to do with my footwear largesse.

"I thought I'd wear them to exotic places they've never been before. You know, like *work,*" which set both of us off all over again.

"You are not *allowed* to make me laugh, Madeline Dare," she said. "It's a goddamn funeral, for chrissake."

"Okay, so here's a serious question," I said. "Why won't Dodie be buried here, in the cemetery? After all the work she put into it . . . the roses."

"It was in her will," said Julie. "She told everyone she wanted to be cremated. Have her ashes scattered at Camp."

"Why?"

"She never explained. I always thought it was because these weren't her people. She wasn't born here. But I heard once that she'd said if she couldn't be next to Jake in the ground, she wanted to be in water. The way he was."

"Gonna be cold up there," I said. "Lake's probably frozen."

"Well then, they'll just have to shoot at the ice until the urn falls through, won't they?" she said.

Julie got up and started loading all the Belgians into a box. "Now take these down the back stairs to the kitchen, so Binty doesn't make fun of you, and then come back in and *have a booze.*"

I told her I would, but when I got down to the kitchen and started to open the swinging door, I could hear Kit's baritone swamping all the other voices.

"Cute story . . . cute story . . ." he said, always the cue for an anecdote about how a friend of his had dropped dead recently on a golf course or while nailing a mistress. I wasn't in the mood for any of the people in that room, so I turned around and kept going right on out the servants' entrance.

I thought I'd go back into the woods, but Lapthorne was leaning against his car, waiting for me.

"Running away from home, little girl?" he asked, grinning.

"Just really didn't want to get into the whole gin-and-tonic scene with everybody, especially Mom and Uncle Bonny."

"I must agree. Even around here we don't need Binty, Bonny, and Bunny in the same room."

"Bibbity bobbity boo," I said, shifting the box of shoes on my hip and eyeing the gleaming Porsche. "Can I drive?"

He took the box from me and threw it into the back seat, then motioned for me to get behind the wheel. I hit seventy in second gear before we even got off Centre Island, slowing down before we passed Burwell behind his usual tree. We went to the Long Island Expressway and back, not talking, just listening to way-early Stones on the tape deck: "Route 66" and "King Bee" and "Not Fade Away."

The wheel felt wider across but thinner in my hands, compared to the Rabbit's, and the car took corners flat and heavy no matter how fast I came into them, with speed left over to accelerate out every time. I knew there wouldn't be food at Bonwit's, except for gelled Tetrazzini Mom would no doubt "liberate" and tell us she was saving for lunch next Tuesday, so we grabbed beer and slices in Bayville to bring back.

When we got there, Mom and Bonwit weren't home yet, so I did a doughnut in the bottom of his driveway, throwing up gravel like a water-skier, and when we got out I broke our radio silence by saying, "If I had that car I think I'd never be unhappy again."

"Oh, you're enough like me, Maddie," said Lapthorne. "You'd find a way."

It was getting dark and colder, so I led him down to the sunporch at the far end of the house and lit a big fire. The flames danced off every windowpane around us, and it was warm close in, but our backs were still cold so I brought blankets down from the third floor after we'd eaten our pizza and thrown the greasy papers into the grate.

When we finished our beers, Lapthorne broke out a silver flask of Scotch and took a drink before handing it to me.

"Do you always have to sneak around, here?" he asked.

"It depends on how much of a masochist you are," I said. "His kids have the run of the place, but if we brought friends home from school, he'd ask them over dinner if they'd ever tried lighting their own farts. If anybody phoned for us, he'd pretend to be an Azorean receptionist at an abortionist's office and then hang up on them."

Lapthorne laughed and I passed the flask back to him.

"And, see, that's the worst part," I said. "If you try to describe it, he just sounds charming and unconventional, and we sound like peevish little shits. Plus, of course, the place is so goddamn beautiful you feel ridiculous being pissed off — you can't ever forget all the starving children in Armenia who'd give their eyeteeth for some of your lukewarm pork and beans on the terrace. Still, there are compensations . . ."

"Such as?"

"The milkman has good dope," I said, "and we're the last house on his route."

I lay down on my belly, facing the fire, and propped my chin on my hands.

"I'm only sorry," I said, "that I never brought Kenny down here. He would have held his own. But then he probably never would have spoken to me again. People think you've betrayed them if they've known you as broke and then find out your mother lives someplace like this."

"Kenny struck me as the kind of guy who would have seen through that," he said. "I imagine you meant a lot to him."

"And look how I repaid the favor," I said.

"You really think that?"

I looked over at him, lying on his side and leaning on an elbow, his long legs stretched toward the fire, the blanket arranged around his shoulders like a mantle. "Yes," I said. "I really think that. If it wasn't for me, he'd be alive right now, and Sembles, too. I think somehow bringing everything up around Simon has led to two deaths, and I think if I don't figure out what the hell is going on, that there'll be more. Kenny told me to look more closely at Simon, and he told me I was right about not going to the cops. There's a connection there, and I'm damned if I'm smart enough to see what it is."

"You're plenty smart enough," he said. "You just need a little more opportunity to garner information, and you shouldn't have to do this on your own anymore. We should both talk to Simon."

"Ted — my boss, real asshole — told me I had to bring Simon up to Camp. Have him get a few rolls of the place for that Adirondacks article I'm supposed to write. I mean, in the middle of a goddamn funeral."

"I think it's a great idea."

"Oh *please*."

"No, really. I think what we need is to get Simon up to Camp. It's perfect," he said. "He's obviously the key to the thing, somehow. And I can't let you do this alone anymore. Too dangerous."

"In the middle of the funeral?"

"Invite him up there to take some snaps when everybody's left . . . maybe Monday or Tuesday. I'll pay the per diem freight."

They'd made it a corporation. Cousins

with dough had divided up shares years ago, paid annual dues to cover the upkeep and taxes. Served on the board. Even then they parceled out time to one another at the rate of five hundred bucks a day. So the per diem to keep the place open through Monday or Tuesday . . . well, it was generous of him.

"That's tremendously kind," I said, "but what good will it do us to have Simon at Camp?"

"The place has a way of opening people up, I've found," he said, then grinned, and added, "chicks especially."

"Like I'm sure you need so much help in that department. But Simon's not a chick."

"I'm just saying that Camp has a formidable effect on people. If you want to find out what Simon's part is in this, you need to get him alone, and there's not a better place to do that than the Adirondacks."

I looked at the fire. "I'm starting to think he's the killer, Lappy. I mean, you want to be in the middle of woods with a violent psycho? I've gotten too many people hurt with this."

"So, your entire paper will know he's up with us on assignment. Why would he do anything? He'd get slammed."

"He's been acting really freaky lately. Temperamental, pissy with everybody.

Complete shift in his personality. He might be getting into what they call 'decompensating.' He knows I'm looking into these murders. He must feel threatened. It's just too dangerous."

"Maddie," he said, "what's he going to do? We know where all the guns are, and he doesn't. Safe as milk."

"Look, he'll still be in Syracuse when this is over. We can talk to him there, with more people around. I'll bring you to the paper. Right now he doesn't think I suspect him of anything specific. I refused to bring him up to Camp and I haven't talked to anyone else about it. If I suddenly change my mind, he'll know something's up. I'm not putting you in danger, or Ellis. You're bringing her, right?"

"Since you're married," he said with a grin, "I suppose she'll have to do."

I didn't know what to say to that, so I took a big gulp of the Scotch. I'm sure whatever he'd have was good, but the stuff always tasted like nail polish remover to me.

"L'Chaim," I said. I finished off the flask and pulled a couple of pillows down off the wicker sofa. The fire was so warm, and the blankets were so cozy, that I was asleep in a flash.

CHAPTER 46

I awoke the next morning to see Bonwit glowering over us, in stained painter's pants and a moth-eaten old pink sweater monogrammed with his daughter's initials.

"Charming," he said, looking from me to Lapthorne.

"My thought exactly," I croaked back. Lappy and I still had our shoes on, for God's sake, not to mention all our clothes. I tried to shut my eyes and ignore him, but he sent Egon out with the gas-powered leaf blower, which he aimed at the bottom of the French doors right next to my head.

"I'm beginning to see what you mean about a certain lack of hospitality extended on your behalf," said Lapthorne.

"The usual rude awakening. I apologize."

Lappy stood up and threw Egon a stiff-armed *Sieg Heil,* which pissed the old guy off so much he shut down the blower and stomped off into the bushes.

"Be careful," I said, laughing. "He'll probably go paint swastikas on your car."

"Fuck 'im," he answered. "Let's drive out to civilization and find some breakfast."

Mom cornered me on the second floor as I was taking the blankets back up.

"I have to say, Madeline," she said, "that I'm *appalled*. Sleeping with your cousin, for God's sake . . . you could at least have had the courtesy to take him up to the third floor —"

"The operative word there is 'sleeping,' Mom, as in 'we fell asleep.' "

"Don't use that bitchy tone with me."

"Fine, then. I'll use a polite one," I said, flaming with moral indignation and feeling perfectly justified in skewering her. "You've just accused me of fucking my cousin in a big glass room, and implied that it would have been perfectly all right if I'd snuck him upstairs and out of sight. Are you more worried we outraged your boyfriend's sensibilities, or that his wife might have dropped by and seen us?"

"I just don't *dig* it," she said.

I walked away.

When I got back from the diner in Bayville, I threw everything into a ratty duffel bag and came downstairs to say goodbye to Mom.

She was in the kitchen, snipping the ends off the year's last roses at the sink.

I hugged her from behind, telling her again that I was sorry.

"There's someone on the phone for you,"

she said. "Bonwit's got it in the green room. I hope you have a good trip. . . ."

I went on into the green room, where Bonwit sat at his desk with a big Luneville cup of boozological tea. He had one hand raised in the air, and the phone dangled from his fingers, spinning slowly back and forth on its coiled cord, the dial tone dopplering.

"Oh, hullo, dear," he said. "It was someone from Canada, but I think they hung up about five minutes ago."

He let the receiver fall to the desk with a thunk, then turned and smiled at me.

Dean must have called the paper, to know I was here. But at least he'd know that even Bonwit wouldn't blow him off if I'd been killed.

"You suck, Uncle Bonny," I said.

"Don't I just?" he said, pulling his glasses back down off the top of his head and reaching for the book he'd been reading by way of goodbye.

I shouldered my duffel and walked out, tossing it into the back of the car on top of my gun, tightening the baling wire on the hatchback so the damn thing would stay shut.

I walked up to Lapthorne's window. "So we're picking up Ellis?"

He nodded. "She's hitching a ride to the Taconic. Gas station right off the Austerlitz exit."

"Race you," I said, and we tore out of the driveway.

■ ■ ■ ■

PART V
CAMP

■ ■ ■ ■

The land! Don't you feel it? Doesn't it make you want to go out and lift dead Indians tenderly from their graves, to steal from them — as if it must be clinging even to their corpses — some authenticity, that which —

Here not there.

— William Carlos Williams,
In the American Grain

CHAPTER 47

Coming into the Adirondack Park was like driving suddenly out of Appalachia and into the forests of Bavaria. From the nearly tree-less expanse of the Mohawk's run between Syracuse and Albany, the road plunged into a landscape dense with brooding, wizard-hatted pines and spruce.

The ill-kept two-lane road jumped and dove ahead of us, revealing, from between the stands of evergreens beginning to blacken in the ebbing light, sudden glimpses of great, still, pewtered lakes or flashes of deciduous trees whose fall color was so intense I continually mistook them for fire.

There were few towns this far north, just sometimes clusters of buildings around the old iron bridges spanning necks between lakes.

I was glad to be tailing Lapthorne and El-lis, as the only indication you get for the four-mile-long dirt driveway in was an inch-high series of code flags painted on a one-foot-square plywood sign: C-A-M-P. He slowed way the hell down at the sign for the town of Macy's Lake.

Camp was on its own "pond" to the south, a fish-shaped three-mile length of water called, redundantly, Little Smalls. Great-grandfather Lapthorne had bought the five thousand acres surrounding this in about 1892, when building "Great Camps" was just becoming fashionable among the rich who wanted to summer more rustically than was possible in Newport or Long Island.

He commissioned a sprawling lodge of dark wood on the edge of the water, connected to its outbuildings by a series of covered walkways through the forest. There was an icehouse and a boathouse, servants' quarters above an octagonal dining room, and an old stable that had been converted to a garage, complete with a Deco gas pump out front.

When I stepped out of the car, I stood for a minute, struck by the stillness of the place, the absolute quiet punctuated only by an occasional loon. And of course gunfire.

From the slow rhythm of the shots, I deduced that those already here were getting in a little target practice off the dining room porch, which stood on a large boulder about thirty feet above the water.

For almost a hundred years now, family members had saved any small bottles to toss out onto the lake. They made great targets because they'd float until hit, and the water just off the dining room got very deep very fast, so broken glass didn't bother anything but the few trout who'd survived the on-slaught of acid rain. The water was frozen from the shore to about thirty feet out, and looking oily beyond that.

I left my gun in the back of the car, since the weapon of choice for this game was a .22, they obviously hadn't run out of bottles yet, and you couldn't set up the trap for skeet below while people were shooting off the porch. I hauled my duffel out and followed Ellis and Lappy up the steps to the front door.

"God, it still smells the same," I said, stepping inside and inhaling wood smoke and spruce and the must of generations.

"Batshit," he said. "They get in through the vents, and the roof is leaking."

"Oh, come on, Lappy," I said, dropping my bag next to a dark wooden hatrack carved to resemble a small bear trying to climb a leafless tree, "allow me a little moment of sentiment. I haven't been up here since I was twelve."

"I had no idea you liked the place. I'm more than happy to drag you up anytime — maybe the four of us should come back for Thanksgiving."

Ellis was beaming and I tried really hard not to look too pathetically grateful, but must have failed miserably because he threw an arm around my shoulder and clenched me in half a hug, saying, "Least I can do, considering."

He led us up the stairs and showed us our room. I had no doubt we'd be rearranging quarters after the grownups had turned in for the night, but for the moment I was bunking with Ellis.

"I'll be right next door," said Lapthorne, "should anything go bump in the night."

In the end we didn't have to shoot at Dodie's urn, or even cut a hole in the ice. We gathered where a brook poured into Little Smalls, and the way the water frothed after tumbling through its cut in the bank kept ice from forming for a radius of ten feet.

We stood in a broad, ragged circle, on either side of the brook, Ellis and Lappy much further up the hill from me. There were no words spoken as Ogden, her eldest son, stepped down to the edge and shook

Dodie's ashes into the water, though I have to say the stuff looked more like gravel to me. Kitty Litter. We were just all silent in the face of the great stillness that seemed to rise off the cold surface of the lake, the hysteria of a single loon bouncing off the dark mountains ringing the water, its voice reverberating in the depth of quiet.

We stayed there with our heads bowed, and I thought about how the perfection of this body of water had been paid for with the utter desecration of Lake Oncas, and how, even so, Little Smalls mattered to me more than anywhere else on earth, more even than most people.

I have no talent for quiet meditation, have never gained an insight on the nature of the universe while having to duck my head in silence for anything. My mind just wanders and jumps. I didn't even have a kind thought left for the flight of Dodie's supposed soul, instead considered Kenny with his halo of coins, the pomegranate seeds, and wished I could have brought him here just once.

People started raising their heads and walking slowly back toward Camp. I stayed in the same spot, just breathing in the cold sharp air and looking out over the water and wondering, now that Dodie was gone, if I'd ever have been allowed to come back here but for Lapthorne.

Binty was the last to start up the hill. I was ready to follow, but she stopped before I took a step, blocking the trail.

When everyone else was out of earshot, she looked down at me, saying quietly, "You realize, of course, that when your parents sold their shares in Camp, they were told it meant their children would never be allowed to buy back in?"

Then she smiled and strode away.

I just stood there, slackjawed in the cold.

CHAPTER 48

Egon was manning a bar in the dining room for most of the afternoon, and by dinner that night I was much the worse for wear. Lappy and Ellis sat with me at the kiddy table, the rest of the family gathered around the great round oak table in front of the fireplace.

"Titanic salad," said Lapthorne, pushing the quarter-wedge of iceberg doused in Thousand Island dressing to the edge of his plate.

"Not a big group for cuisine," I said.

"All too drunk to know what they're eating," he said.

I realized that I was, too. Things were blurry enough that I kept wanting to shut one eye, and I had no interest whatsoever in dinner.

I heard Kit's voice ringing out at the next table, "Cute story . . . cute story . . . friend of mine bought a snowblower and dropped dead of a heart attack . . ."

"So tell me about Dodie," said Ellis. "What was she like?"

"The only thing I know about her is she was a junkie," I said. "I just have this picture of her shooting up with a monogrammed Tiffany syringe in her dressing room, surrounded by all her Belgian shoes."

"Oh no," said Lapthorne. "Dodie never shot up . . . she wasn't into morphine or heroin. She had a more old-fashioned bent."

"What *was* she into, then?" asked Ellis.

"Chloral hydrate," he said. "It was pretty much the first thing they gave for sleeping pills, other than laudanum or opium. She had terrible insomnia after Jake died. The syrup form is what bartenders used to use for knockout drops when they had unruly drunks or rich ones they wanted to roll. Called that a Mickey Finn, after the first guy who made a habit of it in Chicago . . . I guess he ran a pretty notorious dive right around the time of the big fire there."

"So it just makes you sleep?" I asked. "What fun is that?"

"Oh, Madeline, addiction is really never about fun," he said. "It's always about pain."

I bowed my head in concession to that.

"It still seems like a pretty unusual choice for what could be called 'recreational' use," I said, "fun or no fun."

"Well," he explained, "it's one of the few scheduled drugs you can make at home, with a little bit of chemistry background. That's where Jimmy the driver came in. Wonder what *he'll* do now."

"Jesus," I said.

I found myself drifting over to Egon and the bar more than usual that night. At one point, when no one else was within earshot, he looked at me seriously and said, "I hear from your mother you been finding a lot of bodies."

I wondered whether it had become her latest lagniappe of intriguing news, the top of the hit parade for phone calls to her friends: "And you'll never *guess* what Maddie's been up to in *Syracuse. . . .*"

"Someone you know?" he said, more sympathetic than I'd ever seen him.

"The last guy, yeah," I said. "A good friend."

"Not just dead, *ja?* Maybe hurt before they die?"

I nodded.

"I'm sorry. Makes it much harder. I remember with my daughter, when I had to see the body, and they tell me what was done to her before she die."

"I thought she drowned . . ."

"In a bathtub. First they cut her feet maybe a hundred times, and put a knife up . . . you know. Police tell me they find her body, that she was drown after they do all that." He looked down at the white tablecloth, clenched his fists.

The image he'd rendered of his daughter's torture, his sadness, made me bow my head. Who were the people that could inflict this? Could leave echoing, haunted voids where beloved children had been? Egon with that pain at the center of his life forever.

"Death, maybe, it's simple," he said, "*maybe* . . . if you don't see it coming. But when you know the person have to think about it first, have to know . . . Well, I'm sorry for you."

He put his hand on top of mine and gave it a little squeeze.

When the elders had gone to bed, the moon came up, dyeing the ice blue, and there was a stiff breeze riffing on the sluggish, not-yet-frozen water in the center.

Ellis was telling us about taking Lapthorne to see the Winslow Homer watercolors at the Clark Art Institute in Williamstown, saying how glad she was that they'd caught the show before it'd closed last Monday.

I'd stopped drinking cocktails, but suddenly got very thirsty. Egon was long gone, so I cut clumsily through the dark dining room toward the kitchen. When I got through the swinging door, I realized Lapthorne was behind me.

I could see a six-pack of ginger ale on the counter, in the moonlight spilling through a pantry window, and walked over to take one. When I turned around, he was standing right next to me.

"She's right, you know," he said.

"Who?" I said, steadying myself against the counter.

"Ellis. It *is* a crime you're married."

He leaned toward me and crooked his index finger under my chin, tilting my face up.

"Lappy —" I said, worried he was going to try kissing me, worried about what I'd do — all that rum making the edges of everything way too soft and comfortable.

"Don't say a word," he said, placing the

pad of his thumb tenderly over the center of my mouth. "It's just too bad, that's all. Thought you should know."

He stepped away from me and then walked out of the kitchen. I cracked open the soda and decided it was high time I put myself to bed.

When I finally got there and lay down, the bed was spinning and all I could think about was Egon's daughter, floating in a pool of water with her feet cut to ribbons. The image tugged at the edge of my consciousness until finally the bed seemed to take such a dip that I put my foot on the floor to stop it from moving.

CHAPTER 49

"You should get up," Ellis said, sitting on the edge of my bed and nearly sending the contents of my stomach to Tilt. "Everybody's gone but us."

"If they've all left, what's the hurry?" I said, pulling a pillow over my eyes to avoid the painful sunlight. She pulled it away.

I opened my eyes and looked at her. She had a goofy little smile and kept rolling her eyes up to check out the ceiling, avoiding my face.

"What?" I said. "You have that *look*."

"What look?"

"Oh for God's sake, Ellis." I sat up and swacked her with the pillow.

"Okay . . . so Lapthorne . . . last night," she said.

"What?"

"He told me he's in love with me," she said.

It's just too bad, that's all. Thought you should know.

"Wow," I said. "Congratulations."

She held out a fist, then opened it, palm up.

Resting there was a pin, the row of diamonds and emeralds I knew from Dodie's portrait. The one she'd worn on her hip.

"He gave me this, but . . ." she said.

I touched it with one finger. The sunlight hit its stones and the whole thing flashed. Full-spectrum glints from the diamonds, deep blue from the emeralds.

"But what?" I asked.

"I mean, he said this belonged to Dodie. I think it should have gone to you."

"Do you have any idea how happy it makes me? That he gave this to you?" I said. "It's perfect."

"Thank you," she said, still uncertain.

"Ellis, after Dean, you guys are my two

favorite people. Maybe we'll all be . . ."

"The *four* of us," she said. "That would be the best part, wouldn't it? Can't you just see . . ."

"*Everything* . . . the most amazing . . ." I started, then didn't want to add another word, certain that saying the least bit more out loud would jinx all the gorgeous possibilities.

I tried to stop even the delicious rush of visions in my head.

Don't think about all of us together, when Dean comes home. Don't think about us sprawled out on the Naugahyde, talking late into the night, or cooking a big dinner in our kitchen or Lapthorne's.

Don't think about who would wake up first on a Sunday morning after a party and cue up the coffee before starting to collect half-full glasses from all over everywhere, and how I would put on some Puccini but Ellis would want Talking Heads . . .

How there might be a passel of kids, dark-haired and fair, tumbling together on beaches and in canoes, summer after summer . . . all of them falling asleep in the car on the way home, heads slumped on each other's shoulders . . .

How we might all be made whole, at long last.

Ellis touched the jeweled bar in her hand, rocked it to and fro so it flashed in the light.

"Madwoman," she said, "I am so terrified that I'm going to screw this up."

I reached again for her hand and gently closed her fingers over the pin. "Tell you what," I said. "Whenever it seems too good to be true, just think of all those holidays you'll have to spend with Binty . . . Christmas dinners at some long table with too many forks, while she pushes a sliver of goose around her plate, *wincing . . .*"

"*Easter . . .*" she groaned. "Fucking *Thanksgiving . . .*"

"Kit carving the turkey, saying 'Cute story . . . cute story . . .' "

And then we both cracked up, which made my head pound even worse, but after a couple of minutes Ellis looked all serious again.

She got up off the bed and walked over to the windows, a tiny row of them above dark cabinets.

"If it was any other guy," she said, "someone *like* him . . . I mean, I'd be nervous . . . excited about the possibility of it working out, because after all he's beautiful and he's a pleasure to be with and he even has some money, which is not the first thing but it's a thing . . ."

"Of course," I said.

"Except he's *not* any other guy, so this isn't just about me . . . *for* me . . . there's more at stake."

She turned her head to glance back at me, then looked again out the windows.

"That's the hard part," she said. "That's what scares me — why it matters so much that I don't ruin things with him. Not what it would mean for me, but what it would mean for you."

"You *can't* worry about —"

"I can," she said. "I will."

She put the pin down, on top of the dark wood, and dropped her hand. "Because here's this one little object, so beautifully made, and here *we* are in this remarkable place, and up until now, all of it was lost to you. . . ."

"Ellis . . ."

"And if I *don't* fuck this up," she said, "I'll make goddamn sure you have it back. Everything."

"Ellis, I am *incredibly* honored, and you're the personification of all anyone could want in a friend, but there's something you have to know . . ."

She turned around. "Tell me."

I looked humbly at the floor. "When you

say *everything* . . ."

"Yes?"

"Look," I said, "I'm not averse to jewelry or money or fast cars or hunting lodges, but if you *ever* try palming Binty off on me . . ."

"Never," she said, "cross my heart and hope to die."

"Long as we're clear on that," I said, standing up.

A mistake.

"You okay, Maddie? You look a little . . . pale."

"I feel like shit."

"You should eat. Lapthorne's down in the kitchen . . . he said something about pancakes and trout."

"Yummy," I unconvincingly enthused.

"Exactly what I said," she confided. "*I'll* make you something . . . a milkshake."

"Um, could you put some Tylenol in it? Maybe sunglasses and an icepack?"

We walked very, very slowly down along the covered walkway to the dining room, and back through to the kitchen. Lapthorne helped Ellis locate a blender, and they found a pint of coffee Häagen-Dazs in the third icebox they tried.

She put two scoops in the Waring's glass carafe with some milk, and he doped it further with a little maple syrup.

It did help, she was right. Enough that Lapthorne suggested we do some shooting off the porch.

"I've got an old pump-action .22," he said, "I'll run back up for it, and maybe you two can rustle up some bottles."

He walked out through the swinging door, and when I stood up to take my glass to the sink, my head started throbbing again.

"I could still use a little Tylenol," I said to Ellis.

"Should have asked him to grab you a couple from the big house."

"There's, like, servants' rooms up above here," I said, motioning toward the staircase door. "Might be some rattling around."

She nodded and took my empty glass, carrying it and the blender over to the sink.

I took the stairs slowly. Had to stop in the middle for a second because climbing made my scalp throb more. The idea of shooting was excruciating.

There were tiny rooms up under the eaves. Through one door, I caught a peek of a clawfoot tub. I slouched inside with my fingers crossed and opened the medicine cabinet.

Hair spray, toothpaste . . . a bottle of Bayer, thank God. Not as easy on the stomach, but my head was a bigger problem.

I shook two tablets out and cranked the faucet, water shockingly cold because it was pumped direct from the freezing lake.

I held my hair back and leaned down, aspirins bitter on my tongue until I swallowed three gulps of water. It tasted so sweet, after the acrid pills.

I blotted my mouth with a hand towel, then turned back toward the hallway, looking out toward the lake as I passed the doorframe of one tiny room — a lonely cell, painted glossy mint green.

Inside was a narrow bed, its mattress sagging on an old-fashioned metal frame. There was a pillow with no case by the tall headboard, a striped Hudson Bay blanket folded at the foot.

Didn't look as though it had been slept in since before the advent of television, but someone had left a few personal effects: two pictures on the wall, and a battered shelf of books that doubled as a bedside table. I stepped inside, wondering what small comforts the resident had abandoned.

The pictures were the size of postcards. One was a photograph — Lapthorne and his brothers, very young. The second actually *was* a postcard . . . stripes of cancellation ink marring an upper corner.

The image was a typical tourist shot, old

enough that the colors had gone greenish. It showed the Little Mermaid statue that sits on a rock at the edge of Copenhagen's harbor, her legs-melting-into-tail curved along the stone, body twisted at the waist so she looked shyly away from the camera. You can't tell whether she longs for the land or the sea or both.

So I knew who had slept here last. Gerdie, from the Jutland — that peninsula shared by Denmark and Germany.

And then I remembered Egon's daughter, what had been done to her before she died. The girl's feet sliced in a hundred places, a knife shoved up her.

I sat on the bed and wasn't surprised to find a copy of Hans Christian Andersen in the shelf beside me. I flipped through it until I found "The Little Mermaid," then read the words of the Sea Witch:

I will prepare a draught for you, with which you must swim to land tomorrow before sunrise, and sit down on the shore and drink it. Your tail will then disappear, and shrink up into what mankind calls legs, and you will feel great pain, as if a sword were passing through you. But all who see you will say that you are the prettiest little human being they ever saw. You will still have the same floating gracefulness of movement, and no dancer will ever tread so lightly; but at every step you take it will feel as if you were treading upon sharp knives, and that the blood must flow.

I closed the book and put it back, read over the spines of all the rest: *Struwwelpeter* and the Brothers Grimm and *A Child's Book of Greek Mythology.* It had been Lapthorne all along, and I was the stupidest piece of shit who'd ever lived.

Because of course the vial marked "C.H." in his toilet case had been chloral hydrate, and if Ellis had taken him to the Homer show on Monday, he hadn't been in New York the night Sembles was killed, he'd been in Williamstown — three hours from Syracuse, not six.

I remembered Ellis saying how well she'd slept, when she never makes it through the night. How groggy we were the night she and Lapthorne stayed in our apartment, so he must have doped us for practice.

I remembered Kenny's voice from what seemed like years ago: *This was not a rookie. You can be the sickest bastard in the world, but the first time you kill somebody, it's sloppy. This guy knew what he was doing. It had the feel of a pattern to it. . . .*

Of course it did, because he'd killed Egon's daughter first.

I heard the door at the bottom of the staircase squeak open, and rising footsteps too heavy to be made by Ellis.

If he found me in the bathroom, maybe Lapthorne wouldn't know what I'd seen. I stood up too fast, and the ancient bedsprings creaked and twanged. I froze.

"Oh, Madeline," his voice echoed up the stairs, "and here I had my heart *set* on all of us living happily ever after."

Three more steps and he was in the doorway, a pistol in his left hand. I stared at it.

He looked down at it himself. "Oh, of course," he said, as though coming to some deeply entertaining realization. "That little trick your friend the bartender pulled with the bottle. I'm ambidextrous, actually. I just make a habit of reserving my *mano sinister* for the coup de grace. Keeps 'em guessing, don't you know. Wheels within wheels."

I turned away from him.

He laughed. "Took you an awfully long time to put this together. I'm disappointed."

"*You're* disappointed?" I looked back at him with effort.

He shrugged and grinned at me. "Gave you a sporting chance."

"So give me another. Old times' sake."

"Sorry. Already far too much on the day's agenda."

"I want to see Ellis."

"You will," he said. "She's almost ready."

"Can't you just . . . let her go?"

"I think not," he said.

I didn't want to ask what that meant.

"You could keep it in the family, Lapthorne," I said. "Give Ellis a sporting chance of her own."

"Not going to happen."

"Just let me see her." Even if she's dead.

"You'll see her," he said. "You'll see everything. Lovely view from here."

"Can't we be . . . together, me and Ellis?"

"You deserve more style, Madeline. Attention to detail."

"Lapthorne?" *Thalidomide. Dalkon Shield.* How perfectly named he was, after all.

"Sit down." Flick of gesture toward the old narrow bed behind me.

I started to shake. Tremors in my belly, radiating outward. First my legs, then my arms, then even my face — teeth chattering so rapidly I knew he could hear the staccato of bone on bone.

"I can't." I looked at him, wanting to keep my body quiet and still, to keep from crying or begging or falling to the floor.

490

He shook his head. "Not a request."

"If I try I'm going to . . . just . . ." Cry. Beg. Fall.

The shaking got worse. Bad enough to hurt, like when you're so cold your body would just as soon shatter itself to bits for the slightest warmth.

I reached my hand toward him, open, beseeching. "Lappy, *please?* I can't move. Walk. I'm not trying to make you angry. I want to, really . . . anything. Any of this. Going along. Exactly how you tell me."

Lapthorne smiled. Took a step closer. "You are sweet, and I'm so very fond of you."

He lifted his right hand, slowly and with great delicacy, until it was inches from mine. I watched him uncurl his index finger, narrowing the gap.

"Sistine Chapel," he said, amused.

I knew I couldn't flinch when he finally touched me, no matter what.

Only he didn't. He maintained that exact distance, skin from skin. My fingers trembling, his absolutely still.

A test. I was supposed to bring my hand to his.

Or not.

I had to choose, but what bargain would each option strike? Reprieve or submission.

Truth or dare.

Pass/fail.

Deep breath and then I made contact: fingertip to fingertip. Scrunched my eyes shut, waiting for the verdict.

That's when he nailed me. Cracked the pistol butt so hard against my skull it knocked me backwards, airborne. I twisted in slow motion, forever, until the bedframe jackknifed me headfirst into the wall, one last bright flash of pain.

So. Wrong answer.

I was all broken. Lying there crumpled, coughing up sobs that went on so long they choked me when I fought to suck air back in.

Lapthorne came over. To watch.

I was so goddamn angry I could have killed him right then, despite the gun, except I was too damaged to move.

He leaned down and grabbed me by the chin, wrenching my head up off the blanket for inspection.

"Oh good," he said. "Would have been a pity to ruin your face."

He let go, and falling those slender inches back down to the mattress hurt so much I couldn't see.

So I only felt it, him taking off one of my shoes.

I knew, then. What would happen. How I would die.

"Now sit up properly," he said.

I tried moving my head and wanted to puke.

"Can't," I said. "Sorry."

"Do it."

I didn't move. Couldn't. Plus it was stupid. I mean, I was going to die before my time wearing one shoe, for chrissake. I *deserved* to lie down.

He cocked the gun.

I sighed. "What, like you won't kill me if I have good posture? Fuck you."

When he placed the barrel against my temple, however, I discovered I was in fact able to raise myself off the mattress.

It took me a long time, and I couldn't hold myself all the way up, so I just slumped against the wall and stared at him.

There was something uncommonly bright and clear about his face, now that his true hunger glittered on the surface.

"Too, too perfect," he said, looking me up and down: my one bare foot, my patched jeans, my ragged sweater.

" 'She bore it all patiently,' " he recited, " 'and when she had done her work, used to go into the chimney-corner, and sit down among the cinders and ashes, so that they call'd her Cinderella; notwithstanding, she was a hundred times handsomer than her sisters.' "

Cute story . . . cute story . . .

"Big fireplace has that lovely old iron pothook," he said, "anchored deep in the fieldstone. Can't destroy it . . . survives anything. Rest of the place will burn away, but they'll find you."

"It won't matter, the shoe. No one will know."

"I will. That's what matters."

He looked at the door.

"And Ellis?" I didn't want to hear it, but if she was still alive, maybe I could buy her enough time to get away.

"You'll find out."

"Give me a hint."

He smiled. "A pleasing contrast."

"Do tell," I said.

"Haven't the time, I'm afraid."

He shook his head, turned toward the door.

"Not going to tie me up?"

He looked back. "If there were any way out of this room, I would have found it a long time ago. Straight drop to the rocks, out those windows. Door might as well be steel."

I wanted to keep him there — tried to

point at the Little Mermaid, but my hand just flopped vaguely toward her picture. "Egon's daughter, she was the first?"

"If you'd been just a little smarter, Madeline, you'd already know."

"Oh, go ahead, gloat. You've earned it."

"Ah, but *you* didn't. Finding out would've been your prize, but you had to win the contest."

"I'm crushed."

"Good," he said.

Then he locked me in.

CHAPTER 50

Of course the first thing I did was open the windows and check out how damn far the drop was. He'd lied about plenty of other crap, but not that: two stories plus — straight shot to the boulder on which the building perched. Even with an out-of-the-question running start to launch myself past the mass of granite, I would've hit ice. Didn't matter how thick it was frozen, because the water below was only three feet deep.

I heard a door open and close, then his footsteps going up toward the big house. I pushed farther out the window, until I was afraid I'd tip, but couldn't twist around far enough to catch sight of the covered walkway. No way to grab onto the eaves and swing for it, monkey-style. No gutters, no handholds.

Inside, of course, there wasn't a trapdoor in the ceiling. Wasn't even a closet.

When I couldn't hear him anymore, I started slamming against the door, but it didn't so much as quiver and the impact made my head hurt so much I was afraid I'd black out. I slid onto the floor and thought he could have saved time and just cast me as a Rapunzel failure, none of the Cinderella crap.

I could throw the horsehair mattress out the window and pretend it would magically break my fall. I could smash the window and slice my wrists with a piece of glass. I could just sit there and wait like an idiot. Catch up on a little reading.

Then I looked at the bed. The tall headboard and footboard, the long metal sidepieces . . . welded? I moved closer. No, slotted together. I pulled the mattress off, braced a shoulder against the floor, and shoved the length of iron up and out. Had a nice flange or whatever at the end. Dean would know the name but who cared, because the walls were beadboard and I could use the thing to jimmy those skinny wooden strips apart — burrow through to the hallway or the bathroom.

I wiggled the other end free, decided against the bathroom in case there were pipes, and went to work on the corner nearest the door. Once I slammed the metal in hard enough to gain a little purchase, the old wood splintered into matchsticks with barely any effort. I cleared a hole wide enough to slide through, then started on the outer wall. I crept through on my hands and knees and crouched in the hallway, not sure what to do next.

Which way now? Down the stairs or through the bathroom window and onto the walkway roof? Stairs. Out the back and with any luck across the dirt driveway undetected, on into the trees.

Totally brilliant plan, except for the part where Lapthorne was waiting for me in the kitchen, laughing his ass off and holding the gun to Ellis's head.

"Poor you," he said. "Might have made it, *chère cousine,* but for my change of heart about letting you two say goodbye."

Ellis had a black eye and a handcuff on her wrist. Must have been a custom job — the chain was two feet long.

He lifted the second bracelet and held it

out toward me.

I walked over and let him snap it on.

I thought he'd force us through the dining room and onto the walkway, up to the house or down to the water. Instead he shoved us toward the back door, the way I'd planned to escape.

"What about the lake?" I asked. "I thought that was next."

"First the icehouse," he said. "You can have a little chat while I get things ready."

Up the driveway, then . . . a hundred yards past the main building.

He jostled us through the door, and when we reached the two steps down to the road's packed dirt, I pretended to trip and lofted myself forward, yanking Ellis with me. We wheeled through the air and landed hard.

I shoved my mouth up against her ear. "I'm going to fall again at my car. Don't let him get me up."

"You *should* be sorry," she snapped. "Bad enough you drag me into this shit. Now I've got a face full of gravel and my fucking wrist is broken."

Lapthorne came down the stairs and twisted the point of his shoe into my ribs, hard enough I thought he'd pry them apart like the beadboard.

I took my time getting up anyway, apologizing and weaving and falling to one knee before I was halfway standing, like I was going to pass out.

Ellis swung in front of me, got her free hand under my armpit to lift me to my feet. She winced, leaned in close to hiss through clenched teeth, "Watch it . . . totally serious about the wrist."

I made a point of limping when we started walking again, hunched over and leaning into her, but keeping my weight off the cuffs as much as I could.

At first the stones cut into my bare foot, but the ground was so cold I couldn't feel anything after a minute.

A hundred dragging steps and we were coming up on the Rabbit.

I staggered a little, said, "Ellis, I'm so sorry . . . I can't keep . . ." and then lurched one more pace forward and crumpled in what I hoped was a convincing way against the rear bumper.

"Goddamnit," said Lapthorne, "get *up*."

I ignored him and slid fast, the rest of the way down — went all loosey-goosey at the end so my head slapped audibly against the frozen dirt. That hurt so much it was all I could do not to scream, and for a couple of seconds I thought the pain would knock me out for real.

I slitted my eyes open, just enough to see Ellis crouched down beside me.

From behind, Lapthorne twisted a mean foot into my ribs again.

I didn't move, just held my breath.

His shifted his weight, shoes creaking, then stepped right next to my head. "Lift her."

Ellis wormed a hand under me and pretended to try.

"I *can't.*" She started crying.

"Son of a *bitch,*" he said.

"Dead weight. She's totally out."

"Fine, then Madeline goes first," and he kicked my head so hard that Ellis's lie came true.

I started coming around when my arm was yanked into the air. I thought Lapthorne was going to try hauling me up, but then the handcuff bit into my wrist and snapped shut. Good . . . if he'd taken it off, then maybe . . .

He let go, and my hand didn't drop back down to the dirt. I was desperate to see what I was chained to, but didn't dare open my eyes.

"Fuck it," he said. "Works just as well to leave you here."

I didn't move, didn't breathe, listened to

his footsteps crunching against grit, a car door opening, the click as he popped the hood on his Porsche. The door slammed. Two more steps, metallic creak of hinges as he raised the lid. Something heavy hit the ground, then another right after. The second weight sloshed a little.

Then he grunted, lifting. I heard him walk toward the house, slap of leather against dirt, then hollow claps as he climbed the wooden stairs.

Screen door whine, click of the front door latch. Two steps inside and then a tinny snap with a solid boom right on its tail, as both closed behind him.

I opened my eyes and looked up at Ellis. "He's gone?"

"Well, he's *inside.* I can think of better kinds of 'gone.' "

"Can you see him?"

"In the living room."

"What's he doing?"

"Probably dumping out the ten gallons of gas he just took out of his fucking car," she said. "And I hope your brilliant escape plan included getting handcuffed to *your* fucking car, because I'm having a tough time imagining how the hell this was a good idea."

She didn't look at me, just let her eyes drift across the ground in front of her feet, tears streaming down her cheeks.

"It's perfect," I said.

She closed her eyes. "Oh, right, like maybe he'll have a change of heart and set *himself* on fire? I'm *so* sure. Too bad he left that gun on the porch."

"I've got a gun."

"No shit?"

"Right behind us. Is he looking?"

"No."

I got up and checked the line of windows. The little porch's overhang cut reflection on the glass, and Lapthorne was backlit by glare off the lake. He was moving along the length of the living room slowly, head down as he poured out the gas.

"Okay," I said, "put your hand near the bumper so I can move mine. Rest your head on your knees if you think you're going to pass out, okay?"

She did it without a word, but the chain was stretched taut and I couldn't turn to see the baling wire that was serving as the hatchback's lock. I fumbled with the knot of metal, and felt the sharp edge of one end slice across the tip of my thumb, then jog under the nail.

Lapthorne looked at us out the central window. Smiled and waved. I grimaced back at him.

The wire wouldn't untwist. I started bend-
ing it back and forth, hoping to make it snap
if I could get it weak enough at a single spot.

He returned to his task, halfway down the
room now, and pausing when he got to
where I figured the sofas were, to shake
some of the liquid over the cushions.

"What's the matter?" asked Ellis.

I shook my head, working the rugged snarl
of metal for all I was worth. It was getting
easier to bend, softening.

"Maddie?" she whispered. "You have to
talk to me . . ."

"Just have to break the wire."

"He's almost finished . . ."

I glanced up again, just as the thing
snapped in my hand. The lid lifted and I
leaned back against it, holding it closed so
he wouldn't see.

"When he gets behind that wall," I said,
"give me as much slack as you can."

The minute he was hidden from view, I
yanked the wire completely off. The hatchback eased up quietly, just a few inches, and
rested against the back of my thighs.

I worked my wrist into the space behind
it, wishing I could force my elbow to bend
in the opposite direction. I patted the worn
carpeting, seeking the feel of the gun sock
tight around the stock, the barrels, whatever

came to hand.

"Can you give me any more slack?" i asked.

"If I can get my hand behind the . . ." Ellis inhaled sharply, in pain.

The chain gave a little, and I crouched down, shoving my arm in farther.

There it was. . . . I grabbed on and pulled and slammed it against the edge of the door in my haste. Would it fit out the small square of the door? I patted my hand up farther, but the stock was thank God still "broken," angled open in a vee.

"Hurry," she said. "Please."

I slid the gun out, butt first, then shook it hard enough to slap the breech closed before shifting it quickly vertical to hide it behind me.

I checked the windows. Lapthorne's dark head came into view. He wasn't watching us. I started inching the sock down, one-handed. Slowly, in case he turned to look.

I got the sock down past the trigger guard. Slid the safety off with my mangled thumb.

He was walking backwards, into the hallway. I'd only have a second before he got to the next set of windows.

My legs started shaking again. I could hear the barrels rattle against the car.

"Stand up," I said, but Ellis didn't move.

I glanced down at her. She was crying but not making a sound, holding her wrist.

"You okay?" I asked.

Ellis nodded, struggled to her feet. "Really is broken now, if it wasn't before."

"Sorry . . ."

"Won't matter, will it? One way or the other . . ."

I could feel her starting to shake. Between the two of us, the chain jangled like sleigh-bells.

Lapthorne appeared in the last windows. He lifted the gas can and shook it empty, then walked back toward the other end of the room.

He stepped halfway out the front door and tossed the empty into the driveway, then picked up the second can from just inside. I watched him take off the cap, then splash gas onto the porch and each tread of the stairs.

"Do it," whispered Ellis.

"He's gotta be closer."

When the can was empty, he dropped it, and retrieved his pistol from the edge of the porch.

He smiled at me. "Ready, Madeline?"

"Can't wait."

With his free hand, he pulled a key from his pocket.

I tried to look nonchalant, right hand behind my hip.

"Well," he said, "I suppose this is good-bye, though of course I'll have to ask you to walk inside."

"Take me first," said Ellis.

"Have to wait your turn." Lapthorne smirked and tossed the handcuff key down in the dirt, far enough from her feet to make her grovel for it.

He grinned at her. "Pick it up."

I slid my fingers into both triggers.

He was careless with the pistol. Not aiming it at us because he was too sure of himself.

He leaned against the porch and pulled a lighter out of his pocket, a Zippo like Schneider's. While Ellis strained for the key, he flipped the top open and started thumbing it to life, then snapping it shut. Over and over.

"Can't reach," said Ellis.

"Course you can," he said, but he took one step forward, then another, still flicking the lighter.

Ellis pressed her foot against mine, then flinched to the side. I watched his eyes snap to the motion.

I brought the gun smoothly up to my hip just like in *Thunderball* and pulled both triggers, blowing his neck open.

Slow motion, gobbets of flesh smacking down wet as far back as the porch, blood hanging in the air longer, like the smoke of a well-hit shell.

He looked into my eyes, puzzled, his glance all soft again, like he was worried about how it would go for me, out in the world. And then he started to tip into flight, everything suddenly real-time fast again.

His back arched and he was splayed against the air like that last drawing in *The Little Prince* and then his arms and fingers jerked up with one last spasm that raised his pistol halfway in the air, firing off a round as he fell like a sack of meat.

I saw a flash of his shoe soles.

The back of his head hit the stairs before his feet came down.

No movement, then.

Not a twitch in his chest.

No pump of blood from his ragged neck because his heart was finished, stilled by the shock waves of damage.

We were frozen, ears ringing from the concussion of the blast.

Then Ellis arched her back, bellowing like a Pamplona-crazed bull.

And the first blue lick of flame blossomed from under Lapthorne's hand.

CHAPTER 51

There were a few minutes there when Ellis and I just slumped against each other, overwhelmed, but the fire brought us around.

I could feel the heat on my face, so strong it felt like my skin was already blistering.

"Could you undo the cuffs?" I said, motioning to the key.

She reached for it, but had to drag it closer with her foot before she could pick it up.

I could barely fit it into the lock, but then I did and we were free and we ran back from the fire, then both burst into sobs and I put my arms around her, tender and trying not to further hurt the wrist that hung all ugly against her leg.

"I can't believe you did it," she said.

The whole porch was raging.

"We'd better call the fire department," I said.

"He cut the phone line. Let's drive."

The paint on my car was emitting tiny threads of smoke.

"Take the Porsche. Keys are under the mat," she said.

"Okay."

"Least he can do," she said, and we

stumbled over on rubber legs and climbed inside.

We screamed down four miles of dirt road in just under three minutes, got to town in another five.

The fire trucks blazed out of the station, sirens wailing. I let Ellis call home first, and when I told Mom what had happened she started to cry and said, "Oh, Maddie, if you'd died I would have *kicked* you."

It took a few hours for the cops to question us and figure out who'd shot whom.

Camp was destroyed. No way to pump water from the lake fast enough, by the time the crew got there.

It burned so hot my car didn't make it either, so we drove Lapthorne's in fifth all the way back to Centre Island.

The sun was long gone when we got there, but everyone was standing in the driveway waiting for us, Bonwit and Mom and even Egon, and after she gripped me in a fierce hug for about five minutes, Egon stepped up and shook my hand.

"I want to thank you," he said, tearing up, "for my daughter. I never thought she would get justice, but you did it. Just fine."

And then he walked away because he

couldn't stand us to see him sobbing.

Wilt called me the next morning. My hands were still shaky when I picked up the phone.

"You okay?" he asked.

"Better. Glad to be around."

"I'm hip. You did a real hero number."

I couldn't say anything.

"So," he finally said, his voice cracking, "Simon hanged himself."

"Oh, Wilt . . ."

"Those pictures of the girls, Maddie. He took all of them, and there were more. We're still going through his files. All dead people. Hit-and-runs. Fires. Little kids. You wouldn't believe . . ." and he had to stop.

I could just see him covering his eyes with his free hand, slumped at his desk.

"He left a note," Wilt said. "How he paid off cops to give him first crack at crime scenes. Wanted to be like that guy in New York, you know? In the Depression, one who was always soonest to arrive at disasters?"

"Weegee," I said.

"Yeah."

"Oh, Wilt, I'm so sorry."

We were all in the bierstube, and Dean just kept looking at me, reaching for my hand.

"Kenny would be proud of you."

No recriminations. No I-told-you-so. I didn't deserve such kindness. "I got him killed."

"You didn't," said Ellis. "I want you to chant it until it soaks into your bones."

"I should have known right away," I said. "The night we went to his brownstone."

"How could you have known?" she asked.

"Because he said they first saw those girls at the rose garden, but they couldn't have. The photo-booth pictures, the silhouettes . . . they weren't wearing the garlands yet. He hadn't made them, because they went to the garden *after* the fair."

I started crying again.

Dean gripped my hands in his.

"That fucker," said Ellis. She took a sip of my coffee and made a face, pale and exhausted.

I told them about Simon.

"Okay," she said, placing her hands flat on the table, "so Schneider thought this all up pretty quickly when he saw those bodies. First he gets Simon in there. But how did he know Lapthorne had money, enough to blackmail him for?"

"I don't know," I said. "Maybe he found the dog tags."

"He'd know from the tags?" she asked.

"The Lapthorne Works are where Dodie's money came from. In Syracuse. Schneider would have recognized the name."

"But why would he leave them there?" asked Dean. "He wanted to cover up what happened, and he could have used them to hold over Lapthorne's head."

I shrugged. "Hard to say."

Ellis crossed her arms, looking fragile. "So Lapthorne must have wanted Simon's negatives."

"Exactly," I said. "Maybe he thought if he could get rid of them and kill Simon, he'd be off the hook. When he got Simon's name from me, he didn't need us alive anymore."

"So Simon was freaking out because he thought you were getting too close to his secret collection, but why did Lapthorne kill Sembles?" asked Dean.

"He must have been the only person who could place Lapthorne with the girls at the fair. He'd spent the most time with the four of them. Schneider got to him fast, since Sembles was the only thing threatening the gravy train."

"How do we know this? I thought Schneider wasn't talking," said Ellis.

"Vomit Girl is," I said. "Darlene Voorhees. Wilt told me she chatted away to the cops last night. She didn't know everything, because Schneider didn't really trust her, but she knew about the deal he'd made with Sembles."

"And the rest of it?" asked Dean. "How many people . . ."

"Lapthorne wouldn't tell me," I said.

We couldn't figure out what to do about Lappy's car, so Egon finally drove it over to Binty and Kit's. I didn't focus on much of anything for the next couple of days. Ellis snuck into his funeral, saying she figured it was the appropriate thing to do as practically his fiancée. Dean thought that was beyond strange, but I understood. We were both mourning the guy we'd thought he was, not the guy he turned out to be.

I went to the cemetery after they buried him, would have picked roses for his grave, but the bushes were all bare, burlapped for the winter. I sat beside his grave for most of an afternoon, the fresh dirt all humped up over where they'd sunk the casket. I wanted to do something, to mark his passing.

At the end of the day I walked over to my namesake Madeline's grave and asked her to take care of him.

Thursday morning a messenger came to Bonwit's with papers for me. My presence was requested at a lawyer's office in the city, for the reading of Lapthorne's will.

"Strange," said Mom. "That means you're getting something."

"An ear or a hoof, maybe," said Ellis, "like a bullfight."

I was shown into a mahogany-paneled conference room at the law firm, with a view of Wall Street. Kit was there, and Binty, and Lappy's three brothers. None of them would look at me.

The lawyer was an older guy with a great head of white hair and a slew of broken capillaries, vaguely familiar from Seawanhaka. He read through the papers in a fine accent, sounding remarkably like Bonwit, "mirrah" for "mirror," and so on.

My bit was near the end. Lapthorne had left me the Porsche, and two envelopes — one letter-sized, one a large mailer stuffed with a thick sheaf of paper.

I opened the small one and pulled out the sheet of stationery inside — thick ecru stock engraved with his initials above a few hand-scrawled lines.

So, chère cousine, he'd written,

If you're reading this, you were indeed a worthy adversary. I hope it's true that having the car means you'll never be unhappy again. I liked the sound of that.

There's a lot more I should probably say. I think you know, anyway. You're the only one who did.

It stopped there, with no signature. I didn't want to look at the thick sheaf of pages behind. Not yet, not with his family around me. I put it back in the big envelope and tucked in its flap.

Things were wrapping up. The lawyer shook hands around the room, then left us alone. I stood up to follow, but Binty walked over and blocked my path. She wore a black suit and stockings, low-heeled black pumps on her narrow feet.

Her long monkey face was screwed up with fury, and I had no idea what to say to her. She hauled her hand back and gave me a ringing slap across the face.

"You stupid little *welfare* case," she spat. "All those years. All the money to that horrible Schneider man to hush it up. Lappy was getting *well!* The doctors *told* us he was, and you had to ruin everything!"

Reader, I decked the bitch.

■ ■ ■ ■ ■

PART VI
LAKE ONCAS

■ ■ ■ ■

In the end there may not be much more to the special gift of aristocrats than the old image of casual grace. . . . Worse, the image can't seem to stand by itself. Its light must have a field of darkness, some dull impasto of despair with a glint of violence flashing through. Without fear, the image lacks shape and substance, and dissolves into a pale, thin air of American possibility. With it, the image comes clear, and so does the gift of courage.

— Nelson Aldrich, *Old Money*

CHAPTER 52

I stood at the edge of Lake Oncas, watching the pieces of snow come down to disappear instantly on its foul surface, small waves rolling in toward me sluggish and dull as molten lead. The last of our stuff was packed up in the back seat of Lapthorne's car, Dean having already left town with the bulk of the crap in a borrowed van.

We were headed to the Berkshires, to Ellis. The Southern Pacific Railroad wanted two railgrinders with computer interfaces and trapezoidal linkages, putting down enough money to make good our escape.

I'd promised to follow Dean, to stay right on his tail and get on the thruway without a backward glance, but at the last pillar-of-salt minute I'd felt the need to come here, to thread through empty warehouses lining broken streets, pulling onto a blank, weed-infested spot of lakeside gravel in the midst of what locals called Oil City.

Even in the cold it stank, here, and from my perch among the petroleum tanks, I could see the ashen hulk of the Lapthorne Works squatting diseased across the water. *From whence it cometh.*

I mourned the death of what might have been: my last hope to redeem our family.

Of course at root Lapthorne had been a monster, hateful, summing up everything that disgusts me about those smug and didactic and murderous City-on-a-Hill prigs from whom both of us were descended.

And yet, he'd embodied all that had been handsome in the traditions of my people, my tribe, a beauty that is as lost as the passenger pigeon, Krakatoa, the childish belief that a war could end all wars or that a ship was unsinkable.

If you looked hard enough at this water, you could almost see the calling cards and straw boater hats and long three-button kid gloves and chilled finger bowls with paper-thin slices of lemon — the delicate props of empire — floating on the waves, arcing through the toxin-rainbowed slop.

The *Weekly* never published my article. The paper was bought out by a conglomerate from downstate, whose gray-pinstriped minions informed Ted in no uncertain terms that their corporate entity had strict ideas about what was and wasn't appropriate for family consumption, though nothing was changed save me being swept off the staff. Family indeed — as if Binty, or her conglomerate's board of directors, would know.

Had there been an ounce of warmth in Ice Cunt's pale narrow hands, Lapthorne might have been entirely different, might have been what I still believe he was fighting to become — human. A real boy, not some marionette dancing through a world of pain.

Of course I couldn't know what bitter crucible, what lack, had formed the corseted shell of Binty herself. To imagine that, you'd have to look perfectly down the barrel of generations, tracing the flaw.

I was holding Lapthorne's envelope. After I'd first read through what was inside, I'd given it to the cops. They said they didn't need to keep it. There wouldn't be any trials.

The young guy, Franklin, had brought it to Green Street. Maybe a posthumous favor to Kenny.

I opened it up and started wadding up the pages inside, one by one, before throwing them out onto the lake.

It was all there. He'd cut single pages from the stories, then written a name, a date, a city — all the details — in the margins of each, starting with "The Little Mermaid."

The longest entry was a chronicle of events leading up to Lapthorne's murder of his army buddy Chris, penned along the edges of "The Steadfast Tin Soldier."

Lapthorne related how they'd become reacquainted at Fort Drum, recognizing each other from school, discovered they had dark tastes in common.

When he'd told Chris how enjoyable it had been to kill Egon's daughter, the pair decided to try a deadly partnership at the New York State Fair, next time they got a weekend pass.

On the midway, Lapthorne was amused when Delphine demanded he hand over his dog tags in exchange for a kiss — grinned while she slid the prize coyly over her head, knowing she wouldn't be alive to complain when he reneged on the bargain. Only he didn't count on slashing its chain along with her throat. The necklace slithered to earth while they struggled, trampled into the soil so deep that Lapthorne's panicked scrabbling couldn't turn it up again.

"I blame Chris for that," Lapthorne's spiky notes explained. "I'd have had time to find them, but he lost his nerve and made me finish off the second girl. Couldn't trust him afterwards."

Lappy paid Chris back in the jungle, some weeks later. Pitched a live grenade into his tent just before an Indochinese dawn.

The tags stayed buried until Cal churned them up. Schneider never saw them. He'd gotten Lapthorne's name from Sembles. It said so, across the page from *Struwwelpeter.*

It said, too, that Schneider had confessed to altering the records from that night, making it look like Lapthorne and Chris were in the holding cell on his shift.

I balled up the second-to-last sheet, ripped from "The Little Match Girl."

"Ellis Clark, Camp" was inked in the margin, with room to spare for recording the horrors that never happened.

The last page was my own.

I burned it, crumbled the ashes to nothing, and walked away.

Billie Holiday's voice poured out of the Porsche's speakers the instant I turned the key. "God Bless the Child."

The car threw up a fine rooster tail of gravel and shot me straight out of Syracuse.

ACKNOWLEDGMENTS

My thanks to:

Edward Eggert, who got this started. He and his lovely wife, Patricia, have treated their downstate daughter-in-law with endless kindness and patience — as have all Eggerts, Heddens, Murphys, Hydes, and Mittags — no matter how much I bitched about the quality of Chinese food in their fair city.

Alice Kaufman and Muffy Srinivasan, the first two people to read the beginning, who convinced me it was worth doing.

James and Mom and Freya and Mark — day in, day out. Thank you so very much for all your sustenance, kindness, and patience.

Juliette Anthony, whose birthday gift of a class at Elaine and Bill Petrocelli's Book Passage in Corte Madera precipitated a chain of auspicious events, the acme of which was my introduction to Lee Child.

Lee's kind support and advocacy have had an indelible impact on the fate of this book, ever since.

My agent, Rolph Blythe, and my editor, Kristen Weber. You guys are tireless, compassionate, and extraordinary. Also you have kicked my butt. In a good way — like literary Sherpas. Their work on my behalf has been furthered by many people at the Dunow, Carlson & Lerner Literary Agency, and at Mysterious Press — especially publicist Susan Richman.

Andrew Ambrose, of Holland & Holland, London, for making sure Madeline was armed with the perfect gun.

My old compatriots at *The Syracuse New Times,* for being infinitely cooler than the coworkers in this story.

The members of my two writing groups, alphabetically: Dave Damianakes, Gaylene Givens, Sharon Johnson, Charles King, Heidi Kriz, Marilyn MacGregor, Kerry Messer, Karen Murphy, Diane Puntenney, Andy Rose, Fred Turner, Dan Ward, and Robert Clark Young, who waded through high piles of stilted, unreadable crap.

Joyce Ahern, Nelson Aldrich, Candace Andrews, Glenn Andrews, Juliette Anthony, Noreen Ayres, Anne Batterson, Joel Blackman, Jacqueline Celenza, Ariel Zeitlin

Cooke, John Cooke, Lee Culp, Rick Dage, Race Dougherty, Elaine Flinn, Alfred Fussa, Holly Gold, David and Kathleen Goldsmith, Bob and Judy Greber, Michael Guinzburg, Derek Guth, Kira Halpern, Emily Harris, Susi Hartmann, Pia Harwood, Katrina Heron, Caryl Hill and Lee, Bill Hoyt, Julie Hoyt, Winthrop Hoyt, Joshilyn Jackson, Maureen Jennings, LuAn Keller, Harley Jane Kozak, Heidi Mack, Regina Marler, David Montgomery, ALL the Mooneys, Heidi Moos, Tom and Maripat Murphy, Geoffrey O'Brien, Martha O'Connor, Sabrina O'Jack, Linda Palmer, Heidi Vornbrock Roosa, Frank Roosevelt, Hunt Smith, Tracy Smith, Tara Staley and William (who has wings and always will), David Walks-as-Bear, and Sarah Weinman.

Everyone at Epinions.com, who saw me through the darkest hours and gave me my writing chops back: T. Allen "cowboyDJ" Morgan, Laura "Leah" Winzeler, Dwight "Counsel" Moody, Markham Shaw "Mshawpyle" Pyle, Curtis Edmonds, Casey "kcfoxy" Stewart (and "ramsfan" the burlyman), Mr. and Mrs. Dave "Sweeper" Burckhard, David "Grouch" Abrams, Lisa "my$.02" Goldman, Nollequeen, gracef, forkids, DoubleCoog, Lambira, erik_kos berg, nita, stonehousellc, expono, kimmiko, sweetpaulie, gogigantes, 401402, Aggie-Brett, emlin, Redlass, ebolles, wildvirgogirl, auntnono, snark, bonniesayers, Syd_Kick, halfsweet, poseidon, kchowell, mgreber, ccoggins, elegiac, and kmennie, and all y'all who ever clicked "trust cornelia."

Maggie Griffin and Rae Helmsworth, Reacher Creatures par excellence.

And the Sad Anoraks, my band: Andi Shechter, Louise Ure, and Shaz Wheeler.

ABOUT THE AUTHOR

Cornelia Read grew up in New York, California, and Hawaii. She is a reformed debutante who currently lives in Berkeley with her husband and twin daughters. This is her first novel. To learn more about the author, visit www.corneliaread.com.

The employees of Thorndike Press hope you have enjoyed this Large Print book. All our Thorndike and Wheeler Large Print titles are designed for easy reading, and all our books are made to last. Other Thorndike Press Large Print books are available at your library, through selected bookstores, or directly from us.

For information about titles, please call:

(800) 223-1244

or visit our Web site at:

www.gale.com/thorndike
www.gale.com/wheeler

To share your comments, please write:

Publisher
Thorndike Press
295 Kennedy Memorial Drive
Waterville, ME 04901